Angle of Declination

Angle of
Declination

Doug Mayfield
Sally Mayfield

WWW.TWOHARBORSPRESS.COM

MINNEAPOLIS

Two Harbors Press
212 3rd Avenue North, Suite 290
Minneapolis, MN 55401
612.455.2293
www.TwoHarborsPress.com

ISBN-13: 978-1-936198-76-4
ISBN: 978-1-937293-96-3 (eBook Mobi)
ISBN: 978-1-937293-97-0 (eBook ePub)
LCCN: 2011939267

Cover photo © 2010. All rights reserved.

Cover design and typeset by Nate Meyers

Printed in the United States of America

To all the people represented as characters in this novel

Our thanks to

Jim Baratto for continuous help and encouragement; Cheryl Karnowski for her nurturing criticism; Linda Bird, who made *Angle of Declination* a better novel; Tony Brackett at NBC for generously providing film clips and archive footage; Norman (Stands Noisily in One Place) Clark and A. J. (Falling Water) Nickaboine for assistance with the Ojibwe language; Melanie Lindquist for assistance with Canadian French; Lori Jackson for her research at the Kenora Public Library; Attorney Steven Qualley for opinions and explanations regarding relevant points of law; David King for his sensitive, insightful editing; Marna Poole for pushing us across the finish line; and Bill Abbott, who made *Angle of Declination* possible.

By God, if I ever cracked, I'd try to make the world crack with me. Listen! The world exists only through our apprehension of it, and it's so much better to say that it's not you that's cracked—it's the Grand Canyon.

—F. Scott Fitzgerald, from "The Crack-up"

I cannot say how long I was asleep, but when I opened my eyes, all the depths of the wood were filled with sunlight ... the weather had changed to fair, and there was that feeling of peculiar dry freshness in the air which fills the heart with a sense of boldness.

—Ivan Turgenev, from *A Sportsman's Sketches*

Chapter 1

In 1960, when I was a little girl, a man named Bud Carston was killed in Watertown, New York, by an Airedale. But it didn't happen the way it sounds. Bud was crossing a street in the middle of the block—that detail is important—when a truck hit the dog at the intersection and sent it hurtling through the air. The dog struck Bud, killing him instantly.

My grandfather, Hedley Addison, knew Bud and mourned his death, but he also said it never would have happened if Bud hadn't jaywalked when he did. Hedley was one of the people who raised me, and for him, life was about the choices we make. That's why the height of absurdity, as far as he was concerned, was the three-color stoplight, which debuted in northern New York in the late fifties. There was simply no need for yellow lights in Hedley's world—either you chose to stop or you didn't. The way Hedley saw it, Bud made an unfortunate choice when he decided to cross the street that day—two of them, if you count the fact that he jaywalked.

My mother, Ellen Addison Hayes, the other person who raised me, had a different take on Bud's accident. Although she didn't know Bud personally, Bud had been in and out of jail a lot, and this mattered to my mother. By her lights, some cosmic force had finally seen to it that Bud got his just deserts. The Airedale's owner was also on the hook for letting his dog run loose on Main Street, and like Bud, he would eventually get what was coming to him. It was only a matter of time.

That's the way my mother saw everything after my father was killed. She wasn't a religious fanatic or anything like that. But she developed an overheated sense of right and wrong and saw—or tried to see—everything in terms of moral implications and cause-and-effect relationships. So if I caught a cold, that's what I got for going outside with wet hair. If I fell down and scraped my knee, that's what I got for being careless, in a hurry or someplace I shouldn't have been at the time. She wasn't mean about it. My mother just reduced life to its simplest terms, which, for her, were about deeds and their all-too-often painful consequences.

Even when she would read to me at night, the stories generally contained morals, and if a ringer slipped in now and then—a Thurber story or a *Little House* book—my mother would still manage to tease something from the pages about proper conduct and the other kind—the kind you always paid for. All this absolutism grew tiresome at times, but it was also comforting and made life, in its dizzying complexity, seem as simple as a bookmark. I had few questions, and that was a good thing, because Cape Vincent wasn't the place to ask them.

That's where I was born—a little river town in northern New York just across the St. Lawrence from Canada. Life was sometimes hard in the Cape, but it was seldom nuanced, and moral ambiguity—even the idea of it—was unimaginable. But like my mother's stories, Cape Vincent's blinkered worldview made perfect sense, and it continued to make sense until I was twenty-four and married. That's when everything fell apart.

Because I was only three when my father died, my grandfather did his best to fill the void, teaching me those things he felt everyone ought to know. My education included a sizable dose of Hedley's metaphysics, but in addition to learning about choice and free will, I also came to understand that America was the last bastion of goodness on earth, the Russians were the root cause of all evil and smugglers were the lowest form of life on the planet. Hedley despised smugglers, and it wasn't just because they moved contraband across the border. It had something to do with the river. In the Cape, men like Hedley were called river rats, which meant their lives, for better or worse, were wed to the St. Lawrence. To them, smugglers were no better than faithless lovers—they had won the river's favor, learned her closely held secrets and then dishonored her.

Like all river rats, Hedley spent every free moment hunting or fishing, and because he loved these things, he shared them with me. Actually, he *gave* them to me, in the way that we give our children tennis rackets, chemistry sets and piano lessons—in the hope they might mean something one day. My mother, who disliked everything about the river, would have preferred he give me something else, but Hedley had nothing else to give. And there was nothing else I wanted. I was a quick study and soon became a river rat, too.

Years before I was born, Hedley had acquired two hundred acres on Lake Ontario that included a long, rocky point at the southern juncture of the lake and the St. Lawrence River. At the end of the point was Hedley's duck blind—a magic circle of shale and limestone with hay bales for seats and walls high enough that when Hedley stood up, only his head and shoulders were visible. There was no place on earth more exciting.

Hedley had a big Chesapeake named Ace, and together the three of us would huddle low in the blind, and in the darkness we would listen to the wind that roared across the point and to the waves that crashed into it a few feet from where we sat, sending sheets of spray over our heads. Hedley and I rarely spoke, not because he had any

3

scruple against conversation in the duck blind but because it was pointless. The wind did all the talking, and we had to cup our hands and shout to be heard.

Long before dawn, a ribbon of gray would appear in the east, and we could make out huge flocks of ducks flying low on the water, filled with a sense of purpose we could only imagine. Soon after that, we could see the lake itself, covered with whitecaps, and Hedley would lean close and say, "The sheep are grazing this morning, Allie," and I would nod and look at the whitecaps that dotted the lake, and if I squinted a little, they became hundreds of sheep grazing in a dusky meadow. And always, as the half-light spread west, a huge freighter, otherworldly and out of scale, would creep from behind Grenadier Island with clock-stopping slowness and make its way onto the lake.

Without warning the ducks would come, their wings cupped, and they would see the decoys, circle around, then barrel into the spread, pitching and rolling in the wind. Hedley would swing smoothly into each flock, then shoot and reload. Ace would be in the water, clawing his way up the waves and disappearing in the troughs, making one retrieve after another with such urgency that he didn't bother to shake himself off in between.

Then it was over. We would leave the small circle of consecrated stone and almost—but not quite—become who we had been before. We were the same, but we were different, in the way that a lake is the same but different after a storm. I was still a little girl, but I had felt the fury of a thousand waters, and I had seen a ship emerge from behind Grenadier Island like it was God. And in the darkness of that morning, I had heard the shape of the wind take the shape of the blind and believe it. *The same but different.*

In those days ducks darkened the sky over Cape Vincent from October until Christmas, and after the mills began to close, duck hunting, which had always been the Cape's favorite pastime, became its leading industry. "Thank God for the ducks," the people said, as waterfowl in unprecedented numbers poured from the heavens like manna, sustaining the local economy in its time of need. Of course, all the ducks in the world wouldn't have saved Cape Vincent if hunting hadn't become wildly popular in America at about the same time. That concurrence *did* seem providential. But whether it was God, a shifting flyway or a changing zeitgeist that turned things around, the Cape survived, and people were soon coming from all over the country—all over the *world*—to hunt the Seaway and stay at the big clubs that sprang up along its shores.

My uncle Jimmy, my mother's little brother, owned one of the biggest clubs on the American side of the border—the Sable Island Hunt Club. Jimmy bought the club with his business partner, Hap Strattner, but Jimmy ran it, and a lot of famous people hunted there. After several outdoor magazines wrote puff pieces about the club, it really took off, and the third year Sable was open, Jimmy guided two movie stars, three famous athletes and a Saudi prince. He and Hap hung autographed photos of their famous guests on a wall in the bar, and after five years the wall was full.

Jimmy was Hedley's only son, but even so, Hedley didn't have much use for him. They didn't even hunt together anymore. One time I asked Hedley why that was, and he hemmed and hawed and said all the "foofaraw" about the club had changed Jimmy. But his timeline didn't parse. The two of them had quit hunting together long before Jimmy and Hap bought Sable Island, so I decided he just didn't want to tell me.

My mother didn't care for Jimmy, either, and when she referred to him at all, which wasn't often, she called him "Mr. Big Shot." To hear my mother talk, Jimmy's shortcomings were mostly a function of velocity—he drove fast cars, dated fast women and traveled in a fast crowd. I didn't know what Hedley and my mother had against him, exactly. But whatever it was, it had real staying power.

The only person they seemed to dislike more than Jimmy was his business partner. According to Hedley, Hap Strattner was a two-bit chiseler who wasn't worth the powder to blow him to hell. Even for Hedley, that was a strong indictment, but for him life was serious business best left to serious people, not to "scalawags" like Hap and Jimmy.

I had no trouble accepting what my mother and Hedley said about Hap Strattner, but when it came to Jimmy, they were wasting their breath—I was crazy about him.

I wish I could have stayed on the river forever, but when I was twelve, my mother remarried and we moved to Illinois, which brought my idyllic life as a river rat to an end. Tom Nash represented an opportunity for love, which my mother had lost at a very young age, and stability, which she'd never really known. Tom was from Chicago, where he owned two furniture stores, and my mother had met him when he was vacationing in the Thousand Islands. Tom was very kind, and there was a wholesome affability about him that most people found hard to resist—except for Hedley, who had a chromosomal distrust of all men who didn't hunt or fish. But Hedley knew enough to keep his mouth shut, and both he and Uncle Jimmy were there that dreary March morning to see us off.

There was an awkward moment just before we left, when Jimmy and my mother looked at each other, uncertain of whether to embrace. They finally did, sort of. My mother said "Good-bye, Jimmy" in a flat, toneless way, and he said something about being sorry, and that was all. After that, she and Hedley hugged each other, and then it was my turn. I was already crying when I threw my arms around Hedley, but when it was time to say good-bye to Jimmy, I dissolved into tears and couldn't say anything.

I cried all the way to Chicago, through five states and six cities, my face pressed against the cold glass of the car window. My mother tried to cheer me up with talk of new friends, better schools and the chance to go to college, but I was inconsolable. I don't think

I stopped crying until I attended my new school the first day. After that, even when I felt like crying, there wasn't time.

Chapter 2

My new life in Chicago was satisfactory—that's as far as I'll go. I fit in well enough, but when the other kids would ask where I was from, I didn't always tell them Cape Vincent, mostly because I grew tired of explaining where it was. Sometimes, I just said New York. Not only was that easier, it also conferred a certain status, since most people assumed I meant New York City.

Chicago took some getting used to, but by the time I was in high school, no one had to ask where I was from anymore. It's strange, but even with a yearbook in front of me, I can't remember much about that period of my life. It's the same now as it was then, a blur of smelly chem labs, pretentious term papers and the fortunes of the football team—something I tried desperately to care about.

Somewhere near the center of that blur was Paula Zarobsky, my best friend. Inside the front cover of my yearbook, Paula wrote, "Every time you see a cat, please think of me. Love, Zee." Like a lot of best friends, we were nothing alike. Paula was an unaffected, fun-loving girl with a big heart and a brassy Chicago accent. Her father was a bricklayer, her mother a beautician, and the two of us were thrown together one morning during our junior year when we were randomly paired as lab partners in a biology class.

It was the day of our first dissection, and Paula and I were supposed to make a seven-centimeter incision in a cat and remove its spleen to the satisfaction of the instructor. I didn't expect to have any trouble with the assignment—I'd cleaned hundreds of ducks and fish—and I was fine as we extracted the cat from its sealed container and shaved its stomach. But when it came time to make the incision, I couldn't do it. I was sick with the smell of death and formaldehyde, and as I looked down at the sodden cat with the scalpel in my hand, I froze.

Paula was making little clucking sounds of frustration. "C'mon, Hayes, it's a dead cat. You want *me* to cut it?"

"No, no thank you," I whispered. "I can do this."

I held the scalpel above the cat's stomach, but I couldn't make the incision.

Then, very casually, Paula placed her hand on top of mine. "If we're gonna be partners, maybe we should do this together." And that's what we did. I held the scalpel, and Paula moved my hand.

"Jeez, Hayes, you gotta tell me when to stop," she said. "I don't know what a centimeter is, but we practically have old Felix nutted and gutted." Then we both started to laugh and everything was fine after that. I ate lunch with Paula that afternoon and thanked her.

"Don't mention it," she said. "Last winter there was a cat under the hood of my car when I started it, so I have some experience when it comes to cutting up cats. Jeez, what a mess! I guess you're better at talking, huh?"

"Talking?"

"Yeah, you know—*debating*."

"You know about that?"

"You gotta be kidding, Hayes. Your name's in the announcements every day."

It probably was. I lived for Debate Society, and I loved debating—the crisp format, the unflinching certitude. But what I liked most about it was the way every topic could be reduced to a pair of tidy arguments, only one of which would prevail. It was like Cape Vincent—things were one way or the other, never both at the same time. For someone like me, debate was a hothouse environment. It was also a sanctuary of order and permanence at a time when everything in America was beginning to unravel.

I was aware of the Vietnam War when I was in high school—we all were—but in the mid-sixties the war was still popular, and few questioned the domino theory or wondered what really happened that night in the Gulf of Tonkin. All that would come later, after the anti-war demonstrations that swirled around the Democratic National Convention in 1968. That's where I got my one and only whiff of tear gas.

I was no one's idea of a hippie, yippie or student radical, but in late August, I went with Paula to the Chicago Coliseum because I wanted to hear Terry Southern and Allen Ginsberg address the crowd. It was fun, and there was no trouble at the Coliseum or even afterward, when several thousand people attended the free concert in Grant Park.

The only surprise that afternoon was one of the guest speakers, an intense, electrifying young man named Abbie Hoffman. There was so much unbridled rage in him that I thought he might explode. But the crowd loved him. From that moment, I became fascinated with Abbie Hoffman, not because I agreed with his politics but because I wondered what it would be like to live as he did—in a world where right and wrong were matters of perspective.

Because Tuesday had been quiet, I went back the next day to hear Norman Mailer, who was scheduled to speak in Grant Park. I asked Paula if she wanted to go again, but she said once was enough.

"Didn't you enjoy it?" I asked. "You liked Abbie Hoffman."

Paula smiled. "I did. I *do*—he's really cute—but don't you get tired of all that 'power to the people' crap? That stuff just isn't me."

"It isn't me, either."

"Yeah, but I'll tell you something. Yesterday, when all those people were talking about overthrowing the establishment and everything, all I could think about was how two years ago, I was still wearing culottes and monogrammed sweaters."

"Like I've always said, your sense of style is—"

"Hayes, you know perfectly well what I mean."

I did, but I pretended not to. "I used to have the days of the week embroidered on my underpants, Zee, but I don't see what that has to do with anything."

"Yes, you do, Hayes. You may be a whiz kid, but you can't fool me."

So I went alone. I parked my car at the Field Museum, and when I looked up, I could see soldiers on the roof of the building. That should have told me something, but it didn't. I walked over to the park, and there were so many people there that I struggled to reach the band shell, where the speakers were.

But I got to hear Norman Mailer. When the rally was over, many of the people tried to march on the Amphitheatre, where the Democratic Convention was being held, but National Guardsmen had blocked the bridges at Balbo Avenue and Congress Parkway. Things turned ugly in a hurry, and I made my way back to my car and got out of there—but not before the tear gas was fired.

After the Democratic Convention, the Vietnam War fractured the country and seeped into the cracks like rain. By the time it was over, more than two million Americans had served in Vietnam, and fifty-eight thousand had died there. The rest of us watched the war on TV, surprised to find that the battle lines often ran right through our shag-carpeted living rooms.

Nothing was ever the same after Vietnam. Everything came apart, and everyone was touched by it in some way, including me.

Chapter 3

The most important thing that happened to me as a teenager had nothing to do with Debate Society, the war or the social upheaval it left in its wake. It was Hedley's death during the middle of my sophomore year. My mother answered the phone; there was a breathless "*When?*" And at that instant I knew Hedley was gone.

Tom, my mother and I left for Cape Vincent the next day. It was a sad trip, and the only good thing about it was the chance to see Jimmy, once at the visitation and once after the funeral. When he saw me, he said, "My favorite river rat!" and whirled me around. He was handsome, as always, very tan, and he had a blonde woman with him who looked as though she'd arrived in the Cape directly from the pages of *Vogue*. Jimmy had to leave right after the funeral to return to Florida—business, he said. He never came by the house, and I'm sure he wasn't invited.

A day or two after the funeral, my mother received a phone call from Hedley's lawyer, asking her to come to Watertown for the reading of the will. So while Tom was left to sort through Hedley's clothes, she and I went to the lawyer's office to do whatever needed doing.

Watertown was only forty-five minutes away, but there had been so much snow we couldn't see over the plow drifts, and it was like driving in a maze, except that my mother knew where she was going. The law firm of Hancock, Weiss & Wheeler was in old Watertown, and its dark mahogany paneling and sconces oozed Victorian clubbiness. The receptionist led us down a hallway hung with portraits of men in bowties and mutton chops, then motioned us into the office of a man not much younger than Hedley, who came around from behind his desk and introduced himself as Eldon Wheeler. He offered his condolences, and we all sat down.

"I used to hunt with Hedley in the old days, Mrs. Nash," he said. "I'm going to miss him."

"Thank you," my mother said. "So will we."

Mr. Wheeler cleared his throat. "All right, then … this won't take long. Your father's will is in perfect legal order, and you and your brother James are the only beneficiaries. I've attempted to contact James, but so far I've been unsuccessful."

At the mention of her brother, my mother seemed to stiffen. "Jimmy is out of town. I don't know when he'll be back."

Mr. Wheeler smiled and opened a folder on his desk. "Not to worry. I'll catch up with him eventually." He then explained that my mother was to receive Hedley's house and "any and all personal property and financial assets," which, as I remember, amounted to a little over three thousand dollars.

"The property on Lake Ontario," he said, "which is described in the will as Addison's Point, is bequeathed to your brother."

My mother nearly came out of her chair. "To *Jimmy*? That's like leaving it to Hap Strattner!"

I thought I saw Mr. Wheeler nod, though perhaps he just lowered his head.

"What does Hap Strattner have to do with anything?" I asked.

"*Never mind*," my mother said.

She signed some documents, and Mr. Wheeler again offered his condolences. Then we were in the car heading back to Cape Vincent. It was late afternoon, and the winter landscape was changing from white to blue, the way it does in snow country at twilight. Occasionally, when I could see over the drifts, I could make out a farm or hay barn in the distance. Everything looked cold and lonely. My mother was very quiet. I should have been quiet, too, but I was fifteen.

"Why did you say that about Hap Strattner? I think Mr. Wheeler knows him." Other than the things I'd heard Hedley and my mother say about him, I knew nothing of Hap Strattner, except that he was Jimmy's partner in the Sable Island Hunt Club, where Jimmy had introduced me to him one time when we were hunting.

"Everybody knows Hap," my mother said, "just like everybody knows Jimmy." She unwound her scarf and let it fall into her lap. "I shouldn't have said anything back there, but I was hoping Grandpa would leave the point to me. That way it could be yours someday."

"But he left it to Jimmy. That's just as good. You should turn your headlights on—three point deduction."

My mother groaned. "I'll be glad when you finish drivers' ed. You don't know this, Allie, but Hap has been trying to buy the point for years. Your grandpa wouldn't sell, but Hap's odds just got a lot better."

"Now your brights are on. Why would Hap want the point? Is he a duck hunter?"

"Everybody's a duck hunter, but it isn't that. Hap thinks the point is a gold mine—he wants to *develop* it or something." She inflected the word as though it soiled her lips.

"Uncle Jimmy knows what the point means to me. He'll never sell it."

"One thing has nothing to do with the other, sweetheart—not where Jimmy's concerned. Sooner or later, he'll need money, and

Hap will end up with the point." She drove on in silence for a time, then shook her head. "I know you love that place more than anything in the world. I've just never understood why."

"Because it's beautiful, because of the ducks, because of the wind—a million reasons."

"The wind is what Jimmy never liked about it," she murmured, almost to herself.

"Well, wind or not, the point's in good hands."

"That's a matter of opinion," she said. "Hap Strattner is a gambler and a crook. And Jimmy—your knight in shining armor—isn't much better."

"Jimmy isn't a crook. What a thing to say!"

My mother turned to me. "He's a smuggler, Allie. It's the same thing."

I couldn't help laughing. "Eyes on the road please. A smuggler? Next you'll be telling me—"

"You were too young to know anything about him when we lived here, but it's true—he's one of the biggest smugglers on the Seaway. I know you think Uncle Jimmy hung the moon, but you're fifteen years-old now. Where do you think his money comes from? The clothes, the cars, the—"

"From his club on Sable Island. He makes tons of—"

"Hogwash!" my mother said. "The hunt club is one of those big fancy places that never breaks even. I know—I have friends here."

"Then it's just hearsay."

"C'mon, Allie, this isn't one of your debates. Jimmy's been a smuggler since high school and everybody knows it."

"Fine." I was angry and numb. The last thing I wanted was a smuggler for an uncle, especially if that uncle was Jimmy. Smugglers were the lowest rung on Hedley's ladder, and suddenly a lot of things about my family were beginning to make sense. But not in a good way.

It was completely dark now and beginning to snow. After a mile or so, my mother looked over at me. "There's some kleenex in the glove compartment."

"I'm not crying."

"Okay."

"I'm *not*."

"Good. It isn't worth crying over. Jimmy is just … Jimmy."

"People can change," I said. "Uncle Jimmy may have been a smuggler once, but I'll bet he isn't one anymore."

My mother laughed. "That's a sucker's bet, sweetheart. When the fiddle's cracked, it's cracked."

I slouched down in the seat. "I don't know anything about fiddles. But I know Uncle Jimmy will never sell Grandpa's point, not to Hap Strattner or anybody else."

"We'll see. I hope you're right."

"I *am* right."

We were almost to the house before I spoke again. "What kind of a name is Hap, anyway? Is it short for Happy?"

My mother made a little sound, almost a laugh. "Not even close. I've never seen Hap when he was happy, unless it was in some gin mill with another man's wife. His real name is Harold, but his father nicknamed him Hap, and that's what everyone's called him since he was a little boy. He drank and gambled so much his father finally cut him off. That's when he latched onto Jimmy, and the two of them sort of … went into a tailspin."

"Even if everything you say about Jimmy is true, you shouldn't hate somebody—especially your brother—just because he's a smuggler."

"I don't hate him, Allie. It isn't that. It's just …"

"Just what?"

We were pulling into Hedley's driveway, and my mother pointed to the house, where the blue light of the TV was flickering in the window.

"Uh-oh," she said. "I hope Tom didn't quit on us."

Chapter 4

When we walked in, Tom was on the sofa, his feet up, watching a snowy telecast of a football game. He was drinking a beer and eating a can of cocktail peanuts that he'd scrounged in the cupboard.

"Everything go okay with the lawyer?" he asked. "I was starting to worry—the weather took a turn."

Ace was on the sofa, too—something Hedley had always forbidden. He thumped his thick tail against the cushions when he saw me but remained where he was, no doubt afraid that if he climbed off, we'd remember he wasn't supposed to be there in the first place.

"You look worried," my mother said, laughing. "It started to snow outside of Chaumont, but the roads aren't bad. Did you finish sorting Hedley's clothes?"

"An hour ago." Tom got a funny look on his face. "Did you know all your father's clothes are wool? Pants, shirts—even his underwear."

"Well, it gets cold up here," my mother said. "And he just ... liked wool."

"You're telling me. Your father had three kinds of clothes, Ellen—clothes for when it's cold, clothes for when it's *really* cold and clothes for when it's cold enough to freeze the balls off a brass monkey."

My mother wrinkled her nose. "How quaint. You've been here less than a week, and already you sound like a river rat. By the way, those peanuts you're eating are probably older than Allie."

"They taste okay." Tom peered into the can. "How can I get the game to come in better?"

"Just like at home," she said. "Move the antenna."

"I would, but I don't see any rotor control."

My mother pointed to the entryway. "You should've looked on the coat rack by the front door."

Tom got up and walked over to the coat rack. "There's nothing here but a pipe wrench." He took it from its hook and held it up. Ace, who knew all about the pipe wrench, jumped off the sofa and stood by the front door, his nose to the crack.

"That wrench is the rotor control," my mother said. "If you want to move the antenna, go outside and put that wrench on the pipe that's holding it up. Look in the window at the TV while you're turning it. And please take Ace with you. That's what he's waiting for."

Tom looked at her as though she were out of her mind.

"This isn't Chicago," she said. "Things are different here."

"Different? No, no. Spaghetti and linguini are different. Football and rugby are different. Cape Vincent is another *dimension*—I keep looking around for Rod Serling."

I laughed, and my mother gave me a dirty look. "Tom … the dog?"

"Yeah, okay. Let's go, Ace." Wrench in hand, he followed Ace out the door, muttering something about the Flintstones.

My mother then turned her attention to me. "I talked to one of Hedley's friends yesterday about taking Ace. He said he'd be happy to do it. You know we can't take him with us, don't you, Allie?"

"Yes," I lied.

After dinner I helped my mother sort through the kitchen cabinets and drawers for a while. Then I began looking at the books and magazines on Hedley's bookshelf. One of the more tattered magazines contained an article about Jimmy and the Sable Island Hunt Club, which it described as "a duck hunter's paradise."

I enjoyed looking at the old pictures of the club, but everything seemed different from the last time Jimmy had taken me there—the day I'd met Hap Strattner. When Jimmy and I had arrived at Sable that morning, Hap was sitting alone at a table in the main dining room with his head in his hands. The table was covered with poker chips and beer bottles, and Jimmy said, "Hap, this is my niece." Hap, who was bleary-eyed and half asleep, had looked up and winked. I've never forgotten that, because it was the only communication I ever had with him.

If I'd told my mother how Jimmy and I got to the club that day, she would have revoked every privilege I had, then flayed Jimmy alive. That's because the Sable Island Hunt Club, true to its name, was on an island—sort of. A hundred years ago, Sable Island had been connected to the mainland by a narrow strip of land that served as a road. But since then, the water level of Lake Ontario had risen steadily, turning the little road into a ford. You could drive a car on it—you could even pass somebody on it, if you knew what you were doing—but it was dangerous. Most of the time, there was only a couple feet of water over the ford, but on either side, it was eighty feet deep. So if you slipped off the edge, you had to bail out of your vehicle in a hurry.

Jimmy had marked both sides of the ford with buoys that stretched in a meandering path to the island. The trick, of course, was to stay between them, which was harder than it sounds because they were so far apart. But Jimmy, Hap and the employees of the hunt club used the ford regularly, and that's what Jimmy and I did that day, except then I didn't know what was happening. All I knew was that Jimmy had inexplicably driven right past the dock, where his boat was moored, and out into the lake. What I felt at that moment was something no human being can convey to another.

I remember looking at Sable Island, a lifetime away, and plowing through the water as though we were in a boat. But it wasn't a boat. It was a truck, bouncing around like a toy in the hands of a child. I don't know how deep the water was that year, but it was deep enough that I was scared. It came in under the doors, and I looked down to see cigarette butts and candy wrappers swirling up toward me. I put my feet on the dashboard, and the air was suddenly filled with smoke and the smell of antifreeze.

"Don't worry," Jimmy hollered. "I drove out here two weeks ago, and the water was a foot deeper. Open your window. Let's get some of this steam outta here." Then he looked at me and laughed. "Relax, kiddo, this is nothing."

It may have been nothing to Jimmy, but it was certainly something to me. But we made it across, and I had a wonderful time. There were no guests at the club, and Jimmy showed me around before we went hunting. The lodge itself was an old mansion with a carriage house that smelled like cedar because that's where they made the decoys, which were strung from the rafters like garland. There were big freezers, machines for plucking ducks and several punkin seeds in there, too—little clamshell floaters that a hunter could anchor in the middle of his decoys and lie down in. An older man in overalls was painting something, and Jimmy introduced us. His name was Stokes. He shook my hand and turned to Jimmy.

"Hap sure had himself a snoot full last night, boss. Is he awake yet?"

"Sort of," Jimmy said.

"By golly, I don't think he had a winning hand all night."

After we left the carriage house, Jimmy showed me the lighthouse, which stood on a rocky little cliff not far from the mansion.

We took the wrought-iron staircase all the way up to where the light was, and when I looked one way, I could see the rooftops of Sackets Harbor, and when I looked the other way, I could see Stony Island and a raft of ducks, like an oil slick, stretching across the water.

That was also the day I shot my first duck—something else my mother would have been angry about, since she and Hedley had agreed I was not to fire a gun until I was twelve. That was an iron-clad rule. But Jimmy, who was unimpressed with rules, put a little .410 shotgun in my hands and insisted I use it. I made him swear by all deities not to tell my mother or Hedley, but he just laughed.

"Allie, I was seven when I shot my first duck. This button's the safety. Remember to lead 'em."

I was somewhere in the middle of my second box of shells when I finally hit one. I was thrilled, and Jimmy was as excited as I was. He gave me a hug and said I was now an official river rat.

I put the magazine back on the bookshelf. It was getting late. Tom had finished watching the news and weather, and as he turned off the TV he said, "This Vietnam business doesn't look good. McNamara just said it will take 400,000 troops to win this thing. That's almost 300,000 more than we have there now. But I guess if that's what we have to do …"

"I don't know anybody over there," I said.

"You will. Before this war is over, we'll all know somebody who fought there. Are you about done, Ellen?"

"Almost. I've got everything boxed and labeled. Do you know what you're taking home, Allie?"

"Three decoys, Grandpa's shotgun and his hunting coat."

"Okay, good," she said. "Then whatever his friends don't want will go to the Salvation Army."

After a while we all went to bed, but I couldn't stop thinking about Hedley, Jimmy and things that happened a long time ago. But the old memories were all mixed up with new ones, and I began to wonder if our lives really had a past, present and future. Maybe they were events, like atoms, in which everything is interconnected and happening at once. We do our best to live in the nucleus of the present moment, but everything that has ever happened to us—and everything that ever will—is whirling around that nucleus in a confounding, ceaseless orbit.

I could hear Ace wandering around the house, his toenails clicking on the floor. Then I heard him circle a couple times beside my bed and lie down heavily. It was getting cold, and I lay there listening to Hedley's furnace trying to keep up with it and to the nail heads popping in the clapboard siding. Not long after the wind started to blow, I fell asleep.

Two days later we left Cape Vincent for Chicago, and as I climbed into the backseat of the car, I steeled myself against the possibility of tears, my old nemesis. But this time was different. This time Ace was seated beside me, panting with excitement as he watched the Cape flash past the window. I hadn't asked if I could bring him. I just did it. Tom and my mother, who chose both their battles and their terrain very carefully, had offered only token resistance.

I should mention that Ace, who was already past his prime by a season or two when Hedley died, adjusted well to his life as a pet. Tom warmed to him when Ace distinguished himself as a watchdog, and even my mother developed a grudging fondness for him over time. Ace died in his sleep shortly before I moved into my first apartment. Perhaps he planned it that way, unable to reconcile himself to another move. At that time I had just begun my junior year at the University of Illinois Circle Campus in Chicago.

And I was about to meet Mike.

Chapter 5

The fall of 1971 was like being in the eye of a storm. A lot of things were over—Tet, Woodstock, the Summer of Love—but there was an abiding edginess about things to come. A lot of people were over, too—Martin Luther King, Bobby, Malcolm X, not to mention Hendrix, Morrison, Joplin and the Beatles. But for all that, the country was at rest, if only for a moment. Even Abbie Hoffman, the angry young man from the Chicago Coliseum, had calmed down long enough to become a famous author. In 1971, Yeats' widening gyre was as wide as it would get for a while. And so far, the center was holding.

Of course, whatever ideas we may have had about history stopping to catch its breath would vanish the very next year, when five inept burglars were arrested for breaking into the Democratic National Headquarters. But we could not know that then. In 1971 it merely seemed as though a lot of things had passed, some of them forever. What I could not know was that a lot of things in my life were about to begin.

During the week I divided my time between a part-time job and school. Paula and I were still very close—she'd graduated from a two-year technical college and was working at Marshall Field's in the Loop—and the Saturday after Thanksgiving, we went to a party together in Winnetka at the home of a girl I knew from school. The girl's parents, I believe, were in Vail, skiing.

When we got out of the car, Paula looked at the huge house and whistled softly. "Jeez, I don't know what this guy does, but I'm pretty sure he isn't a bricklayer."

"I think he's a doctor," I said. "Everybody in Winnetka is a doctor."

"You wouldn't understand this, Allie, because your parents are rich and all, but every time I'm up here on the North Shore—honest to God—I feel like I'm gonna get carded."

"You're being silly," I said. "It's just a house, and we're going to have a good time. Maybe you'll meet a handsome young surgeon."

Paula checked her hair in the reflection of the car window. "I'd settle for an okay-looking proctologist."

It was a great party, and the house, which was decorated inside and out for Christmas, was full of people who were laughing, talking, having a good time. We'd probably been there a couple hours, when I was making my way through the crowded living room and noticed two young men standing in the foyer. One had his coat on and his back to the front door, as though he was about to leave. The other was imploring him to "stick around for a while." I was almost past the foyer when I heard something that shot through me like a jolt of electricity.

"I'd like to stay, but I'm going hunting in the morning, and I have to get up early."

I stopped mid-stride and turned my head, very slowly, toward that voice.

One of the things that had struck me about Chicago, almost immediately, was that it seemed to be a city without hunters. People played golf, they skied, they went on cruises—they did everything but hunt. So the impact of those words—*I'm going hunting in the morning*—was profound. I had to meet this guy, but before I could figure out how to make that happen, he was halfway out the door. Without thinking about it, without thinking about anything, I followed him onto the porch.

"I heard what you said about going hunting. Are you really a hunter?" I was terrifically embarrassed, and my voice sounded very small and an octave too high, like a cartoon character—a ladybug or maybe a talking flea.

He turned around, somewhat startled. "A hunter? I guess so. I don't have much—"

"Time? I know. It must be hard to—"

"It is. With school and—"

"Yes, yes, I can imagine."

We stood there, each of us wondering what would happen next. I couldn't tell if he was more surprised by the hunter question or the fact that I'd waylaid him on the porch to ask it. He studied me carefully for a moment, then reached behind me and closed the door. He looked a little older than I was, and although he was smiling, his eyes were serious—serious and very green.

"I haven't met a hunter for years," I said. "I didn't know there *were* any hunters in Chicago. Honestly, I don't know a single—"

"You're not from here?"

"No, I'm from New York."

He questioned with his eyes.

"No, no, not the city—a little town called Cape Vincent. Everybody in Cape Vincent hunts. What do you hunt for in Chicago?"

"Parking spaces and cheap restaurants, mostly."

"I meant—"

He laughed. "Yeah, I know. There's decent hunting west of the city. I get a few pheasants, even some ducks once in a while."

"Is that where you're going tomorrow?"

"Yes, if I can manage a couple hours sleep tonight."

"I'm sorry," I said. "You were trying to leave and I'm keeping you." My embarrassment, as well as the Hanna-Barbera voice, had returned.

"You're not keeping me at all. But I'm curious why you followed me out here to talk about hunting."

"I don't know," I said, and it was true. "I used to go hunting when I was little. Sometimes, I get … lonely for it. Did you hunt when you were little?"

"Yeah, ever since—aren't you getting cold out here? Should we—"

"No, no, I'm fine. Really. How often do you go hunting?"

"As often as I can," he said, "but usually in the afternoons. Most of my classes are in the morning."

To this day I can't believe what I said next. Before I realized the words had left my lips, I said, "I'd like to go with you sometime."

Instantly, I felt like an idiot, but he acted as though it were a perfectly reasonable request for one stranger to make of another.

"How about next Saturday?" he said.

"Saturday would be fine." I could feel my face turning red. "But listen, you don't really have to do this. I had no right to—"

"I'll need a phone number." He took a pen out of his pocket and wrote my number on his hand. "And it wouldn't hurt if you were to tell me your name."

"I'm Allison Hayes—Allie," I said in my tiny new voice.

"Well, Allie, I'm Mike Bowman. I'll give you a call tomorrow." He extended his hand and I shook it.

"Thank you. I feel funny about this."

"Don't. I'm already looking forward to it." He smiled, said good night and headed down the stairs.

"It was nice to meet you," I squeaked. Then I went back inside and collapsed on the arm of a sofa.

Paula was instantly at my side. "Well?"

"I'm going hunting," I said stupidly.

"You're doing *what*?"

"I'm going hunting. I just … forced myself on a total stranger."

"Jeez, I thought you knew him or something."

"No, I don't know the first—"

"Then I know more than you do," she said, "because when you two were out on the porch, I asked the guy he was talking to."

"And?"

"He's a Vietnam vet and a grad student in English at UC. He's very good-looking—an Aries if I ever saw one."

"He is?"

"Oh yeah—positively Aries."

I didn't really expect to hear from Mike Bowman the next day, or ever again, and I wouldn't have blamed him if he hadn't called. But he did. We made our plans for the following Saturday in the course of a short conversation, the centerpiece of which was a rather detailed discussion of clothing and footwear.

As soon as I hung up the phone, I felt a sense of relief—now all I had to do was wait. But that proved more difficult than I expected, because I couldn't decide if I were waiting for something good, like a paycheck, or for something unpleasant, like a trip to the dentist. Finally, after toggling back and forth between anticipation and dread, I simplified things by experiencing both emotions at once.

Mike Bowman seemed nice enough, and I looked forward to seeing him again. But I couldn't help wondering what I'd gotten myself into. It was sort of a nightmare, one with Freudian overtones.

Chapter 6

On Saturday morning at exactly nine o'clock, Mike Bowman picked me up at my apartment in a little station wagon—a Volkswagen squareback, to be exact—and we headed west, leaving the city behind us. We exchanged the necessary pleasantries about majors and colleges before inevitably bending the conversation toward each other.

"You were in Vietnam," I said, in a way that was neither a question nor an accusation.

Mike looked at his face in the rearview mirror. "Does it show?"

"Of course not," I said, laughing. "I heard that at the party."

"Yeah, it's the same old story—I wanted to go to college, but I didn't have the money, so I joined the army. I was lucky, though—never got so much as a scratch."

"Maybe I shouldn't tell you this, but I've actually protested against the Vietnam War—twice, in fact."

"Who hasn't?" he said. "If I had time, I'd protest against it myself."

"Really? I mean, it's crazy. We're dropping bombs on people because they want to become Communists. It's immoral to—"

Mike laughed and flashed me the peace sign. "Hey, I agree—and 'immoral' doesn't touch it. But when you're over there, things like right and wrong aren't the issue anymore. It's right to stay alive, and it's wrong to get killed. That's about it."

I played the last few moments of conversation back in my head. "I think there should be a rule against couples discussing death on their first date. How do you like my boots? Are they okay?" I was wearing eight-inch leather hiking boots and held up my right foot for inspection.

"They look fine. Are they waterproof?"

"I think so," I said, "but I've never had the chance to find out. You certainly picked a beautiful day for an outing."

"It's too nice a day to spend in the city—that's for sure."

And it was. It was one of those lovely Midwestern days that sometimes occurs in the narrow seam between the seasons—cool without being cold and a sky so blue that if you were trying to paint it, you'd forego your entire palette for the exuberance of a blue crayon.

It always feels good to leave a city, but it was especially nice leaving Chicago that morning. Soon, the expressways shrank from six lanes to four, the looming office buildings disappeared, and the cavernous feeling of the city disappeared with them. As we drove on, we passed freight yards, smokestacks and factories, which quickly gave way to apartment buildings, strip malls and billboards. And then, without warning, the rows of tract homes became rows of corn, and Chicago was gone.

We were on roads that day I'd never heard of, and the countryside was like parts of northern New York, except there were more crops and fewer cattle. A little over an hour after we'd left the city, we stopped at an intersection in the middle of what might have been nowhere—or anywhere. On one corner was a little mom-and-pop place called the Cloverdale Store, and across from it was the Cloverdale Bar. Both places looked as though they had leaped from Norman Rockwell's easel, and both were the unmistakable work of the same carpenter.

Mike pulled into the bar's empty parking lot. "This is where we'll leave the car. We're going to walk the railroad tracks that run right behind this place."

"Is it okay to park here?"

"Sure, they know me—I hunt these tracks a lot." He looked over his shoulder at the store. "Before we head out, let's grab something to eat. I didn't bring anything for lunch. Did you?"

"Of course," I said. "I brought a fried egg sandwich for each of us."

"You did? Thank you. I've never had a fried egg sandwich."

"They're big in Cape Vincent," I said. "Very popular with hunters."

"What do you put on a fried egg sandwich?"

"Cheese, bacon and catsup."

"Sounds good. I've never heard it called 'catsup,' either."

"Yes, I'm working on that. I've lost almost all of my accent, but I slip up now and then on certain words like 'ketchup.' You should hear how some of the old people talk in Cape Vincent."

"Show me."

"It's noyce dat deez folks let yous pahk da cah heah."

"Wow!" Mike started to get out of the car, then turned to me, laughing. "Listen, we have to stop and say hello to these people. Try not to say anything—you'll frighten them."

When we walked into the Cloverdale Store, a little bell jingled on the door, and a startled cat leaped off the counter by the cash register, but no one was working up front. It was hard to believe anything like the Cloverdale Store could have existed within seventy-five miles of Chicago, or a hundred and seventy-five, for that matter. It had a wooden floor with sawdust sprinkled over it, and in the middle of the store, the tiny aisles stopped abruptly in order to make room for a potbelly stove that was ticking and humming with heat.

I heard footsteps descending an invisible staircase, and then magically, a smiling, heavyset woman appeared to greet us.

"Vaddya know?" she said happily in a thick German accent. "If it isn't the hunter again. But dis time he brings his lady. It is so goot to see you."

"It's good to see you, too," Mike said. "Nedra, I'd like you to meet Allison Hayes. Allie, this is Nedra."

"It is *pleasure*," Nedra said, taking my hand. "You are hunter, too?"

"I used to be," I said. "But today I'm just a tagalong." I could tell she didn't understand the word. "I'm just going to keep Mike company."

"Ah, yes," Nedra said. "He is lucky to have such pretty company. You are nice couple. Michael, you go back und say hullo to Otto. He alvays like to meet pretty girls."

Mike didn't seem the least bit embarrassed by her assumptions, nor did he offer any explanation of my presence. I smiled at the "pretty girl" business, and we walked to the rear of the store, where we found Otto behind the meat counter, above which hung a large picture of a cow that grazed bravely, despite being partitioned into cuts of meat. Otto was heavy, like his wife, and his gray hair was cut very short. He was trimming something on a big butcher block, but when he saw us, he put down his knife and came over to the counter, beaming.

"*Wie geht's*, Otto?" Mike said.

Otto laughed. "*Es geht mir gut. Ganz gut.* Michael, I am so happy you haf come hunting again—und with such a *schönes Mädchen!*"

"This is my friend Allison Hayes." Mike placed a slight emphasis on the explicative for Otto's benefit, and Otto wiped his big hand on his apron and reached across the counter. We shook hands a long time.

"It's very nice to meet you, Otto."

"You are just friends," he said, smiling and holding my hand. "But you go hunting together, so *who knows*? Such a pretty girl, *who knows*? It is nice to meet you, Allison Hayes. You und Michael vill come to the bar later?"

"Sure, we'll stop for a beer when we get back," Mike said.

"Goot. I vill see you den."

We bought two fruit pies and two sodas to go with our sandwiches and walked back across the street to the car.

"Otto and Nedra seem very fond of you," I said.

"You were a pretty big hit yourself. I was beginning to wonder if Otto was ever going to let go of your hand. I'm sorry if they embarrassed you."

"I wasn't embarrassed. They're very nice. How do you know them?"

"My father and I hunted around here when I was a kid, and we'd always stop in to say hello and buy something. Now I do the same thing. I give them a few birds for letting me park here."

I realized Mike was looking at me, studying me as he'd done that night when I followed him out the door at the party.

"What is it?" I giggled. "You're staring at me."

"Am I?" He leaned against the car and smiled, his eyes still fixed on my face. "I was just thinking that Otto and Nedra are right—you're very pretty."

"Thank you. I'll bet you say that to all the girls who make you take them hunting."

"Only when Otto and Nedra say it first."

Mike opened up the back of the Volkswagen, and we put on our heavy coats. Then he filled his pockets with shells and pulled his shotgun from its case.

"I brought a shotgun for you," he said, gesturing inside the car.

33

"I don't have a license. I'll just walk with you."

I was wearing Hedley's canvas hunting coat over a down jacket of my own, and the smell of his coat recalled other times and places. We stuffed our pockets with sandwiches and the things from the store, then climbed the steep embankment up to the railroad tracks and headed west. The tracks stretched before us endlessly, converging in a shiny acute angle on the horizon.

"What I like about these tracks," Mike said, "is that they run by a couple potholes where we might jump some ducks. If not, I know we'll see pheasants."

"What I like is the way they seem to go on forever. Does anybody care if you hunt along them?"

"I don't think so," he said. "The farms are all posted, but we're on a railroad right-of-way. It's like an alley that runs behind the fields, but there's nothing out here. You won't even see a farmhouse."

He was right, and within fifteen minutes we were alone in a vast flatness, a patchwork of fields held together by distant hedgerows. There were fields of winter wheat, whose improbable greenness belied the season, and there were many fallow fields. But most important to us were the cornfields—some picked, some standing—because Mike said the pheasants would stay close to the corn. On either side of the tracks was a thirty-yard margin of grass and weeds, which is where we walked, changing sides now and then, depending on which one had better cover. We walked very slowly and as quietly as possible, so that we could surprise the birds and force them into the air before they had time to run ahead of us or scurry back into the fields. In the first forty-five minutes, we jumped several hens and one rooster that flushed well out of range.

Mike took off his hat and wiped his brow. "This would be a lot easier with a dog. We're probably pushing a lot of birds ahead of us and walking over birds we never see."

"You don't live where you can have a dog?"

"No, I'm in an apartment. Besides, you can't have a dog in the

34

city unless you're home a lot. When I finish my master's, I might be able to get one."

"What's your thesis on?"

"Do I have to tell?"

I laughed. "You do now."

Mike looked like a man confessing to a crime. "It's basically an Aristotelian analysis of post-modern tragic form. Very University of Chicago—a real page-turner."

"I'm sure it is. It sounds terribly serious … like you."

"I hope that's a good thing."

"I have no idea. I haven't read it."

"I meant the part about me."

"I know."

We were walking the left side of the tracks when we came to a place where I could see a large black culvert sticking out of the embankment. Mike said there was a slough up ahead, and if pheasants had been running in front of us, they'd be stacked up somewhere between us and the water, unable to go farther. Mike went first, one small step at a time, in a way that led me to believe something was about to happen.

"You'd better get behind me," he whispered.

So I followed a couple steps behind and watched him. I enjoyed watching him. I liked the way he moved and the way his shoulders filled his hunting coat. I was sure he'd been some kind of jock in high school, football probably.

We were almost to the culvert, and the ground had just begun to squish underfoot when, all at once, the air was filled with pheasants. Mike looked at one rooster, then another and drew a bead on a third that was escaping to his left. He raised his gun and followed it but held his fire until I was sure the bird was out of range. At the last possible moment there was a crash, and the rooster somersaulted in midair and fell beside the slough. Mike retrieved it quickly, trying to keep the water from going over his boot tops.

35

He held it up. "It's a nice one. Look at the size of it."

"It's huge," I said. "I was afraid you were never going to shoot. It was like you were picking out a roast in a grocery store."

Mike smiled. "Not really. Every rooster but this one flew out over the slough. I didn't want to knock one down where I'd get wet retrieving it."

"Why did you wait so long to shoot?"

"I didn't want to blow it up." He tucked the pheasant into his coat. "It's no fun eating birds that are full of shot, so I let them get out there a ways."

That was a new one for me. Hedley was smooth with a shotgun, and Jimmy was fast, but I'd never seen efficient before. It fit him, though. There was something about Mike that was mirrored in his shooting, something confident and considered. I decided I liked that, too.

We probably walked another half mile without flushing a bird when a rooster exploded from under my feet, scaring me half to death. I screamed, and I think Mike was actually laughing when he shot it, once again, at the last possible moment.

"You should've seen your face," he said, slipping the bird into his pocket.

"I can imagine. I think I stepped on that bird."

We ate our lunch beside a pretty little pothole dotted with muskrat houses and surrounded by tag alder. We devoured every morsel, and we were having a good time. We liked each other, and we both knew it, which put us at ease. It was as though we'd known each other for years.

Mike was completely self-assured without a trace of swagger—something I'd felt from the time we met—and there was a quiet steadiness about him that gave the impression that the closer you stood to him, the safer you were likely to be. Some of that was probably a result of Mike's being on his own. The rest of it was simply him.

Mike's father had died while Mike was still in high school, and he said that his mother had died shortly after his return from Vietnam. I told him about Jimmy, Tom and my mother, plus a few things about Cape Vincent. Mike had actually heard of Jimmy and even read about the Sable Island Hunt Club.

"Your uncle is famous," he said. "He's like Jimmy Robinson."

"Who's he?"

Mike looked surprised. "A writer. He owns a big duck club in Manitoba."

Mike asked a lot of questions about Sable Island, because he'd spent several summers working at a similar place—a hunting and fishing camp in northwestern Ontario. I couldn't answer many of them, but I did my best.

At some point during lunch, I went through the pockets of Hedley's hunting coat, looking for the tissues I'd stuffed into one of them, and I found Hedley's compass, old and blotchy with verdigris. I hadn't seen it since I was a little girl.

"Look what I found," I said. "This was my grandfather's."

I handed the compass to Mike, who examined it closely. "Very nice—solid brass. Cape Vincent is sure a long way from here."

"You have no idea," I said. "But how can you tell that from the compass?"

Mike tapped on the crystal. "Your grandfather set the angle of declination at thirteen degrees west, which is what you'd do if you lived a thousand miles east of here. Where we're sitting right now is only two degrees west, if that."

"West of *what?*"

"West of true north."

"As opposed to *un*true north?" I said. "North is north, isn't it?"

"Not really. There are two of them."

"Now I'm really confused. How is that possible?"

Mike furrowed his brow. "Well … *true* north is the North Pole. *Magnetic* north is what a compass needle points to, and they aren't the same. The degree of difference between the two is called the angle of declination, and it varies depending on where you are. So if you're in Cape Vincent, and you want your compass to point to true north, like your grandfather did, you adjust it that way. See where he set the pin?"

I looked, but no light bulbs came on. "I didn't realize a compass was different everywhere you go."

"It isn't," Mike said. "The angle of declination is different. If you ignore the angle of declination, the farther you go, the more you stray from your course. Eventually, you'll get disoriented and lose your way."

"So even though you were following your compass, you'd be headed in the wrong direction? That doesn't seem right. There should be one north."

Mike handed the compass back to me. "Maybe so, but we're stuck with two of them."

"Where did you learn all this stuff about compasses and angles?"

"Geomorphology 101. I needed a science credit."

When we finished our lunch, Mike thanked me again for the sandwich and told me how glad he was that I'd followed him out the door that night at the party.

"I'm glad, too," I said. "It's pretty here, and I like … the company." Far above us, a flock of geese were heading south in a loose V, and I remembered an old trap of Hedley's I'd once fallen into. "When geese fly in a V like that, do you know why one side of the V is always longer than the other?"

"No," Mike said. "Why?"

"Because there are more geese on that side."

He laughed. "Cape Vincent humor?"

"Vintage river rat."

We hunted for a while longer, then headed back under a red enameled sunset that looked as though it might burst into flame at any moment. We walked backward halfway to the car just to watch it. Then, when it was almost dark, we saw what looked like a black cloud approaching rapidly from the northwest. At first we couldn't tell what it was, but as it drew closer, we could see that it was migrating blackbirds, millions of them. It was the largest flock of birds either of us had ever seen, and it stretched for miles on the horizon. Different parts of the flock would swoop or climb all at once, as if on cue, and it looked like a serpent gliding noiselessly across the sky, a serpent made of blackbirds.

"An augur would have issued a major press release if he'd seen something like that two thousand years ago," Mike said, watching the birds disappear in the distance.

"Would it have been a good omen or a bad one?"

Mike put his arm around me and pulled me close. "I think it would have been good."

"I think so, too."

When we got to the car, I said, "That was quite a trek. How far did we walk?"

"About eight miles round-trip." Mike threw his coat in the back and looked at me. "I really had a good time. I don't want to take you home."

"You don't have to, at least not right away. Remember, you promised Otto we'd stop at the bar when we got back."

"You're not too tired?"

"I'm tired, but it's *good* tired. Do you think I could have one of those pheasants?"

"Sure. Do you know how to cook it?"

"Yes, and I have some dinner plans that I hope include you."

Chapter 7

During the next two months, Mike and I saw each other whenever we could, and when we couldn't, I would feel empty inside and know that Mike was feeling the same way, because we were in love. It had happened very quickly, and at first it was a little frightening, at least for me. But it was real and it was good. In February, over the strenuous objections of my mother, Mike moved into my apartment, which was larger than his and in a better neighborhood. He did that the week Nixon went to China, and it had the same vaguely thrilling feeling. It felt significant—momentous, even—but we really didn't know where it would lead.

For the most part, that time was a beautiful, crazy-busy dream. Mike and I joked that our lives were probably an allegory of some sort, because everything in the early seventies was a thinly veiled representation of something else. If you unfocused your eyes, a holographic image of a city skyline might morph into a snow-covered mountain range. And if you unfocused your mind, everything from "American Pie" to *Jonathan Livingston Seagull* seemed to suggest other realities just beneath the surface. We were living in Richard

Nixon's America, where nothing was quite as it appeared. Even Watergate was beginning to look like a morality play, though it would take years to identify referents for the principal players.

The strangest thing that happened during that time occurred late one afternoon when I picked Mike up at the new Regenstein Library. The construction was finished, but there were a lot of workmen there, doing landscaping and paving the parking lots, and as I backed out of our space to leave, one of the workmen backed out from the row behind us at the same moment and we collided. I don't know whose fault it was, but the other driver had no doubts. He jumped out of his car, pointed to his rear fender and started screaming at me. Mike and I got out of the car and tried to calm him down, but he was way beyond that.

"What the hell's the matter with you?" he roared, the veins bulging in his neck. "Are you blind?"

"I'm really sorry," I said. "I didn't—"

"You snot-nose college kids make me sick. You think you can do whatever the hell—"

"Look," Mike said. "No one's to blame. It's just one of those things."

The man was practically sputtering. "One of those things? *That stupid coos backed right into—*"

Mike grabbed the man's throat with his right hand and bent him over the trunk of his car. The man's arms flailed helplessly and he tried to fight back, but he couldn't.

Mike leaned over him, putting more weight on the man's throat. "Watch your mouth, mister. It wasn't anybody's fault. Am I right?"

The man couldn't have said anything if he'd wanted to. He was turning purple, kicking his feet. Weakly, with both hands, he tried to pry Mike's fingers from his windpipe.

"Let him go!" I screamed. "He can't breathe."

Mike leaned down until their faces were almost touching. "It wasn't anybody's fault—nod your head."

He jerked his head, and Mike let go. Coughing and gagging, the man got into his car and locked the doors. He couldn't go anywhere until we moved our car, and when we did, he squealed off, one hand on the wheel, the other clutching his throat.

"My God," I said. "What's wrong with you?"

Mike was clenching and unclenching his fingers. "That guy has a big mouth. Maybe he'll keep it shut next time."

"If he lives," I said. "What's a coos? Is it bad?"

"Pretty bad."

"Anatomical?"

"Yes."

"I thought so." I touched my throat. "Did they teach you how to do that in the army?"

Mike laughed. "Yeah, they … give lessons."

"It isn't funny. Don't ever do anything like that again. I mean it. That was really stupid."

"Never again," Mike said.

That little episode shocked and upset me, but there were no more like it, and I never mentioned it again until we had a fight about my decision to drop a required course. I took it again the next term, but it meant that Mike would finish his master's before I graduated, which wasn't part of the plan. But I was comfortable with my decision. When I found out my art history professor had inflated the grades of two young men in the class so they could retain their 2-S deferments, I dropped it the next day. I didn't want *anybody* to go to Vietnam, but the professor had stepped over the line.

Mike thought so, too, but he couldn't understand what I hoped to achieve through a gesture that accomplished nothing, other than costing us money and altering our "plan." Mike, who was very big on plans, said I was behaving like a child—*ingénue* was the word he used—and it really set me off.

"Don't you dare patronize me like that!" I said.

"It just seems so pointless," Mike said. "Idealism gone to

seed."

"Really? What would you like me to do? Should I strangle the professor until he sees it my way?"

We were both angry, and neither of us seemed to understand where the other was coming from. But like the workman at the library, the dropped course was soon forgotten, and those two contretemps were tiny islands in what was otherwise a sea of happiness for both of us.

Not long after we received our degrees, Mike and I were married, but one of our wedding invitations would have as much impact on our lives as the wedding itself. After giving it a lot of thought, Mike decided to invite Dutch Zimmerman, the man who owned the fly-in hunting and fishing camp where Mike had worked a couple summers. Mike had told me about him that time at Cloverdale, when we'd eaten lunch beside the little pond.

"It's not that Dutch and I were buddies," he said, "but I'd like to invite him. He lives in Rockford. That's only a couple hours from here." So we sent our invitations, and that was that—until we got a letter from Dutch a week later.

It was a sad letter. Dutch explained that he had cancer and wouldn't be able to attend the wedding. But there was more. He also wondered if Mike and I would be interested in running his camp the next season because his doctors couldn't say if he'd be able to do it. He trusted Mike, he said, and he didn't know anyone else he could ask. Dutch also said if he were to close the camp for the season, he'd lose it—the bank would take it over.

Mike and I were sitting at the kitchen table when he read me the letter. I think it knocked the wind out of us, though perhaps for different reasons.

"We need to think about this," I said. "We have a lot going on right now."

"I know," Mike said. "I know."

But what I'd said wasn't entirely true. There was the wedding, of course, but we had no real plans for whatever was to follow. And by then I knew all about Mike and plans—even if we were just running errands, he needed to know which stores we were going to and in precisely what order. He had talked about starting work on his PhD, but he was tired of school. We had both talked about teaching, but that meant I'd have to take four additional classes in order to get a teaching certificate, and Mike would have to find a job at a junior college, which he didn't seem ready to do. So I had a pretty good idea how the Dutch Zimmerman thing would turn out. It took only four days to resolve itself. We were lying in bed.

"Ever since we got Dutch's letter, I've been thinking about the train," Mike said.

I, too, had often thought about the train. The two of us had been hunting one afternoon less than an hour from the city. As usual, we were walking the railroad tracks, and when it began to get dark, we headed back to the car. Perhaps because it was a weeknight, we saw the only commuter train we'd ever seen while hunting.

We saw the light when it was still a couple miles away, and as it drew closer, we walked down the grade and stood on the edge of a soybean field to watch it pass. It moved very slowly, and there were only four or five cars, each one suffused with an eerie yellow fluorescence. The passengers were all men—businessmen coming home from the city—and they sat frozen in the amber light like insects from another epoch, trapped forever in their weariness. One man had his eyes closed and his head tilted so far back that I could see his Adam's apple. A few appeared to be asleep, their chins resting on their chests. The rest of them stared straight ahead with vacant eyes, looking at nothing. Anyone would have supposed them unhappy. They looked like a boatload of damned souls being ferried into the underworld.

When the train had passed, we climbed up the embankment and resumed walking. Mike was quiet for a time. Then he turned and pointed down the tracks. "Did you *see* them?"

"It was awful," I said. "They looked like prisoners—like they were being hauled away to a gulag or something."

"Promise you won't let that happen to me."

"It never will—I promise."

So when Mike said he'd been thinking about the train, I knew we were headed for Canada. It was fine by me.

"What's the name of Dutch's place?" I said. "Skillet River?"

Mike laughed. "Close—*Kettle Falls*. So you're with me?"

"To the bitter end."

And suddenly we had a plan. We would move out of the apartment, sell my car, get married and leave for Canada. There wouldn't be time for a honeymoon, but I didn't care about that. Kettle Falls sounded like a great adventure, and we were both ready for one.

Mike and I were married in my mother's living room in late March 1973. We wanted the wedding to be simple, but that didn't prevent my mother from having rooms repainted, draperies replaced and carpets cleaned. For a while there, she was a veritable white tornado, scouring, scrubbing and sanitizing everything in her path. She even made Tom remodel the downstairs bathroom, where he struggled for a week trying to create a repeating pattern in the floor tile.

But the wedding came off without a hitch. Zee was my maid of honor, and everyone Mike and I cared about was there, including Otto and Nedra. Even Jimmy was there, which meant I won a five-dollar bet with my mother, who'd been sure he wouldn't come. At my urging, Jimmy brought his new girlfriend, Gabrielle, who wasn't much older than I was. She was French-Canadian and very beautiful, with layered, Farrah Fawcetty hair and a charming accent. Gabby was a buyer for Holt Renfrew, which is like America's Neiman Marcus, and she and Jimmy had met in Toronto at a jazz festival. I liked her immediately and wished I could have gotten to know her better, but Jimmy and Gabby were not invited to stay at the house. When I told my mother they had a room at the Drake, she said, "Nothing but the best for Jimmy!"

Jimmy was the life of the party, a role he thoroughly enjoyed. He was in his early forties, trim and fit, with leading-man looks that made him seem younger. Both he and Gabby were "dressed to the nines," as Hedley used to say, but the cut and drape of Jimmy's suit was unlike anything I'd ever seen.

"Armani?" I asked, feeling the sleeve.

"Armani's for fairies," he said. "This is a Brioni."

In addition to being a sharp dresser, Jimmy was a peerless raconteur, and, as my mother said, it was one of few things he'd come by honestly. He had inherited Hedley's faculty for storytelling, but while Hedley had been a spieler, Jimmy was a true performer. At one point, I overheard him telling hunting stories to a group of men who had never been hunting in their lives, but who were sitting spellbound in the den. "Then what did you do?" one of them had asked him.

"Well, I said, 'Look here, Mr. Game Warden, if you're a public servant like you say, why the hell don't you get me a cup of coffee?'"

His audience roared their approval and nodded at each other, as though they were all in on a delightful secret together.

Mike, who had been calling Jimmy "sir" since they'd met, was respectful to the point of stiffness. I remember the three of us were drinking champagne on the veranda when Mike automatically said, "Yes, sir," after Jimmy had asked if he was a Cubs fan. Jimmy put his hand behind Mike's neck and pulled Mike toward him until their foreheads were almost touching.

"Mike, anytime you want to quit 'sirring' me would be just fine. How are we gonna be friends if you keep that up?" Jimmy was smiling and Mike looked relieved.

"I don't know why I've been doing it," Mike said, genuinely puzzled. "I feel like I just met the president."

"Kid, I *have* met the president, and it wasn't that great."

Jimmy had quite an effect on women, too. Gabby was obviously in love with him, and she talked about Jimmy as though he were a knight errant who had posted into her kingdom and swept her off her feet. I'd heard plenty from my mother about Jimmy and "his women," but I'd never seen it firsthand. It was fascinating. Zee stuck so close to Jimmy that my mother remarked on it.

"Have you noticed," she said, "that every time Jimmy stops, your maid of honor bumps her nose?"

Even Nedra, who was slightly tipsy from champagne, took me aside and said, "Your onkle Jimmy, he is so … *entzückend*! So *charming*!" She closed her eyes and clasped both hands to her breast in a gesture of transport.

Jimmy had the kind of easy charm that no doubt made every stoplight turn green for him, but it was hard for me not to think of him out there on the river, sneaking back and forth across the border. Gabby probably knew all about that. I wondered what the men in the den would have thought, but the looks on their faces told me they would have found Jimmy's dark side thrilling. He probably would have been to them what Abbie Hoffman was to me—a mesmerizing foil, an antihero from another world.

Chapter 8

'd wanted to talk to Jimmy while he was in town—I mean, *really* talk—but it had been impossible, and I was sorry, since it might be years before I'd have another chance. I thought he and Gabby had headed home after the wedding, so when he called two days later, I assumed he was already back in New York.

"No, I'm still here," he said. "We decided to stay a few days."

I could hear Gabby's voice in the background.

Jimmy laughed. "Gabby says she won't go home until she's done the three B's, whatever that means."

"Bergdorf's, Bloomingdale's and Bonwit's," I said. "I'm glad you stuck around. Can I see you?"

"That's why I called."

So the following morning, while Gabby was shopping and Mike was in Rockford for his final meeting with Dutch, I met Jimmy at the Drake.

He waved me into the room with a grand gesture. "Good morning, Mrs. Bowman."

"Wow! Nice digs. Positively decadent."

Jimmy looked around absently. "Nothing but the bare essentials."

It was a beautiful three-room suite overlooking Lake Michigan. One corner of the living room was a bar; in an adjacent corner was a baby grand piano.

I ran my hand over the dark wood of its cabinet. "I didn't know you played."

"I can't explain the piano," Jimmy said, scratching his head. "Either it came with the room or the last guy forgot it."

"Have you had a chance to see the sights?"

"Like what?"

"You know—the museum, the aquarium. The zoo. The planetarium." I started to laugh. "I sound like *The Cat in the Hat*."

"I thought you were giving a blessing. No, I haven't had much time for sightseeing. You know what I'd really like to do?" Jimmy pointed to the lake, which under the sunless sky was the color of slate. "I'd like to go over there. I've been looking at it for four days, but I've never really seen it."

"Then let's check it out," I said. "But wear something warm. It's colder than it looks."

"Not for a couple of river rats like us."

A few minutes later we were stepping out of the elevator into the lobby. We passed the concierge's desk and left by the Oak Street entrance, and when we came through the revolving brass door, the doorman touched the brim of his top hat and smiled. We could smell the lake, but we couldn't see it.

"It's great to get a breath of fresh air," Jimmy said. "Do you know where you're going?"

"More or less. I'll just follow my nose."

We crossed Oak Street and walked through the park, following a little cobblestone footpath. The trees were thin and bare-branched, and the wind whistled in their branches. At the north end of the park, the pathway led to an underpass beneath Lake Shore Drive, and when we came out of the underpass, the lake exploded before us like a surprise party.

"Damn!" Jimmy said. "It kinda catches you off guard, doesn't it."

"Every time."

We bought coffee and croissants from a vendor in a snowmobile suit who was using the empty lifeguard station as a windbreak. The croissants were warm, and he wrapped each one carefully in waxed paper. Other than a few college kids who were jogging up the beach from the direction of Northwestern's City Campus, there weren't many people around.

We headed down the shore toward Navy Pier, the wind quartering at our backs, and we could see huge waves exploding against the breakwater of the outer harbor. After a while we sat down at a picnic table and watched the lake, which seemed angry at times and at other times confused.

I closed my eyes halfway and looked at the whitecaps. "The sheep are grazing."

Jimmy smiled. "Hedley used to say that every time we'd hunt the point."

"Do you ever hunt there anymore?"

"It's been a long time."

"How come? Hedley always said it was the best place on the lake."

"It probably is—if the wind's blowing hard enough. But then it's like hunting in a hurricane out there. There are other places more pleasant."

"But none so exciting."

Jimmy brushed some sand from the picnic table with the edge of his hand. "I don't know about exciting. It's more like annoying. Between the wind howling and the waves crashing into the rocks, you can't hear yourself think. And then when the ducks come, your eyes are watering so bad you can't see anything. It's a hard place to hunt."

"Do you still own it?"

"Half of it," Jimmy said automatically.

Something gave way inside of me, and all I could see was my mother's wry, disembodied smile hanging in the air.

"Well, technically I own it all," he said, trying to steer out of the skid. "I mean I sold a half interest to Hap, only it isn't really Hap that I sold it to. We have a legal partnership called Seaway Limited, so when I sold half the point to Seaway, it was like selling it to myself. No big deal."

"No big deal? How could you *do* that?"

"I didn't have a choice, Allie. Everything happened at once. We were behind on our taxes; then I got fined; then the notes came due for improvements at the club; then we needed—"

"Go back to the part about being fined."

Jimmy grimaced. "I got caught baiting."

"Baiting ducks? I suppose you didn't have a choice about that, either."

"I didn't," Jimmy said. "Not if I wanted to stay in business. All the clubs bait. The Wolfe Island clubs, Howe Island, Simcoe—"

"But those are Canadian clubs."

"They're also the competition. The Canucks dump a million pounds of corn on the flats with barges and end-loaders. They hold the birds 'til freeze-up, and the Ministry just winks and looks the other way." Jimmy shrugged and stared down at the table. "I should've bought a club in Ontario."

"Right now I wish you had."

"Life would be a lot easier," he said. "As it is, I've got state and federal wardens dropping by every other day, checking the freezers, checking the coolers, checking licenses, checking everything. You know, the day they busted me, it was like D-Day. Those bastards came from everywhere at once—by boat, by truck, even by air. They set a chopper down on the ford—one of those turbo jobs with floats. Can you believe that? You'd have thought the FBI's ten most wanted were all holed up on Sable Island. And getting fined wasn't the worst of it—they shut me down for three weeks in the middle of the season so they could do their so-called investigation. And I was booked solid."

"I'm sorry, Jimmy," I said. But I didn't feel sorry. I just didn't know what else to say. Jimmy was clearly embarrassed and angry with himself, not because of what he'd done, but because he'd been caught doing it. "Are things going better now?"

"Oh, sure. They still watch me pretty close, but the bust was two years ago." Jimmy's face broke into a smile. "We bought the Bayside Pub. Did you know that?"

"No," I said. "Isn't that the place down by the lighthouse?"

"Yeah. It's funny—Hap and I stopped in there for a beer one day, and when we left, we were the new owners."

But I wasn't in the mood to hear about it. "Jimmy, this is really important to me. I need you to promise that you won't sell the point, not to Hap or anybody else."

Jimmy was still thinking about the Bayside Pub, but his lingering smile disappeared quickly. "I won't sell the point, Allie. And after today, my mission in life is to get the other half back." He reached across the table and put his hand on mine. I thought he was going to offer me further reassurance about the point, but he surprised me. "Your father would be so proud of you."

"Proud? What would he be proud of?"

"Everything," Jimmy said. "You went to college, you've got a future, you got out of the Cape—and now you're married. What father wouldn't be proud?"

"Thank you." I lowered my eyes. "I'm not sure getting out of the Cape should be on the list, but thanks just the same."

I didn't look up right away, and Jimmy tilted his head so he could see my face. "What's wrong?"

"Nothing. I was just wondering if I could ask you something—

something personal."

"Sure. Fire away."

"What happened between you and my mother?"

"You really don't know?"

"Not … all of it," I said. "I've asked, but she doesn't like to talk about it."

Jimmy looked out at the lake, then at me. "How much do you know about how your father died?"

"Just that he drowned and they never found his body. I think he was fishing."

Jimmy shook his head. "He wasn't fishing. He was helping me and three other guys smuggle five thousand gallons of benzene across the river at Featherbed Shoal."

"He was a *smuggler*?"

"Hell, no. Matt Hayes was a straight arrow—same as you. But the mill had just closed, and he was worried about you and Ellen, about paying the bills and losing the house. I used to do a little smuggling when I was a kid, so that night I brought him along." Jimmy closed his eyes. "Jesus, I'd like to have that decision back."

"About smuggling?"

"About bringing your father."

"What happened?"

Jimmy swung one leg over the bench and straddled it. "Basically, Murphy's Law happened. We were on a barge, and it was windy that night—*too* windy. We were a hundred yards from the border when a gust caught the bow and swung it around. We tried to turn back into the wind, but we were drifting sideways by then, and we blew onto the shoal and hit a reef." Jimmy stopped and swallowed hard.

"And that's how he drowned?"

"He didn't exactly drown. There was benzene running all over the deck—a lot of the barrels were rusted out—and when we hit, I think somebody dropped a lantern. There was a fire, then an explosion that they heard all the way to Gananoque. That's how your father died.

That's why your mother and I … well, you know all about that part."
He let the story sink in for a minute. "You don't seem surprised."

I was, but at the same time, I wasn't. "I think I've always known the truth would be something like that. It wasn't your fault."

"Yes, it was. Your father should have been at your wedding, and I'm the reason he wasn't. Matt should never have been on that river."

"None of you should have been on that river—you were smuggling."

Jimmy got a faraway look on his face. "Yeah, but it was different with him. He was just a guy down on his luck. Matt was no river rat. Hell, he couldn't even swim. When the barge caught fire, the rest of us swam to Carleton Island. I kept hollering at him to jump, but he wouldn't do it. I didn't know why until your mother told me."

"Jimmy, my father made the decision to be there. It was his choice, and … it was a bad one."

"You know—I've thought about this a lot—there were five of us on the barge that night, and none of the other guys ever amounted to a tinker's damn. One of them died in Attica, one drank himself to death, and the other was killed robbing an all-night deli someplace. Your father wasn't like that."

"What about you? You aren't like that."

Jimmy shivered and clasped his arms to his sides. "God*damn*! Gabby told me this Burberry was supposed to be warm. Feels like it's made out of cheesecloth."

"You look very nice in it."

"Hey, you wanna go back to the hotel and have a toddy? I'd like to hear more about this camp you and Mike are gonna run."

That was Jimmy's way of ending the conversation, and there was nothing I could do about it, even if I'd wanted to. We walked back up the beach, leaning into the wind, and I tried to feel something for my father, but it was hard because I'd never known him. He was an abstraction, an unrealized sketch. But he was also the type of person I tended to distrust—the type who does the wrong thing, like smuggling, for what he believes is the right reason. In that way he was like a character from my mother's stories.

I was also sorry about the point, half of which was already gone, sucked into the black hole of a partnership from which nothing was likely to escape. Jimmy didn't understand. To him the point was just a place. To me it was an idea, a lost fragment of something huge and important. But it was foolish to think Jimmy could grasp that. He was too busy looking for the pot of gold at the end of every crooked little rainbow.

It was cold on the way back to the hotel. Jimmy put his collar up, and I pulled my hands inside the sleeves of my coat. The wind was straight out of the north now and blowing very hard. There were no more joggers. When we reached the lifeguard station, the vendor and his little cart were gone.

Chapter 9

"Come over here," I shouted to Mike. "You have to read this. It's really interesting."

Yesterday, we'd said our good-byes, left for Kettle Falls and spent the first night of our trip in a little motel in Minong, Wisconsin. Today, we were back on the road, alone at a wayside rest in northern Minnesota. It wasn't a wayside rest in any conventional sense, just a place where the road looped into the woods and came out again. There was nothing there except for a picnic table and a sign indicating that we had arrived at the Laurentian Divide.

Mike came over and joined me, a half-sandwich in hand. "The first chance we get, we should put another bag of ice in that cooler."

I pointed to the sign. "Read this."

Mike read the yellow words routered into the wood and bit the acute angle from his sandwich. The sign explained that if a drop of water were to fall on that precise spot, half of it would flow north into Hudson Bay, and the other half would flow south into the Gulf of Mexico.

"Did you know that?" I asked.

"Sure. The Laurentian Divide is kind of a continental pivot point from the last ice age. It's all that's left of a mountain range that was ground down by the Wisconsin Glacier."

"Let me guess—another tidbit from Geomorphology 101?"

"202," Mike said. "I needed both semesters. You know, twenty thousand years ago the Wisconsin Glacier covered most of the upper Midwest. The ice was two miles thick."

"I'd hate to be a raindrop that falls here. It would be the worst possible luck. Half of you would go one way and the other half—"

Mike threw his arms around me suddenly, pulling me toward him. "That was really close—you were on the wrong side of the line. You could've been swept away to the Gulf."

"While you went to Hudson Bay," I said, laughing. "How awful."

"It would make *Evangeline* look like a comedy."

We kissed, and I pressed myself against him. Moments later we were making love on the cold ground beside the sign. We were two rivulets, then a stream, then the confluence of tantric rivers, tumbling and cascading toward the dark waters of Hudson Bay.

Afterward, half-dressed and shivering, I said, "I can't believe we did that." We were both laughing and a little surprised at ourselves.

"It was the sign," Mike said, looking up at it. "I was overcome by the thought of us going in opposite directions."

I put my arms around him. "We'll never go in opposite directions. Don't you think we should get dressed before someone pulls in here? They won't understand about the sign."

Mike did most of the driving that day. I studied the map and looked out the window, intrigued by the place names and desolation of the countryside. An hour north of Duluth, the landscape changed dramatically. The hayfields gave way to dense forests of poplar and jackpine, and the farms—farms that looked as though they'd been hacked out of the wilderness with a dull ax—became smaller and less frequent. There was a quiet sense of urgency about these little homesteads, and they gave the impression that if their owners were to turn their backs on the tree line—even for an instant—the wilderness would swallow everything in a single, pulsing gulp.

"Don't you just love these names?" I said. "In a few miles we should cross the Rat Root River—try saying that three times fast. And right now we're in the middle of the Kabetogama State Forest. I can't even say that once. Do you realize that every place we've stopped had fish hanging on the walls, even the gas stations? The place where we ate breakfast had lots of fish, plus a bear and a moose. I'm absolutely convinced that food tastes better in restaurants that have fish on the walls, and any place that has fish on the walls *and* catsup on the table should receive five stars."

"*Ketchup* on the table."

"Oh, yes, I forgot. I do that when I'm excited."

"I doubt if there are many people who get excited driving through this part of Minnesota," Mike said. "It's not exactly pretty. But then, you have unusual sensibilities."

"Why, thank you. I'll take that as a compliment. According to the map, we're about to enter the 'Big Bog.' Is that like the Slough of Despond?"

"Probably worse. In most places you couldn't walk across it, and in the places where you could, it would tremble under your feet."

"Like a giant waterbed," I said. "On the map it looks like you could put a canoe in Kabetogama Lake and paddle a thousand miles."

"It's Ka-be-TOE-ga-ma."

"How would you know that? And don't tell me Geomorphology 303."

Mike looked at me and smiled. "I knew a guy who fished it a lot. He lived around here someplace."

"Who?"

"His name was Dale Olsen. He was my lieutenant in 'Nam—one of them, anyway."

"Did he make it? You said *was*."

"Yeah, he made it," Mike said. "But all those guys are *was* to me. Dale used to dream about fishing Kabetogama Lake. It got to be kind of a joke. I'd see him in the morning and say, 'How were they biting last night, LT?' And he'd say something like, 'Mike, it was gangbusters—green jig in twelve feet of water. Tonight you gotta come with me.'"

"You two were friends?"

"We were. He was a good platoon leader—one of the bravest men I ever met."

Mike rarely talked about Vietnam, and I tried to encourage him when he did, but I never had much luck. I was afraid Mike might be done with his story about Dale Olsen, because that's the way his stories usually ended.

"What did Dale do that was so brave?"

Mike stared at the road and didn't answer right away. "It wasn't any one thing. It was all the little things he did to keep us alive. Dale didn't want to be a 'leader of men' or any crap like that. He took ROTC courses in college because they were cheap credits, and when he graduated, he was a second lieutenant, so they shipped him off to 'Nam. The thing about Dale—he didn't believe in getting people killed, even if it meant an Article 15." Mike chuckled. "His motto was 'Let arty do it.'"

"Who's Arty?"

"Artillery. Whenever we'd come under fire, the first thing Dale did was get on the radio and call it in. One time he called in a strike on a minefield just to neutralize it. Command chewed his butt for that one, but none of us got our legs blown off. Don't get me wrong—Dale got the job done. He just never risked our lives unless there was no other way."

I was sure that was the end of it, and I didn't press Mike further, but after a mile or two, he returned to Dale Olsen on his own.

"I've never told you this," he said, "but near the end of my tour, a lot of the guys in my platoon were pretty short. Five of them had less than a month. One guy had eleven days and a wake-up. We were at Pleiku, but it quieted down there, so they sent us up to a firebase in northern Kon Tum Province to do search and destroy."

"I know what that is."

Mike shook his head. "No, you don't. Not really. It means going out on patrol just to see if you can draw enemy fire. There was this bird colonel up there who was bucking for general—he thought it was great stuff. But we took casualties on almost every patrol, and the short guys were coming unglued. So after about a week, Dale says, 'Men, this is bullshit on stilts,' and he put all the short guys on the same squad and took it out of the rotation. We didn't mind doing the extra patrols—the short guys had earned it."

"They must have loved him."

"I don't know about that, but we would've followed him *any-where*." Mike rolled his window down a crack, then went on. "One time that idiot colonel got bored and ordered the whole platoon into the bush—all three squads. We were supposed to go eight klicks to a village, turn around, and come back again—no mission, no objective. He was just using us for VC target practice, tempting the gooks with a big column. We all knew it. That's when Dale said our orders were subject to 'field discretion.'"

"What did that mean?"

"It meant Dale led the platoon a couple klicks outside the wire, spread his maps out on the ground and got on the radio. He made it sound like we were doing search and destroy all the way to Cambodia. Hell, he was so good at it, we almost believed him ourselves. And Colonel Mustard never knew the difference." Mike laughed at the thought of it. "If we could've put Dale in for a medal, we would have."

"I doubt if they give medals for that."

There must have been something in my voice I wasn't aware of, because Mike turned to me and frowned. "Well, they should. There should be a medal for valor in the face of overwhelming stupidity, and Dale Olsen should have one. A lot of guys came home because of him—I was on the short squad myself for eight days."

Just then a deer ran in front of the car, and Mike hit the brakes hard. The little station wagon leaned forward, then settled back again. The deer bounded into the woods on the other side of the highway.

"Sorry," I said. Mike had asked me earlier, after another near miss, to help him spot deer in the ditches, but this one had come out of nowhere.

"It's okay."

"I never saw it until the last second. All of a sudden it was *there*."

"The deer?"

"Yes. What did you …" I realized we were speaking of two different things but let it go. After we'd gone a mile or two, I said, "As long as we're here, should we try to see Dale or at least call him?"

"I couldn't do that."

"Why not?"

"I just couldn't."

"And you won't tell me why?"

"I already did—that part of my life is *was*."

We were both becoming uncomfortable, and whatever Mike didn't want to tell me, I didn't want to know.

"I understand," I said. "And if Dale Olsen is the reason we're together right now, I'd pin a medal on him myself."

Mike nodded. "He just might be."

"I started to ask you before—before we started talking about

Dale Olsen—if Kettle Falls looks anything like this country. What's it like there?"

"It's a lot prettier," Mike said. "It's postcard pretty—Canadian shield, lots of rock. But there's no *there* there."

"As in people?"

"As in anything. It's wilderness. Dutch used to say there's no Sunday north of Minaki and no God north of Kettle Falls. And he's right—it's the end of the line."

"How ominous."

Mike laughed and put his hand on my knee. "What I meant was … it's the end of the road. There are no roads beyond Kettle Falls."

"That sounds much better."

"You're gonna love it. Anybody who finds northern Minnesota exciting will think Kettle Falls is heaven."

"I'm sure I will. I just wish we didn't have to cross the border to get there."

I'd been worrying about going through customs off and on now for several days. Mike had said that during the war they'd been very suspicious of draft-age men and young couples who sought to enter Canada for any reason. He'd had some trouble at the border himself, when he'd worked for Dutch Zimmerman during the summers. It wasn't Checkpoint Charlie or anything like that, he said, but they'd asked him a lot of questions. I hoped that wouldn't happen to us. After all, the Paris Peace Accord had been signed in January, and the POWs were returning home. And six weeks before we left for Kettle Falls, the last American troops had been withdrawn from Vietnam.

But there were other problems. The Canadian authorities prohibited Americans from entering Canada to work unless they had dual citizenship or were landed immigrants like Dutch Zimmerman. Since Mike and I didn't qualify on either count, our plan was to tell the border guards we were on our honeymoon, which, in a way, we were. We would say that we intended to be in Canada for about a week. Once we'd entered the country, our problems were over, according to Mike, because when we would leave Canada in the fall, it would be through U.S. customs, and they wouldn't know how long we'd been north of the border. And they wouldn't care, as long as we were American citizens. It sounded like a classic case of the left hand not knowing what the right hand was doing, but Mike had done it in the past, and it worked fine. That part seemed simple enough.

I was more concerned that we were smuggling several hundred dollars worth of fishing tackle—mostly trolling sinkers and spinner rigs—that Mike had stashed in the squareback's trunk. These items were for the store-cum-tackle shop at Kettle Falls, and Mike had decided to smuggle them in because the import duty on retail items was prohibitive, and they were too expensive to buy in Canada. When he'd told me what he intended to do, I was furious.

"Are you *nuts*?" I said. "This is something Jimmy would do, not us."

But Mike had just laughed. "It's not a problem, Allie. I have a plan. You'll see."

Mike's promise of a "plan" had sustained me until now, but this was the hour of reckoning. The trunk carpet was two inches higher than it should have been, and any diligent border guard would know something was hidden beneath it.

Canadian customs is just across the Rainy River from International Falls in Fort Frances, Ontario, and by the time we got there, I was a wreck. What made it worse was the waiting. Cars were backed up the entire length of the bridge, and there was nothing to do but sit there and look down at the coffee-colored water churning beneath us.

"What's that awful smell?" I said.

"The paper mill."

"I knew I recognized it. I guess if you've smelled one paper mill, you've smelled them all. We're going to end up in jail, you know."

"Everything will be fine, Allie. We're not exactly robbing a bank."

"No, but smuggling is just as illegal."

Mike laughed. "The way I see it, we're neglecting to declare a few things at customs, that's all."

In the time we'd been together, I had discovered that Mike, in addition to his easy relationship with violence, had a certain moral flexibility. But now I began to wonder if there was more to it than that. I couldn't understand how this deliberate, methodical person—the student who'd invoked Aristotle at every turn in his thesis—could be so cavalier about breaking the law. He wasn't the least bit worried. I was terrified.

A car length at a time, we crept closer to the customs station on the north side of the bridge. After a while, we were the eighth car back, then the seventh, then the sixth. About forty-five minutes from the time we'd driven onto the bridge, we were there, stopped in front of a sign that said "Arrêt!" in big red letters. It was our turn.

A beefy man, uniformed but hatless, approached the car and told Mike to turn off the ignition. Then he began asking questions in a rapid, mechanical cadence.

"Where do you live?"

"Where are you going?"

"What is the purpose of your visit to Canada?"

Most of the questions he addressed to Mike, but occasionally he would ask something of me, then stick his head into the car so he could hear my answer. I'd made Mike catechize me on the questions we were likely to be asked, and he'd done an excellent job of it. For a while, there were no surprises.

While this was going on, another guard with a handlebar mustache emerged from the office and began walking around our car, looking in the windows. A couple of times he pressed his forehead to the glass and cupped his hands around his eyes to see better. When the beefy man had finished asking us questions, he looked behind the car at the man with the mustache and nodded.

"Sir, please pull ahead and park your vehicle next to the building for inspection. You and your wife can wait inside."

My stomach immediately turned upside down, and I thought for a moment I was going to vomit.

Mike, however, was unflappable. "No problem, officer."

We parked the car as directed and saw another car being inspected a few spaces away. Two guards were going through it with horrifying thoroughness. The trunk, along with all four doors, was open, and they had taken everything out of the car, including the back seat. One of the guards had removed the ashtray and was sniffing its contents.

My knees were shaking as I climbed out of the car. "Whatever your plan is, it better be good."

We were escorted into a little waiting room with a table and chairs, some magazines and a coffee pot. I picked up a magazine and sat down at the table, pretending to read. Mike poured himself a cup of coffee and sat down across from me. Through the open door of the waiting room, we could see a young man, presumably the owner of the disemboweled car, being frisked.

After fifteen interminable minutes, and without lifting my eyes from the unread magazine, I said, "What are we going to do?"

"That depends on what *they* do." Then he started to laugh. He was looking past me, out the window, to where the guards were going through the squareback.

"Stop that," I whispered. "This isn't the least bit funny."

"I love that car."

"What are you talking about?"

"Turn around, Allie. You've gotta see this."

I turned around but failed to see what Mike found so amusing.

Two guards were looking through the unremarkable items they'd removed from the back of our car—coats, sleeping bags, suitcases. One guard had his hands in his pockets. The other was pointing to the line of cars on the bridge.

"They don't know it's there," Mike said.

"They don't know *what's* there?"

"The trunk. They would've opened it by now if they did. They think the engine's up there. This is the third time I've crossed the border in that car. The same thing happens every time."

"And that was your plan?"

"Pretty slick, huh?"

All I could do was shake my head. The guards were heading back toward the office, having given the squareback the standard station wagon treatment.

I was angry at Mike for the ordeal he'd put me through, all for the sake of some weights and spinners, but it didn't last long, and as we made our way through the labyrinthine streets of Fort Frances, all I felt was relief. By the time we reached King's Highway 71, which a sign described as the *Circuit des Explorateurs*, I had recovered, and we were once again *explorateurs* ourselves. We had left the nightmare of the border behind us and were heading north again. There would be no more east or west on this trip. North was all that remained for us, and we felt as though we'd passed the last milestone. We were only a hundred and twenty-five miles from Kenora, and by late afternoon, we would be there.

Chapter 10

Kenora lies at the north end of Lake of the Woods, where the Winnipeg River flows out of the lake at Rat Portage, eventually making its way to the frozen tundra of Hudson Bay. In order to reach Kenora from Fort Frances by car, you have to drive around the east side of the lake, which Mike and I spent much of that afternoon doing. The scenery was breathtaking, and by the time we reached Sioux Narrows, the sun was out, which helped me realize what Mike had meant earlier by "postcard pretty." There was almost always a lake on one side of the road or the other, sometimes on both. They were pristine, garnished with small islands, and as the road wound its way around their convoluted shorelines, our windshield held the scrolling serenity of a beer clock.

After Sioux Narrows, the country became more rugged, with many cliffs, rocky outcroppings and rivers swollen with runoff. There were no leaves on the trees, and the only color was provided by the blue of the water and by the pine trees, which stood in bold relief against the gray backdrop of leafless aspen. Some of the smaller lakes were open, but as we neared Kenora, most of the larger lakes and bays still held ice.

Kenora doesn't catch you by surprise the way a lot of small cities do that have sprung up, for one reason or another, in the middle of nowhere. I could tell when we were getting close, because it was like coming into Cape Vincent or almost any town along the Seaway. There was the telltale smattering of houses, then the gas stations, then more houses, followed quickly by the small businesses that struggle on the outskirts of all towns near water—the bait shops, prop shops, sport shops and marinas. After the marinas came Kenora. We arrived a little ahead of schedule and with plenty of daylight to spare.

Kenora was larger than I'd thought and more beautiful than I could have imagined. It doesn't turn its back on the water, as many lakeside cities do, but embraces it frankly and without hesitation. Mike gave me a quick tour of the business district, which was five charming blocks long, and after that, we headed for the Kenora Inn, where we had a reservation.

The Kenora Inn wasn't what I'd expected, either. It was nine stories and had the same columnar, corn-cobby look as the Marina City Towers in Chicago, which had obviously inspired it. But despite looking out of place, it was very nice, and when we saw our room, we knew immediately what the architect had been thinking. We were in a large lakeside room on the seventh floor, and we could see forever.

"Let's get cleaned up and check out the dining room," I said. "I'm starving."

"Me, too."

The dining room was on the ninth floor, and because it wasn't crowded, the smiling maitre d' led us to a table by the windows, seated us and gestured to our waiter. The view was like the view from our room, only better because of the sunset. The sun was just below the trees, and the lake, most of which was still covered with black ice, looked cold and forbidding beneath the red sky. There were eagles everywhere, apparently migrating north again after wintering in warmer climes. They glided past at eye level, then swooped down to join their companions, who were sitting on the dark ice below. Everything was perfect, and I knew if I were any happier, I'd burst into blossom.

The next morning we got up early. I was determined that Mike and I would check out every store in downtown Kenora, and by one o'clock that afternoon, we'd nearly done it. As we walked the streets of Kenora, I felt as though I were in a foreign city— a distant city, as opposed to one a hundred and forty miles from our border. Most of the names on the storefronts were Scottish— Campbell, McTaggart, Gibson—and the people I spoke with had a pretty brogue that animated their western Ontario accent. In the seventies, Canadians were famously saying "eh" at least once per sentence, and in Kenora it didn't matter whom you were talking to—even professional people said it, though less often. There were little syntactical differences, too, like Kenorans' habit of using pronouns in apposition to nouns, as in "The snow, it's aboot gone, eh." After thirteen years of Chicago's flat, guttural English, I loved what I heard on the streets that morning. It was as though someone had turned the dial from AM to FM.

Mike, who was growing a little weary of following me in and out of stores, suggested we stop for lunch, so we went to the Kenwood Hotel and had a hamburger in the quiet darkness of its subterranean dining room.

"So what do you think of Kenora?" he said.

"I love it. It's familiar and foreign at the same time."

"While we're in town, we should put an ad in the *Daily Miner* for some employees."

"You want that pickle?"

Mike speared the pickle with his fork and put it on my plate.

"Thanks. I thought you said we'd have the same crew back as last year."

"We'll have our core group back," he said, "but we'll need other people, too. You could help with that if you want to."

"Your wish is my command."

"Good. The ad will say that anybody who wants to work for Kettle Falls should come to the Kenora Inn on … let's say, April twenty-fourth, and you can interview them."

I laid my napkin beside my plate. "Good hamburger. How will I know which people to hire?"

"Hire the ones with the most teeth."

"You're kidding, right?"

Mike shook his head.

After lunch we walked along the harbor front toward McCleod Park. It was getting colder, and a north wind had pushed the ice away from the shore, creating a small ribbon of open water in which several otters were playing, diving and surfacing together like synchronized swimmers. We watched them for a while, then headed back toward town.

By the time we reached the hotel, it had begun to snow, and we sat at the table in our room, drinking room-service champagne and marveling at the huge spring snowflakes. We'd placed the ad in the newspaper, and I was becoming curious about the scope of my responsibilities at Kettle Falls. From earlier conversations, I knew I'd be helping in the kitchen and doing a lot of bookkeeping, but beyond that, I didn't really know what was expected of me.

"I think it's time I knew exactly what my job description is," I said.

"I was thinking you'd do what Katherine did—Dutch's wife."

"You said she divorced him. Are you trying to tell me something?"

Mike laughed. "I meant before that. She and Albert ran the kitchen. Katherine also did the payroll, helped with the books, tended bar and oversaw the female staff."

"No wonder she left."

"It wasn't that," Mike said. "Dutch had girlfriends."

"I see. Who's Albert?"

"Albert is the best camp chef in Ontario. He used to be a *sous-chef* for some big hotel in Winnipeg. His name is Albert Slimm, but everybody calls him 'Biscuit'—not to his face, of course."

"Why *Biscuit*?"

"Hot Biscuit Slim was Paul Bunyan's cook." Mike refilled both our glasses and set the bottle between us. "Kettle Falls is known for its food, and Albert's the reason why."

I raised my glass. "Then here's to Albert. How many people are on the Kettle Falls payroll?"

Mike paused for a moment to add them up. "About forty. Louie and Pop are my mainstays. Louie lives there—he'll be my right-hand man. Pop's the motor mechanic. Then there are waitresses, the women in the laundry, at least sixteen guides, the minnow man—"

"The minnow man? That sounds like a carnival act."

"Every camp has one. Nobody can afford to buy a hundred dozen minnows a day, so someone has to trap and net them full time. We'll also need a couple dock boys and a grounds crew. And a pilot—I forgot about that. Dutch did all the flying, so without him we'll need somebody on retainer, especially in the fall, when we've got moose hunters at outpost camps."

"That's a big staff."

"That's what it takes to keep our guests happy." Mike's face grew serious. "Here's the thing—Dutch's business is 95 percent corporate, so if we lose a customer, it's not like we lose one guy who won't come back again. We lose an entire corporate account—and a ton of money."

"Who do these corporations send there?"

Mike leaned back in his chair. "Oh … it depends. It might be their top-selling salesman or maybe their best customers. Or both—

that's what Whirlpool does. We have a hundred and twenty men coming in June from Whirlpool in four consecutive groups of thirty. Whirlpool is all we do in June."

"Any women?"

"Not very often. Kettle Falls is a fishing and hunting camp. I think the companies we deal with give their female employees other options, like cruises or maybe a few days in the Caribbean—that sort of thing."

"I'd take the fishing trip," I said.

"But you're the product of an unusual culture."

"That's true. I'm a river rat."

Mike leaned forward, all the way across the table, and kissed me. "And that's one of the many, *many* reasons I love you."

"What about my mind?"

"I love that, too."

"And my body?"

"That, too."

But I could tell Mike wasn't thinking about either one just then. He was staring out the window, and something in his face told me he was sixty miles up the road at Kettle Falls, solving one problem after another, doing his best not to lose one of Dutch's plum accounts. It was going to be hard. We both knew it.

"We can do this," I said. "Just remember the train."

Mike, still looking out the window, stood up and pointed. "I wonder what the hell *he's* up to."

Far below us, a small boat was attempting to make its way across the ice-filled bay to Laurenson Creek, which was open. The driver was alone, standing up in the stern, with one hand on the outboard's tiller. He was trying to follow the little leads that had opened up in the ice, but it wasn't going well. He'd follow a channel until it dead-ended, then back up into the open water and try another. He didn't appear at all discouraged, and each time he chose a different route, he made it a little farther than the time before. Yet in the fifteen minutes we watched him, he only managed to go fifty yards.

"I should go down and offer that guy a job," Mike said. "Perseverance like his shouldn't go unrewarded."

"I'll bet anything there's a woman involved in this—probably a woman he hasn't seen all winter."

Mike looked at his watch. "He's probably trying to get to the liquor store before it closes."

"How *romantic* you are."

"I am." He nodded toward our huge bed. "Let me prove it to you."

Chapter 11

The following day Mike made it a point to stop in and say hello to the merchants and wholesalers with whom Kettle Falls would soon be doing business again, assuring them that the camp was heavily booked and in good hands. Most of the people we talked to had heard about Dutch's cancer, and when Mike updated them on his condition, they just shook their heads, as if to say, "You don't never know, eh."

At the Royal Bank of Nova Scotia, which held the mortgage on Kettle Falls Lodge, one of the men—I would eventually know him as the bank president—pulled us into his office and explained that the bank had very nearly foreclosed on Kettle Falls when they found out Dutch wouldn't be able to run it.

"You were the deal-maker, son," the man said, clapping Mike on the shoulder. "Dutch swore you knew the business top to bottom." Then he smiled broadly, looking at me to make sure I appreciated his unselfish confidence in my husband.

"I think Dutch may have exaggerated a bit, sir," Mike said. "But the camp is booked pretty tight, and you and Dutch will get the best

I've got."

"I don't doubt it for a second," he said. "And I'm glad that mercury business over in Dryden isn't a problem for you, eh."

I had intended to ask Mike what he meant by that remark and then forgot.

We had planned to spend three days in Kenora—a honeymoon of sorts—but by the end of the second day, we were both getting antsy. For my part, I was anxious to see Kettle Falls, the closed, collateral universe in which we'd be living, and Mike was eager to address all the problems, real and imagined, that awaited him there. So around noon of the third day, we agreed it was time to head for the camp and bring our northern journey to its conclusion. Mike suggested that if I wanted to make any phone calls, I should do it before we left, because the phone at Kettle Falls wouldn't be connected for a few days. I took his advice and called home, but no one was there, so I called Paula at work and told her we were heading into the bush. Paula said it sounded as though Mike and I were living in a romance novel.

"I'll let you know," I said.

It's thirty-seven miles from Kenora to Minaki, and only the first few miles were paved. It was rough-looking country, and I didn't see a house or a person the entire way. We picked up the mail in Minaki, practically a suitcase full, and spent a few minutes looking around. There was a Hudson Bay store, a liquor store and a little train depot. That was about it. There were a few Indians standing in front of the post office, and except for them, there were no signs of life. Mike bought a bottle of brandy for Louie Labonté, the only year-round resident of Kettle Falls Lodge, and when Mike asked the man behind the counter if he happened to know Louie's brandy of choice, the man took a bottle from the shelf and handed it to him. "Old Louie, he's not too fussy, eh."

It's twenty-six miles from Minaki to Kettle Falls, and the road was unpaved, ungraded and nearly impassable in places. Frost boils had created holes in the road that were almost as big as the square-back, and the beaver had seen to it that many of the creeks that were supposed to flow under the road were now flowing over it. In one of those places, we got stuck, and I got behind the wheel while Mike pushed us out somehow. It was very early in the season, Mike said, and no serious road work would be done until all the frost was out of the ground.

A little more than halfway between Minaki and Kettle Falls, we crossed a huge dam at Twin Rivers Rapids. I was surprised to find no one tending it, but Mike explained the dam's automation in terms that sounded like the divine watchmaker theory of creation. The water was a couple feet below us on the right side of the car, and perhaps thirty feet below us on the left, where it boiled from the turbine gates. There was a one-lane road across the dam, which was about a hundred yards long.

"What river is this?" I asked.

"This is still the Winnipeg."

"It's beautiful. This isn't the river that Kettle Falls Lodge is on, though, is it?"

"Technically, no," Mike said. "Kettle Falls is on the English River, which is what the Winnipeg is called after it flows into the English and heads north."

"I love that name—the English River."

"There's another dam north of Kettle Falls Lodge. That's where the camp gets its power—we're 100 percent hydro, which is a very good deal for us."

After we crossed the dam, the road turned to washboard that nearly shook the fillings from our teeth.

"This is the roughest stretch of road I've ever been on," I said, bouncing my finger between my lips for effect.

"It won't be much longer."

There was a road on the left, marked by a hand-painted sign that said "Pennington 33."

"What's that?"

"The Twin Rivers Indian Reserve. It's only about seven miles from the camp, so we use people from there sometimes—if we're really desperate. It's a tough reserve."

"In what way?"

Mike shrugged. "It's just … unfriendly. They don't like white people at Twin Rivers. They always have white teachers, though. We'll have to stop by and meet them when we get a chance."

"Won't they be leaving soon for summer vacation?"

"Most reserve schools run year-round."

After that we pounded along in silence for what seemed like a hundred miles. Then Mike pointed to something.

"See that sign up ahead? That's our road—our driveway, so to speak. Only three miles to go after that."

"Thank God."

We made the turn, and the road improved some. We'd gone about a mile in when I saw a road—more of a cartway—leading off into the forest.

"Where does that go?"

"To an old feldspar quarry," Mike said. "Great place to seine minnows when they aren't running anywhere else."

Fifteen minutes later, I could see sunlight streaming through the trees in front of us, as though there might be a clearing ahead. Then the forest fell away suddenly on all sides, and we were there.

"This is it," Mike said. "This is where we live."

I leaned over and hugged him. "I can hardly believe it. I know we're going to love it here."

Before we had quite reached the cluster of buildings that was the resort itself, Mike turned left onto a muddy path that led to a cabin tucked back in the trees, almost out of sight. It wasn't much to look at, just a roof and four walls sheeted with weathered particle board. Beside it were the remnants of a wood pile and a leveled-off tree stump with an ax stuck in it. But other than the smoke coming from the chimney, there were no signs of life. We were just getting out of the car when a large dog—a Lab mix of some kind—came running to greet us, barking and wagging its tail at the prospect of company.

"I guess Louie's got a roommate." Mike knelt down to pet the dog. "I wonder where he is."

No sooner had he said that than a man emerged from the cabin cradling a rifle in his arms. He was about sixty, lean, with wildly tousled gray hair, and a large nose that seemed to complete, without interruption, an angle that began at his hairline.

"Hello, Louie," Mike said. "We were beginning to think you weren't here."

"Where the hell else would I be, eh? I was takin' a nap when I heard Molly barkin'."

"It's been a long time," Mike said as the two of them shook hands.

"Yeah, it's been a while. This good-lookin' gal your wife?"

"For about a week now. Louie, this is Allison Bowman."

"Please call me Allie." Louie and I shook hands, and I noticed that his eyes, which were very blue, seemed filled with mischief.

Louie turned to Mike. "I don't know how the hell you expect me to get any work done with such a pretty girl in camp, eh."

"You don't get any work done anyway, you French goldbrick."

"Allie, what the hell did you marry this smart aleck for, eh? You coulda done better."

"I know," I said. "But Mike promised to take me to exotic, faraway places."

Louie switched the rifle to his other hand. "Well, he wasn't lyin' about faraway. But this place is about as exotic as a tin shithouse, eh." He looked at Mike closely, as though he hadn't actually seen him until that moment. "You look good, kid, for a wet-behind-the-ears Yank. What's it been, a couple years?"

"Three," Mike said.

"Well, I'm glad you made it. I thought your letter said you weren't comin' 'til tomorrow, eh."

"It did, but we were anxious to get here."

Louie laughed. "That's funny. All I want to do is get outta here, but I'm lucky if I get to town once a month ... think I'm goin' bush-batty. Well, you two might just as well come in, eh, 'stead of standin' out here. Goddammit, I would have tidied up some if I'd knowed you was comin' today."

The cabin was warm and far cleaner than Louie led us to believe. It was a single large room with two bedrooms on one side. The bedroom walls stopped halfway to the ceiling, and instead of doors, there were curtains hung across their entrances. The curtain to Louie's bedroom had been pushed aside, revealing the framed photograph of a woman on the far wall.

Everything looked bachelor-efficient, right down to the large freezer chest that occupied one corner of the kitchen. There was a sink that appeared to drain into a five-gallon bucket, a gas range, a refrigerator, a big wood stove and several open cabinets filled with pots and pans. There were shelves above the sink and stove, where no women would ever have put them, but there was very little *on* the shelves—just coffee, salt, flour, Red River cereal and a can of Crisco. In the middle of the cabin was a large table covered with red oilcloth that bore the dark scars of innumerable cigarette burns.

Louie motioned for us to sit down. "'Course, I'd offer you a drink if I had one, eh."

"Hang on a minute, Louie. I almost forgot." Mike went out to the car and returned with the bottle of brandy.

When Louie saw it, he smiled. "Yank or not, I take back every bad thing I ever said about you."

"I sort of figured this would do it," Mike said, handing him the bottle.

Louie poured us all a drink and asked about Dutch. When Mike told him that it didn't look good, Louie was quiet for a time. Then he snarled, "Goddamn cancer."

Mike began rattling off a long list of all the things that had to be accomplished in the next few days, but Louie finally cut him off.

"Hell's bells, kid, take a breath. We'll get it done, eh, just like we always do."

"Yeah, but we need to make a list of the most important—"

"A list, eh?" Louie smiled at me, his blue eyes quickening. "How do you live with this guy, Allie, with his lists and all?"

"You should see him pack a suitcase," I said. "Mike is very organized."

"He's gonna organize himself into a goddamn ulcer."

Mike raised his hands. "Okay, okay—no lists. But we've got Texas coming the first of the month. That doesn't give us much time. The first thing we'll do tomorrow is fire up the pump and check the lines. After that we can hook up water to the cabins and—"

"You're worse than Dutchie, eh," Louie said. "How does the season look?"

"Real good, so far. Dutch couldn't do the sport shows this winter, but we've got enough repeat business that this year should look a lot like last year."

"Last year was a dandy," Louie said. "We had Bobcat, Whirlpool, Harvester and them drunken galoots from Lone Star Hydro-something-or-other."

"Lone Star Hydraulic Couplers out of Dallas."

"Yeah, them. I thought maybe the mercury scare would keep people away, eh, but I guess it ain't gonna."

"That's the second time I've heard somebody mention mercury," I said. "Are we talking about the stuff they put in thermometers?"

Louie looked at Mike, but Mike parried the question. "I'll tell you all about it later. Right now I think we should take a look around the place before it gets dark."

"Good," I said. "I'm dying to see it."

"Just don't be makin' no lists, eh," Louie said. "You two might as well bunk with me until we can get power and water to Dutch's cabin—that's where you plan on stayin', isn't it?"

"Yeah," Mike said. "We'll be back in a little while. Don't climb in that brandy bottle."

"Go to hell, Yank."

Chapter 12

Mike and I left the cabin and headed down to the resort for my tour, accompanied by Molly, who ran happy circles around us and chased after all the squirrels having the temerity not to flee at our approach.

"Louie is like men I remember from Cape Vincent," I said. "He's probably what river rats were like a hundred years ago. There's a picture of a woman in his bedroom—who is she?"

"That's his wife," Mike said. "Her name was Angelique. Louie brought her out to Kettle Falls in the early fifties, when he got a job with Ontario Hydro building the Kettle Falls dam. It's just like the one we crossed at Twin Rivers Rapids, only twice as big."

"And they never left?"

"They liked it here. They eventually went to work for the guy who owned Kettle Falls before Dutch bought the place. Angelique died right there in that cabin. In fact, Louie buried her around here, but nobody knows where."

We were walking along a gravel path, but when I heard that, I stopped. "She's buried in an unmarked grave?"

Mike saw me looking at the ground and laughed. "In the woods someplace, not *here*. Louie was afraid they'd exhume her body so … yeah, he hid the grave. Sometimes, he disappears for hours, and I think that's where he goes. C'mon, we've got a lot to see." He took my hand and we continued walking.

"That's a sad story."

"Very sad … I hope it isn't locked."

We were standing in front of the main lodge, which, like the eight guest cabins, was made of hand-hewn logs. We climbed a flight of steps, and Mike tried the big wooden doors that had elk antlers for door pulls. "It's open."

Inside the lodge it was very cold, and somehow the chairs placed upside down on all the tables made it seem even colder. But it looked precisely as it should, with a huge vaulted ceiling over the bar and dining room and dozens of mounted fish and game heads on the walls—mountain goats, elk, deer. There were even full mounts of two bears and a wolf that stood guard inside the main entrance, plus a huge bearskin rug that someone had draped over a table.

Molly had apparently never been in the lodge, and the mounted animals frightened her, especially the bearskin rug, which must have seemed particularly menacing at that height. She growled loudly, and the hair on her back stood up.

One side of the dining room was all windows and faced the river. The opposite wall contained an enormous stone fireplace that Mike told me Albert sometimes used for cooking a cauldron of soup or stew.

The kitchen was large and well-appointed, like a restaurant kitchen, with a big walk-in cooler, a walk-in freezer that was only slightly smaller, a storage room and a little office, where I imagined Albert compiled his staggering grocery list each week. Behind all that was a long, narrow room, with trestle tables running the length of it.

"Staff dining room," Mike said.

When I had satisfied my curiosity about the lodge, we left by the door we had entered, with Molly growling over her shoulder at the bearskin rug, which she clearly believed would attack her the moment her back was turned.

"This place is really fancy," I said. "It must cost a fortune to stay here."

"It does," Mike said. "You and I are going to make a lot of money—after we pay Dutch and the Scotia Bank."

"And the forty-odd people on the payroll."

"Some odder than others."

As we walked around the resort, I saw that we were on a blunt, south-facing point that was about three hundred yards long and a hundred yards wide. On the east side of the point was a little bay, partially covered with ice, and on the west side, where the lodge and the guest cabins were, was the river, which was open and flowing very fast.

Half of the point was wooded. The staff buildings—the bunkhouses, showers, laundry facility, fish-cleaning house, tool shed and garage—were more or less hidden from view by a screen of trees. The other half of the point, the half that would soon be occupied by guests, was park-like and open in an effort to reduce the mosquitoes. Between the guest cabins and the staff cabins was a large greensward, a sort of no-man's-land, with three martin houses and two flagpoles of equal height, one for the Stars and Stripes and the other for the Maple Leaf. There was also a tower with something like a TV antenna at the top of it.

"That tower doesn't have anything to do with TV, does it?" I asked.

"That's the radio-telephone tower. I'll hook the phone up first chance I get. I hope it works."

"I'll be able to make phone calls?"

"Sort of."

"Will I be able to call Paula and my mother?"

"Sort of. It's a radio phone. You'll see."

We went into all the guest cabins to check for damage, and shortly after entering each one, I would hear Mike say "cracked toilet" or "ruptured water line" or whatever it was that had failed to withstand the brutal temperatures of the recent winter.

We eventually made our way to Dutch's cabin, which I was especially anxious to see. It was at the far end of the row of guest cabins and quite lovely. Like everything else at Kettle Falls Lodge, it was a model of studied rusticity, with interior walls of rough-sawn cedar and a queen-size bed made of peeled logs that Molly jumped up on as though she knew something we didn't.

When we'd finished looking at Dutch's cabin, which Mike noted had a shattered sink trap, I said, "You haven't shown me those two buildings way down by the water."

"That's where we're headed next. The little one on the left is the outboard shop. The big one next to it is the store, the office, the staff rec room—a little bit of everything. The marina's down there, too. I've been putting that off."

"Why?"

"Because there's probably a lot of ice damage to the docks, and we can't do anything about it until the crew shows up."

When we got there, we found the docks to be in reasonably good shape, but Mike said the high water would require an additional crib and dock section because there was a large pool of water between the shore and the dock. That didn't stop Molly, though, who splashed through the water and was soon scampering all over the docks and jumping in and out of Louie's boat, the only one in the marina. The main dock was about twelve feet wide and thirty yards long, with four narrower, perpendicular docks running off it into the shelter of the bay. One of them was much longer than the others and had a large platform at its terminus with a bulk fuel tank in the middle of it.

"That's the seaplane dock," Mike said. "Most of the time there will be two or three planes tied up there. We take good care of the pilots—we feed 'em, fuel 'em and give 'em a bed for the night if they want."

After looking at the docks, we walked through the store, which, because it was closest to the water, was colder than any other building we'd been in. There was a long counter, a cash register and some empty shelves that would eventually hold things like insect repellent, sunglasses and candy bars. One corner of the store was a miniature tackle shop with line, lures and sundry items for catching fish in the English River. Mike saw me looking at the tackle.

"That's where, uh … remember those spinners we brought with us?"

"Don't remind me."

"Okay, I just thought—"

"Stop," I said.

There was a door behind the counter that led to Dutch's office, where I knew Mike and I would be spending a good deal of time. We looked in briefly, then went back into the store and walked down a little flight of four stairs at the far end that led to another level of the building—an area three times the size of the store itself. It was basically just a big room, but it had a couple of pool tables and a ping-pong table, a stove and refrigerator, a jukebox and a dance floor. It was a place where the staff could gather in the evenings, have a beer, make popcorn or throw a frozen pizza in the oven—a place for them to get away from the guests.

The part of the building closest to the water was a large pantry with barn-style double doors that opened on the docks. This is where Mike said the guides would come in the mornings to fill their coolers and pick up everything they needed to prepare a shore lunch for their guests. There was a walk-in cooler off the pantry, but it was much smaller than the one in the lodge kitchen, since it would hold only shore lunch supplies. The cooler smelled musty, and the floor was sticky underfoot because someone had left an entire case of Orange Crush sitting on a shelf, and the cans had frozen and exploded. There were also what appeared to be a few desiccated potatoes on the floor. Molly sniffed one of them, then backed out of the cooler as though she were offended. We followed her, our shoes crackling on the concrete.

When we got back to Louie's cabin, he was standing at the kitchen counter, slicing an onion. "So what do you think of the place, Allie?"

"It's beautiful," I said. "It's much fancier—much *grander*—than I expected."

He looked at Mike. "What about you?"

"Well, we've got two cracked toilets, three cracked toilet tanks, at least half a dozen ruptured water lines, one ruptured water-heater tank and a dozen doors that aren't closing because of frost heave. And the cooler in the store looks like some kid's science project."

Louie reached for another onion. "Just so you didn't go makin' no lists, eh. Have a drink, why doncha? Let's *all* have a drink. I oughta have supper ready in about an hour, eh."

"Louie, please let me make dinner," I said. "I can do it if you tell me where things are. Sit down and catch up with Mike."

"By God, I think I'll take you up on that, eh. I'm kinda tired of my own cookin'. Thanks, young lady."

"You're welcome. What am I making?"

"You're makin' the only thing we got, eh—moose liver and onions."

I didn't say anything, though I was inwardly retching.

Mike was less timid. "You mean the only thing in that gigantic freezer is moose liver?"

"Well, goddammit, I been eatin' out of that freezer for the last six months, kinda workin' around the liver, but that's all that's left now, eh. I been eatin' it for over a week. Except for yesterday. Yesterday I et the porcupine that chewed the handle off my ax. You want I should find you a porcupine?"

"What did it taste like?" I asked, hoping to change the subject.

"Oh, I dunno," Louie said. "It kinda tasted like—"

"Like chicken?"

"Yeah, it did in a way, but I was gonna say turtle, eh."

"I think I'll pass," Mike said.

"Then we're right back to where we started," Louie said. "How the hell does moose liver sound?"

Mike laughed. "It sounds better all the time. But we definitely need to get some groceries in here. If we'd known you didn't have any food left in camp, we would've brought some from town."

"We got plenty of bread, spuds and onions," Louie said, "and beyond that you don't need to worry, eh. I'll take care of the groceries myself."

"How?"

"None of your business, ya finicky Yank."

Dinner, as it turned out, wasn't as bad as I expected. I found garlic powder, celery salt and a few other spices that smelled as though they might have the potential to make moose liver palatable, and they very nearly did, although I doubt even Albert could have made moose liver taste like anything other than what it is. The worst thing about it was its extraordinary toughness—the more I chewed each bite, the bigger it got.

Even with the overhead light on, it was soon dark in the cabin, so Louie put a Coleman lantern on the table, and after dinner we talked for a couple hours to the soft accompaniment of its sibilant hiss.

When it was time for bed, Mike and I went out to the car to bring in a few things, and when we did, I saw the northern lights in a way that bore no resemblance to their poor relations in upstate New York. To the north the sky was alive with neon greens and blues that rippled in the night like curtains. Every few seconds, the colors would deepen and freeze, then burst into glittering shards, creating a tapestry of light.

Finally, Louie stuck his head out the door. "What the hell are you two doin' out here? I thought maybe a bear drug you off, eh."

"It's the northern lights," I said. "I've never seen them so beautiful."

Louie looked up. "Yeah, they been pretty sightly this spring. They was red a couple nights ago. Don't often see that, eh."

When we returned to the cabin, Louie let the fire in the stove go out, and the three of us finished the rest of the brandy and went to bed early. I awoke once during the night to the sound of wolves howling, and I could hear Molly, who was at the foot of our bed, growling softly in response to their ghostly, primordial voices.

Chapter 13

I t got very cold in the night, and the next morning there was frost on the windows and skim ice in the big bucket next to the sink. Water was a problem, not because it froze, but because every drop we used had to be carried from the river, boiled for drinking and, above all, conserved. Serious bathing was out of the question, and as I splashed the icy water on my face, I hoped by the end of the day that Mike and Louie would succeed in routing water to at least one of the camp's water heaters, so I could take a shower.

After a milkless bowl of Red River, I went to the lodge and worked in the kitchen until noon, when I decided to see how the boys were doing. They were down at the pump house, mercifully addressing the water situation, and had just finished priming the pump. It had gone well, and Louie said he was going to take a break and go "grocery shopping."

"Let's talk about that," Mike said. "You'll do whatever the hell you want anyway, so you might as well tell me how you plan to feed us."

"Squarehook."

Mike's face was part anger, part disbelief. "For a second there, I thought you said 'squarehook.' But you couldn't have—the Ministry would shut us down for that."

"Don't worry about it, eh."

"Don't *worry*? What if—"

"Look, kid, if you think I'm gonna listen to you bellyache about eatin' moose liver again, you're crazier than an acre of snakes. And just in case you forgot, that's what we're havin' for supper tonight, and *every* night unless we do somethin' about it, eh. I don't know about you, but my teeth won't survive much more moose liver. It's like chewin' on a goddamn fan belt."

Since no one felt compelled to explain, I said, "All right, I give up—what's a squarehook?"

"It's a gill net," Mike said, "and gill nets are illegal in this district unless you're an Indian." He glowered at Louie. "They're so illegal I can't think of anything to compare them to."

"Well, while you're tryin' to come up with somethin', I'm goin' fishin'."

"Great," Mike said. "I'm glad we had this talk."

"Me, too, kid."

"Just hide the net when you're done. I don't want the MNR ending our season before it starts."

"I'll take care of it, eh. Whaddya think, Allie—you wanna come with me?"

"No way," Mike said. "This camp can only afford to bail one person out of jail at a time."

Louie gave me a little sideways smile. "Whatever you say, Yank."

Mike started testing the water lines, and I went back to the lodge to finish cleaning the kitchen. I hadn't been there long when I saw Louie's boat come around the point from the marina, then disappear behind four little islands not more than two hundred yards from where I was working. Half an hour later, he was heading back to the marina, and not long after that, he walked into the lodge, rubbing his hands together.

"I gotta remember my rubber gloves next time," he said. "Water's so damn cold it burns, eh. Do I smell coffee?"

"Let me get you a cup." I got us each a cup of coffee, and we sat at a table and talked as we looked out at the river.

"This is good, eh," Louie said, holding the cup with both hands.

"The water I made it with was probably ice yesterday. Did you put your squarehook out?"

"It's right behind them little islands." Louie turned and pointed to the kitchen. "Did you come across any cornflake crumbs in there?"

"I did, actually. Mice got into a few of the boxes, but there are at least half a dozen that are fine."

"Good. We'll need it for the fish, eh. We're gonna have a big supper tonight."

I rapped my knuckles on the table. "Only if you catch something."

"No need to knock wood, Allie. I'll catch lots of fish. You'll see."

We had another cup of coffee, and in twenty minutes Louie had elicited my life story without offering much of his own. He was smart and tough, and I liked him a lot. There were things about him that reminded me of Hedley.

Finally, Louie decided it was time to get back to work. "I s'pose I should go find your worser half, eh. Thanks for the coffee." He ground out his cigarette in the ashtray and stood up to leave but then stopped to pet Molly, who was stretched out at my feet. "She sure has taken to you, eh. Even Molly knows you're the nicest thing to happen around here in a good long while."

"Why, thank you, Louie."

Louie nodded and trudged out of the lodge in search of Mike.

The next time I saw him, about an hour later, he was walking up the hill toward the fish-cleaning house with a wash tub. The tub was heavy, and it was all he could do to carry it.

Mike had seen Louie, too, and we met on the way to the fish house. When we stepped inside, Louie was smiling from ear to ear, and he had fish all over the place.

"I done pretty good, eh—fifteen walleye and a ten-pound jackfish."

Mike took a knife from the rack. "Let's cut these fish before the local conservation officer drops by for a chat. Even that northern is out of season."

"There ain't no CO within fifty miles of here, eh."

"Just the same, I want these fish out of here—the guts, too."

"I'll dump 'em in the river."

"Okay, but do it on the current side, not the marina side."

Louie checked his knife for sharpness. "Good idea. Bein' a moron an' all, I woulda tossed 'em in the marina, eh."

"I just meant it would be—"

"Go to hell, Yank."

I didn't get a shower that day, but dinner that evening almost made up for it—potatoes and onions and fresh, flaky-white walleye, breaded with cornflake crumbs.

"So how do you like English River walleye?" Louie asked between mouthfuls. "Pretty tasty, eh?"

"It tastes sort of … illegal. Good, though," I added quickly.

Louie laughed. "Eatin' somethin' illegal always makes it taste better, eh. I think that's why, if I had my druthers, I'd sooner eat a whooping crane than a goose."

"Oh, come on. You wouldn't really eat a whooping crane."

"No, you're right about that, eh." Louie's eyes were full of their usual mischief. "Whooping crane's almost as stringy as trumpeter swan. Damn sight better than bald eagle, though."

"Now, I know you're teasing me."

"I am. I ain't never et a trumpeter swan."

About halfway through the meal, Louie got up to turn on the radio so he could listen to the hockey game. Louie loved hockey, and that night the Winnipeg Jets were in the playoffs. To his amazement, neither Mike nor I knew very much about hockey, but it didn't matter because the game was broadcast in French.

"They'll switch to English after the first period, eh," Louie said. "I know enough French to get you by 'til then."

So we listened to the game as we ate, following the announcer's voice up and down the scale, and Louie translated the highlights. After a while, the names of the players—at least the ones that got mentioned a lot—became oddly distinguishable from the general babel, so when the announcer switched to English, we had a leg up on the action. The game wasn't nearly as interesting in English, but it gave me the confidence to ask a question.

"Why did they take Rondelle out? He was the best player!" I pointed to the radio. "They were calling his name all the time."

Louie looked at me, then started to laugh. He was soon laughing so hard I thought he'd never stop, and when he tried to speak, he couldn't. Finally, when he was able to talk again, he said, "Allie, *rondelle* isn't a person—it's French for *puck*." And then he began to laugh all over again. Louie never let me forget that, and in the months that followed, the *rondelle* story would be subject to endless telling and retelling, especially when Louie encountered French-speaking Canadians.

After dinner Mike said, "Louie, if you've recovered enough to walk, we should take a look at the substation while it's still light. That's the first thing I should've done today."

Louie agreed, and the three of us picked up a path behind Dutch's cabin and followed it about fifty yards into the woods to a small clearing. In the middle of the clearing was the substation, a collection of cylindrical transformers and green metal boxes resting on a cement slab. It was surrounded on all sides by an eight-foot chain-link fence with a padlocked gate, and the fence was topped with a strand of barbed wire. Inside the fence, the substation sat God-like and serene on its concrete altar, humming its incessant syllable into the forest. The substation supplied the camp with its lifeblood—220 volt alternating current—that it alchemized from the raw hydro power supplied to it by the Kettle Falls dam.

We stood before the substation, and Mike and Louie assayed its health in hushed tones.

"It looks okay," Louie said.

Mike nodded. "Yeah ... it does."

"I mean there's no trees down across it—nothin' like that, eh."

"No—no trees."

"Why are you two whispering?" I said. "Should I cover my head?"

Mike snapped out of his little reverie. "Louie, let's get four timed floodlights on this thing and run a couple more strands of barbed wire across the top of that fence. And let's cut some of this brush back, too."

"I'll get on it tomorrow," Louie said with surprising alacrity.

By the time we returned to the cabin, dusk had given way to nightfall, so Louie lit the Coleman lantern and put it on the table. As the darkness congealed around us, we were drawn to the light like moths and were soon sitting within the radius of its glow.

"I don't understand something," I said. "Since the substation isn't likely to climb the fence and escape, why do you need barbed wire around it?"

Louie laughed. "You might as well tell her, kid."

"Yeah ... I suppose so." Mike looked at me and turned up the lantern. "Do you remember when you asked me about mercury yesterday?"

"Yes," I said. "The man at the bank mentioned something about it, too."

"Do you know what it is?"

"It's toxic. That's all I know."

"That's the part that matters," Mike said. "A lot of what people are saying is just speculation—nobody knows all the details yet—but a paper mill in Dryden supposedly dumped some mercury into the Wabigoon River a couple years ago. That's what Dutch told me."

"How far is Dryden from here?"

Mike looked at Louie.

"Oh, 'bout a hundred and fifty miles, give or take," Louie said. "But it ain't about the distance, eh. Everything's connected. The Wabigoon flows into the English a hundred miles east of here, so that mercury is in all the water in this part of the province, includin' the Winnipeg River—if you believe what you hear, eh."

"What it means," Mike said, "is that there's now a corridor from Dryden in the east to Kettle Falls in the west that's contaminated with mercury."

Louie grunted dismissively. "Or so they say. There ain't been enough testin' done to know for sure, eh."

"Not only that," Mike said. "A lot of people say mercury exists naturally in these watersheds. They've found mercury as far east as the Nipigon River, and there's no way it got in there from the Wabigoon. So no one really—"

"If all this happened two years ago, why all the fuss now?"

"It took that long for the word to get out, and now the newspapers and environmental groups are having a field day with it. People are scared, especially camp operators."

"I can see why," I said. "But what does it have to do with the substation?"

Mike turned to Louie again, who made a rolling motion with his finger. "Go ahead, kid. You're doin' fine."

"Well, most of the big camps have already closed down. They're suing the provincial government and the paper mill that put mercury in the Wabigoon."

"I can understand suing the paper mill," I said, "but how can they sue the government?"

"They say the province is running interference for the mill, trying to cover things up. Isn't that their beef, Louie?"

"Yeah, but there's a lot of monkey business goin' on, eh. Most of them camp operators are old-timers lookin' to sell. Thing is, their camps is worth so much money nobody could ever buy 'em, eh—except maybe the government. So the owners, they figure if they shut down and scream bloody murder, maybe they'll get a big chunk of money to retire on. They don't care where it comes from, eh."

"And our substation?"

Mike got up and fiddled with the stove damper. "There's … sort of a war going on."

"A war? What kind of war?"

"The closed camps are forcing the open camps to close down, too," he said. "If a camp stays open and makes money, it hurts all the closed camps in court."

"And it's gettin' pretty nasty, eh."

Then Mike and Louie explained how this war was being waged, and short of murder, anything the closed camps could do to make an open camp shut down was being done. There were endless threats, mysterious fires and acts of vandalism to boats, bulk gas tanks, vehicles and airplanes. But nothing was as devastating to an open camp as an attack on its power supply, because a camp that lost power would also lose the food in its coolers and freezers. Few camps could survive a hit like that. The saboteurs knew this and had recently begun attacking the generators and substations of the open camps. That's why Mike wanted floodlights and more barbed wire around the substation. And that's why Louie had been so willing to do it.

"It's one helluva mess, eh," Louie said. "No tellin' how it's gonna end."

"Is that why you came out of the cabin carrying a rifle when

Mike and I first got here?"

"Yep. I been sleepin' with that rifle since last fall."

I turned to Mike. "You might have told me about this before. It wouldn't have changed my mind about anything, but you should've told me."

Mike closed his eyes and nodded. "I would have, but I didn't know the worst of it until we got here, and Louie filled me in. Dutch told me about the mercury, but he never said anything about the rest of it. If I thought you were in danger, we never would've come."

"What are the police doing about all this?"

"Ain't much the Mounties can do, eh," Louie said. "This is bush country, and there's a lot of it."

"We couldn't contact the authorities anyway," Mike said. "Remember, we're illegal immigrants."

"So we're on our own?"

"Yes, but out here, everybody's on his own."

Chapter 14

Three days after Mike and Louie told me about the mercury war, Albert "Hot Biscuit" Slimm showed up. He was a slight, soft-spoken man with wavy black hair and a small, nervous mouth that tended to pucker when he was worried, which was most of the time. Albert had his own cabin, as befit his station, and he cooked delicious meals for us in Louie's little kitchen until the crew began to arrive. After that he moved his base of operations into the lodge and fed us all in the staff dining room, ringing the big bell outside the back door promptly at six o'clock in the morning, again at noon, and again at six o'clock in the evening.

Albert was excessively deferential to me, courteous to a fault, and no matter how hard I tried to be his friend, I couldn't draw him in. I was the boss's wife, and it was Albert's clear intention to treat me with unflagging respect whether I liked it or not.

"Mrs. Bowman, I believe I have this year's menu very nearly ready. I'm doing a great many things with berries—roasted blueberries, juniper glazes and a wild cranberry pellicle on the pork. Oh, yes, and I'm switching from a goose liver pâté to a mushroom pâté on the beef Wellington. And with your approval, ma'am, I thought I might try a wild rice and chestnut stuffing with the pheasant this year. Would you care to review the menu now, Mrs. Bowman?"

"I will if you want me to, Albert, but everything sounds delicious. I'm only here to help you."

"But Mrs. Bowman, you've already done so much. It was very good of you to clean the kitchen. I must apologize for—"

"Albert, do you think you could call me Allie, like everyone else does?"

"Yes, ma'am. I've also rethought some of our desserts, and I want to get away from all the pies …"

As April twentieth approached, our crew began to trickle in by twos and threes, and on the nineteenth, it seemed as though people were arriving in camp every hour or so. Nevertheless, Mike determined by the twenty-third that we would need eight or nine additional employees, so I went to Kenora the following day to see who would show up at the Kenora Inn to answer our ad. We had a good turnout, but I was so busy trying to count everyone's teeth that twice I had to ask people to repeat things.

I hired nine people altogether: two college boys who were home from the University of Manitoba for the summer; two high school boys from Keewatin; three teenage girls—two of them sisters, plus their cousin, who was visiting from Thunder Bay. My personal favorites, though, were two twenty-year-old girls from British Columbia named Marcy and Collette, bell-bottomed free-spirits who had planned to hitchhike from their home in Victoria all the way to Nova Scotia. A lot of kids were doing it, they said—hitching across the country, following the TransCan as far as they could. Fortunately, for me, these two had grossly miscalculated the cost of the trip and run out of money in Kenora.

It was the next day that Edward "Pop" Smith, the outboard

mechanic, arrived in camp. He and Louie were good friends, but I couldn't see that they had much in common, other than their age and a genuine fondness for each other. In fact, Pop was the antithesis of Louie. He was a sweet, gentle soul, bookish and well-spoken, who seemed altogether out of place in a fishing and hunting camp. But I liked Pop immediately, and we would become lifelong friends.

The Indian guides and their families were the last to show up. They arrived in two groups, one from the Grassy Narrows Reservation and the other from the Shoal Lake Reservation. Mike said most of them had been with Dutch a long time. The Indians were a taciturn, brooding bunch, and as soon as they arrived, they went directly to their big bunkhouse, drew the blinds and rarely left, except for meals, which they avoided taking with the rest of us. They would come over to the staff dining room together about the time everyone else had finished eating and speak only in Ojibwe, even though they all knew English. We desperately needed the Indians' help to get the camp up and running, but unlike in previous years, they refused to offer it.

Everyone else was working twelve-hour days, and we had crews raking leaves, working on the docks, staining cabins and laundering a thousand sheets and pillowcases. Wherever I looked, there was someone doing something. Louie was running from one job to the next, helping each crew. Pop was ministering to the needs of his two dozen outboard motors. Orin, our minnow man, was netting minnows by the thousands in the feldspar quarry and nearby creeks. Albert was breaking in his kitchen staff, instilling in them the virtues of serving from the left and clearing from the right.

And every day, the staff was becoming increasingly unhappy with the Indians. They didn't say so, at least not to us, but it was clear that they were annoyed by the Indians' refusal to lend a hand at this busy time of year.

After we'd spent a week wondering what the problem was, Louie, who had friends among the Indians, found out they were angry about Wounded Knee, where a stand-off was still going on between the U.S. government and Indians from the Pine Ridge Reservation. But knowing why the Indians were out of sorts didn't change our situation, and Pop and Louie showed up on our porch one morning to point that out.

Pop was clearly uncomfortable. "Michael, I'd never tell you what to do—and Lord knows you can run this camp any way you see fit—but we have to deal with the Indians." He shifted his weight from one foot to the other. "It's beginning to have an effect on morale."

"He's right, kid," Louie said. "Them Piutes won't do sweet fuck-all. Everybody's workin' to beat hell, eh, while they sit in the bunkhouse playin' euchre."

Mike was already heading for the door. "I'll deal with it. I should've done it right away."

"Be careful, eh. It wouldn't hardly do if you was to get your nuts cut off."

But Mike was halfway down the stairs.

The three of us sat at the table in our cabin and waited, wondering what Mike would say, wondering how the Indians would take it.

After half an hour, Mike walked in the door, pulled a chair away from the table and straddled it backward. "I took care of it."

"So they agreed to help out?" Pop asked.

Mike shrugged. "We'll know soon enough. They didn't want to talk to me, but they said there's some kind of boycott going on, and they aren't supposed to work for the *zhaagnaash* until the business at Wounded Knee is over. What the hell does *zhaagnaash* mean?"

"It means white man," Louie said. "And it ain't exactly a compliment."

"Are they going to pitch in or not?" Pop said.

Mike stood up. "I told them to get to work or be gone within the hour."

Louie laughed. "Jesus Christ, kid. If them Indians pack up and leave, we'll be usin' cabin girls for guides, eh."

"They aren't going anywhere," Mike said. "They wouldn't be here if they didn't need jobs. Most of the other camps are closed, and they know it."

Forty-five minutes later, the Indians all came out of the bunkhouse, dispersed and joined the other crews working around the camp. And at six o'clock that evening, every one of them showed up for dinner and visited with us in English for the first time since they'd arrived. They weren't happy, and the mood in camp remained somewhat tense, but we got the help we needed.

The Indians gave Mike a wide berth for a time, and the only Ojibwe I heard in camp was Mike's new nickname, *dayewe`igedjig*, which means "he who beats drum." Eventually, they would call him *ogimaa*, which means "boss," but this would not happen until after May 8, when the Indians at Wounded Knee laid down their weapons after seventy-one days and made an uneasy peace with the federal government.

Chapter 15

E very day for a week before our first guests were due—a group of bear hunters and fishermen from Fort Worth—supplies arrived in camp from morning till night. Most of the frozen food was delivered by seaplane, and as I sat at my desk in the store, adding up the cost of it all, I could look out the window and see DeHavilland Beavers and big Twin Otters coming and going from our docks all day long. As soon as they were unloaded, the planes would taxi from the marina into the river's main channel and roar into the air.

It was when our coolers and freezers began to fill that Mike unlocked the gun cabinet in our cabin and removed one of Dutch's rifles, which he loaded and placed in the corner of the bedroom on his side of the bed.

"Until now," he said, "we haven't had a whole lot to lose. But from here on out, we'll have to be more careful. If we lose the food, that's the ball game."

"You can't shoot someone over food."

"It isn't about food. These cowards who sabotage camps don't

just destroy property—they destroy livelihoods. I'd have no problem putting a bullet in one of them."

And two days later, had he caught the saboteurs that attacked
the camp, he probably would have. Dutch's cabin—our cabin—was
the farthest building from the marina, so we couldn't see anything
down there except the yellow glow from the big mercury-vapor light
that illuminated the docks. That's why we had no idea anything was
wrong that night until Molly started whining. Then, before we could
turn on the light to investigate, Louie was pounding on the door.

"Get up!" he yelled. "The seaplane dock's on fire."

Mike tried to ask him about the fuel tank at the end of the dock,
but Louie was already gone. We scrambled to get dressed.

"Has the avgas tank been filled?" Mike was hopping toward the
door on one foot, trying to pull his other boot on.

"No, aviation gas comes tomorrow."

"Lucky for us."

We ran all the way to the marina. When we got there, most of
the crew was already on the scene, but they were crouched behind
trees or huddled behind the motor shop and the store. No one was
anywhere near the water, let alone out on the docks. Pop and Louie
were among those standing behind the shop, sort of peering around
the corner. Mike started to ask them what they were hiding from,
but at the sound of Mike's voice, Pop turned and shouted, "Stay
outta the light, Michael—they're shooting from the river."

No sooner had he spoken than a bullet ricocheted off a rock at
the water's edge and rattled through the trees. Mike and I ran for the
shadows and took cover behind a large boulder a few yards from
the shop. As we did, we heard another bullet hit the dock. We were
hearing the gunshots a split-second after the bullets' impact.

Mike stared into the darkness. "Goddamn cowards. They're
way out there."

Through the trees we could see that the seaplane dock and refueling platform were completely engulfed by the fire. The gas tank

hadn't exploded, but it was just a matter of time. It was a thousand-gallon tank, and even though it was almost empty, it was still dangerous—perhaps more dangerous than a full one.

Pop and Louie motioned to us, and we made our way over to them.

"When we first got here," Pop said, "we all ran out on the docks to see if we could do anything about the fire. That's when the shooting started."

Two more bullets whizzed harmlessly overhead, sending down little showers of pine needles.

"They aren't trying to hit anybody," Mike said. "They just want to make sure we can't put the fire out."

"They're doin' a damn good job of it, eh," Louie said. "We can't do nothin' but watch."

Mike looked around at all the people. "We have to get them out of here."

At that moment there was a shrieking sound from the fuel tank, and a huge arc of flame shot over the water. Then the tank exploded. It was more of a flash than a fireball, more of a crack than a boom. But it shook the ground. Several girls behind the store screamed.

Then it was very quiet, and we heard the shooters start their motor. There was no more gunfire. The gas tank, the refueling platform and perhaps fifteen yards of dock were gone. Little islands of gasoline were burning on the water, and one of our boats was on fire, but a few of the staff scrambled onto the docks and put it out before any serious damage was done. Mike told several young men to get buckets and soak down the burning end of the seaplane dock to keep the fire from spreading to the marina. Then he and Louie got their rifles and prepared to go out on the river.

"What can you possibly accomplish out there in the dark?" I said. "Whoever did this is miles away by now."

"Maybe," Mike said. "But they only have a ten-minute head start. They could be in a slower boat than ours."

But when Mike walked into the cabin just before sunrise, he said whoever set the fire had gotten away clean. He was angry and frustrated, but there was nothing we could do. We certainly couldn't report it.

"We just won't have any avgas this year," Mike said. "We can get by without it—it's more of a convenience for the pilots than anything else."

"We were lucky," I said. "They could've blown up one of the bigger tanks, like the boat gas tank. That would've burned down the store—maybe the entire marina."

"They hit the seaplane dock because it was easy. It sticks out there in the bay all by itself, just begging to be set on fire."

After that we posted two guards around the camp at night who sometimes managed to stay awake. The fire was an emotional bump in the road, but two days before "Fort Worth" was due to arrive, we were ready for business. We had the crew, guides, food, beer, liquor and gasoline required to set the camp in motion. Gasoline was extremely expensive that year, and we needed a lot of it—regular gas for the pump by the garage, and mixed gas down in the marina for the boats. Not having to buy avgas actually worked in our favor, although I doubt Mike would have agreed. Our start-up costs were staggering, but Mike and Dutch had calculated the initial expenses carefully, and we were able to cover it—barely.

It was the morning before our first group arrived that I talked Mike into taking me out on the river. I had heard the guides discussing the places they'd fished last year and places they planned to take our bear hunters when they arrived. I was anxious to see what people were willing to come thousands of miles and spend thousands of dollars to enjoy, so I asked Albert if he would put together a picnic lunch for Mike and me, and he was only too happy to oblige. Within an hour, he came down to the store, carrying one of the freshly painted shore lunch boxes, sans cookware, that he had transformed into a picnic basket. It was full of cold fried chicken, sandwiches and a bottle of wine wrapped in a towel.

"I don't know how long the chardonnay will remain chilled, Mrs. Bowman, but I was thinking perhaps you could put it in the water for a few minutes before you eat."

"Albert, thank you. I didn't mean for you to go to all this trouble."

"It was the least I could do, Mrs. Bowman—a token of my appreciation for everything you and your husband have done to help me this spring."

I thanked him again, and in a few minutes Mike showed up, shouldered the picnic basket, and we walked to the dock, where Pop was sitting in a boat, working on its motor. He had the cowling off and was muttering to himself.

"Which boat should we take?" Mike asked.

"Number eleven," Pop said. "It's got two full tanks, and I just put a carb kit in it. Let me know how it runs when you get back."

"Will do."

Number eleven started with one pull of the rope, and Mike gave Pop a thumbs-up as we backed out of the corridor between the docks. I felt the motor clunk into its forward gear, and we made our way to the river's main channel, where Mike opened the throttle and brought the boat up on plane. We headed south, and there was beauty everywhere I looked—craggy cliffs, quiet little bays and islands covered with tall pines, many of them gnarled by the lightning of a thousand passing storms.

Five miles below Kettle Falls, the English River became a vast, sprawling flowage of interconnected lakes, some of which were huge and filled with islands, and only in the channels between these lakes was there any sense of current. There, the water swirled and behaved in odd ways, and if it weren't for that, I wouldn't have known I was on a river at all.

"What's the name of this one?" I said, as we came around an island and entered a lake that was at least ten miles long.

"Tetu," Mike said over the motor. "Tetu Lake."

"It's gorgeous."

The sun had come out, and the waves flashed silver as the sunlight shattered on the water. I pointed to a cluster of red buildings with gray roofs on the west side of the lake.

"White Elk Lodge," Mike said. "That's Kenny Morgan's place. He's our only neighbor, and he's still open—God love him."

From Tetu we went south to Swan Lake, which, Mike explained, was where the Winnipeg River flowed into the English. Then we headed north until we came to a forty-foot-wide notch in the shoreline that led to something Mike clearly intended to show me.

"This is North Boundary Rapids," he said.

"Are we really going through there?"

"Hang on."

I looked at the channel in front of us. Two very determined rivers were trying to force their way through that tiny cleft at the same time. The water was boiling and white in the narrows, and as we entered, I could feel the boat being lifted up several inches and hear the pitch of the motor change as we lunged forward with the current.

Once we'd passed through the narrows, it was even worse. For a hundred yards in every direction, the water bulged up around us like lava, like horrible black flowers that burst outward from the center, creating deep whirlpools and swirling eddies that flung the boat in all directions. Finally, we went around a point and it was over. Once again, we were on a big lake, and the current seemed to disappear.

"I didn't much care for that," I said.

Mike laughed. "I could tell by the way your knuckles turned white."

"It's a scary stretch of water."

"It's a river."

"*Two* rivers," I said.

We ate our lunch beside a waterfall that Mike called South Boundary Falls. I set the wine in a rocky pool and let the water wash over it for a few minutes as we unpacked the lunch box.

"I'd have bet anything Albert wouldn't remember to put in a corkscrew," Mike said, holding one up. "There's even a little table-cloth in here … and wine glasses."

We spread the tablecloth on a flat rock and placed everything on it. A picnic by a waterfall is hard to beat, and ours was made even better by the fact that it was too early in the year for black flies or mosquitoes.

Mike pulled the cork from the wine and pointed overhead. "Now, *there's* a fisherman." An eagle floated high above the falls, hanging there motionless, as though it were nailed to the sky.

I shook my head in wonder. "If you painted this scene, no one would believe it. It's just too perfect."

We ate our lunch slowly, partly to savor it and partly because we didn't want to leave. As we sat beside the waterfall, it seemed as though the camp and its tribulations were a million miles away, and we were very much aware that it was the first time in days that we weren't being asked two or three questions at once. But after a couple hours, we reluctantly packed up and headed back. Our passage through North Boundary Rapids was even less enjoyable the second time because we were going against the current. Like all the Kettle Falls boats, number eleven had a thirty-five-horse motor, but even wide open, we crawled across the roiling water at a snail's pace. With any less of a motor, we wouldn't have made it at all.

Molly was waiting for us on the dock when we arrived, a little put out that we hadn't taken her with us. But everything seemed to be fine. Nothing had burned down, no calamities had struck, so Mike, Molly and I sneaked back to our cabin, pretending to be invisible.

The next morning at ten o'clock, sixteen happy Texans, with enough gear for a protracted stay in the subarctic, taxied up to the dock in two float planes, and an hour after Albert had served them lunch, we had them out hunting. It was the perfect sized group for us to cut our teeth on. There would be a second small group of Texans to follow, then a short break. But after that we would have thirty guests in camp almost every day until the end of August—barring cancellations, which we didn't want to think about.

The Texans hunted bear morning and evening and fished during the afternoon. The walleye season wouldn't open for twelve more days, but the Texans hadn't come to catch walleyes. They wanted to catch big northerns, and they did. The northerns were still in the bays, and most of the Texans took a fish over twenty pounds, so they were happy whether they got a bear or not.

At the end of four days, the second group of Texans arrived, and we sent the first group out on the same planes, along with their fish and bear hides. Both groups from Texas came and went without incident, and Kettle Falls functioned with a jeweled precision that surprised even Mike and me.

As reassuring as that was, we knew Kettle Falls had not yet proven itself, nor had it operated at anywhere near capacity. That would begin on Saturday, May 12, the opening of the walleye season, which for us meant the arrival of thirty men from Harding Tool and Die in Milwaukee, Wisconsin.

Chapter 16

The combination of the high water and a late spring delayed the walleye bite somewhat, and for the first week of the season, our newer guides had trouble finding fish, although their guests always managed to catch enough for shore lunch. But by the middle of the second week, the fishing, which had been sputtering like a wet fuse, caught fire in places like Swan Lake, and within days the bite was on everywhere. Our guides could do no wrong, and our delighted guests were coming off the river each day with limits of big walleye and stringers of smallmouth bass between three and four pounds, sometimes more.

As the fishing heated up, so did Watergate. Mike and I were far too busy to give it the attention it deserved, but each group of guests that arrived wore Watergate like a mantle. They would be talking about Watergate as they stepped off the plane and continue talking about it through dinner the first evening. They would speak breathlessly of "hush money" and "secret tapes." And they would recite the names of Ehrlichman, Haldeman, Mitchell and Dean like a dactylic mantra.

This would continue until they went fishing. After that, Watergate would cease to exist for them, and all subsequent talk was of fish and the places and depths that produced fish. I concluded by mid-May that there was nothing in life, including politics, capable of surviving a collision with the American archetype of fishing. The English River was like the waters of Lethe, and in a short time our guests forgot everything in their former lives that had once seemed important, even themselves.

There were very few problems, and in no time the camp acquired the habit of rhythmic efficiency. By eight o'clock each morning, thirty guests and fifteen guides would leave the marina. At five o'clock they would return, and the guests, sunburned and exhausted, would shower, then drag themselves into the lodge for a drink or two, after which they would attack Albert's meals with terrifying ferocity. Dessert and coffee finished, they'd sit in the bar for a couple hours before repairing to their cabins and the comfort of their beds. Mike and I would tend bar and schmooze throughout the evening, making sure that each guest had experienced the nicest day possible.

"How did you do today?" we would ask.

"Terrific! Rudy really kept us in the fish. We saw two moose at Tetu Narrows."

"Great. Well, if you need anything—anything at all—just let us know."

After the guests and our staff had gone to bed, Mike and I would do the same, falling into a deep, dreamless sleep, with Molly on the floor beside us—unless there was a thunderstorm, in which case Molly would climb into bed with us and tremble at the noise. Molly had adopted us the first week we were there, and she rarely let me out of her sight.

With the beginning of June came our first flight of Whirlpool men, with three more to follow. Within twenty-four hours of their arrival, Kettle Falls looked like something from Picasso's blue period. Everyone on our staff was wearing blue Whirlpool jackets, blue caps and blue T-shirts which had been given to them by the blue salesmen, who felt a hegemonic compulsion to see the Whirlpool swirl everywhere they looked.

Most of these men had been to Kettle Falls before, and they had favorite guides to whom they offered large sums of money to guide them again. Mike believed that guests like ours—people who weren't paying for their trip—were the easiest folks in the world to deal with because they threw a lot of money around and seldom complained about anything. Most of the time that was true, and the only trouble we had came as a result of Whirlpool's big fish contest. And it happened with the first group.

It was Whirlpool's custom to offer each group it sent to Kettle Falls a thousand-dollar cash prize to be awarded to the man who caught the biggest fish. The winner, in turn, would award half the prize to his guide. The competition was fierce—not among the guests, to whom five hundred dollars might represent a couple payments to their child's orthodontist, but among the guides, to whom five hundred dollars was a dangerously large sum.

Jay Two Hawks' boat caught a twenty-two pound northern the second day out, and everyone thought it would probably be the money fish, since the big northerns had left the bays and become harder to catch. But on the last day, George Fox came in with a twenty-four pounder. The problem was that the guest who caught the fish had taken it on a big perch, which—at George's behest—he had trailed in the water all day on a second fishing pole, thereby making the northern illegal on two counts.

When word of this got out, Two Hawks was furious, and because he was from Grassy Narrows and George Fox was from Shoal Lake, there was a tribal rivalry involved as well. It was very unpleasant, and dinner that evening was punctuated by Two Hawks sniping at Fox, who maintained that even if the fish were taken by illicit means—something he never actually confessed—the biggest fish was the biggest fish, no matter *how* it got into the boat.

That evening, like most evenings, Mike and I split up after dinner. I went down to the store to help Marcy and Collette, my hitchhikers, and Mike remained in the lodge until everyone had left. I'd been in the store about twenty minutes when Jay Two Hawks, who had drunk too much beer, gave George Fox a shove.

"*Gigii gazenzhinge!*" he shouted. "You cheated."

"*Gi giiwanim!* That's a lie!" George shouted back.

"*Ini gaayendaagoz,*" Two Hawks snarled. "You sonofabitch."

And with that, Jay Two Hawks pulled his fillet knife from its sheath and plunged it into George's belly.

George got a strange look on his face. He stared down at the knife, and when he did, he saw that he was standing in a pool of blood that had filled his shoes and was now spilling onto the floor. He pulled the knife from his stomach and said quietly, "My shoes." Then he collapsed.

"Somebody get Mike!" I screamed.

There were probably twenty-five people in the store at the time, and within seconds they were crowded around George, asking each other what had happened and, like me, uncertain as to what they should do. I was holding George's hand, and George, who was still conscious, was looking up at me with terrified eyes. And I was as frightened as he was.

"George, you're going to be okay," I said. "Mike's on his way."

"I'm not gonna die?"

"No, you're going to be fine," I said, having no idea if it were true.

Mike burst through the door and hollered for everyone to get out of the way. He told Collette to call the Kenora hospital and have them send the air ambulance immediately. Then he knelt beside George, ripped open his shirt and examined the wound.

"Get me a couple of those sweatshirts," he said, meaning the

Kettle Falls sweatshirts we sold in the store.

Somebody handed them to him, and he wadded one up and placed it beneath George's head. The other he pressed against the wound. "I need somebody to keep pressure on this."

Billy Red Deer knelt beside him. "I can do it."

"You'll have to press hard. *George, can you hear me?*"

"I hear you," George said weakly.

Mike looked at me. "Who did this? *Hang in there, George.*"

"Jay Two Hawks," I said.

"*George, I need you to stay with me. Can you do that for me?* Where is he?"

"He ran—I don't know."

"I'm ... cold," George said. He was very pale.

Mike checked George's pulse and looked carefully at his eyes. "He's getting shocky. I need boat cushions and a blanket."

Marcy ran to the back and returned with an armful of cushions that Mike used to elevate George's legs, and Neil, one of the college boys I'd hired in Kenora, ran out the door and returned with his own sleeping bag.

Mike took the bag and quickly unzipped it. "Help me get it over him. *George, don't you go to sleep on me. You hear me?*" He grasped George's jaw with his left hand and turned George's head toward him. "*Do you hear me, George?*"

"I hear you."

After a few tense minutes, George's color had returned, and he was breathing evenly. Mike checked the bleeding, and it had nearly stopped.

"I'm thirsty," George said.

"Sorry, partner. I can't give you any water."

"I need a doctor."

Mike put another sweatshirt under George's head. "Help's on the way. How about a salesman, George? We've got a whole camp full of them."

George looked at Mike and tried to laugh. "No salesman."

George would be okay. The air ambulance took him away that evening, and three weeks later he was back at Kettle Falls, showing off his surgical scar like LBJ. Mike had been afraid the knife might have nicked an artery, but George had been lucky.

Jay Two Hawks was lucky, too. He was seen going into the laundry building by Tina, one of our cabin girls. Mike dragged him out of there, and we had no choice but to call the Provincial Police, who apologized but said they couldn't send anyone for Two Hawks until the following day. That meant we had to do something with him in the meantime, and other than locking him in one of the coolers, we had no place to put him. Mike talked it over with Pop and Louie, and the consensus was that Two Hawks should be placed overnight on one of the tiny islands near the marina.

"There ain't but one Indian in a hundred that can swim, eh," Louie said.

So Mike and Louie took Two Hawks out to an island and left him there.

That night we lay in bed and talked until almost dawn. We were worried about George and worried that when the police questioned us about the stabbing, they would discover we were illegal immigrants. If not, Two Hawks would probably tell them. Mike was as low as I'd ever seen him, and there was no denying that deportation for us was a real possibility.

"And all because of a goddamn fish," Mike said. "Tonight was a disaster, a major—"

"You're tired," I said. "And you're forgetting something—you probably saved George's life tonight. How did you know what to do?" I nudged him. "Was it Geomorphology 101? No, I bet it was 202."

Mike smiled but not very much. "That was 100 percent 'Nam. You know, when guys go into shock like that, they don't usually ..." He groaned and tugged at the blanket. "We'd better get some sleep or we're gonna be worthless tomorrow."

We tried, but at sunrise we were awakened by Louie stomping up the steps.

"Damned if I know how he did it, kid," he said through the screen door, "but Two Hawks ain't on that island. I could see from the marina that he wasn't, eh, but I went out there to make sure, and he's gone."

Mike went to the door, rubbing the sleep from his eyes. "He must be the hundredth Indian."

"Whaddya mean?"

"The one that can swim."

"Yeah, maybe," Louie said, "but I don't believe it. You'd better ring up the Provincials and tell 'em our prisoner flew the coop."

"I'll take care of it," Mike said. "Ask around and see if anybody knows anything."

But no one did. Or if they did, they never admitted to it. Mike called the police and told them our prisoner had escaped, and they said they would talk to George at the Kenora hospital, but they never did. George told us later the police had sent over a form that he was supposed to fill out, but because he couldn't read, he'd thrown it away. That was the end of the matter, as far as he knew.

In the following days there was considerable speculation about the fate of Jay Two Hawks, and a lot of the crew wondered if he'd drowned trying to swim to shore. But a little over a week from the time he'd found his way off the island, I saw him on the streets of Kenora, hobbling down the sidewalk with the help of a cane. His left arm was in a sling, his nose was obviously broken, and his face was so swollen and discolored that I hardly recognized him. Mike and I thought some of George's friends from our Shoal Lake contingent might have paid Two Hawks a visit while he was on the island, but we never found out. For all we knew, Two Hawks' punishment could have been meted out in town.

There may have been no God north of Minaki, but there was

apparently a fierce brand of justice that had kept Mike and me from having to deal with the authorities. As fortunate as that may have been for us, I was unhappy about the way the Provincial Police had dropped the ball, and I said so to Mike.

"The way they blew the whole thing off—it's *disgusting*. Two Hawks is walking around the streets of Kenora after almost killing a man over a fish."

"Allie, from what you told me, Two Hawks isn't walking. He's limping on both feet, and if the police did the right thing, we'd be deported, we'd lose a lot of money, and the camp would probably close. We caught a break on this one, and Two Hawks didn't exactly come out clean. Let it go."

"It isn't right."

"No, it's a whole lot better than right."

Chapter 17

The day I saw Two Hawks in town there was a letter from my mother in the mail that I picked up in Minaki. My mother and I talked on the radio phone occasionally, but it was difficult because I had to hold a button down when I spoke, and we both had to say "over" every time we completed a thought. It was impossible for us to interrupt each other, and until I'd called Paula and my mother a few times from Kettle Falls, I hadn't realized how essential this is to feminine conversation. The men didn't have any objections to the radio phone. All the women hated it.

In her letter my mother told me that she and Tom had gone to Cape Vincent for a high school reunion. It was a lot of fun, she wrote, but she also mentioned that she'd talked to a friend of hers who sold real estate, and according to her friend, Hap Strattner was trying to get his half of the point surveyed so he could sell it. I was upset and confused by this development and called my mother that evening.

"But Hap doesn't really own *half* of it," I said. "He's a half-owner of the whole thing—over."

"I don't think he sees it that way—over."

"Jimmy must be furious—over."

"From what I heard at the reunion, he's got his lawyer working on it—over."

"Did you see Jimmy when you were out there? Over."

"No—over. Why do we have to talk this way?"

I didn't know what to make of my mother's news from Cape Vincent, but it sounded as though there was increasing friction between Jimmy and Hap. But I supposed they would get past it somehow, so they could focus their attention on more practical matters, such as making a million dollars by cornering the market in something or by seizing upon some opportunity the rest of the world had overlooked on its way to work. When I'd last spoken with Jimmy that windy morning by Lake Michigan, he promised to do everything in his power to regain full ownership of the point. Now, only three months later, he was fighting to keep Hap from converting a 50 percent interest in it into actual feet of lakeshore and explicit acres of land. It was hopeless.

When I told Mike about it, he just shook his head. He didn't want to get caught in the middle. He knew what the point meant to me, but he really liked Jimmy. Of course, other than my mother, *everybody* liked Jimmy. But Jimmy was a mistake, like that piece of furniture you buy—the one that looks terrific in the store, but when you get it home, you realize it doesn't go with anything. That's how it felt. And as far as my house was concerned, Jimmy clashed with everything in it.

It was during the second week of Whirlpool, as we referred to June, that I walked into the lodge one morning and found Mike talking to a haggard, sad-looking old man. They were seated on a sofa in the bar, drinking coffee, and the man was slouched forward with his elbows on his knees. He was wearing a red windbreaker with something printed on the back, but the only word I could make out was "Elk." When Mike saw me, he introduced us.

"Allie, this is Kenny Morgan from White Elk Lodge. We went by his camp last month when we were sightseeing on the river."

"Yes, I remember. It's a pleasure to meet you, Kenny."

Kenny raised himself part way off the sofa, shook my hand and sank tiredly back down.

"Kenny got hit last night," Mike said.

"Sabotage?"

Kenny nodded. "My generator. Somebody took bolt cutters to it, cut all the power cables. Even put sugar in the fuel tank, eh. Got the backup generator, too."

"What are you going to do?" I asked.

"Not much I *can* do. I'll lose most of the food ... the minnows. I'll have to shut down for a couple weeks, buy another generator and get it out to the island somehow—I'll be in hock up to my arse, eh." Kenny's eyes narrowed to little slits. "But I'll tell you what *ain't* gonna happen. I ain't gonna close." Kenny was angry and defiant, but he'd already lost the season. Nothing could change that now.

"I'm really sorry," I said. It didn't seem like enough, but it was all I had to offer.

"Me, too." Kenny leaned forward again, elbows on his knees. "I wish I coulda caught the bastards that did it, eh. I woulda taken them on their last airplane ride, that's for sure."

"Where do you think they came from?" Mike asked.

Kenny shrugged. "Hard to say. Maybe Twin Rivers. Maybe not. Hell, they coulda been my own guides. I got people working for me that would do a lot of things for a couple hundred bucks, eh. That's the going rate—two hundred dollars to put a man out of business."

Mike put his hand on Kenny's shoulder. "Why don't you put your food in our freezers. We'll help you get it over here."

"Thanks. Nice of you to offer." Kenny laughed bitterly. "You two should come for supper, eh—I got a hundred pounds of rib-eye thawed."

I left Mike and Kenny in the lodge and went down to the office, thinking about the violent, anomic wilderness in which we'd chosen to live—a place where people struggled against all the adversity of nature yet weren't satisfied until they could fold criminality into the mix.

When we were getting ready for bed that night, I asked Mike what Kenny had meant about taking the saboteurs on "their last airplane ride." Mike climbed into bed, chuckling to himself, and told me that, years before, one of Kenny's guides—a man with a lengthy history of causing trouble—had gotten drunk and fired a rifle several times into the dining room while the guests were eating dinner. No one was hurt, but Mike said Kenny had gone "a little crazy." He'd subdued the man, tied him up and thrown him into his Cessna, supposedly to fly him to town, where he could be turned over to the police. Kenny took off for Kenora, all right, but according to the staff at White Elk Lodge, he returned thirty minutes later—without his passenger.

"My God," I said. "Did he throw him out of the plane?"

Mike turned off the lamp on his nightstand. "That's the story. I think he's capable of it."

"No surprise there—you think we're all capable of anything."

"Pretty much," Mike said. "Are you coming to bed?"

"In a second. And nothing ever came of it?"

"Nothing comes of anything in the bush, Allie. There's no rule of law out here, except what each camp operator enforces. That's why the mercury war is going on."

"That may be," I said. "But just because a handful of people make up the rules doesn't mean they're right."

"Maybe not. But you and I aren't going to change it."

I climbed into bed beside Mike and kissed him. "I don't want to change anything. I just want to know what you use for moral coordinates when everyone is making up the rules as they go."

"I sort of navigate by the stars," Mike said, yawning.

"What does that mean?"

"I wing it. *Gosh*, I'm tired."

"You can be very frustrating. You know that, don't you?"

Mike turned to me and smiled. "Yes, but I have oodles of charm. You told me that once—oodles of charm."

By that point I was laughing. "I must have been out of my mind."

As I lay there in bed, I supposed it was possible to navigate by the stars, but I wondered how much help they would be in dangerous shoal water where a few yards either way might mean the difference between a close call and a moral shipwreck. A compass would be better, but then there was that business about the angle of declination. To ignore it was dangerous—*you'll get disoriented and lose your way*. That's what Mike had told me that day by the pothole, and I believed it. Maybe it was already happening. Maybe I was stuck between the two norths—true north and the other one, the one you couldn't trust. One thing was certain—finding your way in a wilderness requires special skills and great precision.

I fell asleep that night wondering how many places were left in the world like the one we lived in—places where people set fire to your property and then shot at you from the darkness. Places where a man could be stabbed over a fish or thrown from an airplane. Before I'd come to Kettle Falls, I hadn't known there were places like that, though perhaps I should have.

Chapter 18

I t was the fourth week of Whirlpool and things were going well. Fishing was excellent, and the big fish contests had been un-eventful since the first one. Then, the Saturday before our last group was scheduled to fly out, they took it upon themselves to throw a party for the entire camp—a big one. Mike and I didn't know anything about it, and no one on the staff dared mention it to us for fear we'd stop it the minute we found out. We were having dinner with the crew that evening when we heard a float plane ar-rive, but we didn't think anything of it since planes came and went from our docks on a regular basis.

When Mike had finished eating, he said, "I think I'll walk down and see who our visitor is. He'll probably want us to put him up for the night."

I went with him, but the plane left before we got there. The pilot didn't even taxi into the channel. He took off from our little bay, barely clearing the islands in front of the camp.

"That guy was sure in a hurry," Mike said.

At the marina we saw at least fifteen cases of beer and three cases of whiskey sitting on the main dock, along with a couple cases of mix and some crates of frozen pizzas. Several of our blue-clad Whirlpool guests had already begun carrying everything into the store.

"What's going on?" Mike said. "I didn't order this stuff."

"We did," one of the blue men said. "This was the greatest fishing trip we've ever had, so we decided to throw a party for the whole camp."

"You paid for all this?"

"Yessiree, we sure did," he said. "We got everything but hats and horns. We called the Kenora Air Service on your radio phone, and they flew it out here for us. We had to pay extra because it's Saturday, but we didn't mind. It's a surprise."

Mike looked at the whiskey. "It certainly is."

The man knelt down and picked up a case of beer. "They didn't want to deliver it tonight, though—said there was a big storm headed our way. That's why the pilot high-tailed it outta here." He hoisted the beer onto his shoulder and headed for the store.

Mike and I looked to the west, where we could see dark thunderheads gathered on the horizon. But it wasn't the weather Mike was concerned about. Alcohol caused more problems in camps like ours than everything else combined, and the last thing we wanted was for our well-intentioned guests to plunge Kettle Falls into a bacchanal. One stabbing was enough. But we were in a tough spot because the staff already knew about the party. If we were to stop it, both the staff *and* Whirlpool would be angry. So we stood there, weighing our options, while our guests carried case after case of beer into the store.

"What are we going to do, *ogimaa*?" I asked.

"I guess we're going to a party. Do you see any way out of this?"

"Not really. All things considered, the timing isn't bad. All we have to do tomorrow is put these men on planes and send them home. We don't have another group coming in until the next day."

"Yeah," Mike said. "Weyerhaeuser. I suppose it'll be okay. Everybody has worked hard. They deserve *some*thing. I just wish it could've been something else."

But the staff didn't want anything else, and by eight o'clock there were seventy happy, drunken people in the store. Even Albert came down to check things out. We turned the jukebox up as loud as it would go, and people had pushed the tables out of the way and were dancing. The thousand dollars for the biggest fish was awarded, and the lucky fisherman counted out five hundred-dollar bills and gave them to his guide, Duncan McAllister. Duncan was my other college boy from Kenora, and his inamorata for the summer was none other than Collette, one of my hitchhikers.

Louie, who was hardly gregarious, showed up after the party was well underway but didn't stay long. Ten minutes after he got there, he walked over to the counter, which had been converted to a bar for the evening, grabbed a bottle of Scotch and slipped out the door. He and Pop played cards together almost every night, and I was sure he'd retreated to his quiet cabin and his own small society.

For most of the night, Mike and I worked the room, visiting with everyone we could. Mike was uneasy about the heroic quantities of liquor being consumed, but he was a good sport about it, nursing a beer as he kept a watchful eye on everything. But there wasn't a hint of trouble. The party was just a harmless, drunken gala, due in part to the storm, which rolled in shortly after Louie left and kept everyone confined to the store. It was the worst storm we'd seen at Kettle Falls, and the rain slashed down in torrents, driven by high winds that could be heard even above the jukebox.

By one o'clock, things were winding down, and people had begun making their unsteady way through the rain to their beds. At that point I felt comfortable leaving, so I told Mike I'd wait up for him and went back to our cabin to write Paula and my mother, who'd both sent letters recently. When I left the store, Molly was sitting outside the door, cold, bedraggled and very upset by the storm. I hadn't known she was there.

"Poor Molly," I said, talking baby talk to her. "Wouldn't anyone let that poor little puppy inside? Let's go back to the cabin so I can dry you off." Molly wiggled excitedly and ran with me all the way.

When I got there, I dried Molly and took a shower, but I didn't feel like writing letters anymore. I sat at the table, toweling my wet hair, and watched the lightning rip the night to tatters. All the while, Molly huddled beneath the table, making sure that some part of her body was in continual contact with my foot. There were many lightning strikes close by, several just across the river, and the close ones rattled the windows.

It wasn't long before Mike walked in, soaking wet, and announced that the party was over.

"So," I asked, "any shootings, stabbings or other unpleasantness?"

Mike hung his jacket behind the door. "No, everything was fine, except for right at the end. One of the cabin girls got up on a table and did a striptease."

"Who was it?"

"Uh … Tina, I think. It was one of those sisters you hired in Kenora—Tanya and Tina. I can't keep their names straight. Hell, I can't even tell 'em apart."

"Was she any good?"

"She seemed to grasp the fundamentals. Naturally, I put a stop to it before she—"

"Oh, but of course," I said, laughing. "I'm sure you were conflicted, but it was very gallant of you."

"Stupid is more like it." Mike sat down on the bed and pulled off his shoes. "I just stopped a girl from taking off her clothes in front of a bunch of drunks with knives—not something I recommend."

There was a flash of lightning and an explosion of thunder, one right on top of the other.

Mike went to the window and looked out. "That was close. How long is this storm supposed to last?"

"Most of the night, according to the radio."

"Let's call it a day," he said. "I'm beat."

Mike got undressed, climbed into bed and was sound asleep in less than five minutes. I opened the window on my side of the bed, and when I was sure the rain wouldn't blow in, I turned off the lights and climbed into bed, too, followed by Molly. We lay there listening to the thunder and wind, both of which were unrelenting.

I think I'd just fallen asleep when I was awakened by something. I didn't know what it was at first, but it was Molly, growling in a strange, frightened way that sounded like ripping canvas. I couldn't see her, but I reached down and felt the hair bristling along her back. In the next flash of lightning, I could see that her ears were up and that her eyes were riveted on the open window, beyond which, I supposed, lurked one of her many demons.

"Molly, be quiet. You'll wake up Mike."

But Mike was sleeping peacefully through the thunder and lightning, and short of a tree falling on the cabin, I doubted that anything could have awakened him. Molly stopped growling for half a minute, then started in again—even louder than before—and the bed, which had become an extension of her fear, was trembling as though it were alive. At that point I turned on the light and woke Mike up myself. I shook him gently, but for a few moments he remained inside his dreams, mumbling something about a propane tank.

"Mike, wake up."

"Put it on a plane and *fly* it out here," he said.

I shook him harder. "You'd better wake up. There's somebody outside."

He woke with a start and sat up, opening and closing his eyes. "I'm awake, I'm awake … what's wrong?"

"It's Molly—look at her."

Molly was still growling, still staring at the window.

"It's probably a bear," Mike said. "They walk right past the cabin on their way to Albert's garbage cans."

"Are you going to check it out?"

"Yeah ... I'll take a look."

"I'll go with you," I said. "Who's watching the camp tonight?"

"Nobody. It was Duncan and Neil's turn, but they were too drunk to do it. So was everybody else. I thought we could get by tonight because of the storm, but ..."

"We'll do it ourselves," I said. "What about Molly?"

"Bring her. Bears are afraid of dogs."

"Hear that, Molly? Good news for you." But Molly was too busy growling to pay any attention.

We pulled on our clothes, and Mike grabbed the rifle and flashlight. When we opened the door, Molly squeezed through it, growled all the way down the stairs and disappeared. It was raining hard, and the entire camp was dark, except for the confused flashing of the marina's mercury-vapor light, which was turning itself off and on with the lightning. When we made our way around to the back of the cabin, we found Molly staring down the path that led to the substation, unwilling to go farther.

"I don't like it," Mike said.

"Is it a bear?"

"I want you to take Molly and go back to the cabin."

"Not a chance," I said.

"Then take the flashlight. But don't turn it on unless I tell you."

"Okay."

We walked past Molly, who was frozen in place, and headed toward the substation with Mike in the lead. When we were halfway there, we could see the light from the floodlights filtering through the trees, and we made our way carefully toward it. Once, I nearly screamed when lightning struck so close I could feel its concussive breath on my face.

When we reached the edge of the clearing, it was very bright, and at first I couldn't see anything because of the rain and the flood-lights in my eyes. Then Mike pointed to the open gate, and when I saw it, I knew something was terribly wrong. A moment later I saw a man kneeling inside the fence.

He was down on one knee in front of the substation, looking at it, apparently deciding what to do. His left profile was toward us, but even so—and even through the fence—I could see that he was holding a rifle in his right hand.

Mike gestured that I should stay put. Then he moved three or four steps to my right, where he could see the man through the open gate. Mike raised the rifle to his shoulder, and when he did, the man saw him.

"Put the gun down!" Mike shouted. "Put the gun down and come out of there!"

The man stood up slowly but hung onto the rifle.

I heard Mike click the safety off. "Drop it!"

But he just looked at Mike, as though he didn't understand. Then he brought the rifle around in front of him and started to raise it, and when he did, Mike shot him. The man lurched backward, dropped the rifle and tried to take a step, but his legs wouldn't work and he fell heavily to the ground.

Part of me realized what had just happened, but there was an-other part of me that said it couldn't be true, that it was all a terrible dream and at any moment I would wake up back at the cabin. I closed my eyes and willed myself to wake up, but it didn't work. When I opened my eyes again, the man inside the fence was still there, and Mike was approaching him cautiously. I followed Mike through the open gate but hung back a few feet, afraid to look.

Mike stood over the man and prodded him with his foot. "He's dead."

I looked, then looked away. The man was lying on his back with one leg bent beneath him. I could tell he was an Indian, but I didn't recognize him. One of his eyes was open, and there was a bloody spot the size of a fist in the middle of his chest. On the ground next to him was a large bolt cutter, and when I saw it, I began to shake.

There was no rifle. There had never been a rifle.

"He didn't have a gun," I said, my voice quavering. "He was trying to show you the bolt cutter."

"He should've dropped it," Mike said. "It's a good thing he isn't one of our own staff." He took the flashlight and shined it on the substation, moving the beam around very slowly. "I hope to hell the bullet didn't go through him and hit something. *Hello* ... this ought to make you happy."

I looked where Mike was pointing the flashlight and saw a rifle leaning against one of the green metal boxes.

"Mike, what have we done?"

"We've kept this guy from putting us out of business—or shooting one of us." He looked down at the man again. "Whoever he is, he reeks of whiskey. You ever seen him before?"

"No, never."

"Where the hell did he come from?" Mike knelt beside the body, looking for answers. I was horrified at how casually he rolled the man over and inventoried the contents of his pockets. "We've got a wallet."

I didn't look, but I could tell Mike was going through it. After a few moments he said, "His name is Leon Thin Bird, but I can't tell where he's from. Some of the stuff in here is from Hollow Water, which isn't that far away. But he's also got a social insurance card and tribal ID from the God's Lake Reservation, which is way up north. He must be Cree. Look at this." Mike waved something in the air. "Leon's got himself a brand new hundred-dollar bill. I'll bet that was a down payment for services to be rendered here tonight."

"We have to call the police."

Mike stood up and walked over to me, shaking his head. "No

way. If we do that, a lot of things will happen, and they're all bad. You'll get deported, the camp will close, and I'll be put on trial in a Canadian court. I shot this guy in self-defense—or so I thought— but I can't prove it. And the fact that I'm an illegal alien wouldn't exactly work in my favor."

"So what do we do?"

"Unless you have a better idea, I'm going to bury him."

"Mike, we're not talking about a dead hamster."

"Goddammit, I know that. I don't like it any more than you do, but it's better than he deserves. What choice do we have?"

All at once I was unable to breathe. I tried to make it to the base of the substation to sit down, but my legs gave out before I got there. I felt myself falling, but it was like falling through some trap door in my mind. I was aware, in a disinterested way, that I'd struck my head on something, but I didn't feel any pain. Just before I passed out, I heard a sound like the angry buzzing of bees.

When I came to—even before I'd opened my eyes—I felt the rain and heard the bees again, all mixed up with Mike's voice, and I realized I was propped up against one of the transformers, listening to its beatific hum. Mike's hands were on my shoulders, and he was looking into my eyes, talking to me. I put my hand to the side of my face, and it came away sticky.

"Allie, you're bleeding—you hit your head. Can you walk?"

"I don't know." I was very cold.

"You're shivering—I'll get you out of here."

Mike scooped me up and carried me all the way back to the cabin. When we got there, he helped me out of my wet clothes and put me in the shower. Then he got in the shower with me, clothes and all, and sort of held me up while he cleaned the cut above my ear. A short time later, I was in bed with two blankets over me, and Mike was beside me, smoothing my hair. He was talking, but his voice sounded as though it were coming from someplace very far away.

"What did you say?"

Mike's face came closer. "I said the bleeding stopped. It's just a cut."

"Where's Molly?"

"Right here on the floor. Listen, I have to go. I have to bury that guy before it gets light."

"Mike, you can't."

Mike pulled the blankets up to my chin. "What's the alternative? Everyone in camp is drunk and asleep—they wouldn't have heard a bomb go off over this storm. And the only people who could ever ask questions about this guy are the ones who sent him here, so that's not gonna happen." Mike kissed me, then stood up and headed for the door. "I'll bury him, but like I said, I don't think he deserves a hole in the ground."

"Did he deserve to be killed? It doesn't feel like it."

"Deserving has nothing to do with it. If he'd dropped the bolt cutter, I wouldn't have shot him. Things took a bad bounce."

"A bad bounce?"

Mike was halfway out the door, but he closed it and turned around. "Allie, I know how you are when it comes to ... certain things. I know you think this is terrible and wrong—and it is. But there's nothing we can do about it now that wouldn't make it worse."

"But you can't just—"

"Sure I can." Mike came over to the bed. "We're not going to fall on our sword for Leon Thin Bird. He isn't worth it, Allie. I'm sorry—I have to go."

Not long before the sun came up, Mike returned, carrying Dutch's rifle. Molly was on the bed with me, and it was still raining, but there was no more lightning or thunder. Mike said that he'd buried the man, along with his rifle and bolt cutter, where he'd never be found, and when he had finished the job, there was no indication that a hole had ever been dug there, let alone a grave. The rain had helped with that, he said.

"It's all over. The last thing I did was rechain the gate."

Mike took a shower, and by the time he was finished, it was light enough that I could see the soft silhouettes of trees through the window and smell the faintly fishy smell of the river—its morning smell. When he came out of the bathroom, Mike was frowning.

"I never thought of it until I was in the shower, but how the hell did he get here? He couldn't have come by boat in that storm, and he didn't have any car keys." Mike brooded on the possibilities. "But he might have left the keys in his car. I need to know if there's a car around here someplace."

"Please don't leave me alone again," I said. "*Please* don't."

"Allie, if he left a car parked on the road, I need to get rid of it."

I don't know how long Mike was gone the second time, but when he came through the door, it was still gray outside, and I could tell he was relieved the instant I saw him.

"No car," he said. "I went all the way to the main road."

"What would you have done if you found one?"

"I would've driven it into the feldspar quarry. There's a hundred and fifty feet of water in that pit."

"A plan for every contingency."

Mike looked at me suspiciously. "That's right."

Mike didn't get into bed right away. He sat shirtless at the table and cleaned Dutch's rifle before returning it to its place in the corner. I watched from bed, and there was nothing about him that suggested this night might have been different from any other. Before he turned off the lights, he tried again to reassure me.

"Allie, I know you're upset, but I'm telling you it's finished." Then he came over to the bed and kissed my forehead. "Please don't make more of this than it is. Nothing will ever come of it."

But Mike was only partly right.

Chapter 19

The next day I couldn't make myself get out of bed, let alone leave the cabin.

Mike looked in on me every hour or so. He said no one suspected anything, and everyone had slept through our ordeal of the night before. The entire staff was badly hungover yet had somehow managed to put our equally hungover guests on planes that would fly them to Kenora, where they would get on bigger planes that would eventually deliver them to their wives, their children and their unassailable suburban lives.

Mike was very solicitous and said everyone assumed I was ill— a conclusion he must have encouraged, because when I didn't show up for dinner that night, Albert came to the cabin door with a tray full of covered dishes that included things like chicken soup and green tea. I vowed to put a stop to that, so the following morning, I made sure I was in the lodge for breakfast promptly at six. The cut above my ear was hidden by my hair, and there was a bruise on my face that I said was the result of a fall I'd taken while running back to the cabin with Molly. What Mike had said was true—no one suspected anything. Not even when the police showed up.

Our next group of thirty fisherman wasn't due until one o'clock that afternoon, so the entire crew was in the staff dining room eating lunch when two vehicles arrived in camp. One was a squad car bearing the familiar black and yellow insignia of the Ontario Provincial Police. The other was an old blue pickup truck with a headdress painted on the side. They pulled up to the dining room door, and we all went outside to see what they wanted, even Albert and his girls. I tried to make eye contact with Mike, but he wouldn't look at me, even though I was standing right next to him.

The OPP officer looked like a recruiting poster, smiling and ruddy-faced, in a navy blue uniform with a Sam Browne belt and trooper's hat. "Good afternoon, everyone. I'm Leftenant Sinclair, and this is Officer Stone Bear from the tribal police in Hollow Water."

Stone Bear made a curt little nod but did not smile. He was a barrel-chested man who might have been thirty-five or fifty. His hair was plaited in heavy braids, and he didn't wear a uniform, just an insignia sewn on the sleeve of his jacket like the one on his truck.

Sinclair surveyed the group. "Officer Stone Bear and I are looking for an individual who may have passed this way recently, eh. Is Mr. Zimmerman around?"

Mike stepped forward. "Dutch, he isn't here, eh."

"When do you expect him back?"

"Hard to say," Mike said. "He took a little vacation, eh."

Stone Bear turned and fixed his small dark eyes on Mike. His mouth opened a little, as though he were about to say something, but he let Sinclair continue.

"Well, then, who's the straw boss of this outfit?"

"I am," Mike said.

"And you are?"

"Mike Bowman."

"Mr. Bowman, we're here to inquire about a man named Leon

Thin Bird who's been living on the Hollow Water Reservation. We need to know if you or anyone in this camp has seen him, eh."

When I heard the name, I felt light-headed and sick.

Sinclair pulled a piece of paper from his breast pocket, unfolded it and handed it to Mike. "This is an old mug shot. It's all we have. You recognize him?"

Mike looked at the picture. "I've never seen him before. He's done time, eh?"

"Yes, sir," Sinclair said. "Thin Bird has arrests for arson, forgery, car theft, burglary—he's a jack of all trades."

Mike was still reading. "It says here he got drunk and tried to steal a plane up in Thompson ... but he can't *fly*. This guy, he's not too bright, eh."

For a moment I thought Stone Bear, who'd never taken his eyes off Mike, was going to smile. His face lost its saturnine expression, and the corners of his mouth turned upward slightly. But only for an instant.

"That's old news," Stone Bear said. "Thin Bird, he kills people now, eh. Two weeks ago he robbed a liquor store in Broken Head. Shot the owner."

"You don't say."

Stone Bear was like a dog on point, staring at Mike as though nothing else existed for him. I didn't know what was going on, but there was something scary about it.

Sinclair didn't seem to notice. "Mr. Thin Bird has also been linked to a couple acts of felony vandalism, eh."

"Camp sabotage?" Mike asked.

"Yes, sir, two camps west of Dryden."

Stone Bear walked over to Mike and stood directly in front of him. "You sure you never saw him before?"

"Yeah. I already told you that. What makes you think he's around here, eh?" Mike handed me the piece of paper.

The thought of seeing Thin Bird's face again was too much, so

I gave it to Louie, who looked at it and passed it on.

"We got a tip," Stone Bear said brusquely.

"Thin Bird was seen in Minaki three days ago," Sinclair said. "He was trying to get a ride to the Twin Rivers Reservation, but we haven't determined if he did. No one we spoke to at Twin Rivers remembers seeing him. What about the rest of you, eh? Any of you people seen this man?"

The staff looked at each other blankly, shook their heads and murmured a thin chorus of no's.

"Then I suppose we're done here," Sinclair said. "This man may still be in the area. If any of you should see him, please contact the OPP right away. Thanks for your time, folks."

Mike and Sinclair shook hands, and Sinclair headed for his car, casting a backward glance at Stone Bear.

"You go ahead, eh," Stone Bear said.

Sinclair hesitated. "Yes, but if I'm not here ..." Then he shrugged. "Oh, I suppose it's all right. Have a good day, everyone."

After Sinclair left, most of the shore crew went back inside to finish eating, and the guides headed to the marina to clean and gas their boats. Mike and I, along with Pop and Louie, remained outside with Stone Bear, who said nothing. He lit a cigarette and leaned against his truck, smoking and looking around with eyes that moved slowly, focusing on one thing, then another, as though each image were a part he was trying to relate to some indefinable whole.

Finally, Louie said, "If you got somethin' to say, have at it, eh. We got work to do."

Stone Bear pointed to Mike. "I wanna talk to him, not you."

"This ain't the rez, eh," Louie said. "You got no authority to talk to *anybody*."

"Which is why the OPP came along, isn't it?" Pop said.

Stone Bear looked at Pop and Louie in the same deliberate way he'd looked at everything else. "Who are you two geezers?"

Louie thrust out his chin. "We're the geezers who are gonna

kick you the hell outta here, chief—"

"It's okay, Louie." Mike put his hand on Louie's arm. "Why don't you and Pop go on down to the store. We'll be along in a minute."

"You sure, kid?"

"Yeah, go ahead."

Pop and Louie glowered at Stone Bear, then headed for the marina, turning around every few paces to make sure they weren't needed.

"Friends of yours?" Stone Bear asked.

Mike nodded.

Stone Bear watched Pop and Louie until they disappeared below the crest of the little hill leading down to the water. Then he spoke to me for the first time.

"Who are you, eh?"

"I'm Mike's wife." My throat was so tight I had to force each word out. "I'm Allison Bowman."

"You ever seen Leon Thin Bird before?"

"No."

"How would you know, eh? You didn't look at the poster."

"Yes, I did. I've never—"

"How'd you get that bruise on your face?"

I touched my cheek. "I was running and I fell."

"Who were you running from?"

"No one. I was just … running."

Stone Bear nodded. "Uh-huh. You an American, too?"

I looked helplessly at Mike and saw that he was also caught off guard.

"Look here, Stone Bear," he said. "We don't have to answer any—"

"Take it easy, Yank. I don't care if you're illegals, and Sinclair— Mr. Spit 'n' Polish—was in too big a hurry to notice, eh. But lemme tell you something. Canadians don't go on 'vacation.' They go on holiday, eh. And only Americans get 'drunk.' Canadians, they get ginned-up or pissed-up, eh." Stone Bear laughed to himself, a low, rumbling laugh that seemed to get stuck somewhere in his huge chest. "They go on holiday and get pissed-up."

"I'll remember that, Stone Bear. Is that what you wanted to talk about?"

"You had any sabotage?"

I wasn't sure what dots Stone Bear was trying to connect, but my heart began to race.

"Somebody blew up our avgas tank last month," Mike said. "We never saw who did it."

"Did Zimmerman report it?"

"What good would it have done?"

Stone Bear mulled things over for a while and nodded to himself.

"What about the fact that we're Americans?" I said.

"Not much I can do about that, eh—no jurisdiction." He spat the word out as though it were distasteful. "Somebody should have a little talk with Zimmerman, though—he's just as guilty as you two, eh." Stone Bear turned and headed for his truck but wheeled around before he got there. "I could report you to Immigration, but I don't wanna do that."

"No?" Mike said. "And why not?"

Stone Bear smiled for the first time. "Because they'd throw you out of the country. I kinda like knowin' where you are, eh." Then he got in his truck without another word and drove off.

Mike and I stood there, watching his truck disappear into the trees.

"*Shit*," Mike said. "Even when I was talking to Sinclair, I could tell Stone Bear had a weed up his ass, but I couldn't figure out why. It never occurred to me I was mangling the idiom."

"He doesn't believe us," I said. "He'll be back."

"It doesn't matter. What matters is that he won't tell

Immigration."

"But he knows we lied. If we lied about one thing, he'll think—"

"He won't think anything. All he knows is that we aren't Canadian, and we never said we were. We'd better get down to the store. We've got fishermen coming any time now."

When we got there, Louie and Pop were waiting in our office.

"So what did Chief Pain-in-the-Arse want?" Louie said.

"He knew we were Americans," Mike said.

Louie bristled. "Who told him?"

"I did. I blew it."

We could hear people in the store, and Pop swung the door closed with his foot. "Was it that business about Dutch being on vacation?"

"Yeah ... and what I said about the guy they're after getting drunk."

"I missed that one," Pop said.

Louie laughed. "Hell, I missed 'em both—been around too many Yanks, I guess. Sergeant Preston, he must've missed 'em, too, eh?"

"Sinclair? Yeah, I guess so," Mike said. "I think he just wanted to catch a murderer and make it back in time for dinner."

"The important thing," I said, "is that Officer Stone Bear isn't going to turn us in. At least, that's what he told us."

Louie waved his hand. "I wouldn't worry 'bout no ragtag tribal cop, eh. He can't even give a speeding ticket off the rez."

But I did worry, although I wasn't nearly as concerned about being deported as I was about Mike's having killed a man and disposed of the body without so much as a shiver. And I was no better—I'd let him do it. The guilt I felt surprised me, and the fact that Leon Thin Bird was a murderer did nothing to diminish it. Mike thought once I knew that, everything would be fine. And in a way, it should have. It would've been more than enough for my mother—

probably for Hedley, too—but it was no longer enough for me, and I couldn't understand why.

It wasn't that Thin Bird's death had suddenly put my values to rout. The problem was the values themselves. I didn't know what Thin Bird deserved, and I wasn't sure it mattered. Nor did I know what choices he might have made that led him to the substation that night. It would've been easier if I cared about those things, but I didn't.

Mike didn't care about them, either, but only because he didn't require additional justification for what he'd done—Thin Bird's intentions and his refusal to drop the imagined rifle were enough for him. But that didn't stop Mike from using Thin Bird's past to backfill his own actions, and the way that he did it for my benefit angered me. Mike didn't understand that Thin Bird was only part of the problem. Some of it had to do with the way he'd behaved afterward—as though it were nothing. The rest of it had to do with me. I tried again and again to explain this to Mike, but I never got anywhere.

"Allie, I couldn't take any chances, not with you standing right there. I thought he had a gun."

"So did I. I'm not talking about that. I'm wondering how we could do something so horrible. And your reaction to it is—"

"Listen, I wish it hadn't happened, but it did."

"But you can't *do* things like that. We don't get a free murder, Mike. It isn't—"

"Thin Bird's the murderer, not me."

It was as though Mike and I were speaking different languages, and after a while our lives were like Kabuki theatre—everything was significant except for what we said. The world may have been a better place without Thin Bird, as Mike insisted it was, but it was hardly a utilitarian impulse that had caused Mike to shoot him, let alone to bury him behind the substation. And the real issue had more to do with my past than Thin Bird's.

The cut above my ear healed quickly, and soon all that remained of it was a welt in the shape of a check mark that I traced continuously with my fingers. I wouldn't even know I was doing it until Mike would say something like, "Is that still bothering you? Let me take a look." And I would pull my hand away quickly, saying it was fine.

That part was true. It was the inside of my head that was the problem. Nights were the worst, when I would dream about the shooting, living it over again just as it had happened. I would see the figure kneeling inside the fence, and I would see Mike raise the rifle to his shoulder. Then I would hear the shot and see Thin Bird take that little half-step and collapse.

Each time he fell, I was relieved, because at that point in the dream, it was almost morning, and even though I was dreaming, I could smell the river. And I knew—without knowing—that if I opened my eyes, I would see the soft gray dawn through the window, and the dream would be over.

After that I would follow the well-worn grooves of my routine, clinging to it as though it were a rite that would protect me from my own nagging doubts. Mike and I would eat breakfast with the staff and have our guests on the water by eight, after which Molly and I would go down to the empty store and do bookwork.

When I'd finished paying the bills or doing the payroll or balancing the books, I would help Albert in the kitchen or lend a hand in the laundry. Generally, when I'd finished doing that, it was time to get cleaned up for dinner and go over to the lodge, where Mike and I would mingle with the guests. My evenings usually concluded in the store, where I'd help Marcy and Collette until eleven o'clock, when Mike and I would head for our cabin.

As the weather warmed up and the days grew longer, the crew spent less time in the store and more time at the old feldspar quarry, which added a new dimension to the camp's social life. Thirty years ago the quarry had been an active mine, but now it was our personal swimming hole. Our stretch of the river was too cold and dangerous for swimming, and because the quarry was only a couple miles away, many of the crew went there in the evenings to party or dive into the gin-clear water from rocks that towered above it on two sides. On those evenings when it was quiet in the store, I would tell Marcy and Collette to take the night off, and they would thank me effusively and race out the door and up the hill in search of Louie, who always had the keys to the Jeep.

We were very busy during the first two weeks of July. We had only two cancellations due to the mercury scare, and both were small groups. Staying busy helped to keep my mind off things, and I eventually reached a point where I even forgot about the shooting for brief periods, the way someone with a terminal illness might forget about it for an instant now and then. I don't think anyone noticed anything peculiar about my behavior, except for Pop. And Mike, of course.

After a while, I quit trying to talk to Mike about what had happened. It wasn't just that he couldn't understand. It was because I couldn't understand, and that made me afraid. I was afraid because nothing I believed in could explain Thin Bird's death. There was no moral in it, no meaning, no causality that I could snuggle up to for comfort. There was only guilt. And the weight of it was crushing. I wanted desperately to make it right, to atone for it in some way, but I didn't know where to begin—or how.

I sensed nothing of this in Mike. The workman he'd throttled in the library parking lot should have been a warning, and I wondered if this was what happened to men who went to war. Maybe for them violence became an acceptable response—a sort of psychic default unattended by remorse. That *really* scared me, and it wasn't long before I was afraid for our marriage, which scared me even more.

And every day, I felt as though something was creeping up on me from behind—something like the Wisconsin Glacier, waiting to seal me forever beneath a million lightless years of ice.

Chapter 20

One hot, sticky night toward the end of July, things sort of boiled over. I'd become quite forgetful, and Mike, for the most part, tried to overlook it. But that morning we'd run out of gas in the marina because I hadn't paid the bill. That meant we had to measure oil into thirty-two gas tanks, load the tanks into a pickup, fill them at the pump by the garage, then haul them back down to the marina. Mike hadn't said anything at the time, but he was angry all day, and I knew it. That night when we were alone in the cabin, I wanted to talk about it.

"Look," I said. "I'm sorry about the gas. I didn't pay the last bill because I wanted to ask them about it—I'm still confused about the stupid Canadian gallon. But I never called them, and the bill never got paid."

Mike was going from window to window, opening each one as far as it would go. "It's hotter than hell in here."

"Did you hear what I said?"

"Yeah. Forget about it."

"That's your solution to everything, isn't it?"

"What's that supposed to mean?"

"Nothing," I said. "I'm just not sure that forgetting about things is always the answer."

"Why do I get the feeling you're not talking about the gas bill?"

"I can't imagine. What other issue could we possibly need to discuss?"

Mike quit on the windows and wheeled around. "Goddammit, I've run out of ways to tell you that I'm done talking about Thin Bird. It's *over*."

"Not for me," I said. "And what about regret? What about guilt? I thought I knew you, but I'm not sure anymore. Whatever this thing is that you do—this compartmentalizing thing—I can't do it. Maybe you can kill a man and forget about it, but I can't."

"So what's the alternative? Do you plan to carry on like this forever?"

"I am not carrying on. I'm trying to cope."

Mike mumbled something, peeled off his T-shirt and threw it into the laundry basket.

"What did you say?"

"I said if you're trying to cope, you're doing a lousy job of it. You can't remember anything. You're constantly making caustic little remarks—just like you're doing now—and you mope around camp like you're in the third hell of depression. Not only that, you cry over every little thing."

"That's not true."

"Isn't it? What did you do when you were writing a letter to Jimmy the other night? Or a couple nights before that when Molly didn't show up for dinner? And what about right now?"

I put my hand to my face and felt disobedient tears coursing down my cheeks. "I can't help it. What we did was—"

"I did it, not you."

"We *both* did it. And the worst part is how much I hope we get away with it. My God, I'd give anything if I could press a button and make it right somehow."

Mike shook his head. "You can't."

"But I feel so … *awful*. I've never felt like this before."

"Then you've been lucky. Sooner or later, everybody gets tagged."

"Would you care to explain that pithy bit of wisdom?"

Mike sighed in frustration. "You want to be the guy in the tuxedo who walks through the pie fight and never gets hit. It doesn't work that way."

"It does for some people," I said, still crying. "Are you saying that you've done things you actually regret? I find that hard to believe. Where could you possibly find room for regret in your situational scheme of things?"

"I've got plenty of regrets." Mike flung the little pillows from one end of the sofa and sat down. "But what I regret most is that Thin Bird was holding bolt cutters instead of his rifle—that really matters to you. But you never stop to think that if he'd been holding the rifle, he probably would've used it, like he did at Broken Head."

"What happened to Thin Bird was terrible, but I think I could handle it if you thought it was terrible, too. But you don't." Then I said something I'd often wondered about. "You've killed people before, haven't you? Do you ever feel guilty about them?"

Mike glared. "I was in a war, for chrissake. I've got ghosts like everybody else, but I do what I have to do, then I move on. I don't wallow in it."

As angry as we both were, I think we realized that a line had been crossed, that we were now trespassing in explicitly forbidden territory.

"Sit down," Mike said, his voice suddenly softer. "I want to tell you something that happened to me over there."

"I don't want to hear any stories."

"You'll like this one," he said. "I'll skip the story about the farmer I shot because I thought he was spotting mortar fire. And I'll save the one about the old papa-san who surprised me on the trail for another time. This story is special, and you'll like it because I regret the way it turned out—in fact, I regret the hell out of it."

I sat down at the opposite end of the sofa but refused to look at him.

"When I'd been in-country about five months, we were on patrol, and we came to this little village. We'd been there before, and it was always friendly, but there were VC in the village that day, and they ambushed us. I got caught in the open and hid behind a well that was in sort of a courtyard. There was a little mud wall on one side of it, and that's all the cover I had. Dale got the—"

"Dale Olsen?"

"Yeah. He got the rest of the squad to a row of hootches about seventy-five meters from me, and they traded fire with the VC for a while, but eventually they tried to flank us. I don't think the gooks knew I was there, or maybe they thought I was dead, because they sent two men across the courtyard behind my position, and I dropped one of them. He was carrying an RPG, and he would've had a perfect shot from the other side."

Mike stopped talking. He seemed to be looking at something that wasn't there.

"What is it?"

"Nothing. I was just thinking that you're the only person I've ever told this to."

"If you don't want to tell me, then don't. I'm not sure I want to hear it anyway."

"Well, you're going to. I don't like talking about it, but it's *was*, just like all the other shit that happened over there."

"Then go on. Get it over with."

Mike looked at me coolly. "Like I said … I killed the guy carrying the RPG, but his buddy made it across. I was trying to keep an eye on him when I saw a little kid walk right into the open from the same place that VC had gone. This kid couldn't have been more than eight or nine. At first I couldn't figure out what the hell he was doing. Then I realized he was heading for the dead gook, the one I'd just shot. I hollered at him and tried to wave him away, but he just kept coming. When he got to the guy, I knew what had happened. The bastard who'd made it across had told this kid to walk out there, get the RPG and bring it to him. He probably told the kid no one would shoot him."

"I've heard enough."

"You haven't heard anything. I was screaming at the kid not to do it, but he didn't pay any attention. He tried to pick up the RPG and carry it, but it was too heavy, so he started dragging it across the courtyard. I fired a burst over his head, but he just kept walking. I knew I couldn't let that RPG—"

"Please stop. I know what you did. I don't need to hear it."

Mike looked surprised. "You think I killed him?"

"Didn't you?"

"I wanted to, I tried to, but I couldn't pull the trigger. He looked so little and weak … I let him go."

I'd been holding my breath and exhaled all at once. "Thank God. I was sure you—"

"Half a minute later, the VC who sent him out there fired an RPG that killed Bill Falsky—a good friend of mine—and put Dale Olsen in the hospital. If you want to talk about regrets, that's mine— I should've shot that kid dead-bang, no hesitation, no thinking about it. I learned something that day, and I never want to forget it." Mike looked over and shrugged. "Allie, when it comes to regrets, Thin Bird doesn't even make my top ten."

I was crying again. "You're wrong—I don't like *any*thing about that story."

"Either do I. But I don't have to like it. I just have to live with it. I wrote to Falsky's parents. It was one of the hardest—"

"What about Dale Olsen?"

"He was okay, no thanks to me. His left arm and the side of his face were burned. Falsky was standing right next to him—he was Dale's RTO—and little pieces of the radio got blown into Dale's arm and leg. But he was lucky. Or maybe he wasn't—he was back in three weeks." Mike put his hands to his head. "A couple hours after the ambush, I was helping load Dale and what was left of Falsky into the chopper that took them to Pleiku. I kept telling Dale how sorry I was, and just before they lifted off, he grabbed my hand and said, 'Let it go. I wouldn't have shot that kid, either.' But I've never believed that. Then he sort of smiled and thanked me for the Purple Heart. That was it."

A sort of numbness had spread through my body. I could hardly speak. "He meant a lot to you. We should have stopped to see him on the way up here."

"Maybe. But I couldn't have done that. Things were different after the ambush. I don't know how to explain it, but that part of my life is *was*. It's better that way."

"I'm sorry for everything you went through. I can't even imagine it. But killing Thin Bird doesn't change anything that happened in Vietnam."

Mike jumped up from the sofa. "You think I don't know that? I killed him to keep it from happening again. Maybe if you hadn't been standing there, I wouldn't have shot him, but ... I don't take chances anymore. And I don't think about what I ought to do. Thinking will fuck you up every time."

"And I'm living proof, right?"

Mike didn't say anything.

"I can't help it," I said. "I'm trying to deal with everything, and I'm really struggling. You don't seem to care about any of it."

Mike shook his head. "It isn't that I don't care. It's over. Thin Bird is *was*."

"What about me? Am I *was*?"

"Allie, what the hell do you want from me?"

And that's where the fight ended. I felt bad for Mike and for what he'd been through in Vietnam. I tried to put it into some kind of context, but of course I couldn't. The only context for Vietnam was Vietnam—it was the ultimate you-really-had-to-be-there ex-perience. I knew Vietnam explained a lot of things about Mike, but when you love someone, you worry more about effects than causes.

We had other fights, always at night, when we were alone in the cabin. After each one, I'd lie in bed and listen to the terrible dark-ness, afraid to fall asleep, afraid of being overtaken by my dreams. It wasn't as though Mike and I didn't get along. During the day we still worked well together, but there was an ignored tension that nev-er went away. Despite everything, I tried to go on as though nothing had happened, muddling along as best I could. But it was hard to maintain the shell of my life when the core of it was dissolving.

Pop was the only one I could really talk to, and even so, I could never tell him what happened. He knew something was wrong, but he never asked me about it directly—he was too much of a gentle-man for that. Pop's outboard shop was only a few steps from the store, so I got in the habit of walking over there with Molly when the credits and debits would begin swimming before my eyes.

Whenever I came through the door, Pop would stop whatever he was doing, as though nothing were as important as the fact that I was there. He would get us each a soda from his little refrigera-tor, then say to Molly, "I wonder what I've got for a good dog like you." Molly would wag her tail, and Pop would take a box of dog biscuits from the shelf and give her one. Then Pop and I would sit at the table by his workbench and talk amidst eviscerated outboards. On one of my visits, he asked if I was unhappy about something.

"Do I seem unhappy?"

"A little," he said.

"Things are just hard right now, Pop. I feel like one of these motors—I want somebody to put me back together again."

Pop removed some tools from the table and sat down. "I'm just an old wrench-bender, Allie, but I think we all feel like that sometimes."

"But it's scary, Pop. I don't like what's happening to me. I don't even know what's right and wrong anymore—everything is so confusing here."

"Right and wrong are pretty confusing everywhere," Pop said. "Sometimes, I think they're the same thing, Allie. Or maybe they don't exist at all—not in the way you think."

"That's too easy, Pop."

"To the contrary, that's when it's really hard."

I was listening, but at the same time I was watching a moth pattering out its life against the grimy window. "I'm like her," I said. "I know my world is still out there. I'm just not part of it anymore."

Pop went over to the window, cupped the moth gently in his hands and released it out the open door.

"I wish it were that simple," I said.

"Maybe it is."

"I don't think so, Pop. Mike and I are so different. I never realized it back in Chicago, but up here ..."

"Ahh," Pop said. "*Now* I understand. You've discovered marital discord."

"It's more than discord. I feel like I'm trapped in an elevator with a perfect stranger."

Pop laughed. "I'm no expert, Allie, but I think marriage is like that at first—it's bound to be. Marriage takes two people, with all their burrs and imperfections, and grinds 'em to fit."

I shook my head. "It's not working."

"Give it time. The way I see it, married people are like pistons—they take a while to wear in, but once they do, everything works just fine."

"I hope you're right, Pop. Mike is just ..." I sighed and lowered my head.

"Well," Pop said, "I don't doubt that Michael has his faults, but he's one of the steadiest, most level-headed men I know. If I were in a jam, he's the one I'd want in my corner."

"Who wouldn't? Mike is very talented when it comes to jams and corners. With him there's never any ethical clutter—it's full speed ahead and damn the torpedoes."

"And your taste runs more to Hamlet than Fortinbras?"

I looked at Pop across the table. There were things about him that had always intrigued me, and all at once I was reminded of them. "Pop, I want to ask you something—and you don't have to answer unless you want to. There isn't another person within a hundred miles who would've said what you just did. You're a college man, aren't you?"

Pop grinned. "University of Michigan, class of 1933. You found me out, Allie. Only you and Louie know that."

"You're an American!"

"Once upon a time."

"I knew there was something different about you. Right from the start, I—"

"Allie, the only thing about me that's different is that most outboard mechanics don't have engineering degrees." Then he laughed. "Most of them don't live out in the bush, either, but I fancy camp life. I really do."

"Have you always worked in camps, fixing motors and things?"

"Lord, no," he said. "I was an automotive engineer. I had a beautiful home in Detroit, a wife and son. I had life greased on both sides."

"What happened? *Oops*—sorry."

"I don't mind, Allie. It was a long time ago, and there's a simple answer." Pop sat back, ramrod straight, and squared his shoulders. "I drank myself out of every job I ever had. My wife left me, and my son hasn't spoken to me in twenty years. I eventually drifted north of the border, and here I am."

"I'm sorry. I shouldn't have—"

"No, it's okay. Like I said, it was a long time ago."

"Does it still hurt—I mean, in the same way?"

"Of course it does. I'd give anything to go back and relive my life, but ... we don't get do-overs."

I picked up a spark plug and examined it as though I'd never seen one before. "Maybe Louie has the right idea, Pop. Maybe we should all live in cabins in the middle of nowhere—you know, far from the madding crowd."

"And you think that would keep you safe?"

"It would make life a lot simpler. It seems to work for Louie."

Pop's face was almost stern. "If you really believe that, then maybe it's time I told you something—provided it stays between you and me."

"Of course ... if that's what you want."

"It is, because not even Dutch knows this." Pop leaned forward and clasped his hands in front of him. "Have you ever noticed the picture on Louie's bedroom wall?"

"Yes, and I know the story. It's Louie's wife—her name was Angelica—and when she died of cancer, Louie buried her on this point someplace, but nobody—"

"Her name was Angelique, and Louie loved her as much as any man could ever love a woman. Those two were like ..." Pop abandoned the simile with a wave of his hand. "You're right, though. She did have cancer, and Louie did bury her on this point. But that isn't the part I wanted to tell you."

"There's more?"

"A lot more. Angelique was in the hospital dying of cancer, but she pleaded with Louie to bring her home to that cabin. He didn't want to do it because he couldn't take care of her—she was in so much pain. But he did it anyway because ... that's what she wanted."

"She shouldn't have asked."

Pop shrugged. "Maybe not. Louie said the hospital sent her home with a bottle of Demerol, and when that ran out, Angelique asked him to kill her, begged him to stop the pain. She told Louie that's why she wanted out of the hospital—she knew he wouldn't let her go on suffering. So the next morning ... he ended it." Pop shook his head slowly, then gestured toward the camp. "Everybody knows the part about how she's buried around here someplace. But only Louie and I—and now you—know the rest of it."

I could feel my eyes filling. "When did he tell you?"

"I was living in Winnipeg—it was late fall—and Louie showed up at my door that night drunker than seven hundred dollars. He could hardly talk, but it didn't take me long to figure out what had happened. From that day to this, neither of us ever mentioned it again."

"Is that what you meant when you said right and wrong are sometimes the same thing?"

Pop chuckled. "Maybe. Or maybe I'm just too old to know the difference anymore. These days I try to concentrate on the important things."

"Like what?"

"Like sitting here right now, talking to you."

Chapter 21

The only comic relief for Mike and me that summer was provided by the two couples who taught school at Twin Rivers. They'd driven over to introduce themselves in early May and had stopped by a number of times after that. They knew we were Americans, and we liked them right away, but our lives were so tightly scripted that all Mike and I could do was say hello and agree that we should get together very soon, which we were far too busy to do.

They were all older than Mike and I, though not enough to matter. Nick and Jamie Ralston had joined the Peace Corps after graduating together from Brown, and since then they'd been everywhere—Africa, India, the Mideast. Most recently, they'd been in Chile, and when their hitch was up, they came back to the States to be married. They were brilliant, selfless idealists who had taken the job at Twin Rivers temporarily because no one else was willing to teach there.

Jack and Suzanne Kohl were from eastern Ontario. They'd met and fallen in love while working in a high school in Sudbury—

Jack was teaching history, and Suzanne was the school nurse. Unfortunately, they were both married to other people at the time. When their affair was discovered, Suzanne was fired, and Jack was given the choice of being headmaster at an Indian reservation or forfeiting his teaching certificate. He chose the former, they each got a divorce, and when Jack heard that Twin Rivers needed both a headmaster *and* a nurse, he took the job on the condition that the Department of Indian Affairs would also hire Suzanne.

We were between groups one Saturday in early August when the four of them rolled into camp in their decrepit van—the van I waved to at least once a week on the road to Kenora. When they slid the door open, half a dozen empty beer cans cascaded to the ground.

"We've been partying," Suzanne said, laughing. "Would you care to join us?"

"Absolutely," Mike said, "but we'll never catch up."

Jack handed Mike and me a beer. "You must think positively, neighbor. The four of us have been thinking positively all day, and it's done us a world of good. We went all the way to Minaki to get the beer, but since we can't drink it on the reservation, we thought we'd go to the quarry, where we can swim and continue to think positively." Jack was enunciating very carefully, as though he was afraid his tongue might get in the way of his words.

Mike laughed. "We're further behind than I thought."

"We were really hoping you guys might come along," Suzanne said.

Jamie rolled her eyes. "But of course you can't because—let's see—you're really busy, we caught you at a bad time and there's a plane full of American millionaires arriving in ten minutes."

"Actually, we have an empty camp today," I said. "We can leave for a little while."

Jamie turned to Suzanne. "Well, I'll be damned. And here I thought the Bowmans were just snooty."

"No," Mike said. "It's just that the Bowmans are up to their ass in alligators most of the time."

"Did I ever tell you about the time I was attacked by an alligator?" Nick said. "We were in the Congo. Actually, it was a crocodile—"

"They don't call it that anymore," Jamie said.

Nick looked confused. "A crocodile by any other name is still—"

"No, I mean the *Congo*, silly. It's called Zaire now."

"Oh, yes, of course—Zaire today and gone tomorrow. Anyway, I really was attacked—"

"*Please*—not the crocodile story again." Jack put his fingers in his ears. "The first time I heard that story, it was a baby crocodile. It gets two feet longer every time you tell it."

"But it's a good crocodile story. In fact, it's my best—"

Jamie put her arm around him. "We'll let you tell the crocodile story on the way to the quarry, Nicky. I promise."

"A promise made is a debt unpaid," her husband said. "And in return, you have my word that I won't show anyone where it bit me."

I was about to thank Nick for that when I saw Albert motioning to Mike and me from the back door of the kitchen.

"Now what?" Mike muttered.

"Oh, I'm sure it's a catastrophe of some sort," Suzanne said. "And just when I thought we might succeed in dragging you two away from this place for a couple hours."

Mike and I excused ourselves and went into the staff dining room to see what the problem was. Albert looked a little embarrassed and even more unsure of himself than usual.

"I don't mean to be presumptuous," he said, "but I was thinking—wondering, actually. I was wondering if you would care to invite your friends for dinner this evening. I could serve something very nice if you wanted to ask them."

"But Albert," I said, "you have the night off—no guests. We wouldn't ask you to do that."

"But you're not asking me at all. It's my idea, and I enjoy preparing something different once in a while—I feel like I'm in such a rut sometimes. It wouldn't be fancy—just leftovers. I don't mean to be pushy. If it's a bad idea ..."

"It's a great idea," Mike said. "But I don't expect you to do it for nothing."

"Oh, but payment isn't necessary, Mr. Bowman. Really, it isn't."

"You've just heard our terms, Albert," I said. "It was kind of you to offer."

Albert looked down, and I think he blushed a little. "It's really nothing, Mrs. Bowman. It will give me pleasure. Dinner at seven?"

"Seven is fine," Mike said. "Thanks, Albert."

We found our swimsuits and went back outside to join the others.

"Let me guess," Suzanne said. "You're out of LP, the coolers have shut down, and the United States has just declared war on the Soviet Union."

"I don't know about the last part," Mike said. "But the LP and coolers are okay. Allie and I would like you to join us for dinner tonight—if you're not busy."

The four of them looked at each other in mock disbelief. There was quite a bit of nonsense about having to check calendars and reschedule appointments, but in the end, it turned out no one was busy.

We had a good time at the quarry, and I only thought about Leon Thin Bird once, when we first got there, and I remembered how Mike had planned to drive his car into it, if he'd had one. There were a few of our crew swimming down at the far end. They waved and we waved back.

The quarry had a strange feel. I'd been there with Mike three or four times in May to seine minnows, and it seemed even stranger now. After living in the shapeless chaos of the forest, it was something of a shock to arrive at the quarry, a sunny clearing filled with the geometric perfection of blocks and cubes of stone. It was like frozen music, a chorus of still water framed by angular, hard-edged verses.

We hadn't been there five minutes when Jamie grabbed her swimsuit, walked to the water's edge and started taking off her clothes. She was down to her panties before we started clapping— all we could think of to do—and when Jamie turned around, there was a look of genuine surprise on her face.

"*Oh, God, I'm sorry.*" She tried to cover her breasts with her hands. "I didn't even think."

"No," Jack said. "Don't stop. You were doing great."

Nick, who had been lying on his back on a flat rock, raised himself up on his elbows just enough to see what was going on. When he saw Jamie, he laughed. "I'm afraid we lost our instinct for modesty somewhere along the way."

I'd never known anyone like Nick and Jamie, and it was easy to imagine them deep in the jungle, casting off the niggling trifles of civilization one by one.

"Well, I'm past the point of no return," Jamie said. And with that she finished what she'd started, put her suit on and waded into the water.

"Look at them," Mike said.

At the other end of the quarry, the half-dozen members of our crew were watching us intently.

"They're wondering if we have a second act," Jack said. "Who's next?"

"Not me," Suzanne said. "At the risk of being a prude, I think I'll change in the van."

"Me, too," I said.

The water was cold, but not too cold, and we had fun swimming and batting a beach ball around. Later, when we were tired, we sat in water up to our chins and talked. At six-thirty, we headed back to camp, where Albert was waiting for us. We had a drink at the bar while he finished feeding the crew, and after he'd shooed the last of them out the door, he led us to a beautifully set table, complete with a little centerpiece of wildflowers. Our guests were very impressed.

"I should have worn a tie," Jack said.

"No kidding," his wife said. "I feel like a rich American tourist."

Nick and Jamie agreed. "I want you all to know that I'll do my utmost to prevent my wife from disrobing at the table."

Jamie smiled sweetly. "Nicky, you can be *such* an ass sometimes. Be nice or I won't tell you which fork to use."

As Albert was seating us, I complimented him on the table and asked what he was serving.

"Nothing special, Mrs. Bowman. Just some leftovers I had in the cooler."

"I'll bet," Mike said under his breath.

The "leftovers" were a beautiful *cassoulet*, which was the centerpiece of a meal that Albert served in five delicious courses. There was much wine and good conversation, and I felt better that evening than I had in a long time.

Jack and Suzanne talked about the challenges of working at Twin Rivers, and Nick and Jamie, because they were Americans, talked about Watergate.

"Tricky Dick is going down," Nick said with conviction. "Did you hear about this guy Butterfield?"

"I was reading about him in the Winnipeg paper," Jack said. "Isn't he the one who taped everything?"

Jamie shook her head. "Butterfield is the guy who mentioned to the Senate Select Committee—very casually—that Nixon taped all his conversations in the Oval Office. It was a major bombshell."

I looked at Mike and he shrugged. "I guess we missed that bombshell."

"We saw the Paul Butterfield Blues Band in Chicago a few times," I said. "Does that count?"

"I'm afraid not," Nick said. "You two children of Eisenhower are living in a vacuum out here. You don't even read a newspaper."

"The only thing we do with newspaper at Kettle Falls is wrap fish in it," Mike said. "We don't have time to read one."

Suzanne wagged her finger. "You should make time. You Americans will be better off without that warmonger in the White House. And you're right, Nick. Nixon will never survive this."

Nick raised his glass. "Then let us toast the benevolent Mr. Butterfield."

I think we drank several toasts to Mr. Butterfield that evening, as well as a couple to Paul Butterfield. Later, over dessert and coffee, Jamie told us that Nixon was the reason she and Nick had left Chile two years ago.

"What do you mean?" I asked.

"He and the CIA put us in a tough spot."

"In what way?"

Jamie traced the rim of her coffee cup with her finger. "It's … complicated."

"I'll give it to you in a nutshell," Nick said. "The president of Chile is a socialist named Salvador Allende. In 1970, our first year there, he was elected despite the notable efforts of the CIA. They even staged a coup to keep him from being inaugurated, but it failed."

"But that didn't stop them," Jamie said. "And it was a problem for us because the CIA used the Peace Corps as a resource. What's their term for it, Nicky?"

"A force multiplier," he said.

"Yes, that's right. But we got tired of being force multipliers, so we left."

"Actually, we got kicked out," Nick said. "Everybody did. But that was all right with us. We didn't want to undermine Allende. He's a good man, and most Chileans support him. We actually met him once at a rally in Santiago."

I was confused. "So you left the Peace Corps?"

Jamie dabbed at the corner of her mouth with her napkin. "No, we left Chile. We're still in the Corps. They'll reassign us eventually. We're on … a leave of absence."

"I didn't know it worked that way," Mike said.

"It does with us," Nick said. "We also work for the government."

Mike laughed. "I'll be damned—you're spooks!"

Nick and Jamie looked at each other, and I knew it was true.

"We prefer to think of ourselves as assets," Nick said. "The way we see it, we're PCVs who do a little business with the Company on the side. We feed them a little information, and *voilà*—we have penicillin or a new school, or maybe the engineers show up and build a dam. It's a nasty little quid pro quo, but it works."

"We joined the Peace Corps to make people's lives better," Jamie said. "But sometimes you have to dance with the devil to get anything done."

Jack tapped his wine glass with a spoon. "Ladies and gentlemen, I give you Mr. and Mrs. Bond—007 and 8, respectively. Say, did Q give you those special wristwatches?"

We all laughed, and Nick said we'd seen too many movies. "And I should remind you," he said to Jack, "that Q was *British* Intelligence."

Jack put his hand over his heart. "My people come from Quebec. There's no such thing."

"Maybe not," Nick said. "But there's definitely American Intelligence, and it's working overtime in Chile. Keep your eyes on Allende in the next few months."

"Why?" we asked.

"Because both the CIA and Nixon want him ousted."

"They're backing a right-wing general named Augusto Pinochet," Jamie said. "He'll be the next president of Chile."

Suzanne looked at them, her mouth open. "For a couple of hippies who make eleven cents an hour, it's scary what you two know."

It was late when our little party broke up. Mike and I saw our guests off and went to bed without arguing, which was unusual. I was surprised by what Nick and Jamie had said about working for the CIA, and it was hard for me to reconcile that part of their lives with their Peace Corps altruism. For them, life was a negotiation, and everything was on the table. They couldn't afford luxuries like conviction or fixed principles because those things didn't help people. They just got in the way. The cool, dispassionate compromises that informed Nick and Jamie's life seemed very mature. And very much beyond me.

I remember dreaming that night, but it wasn't the usual dream. It was more like a jerky old newsreel—or a Fellini sequence. I was in Santiago, but it looked like Kenora with palm trees. There were throngs of people and automobiles everywhere, and Richard Nixon was directing traffic. He asked me if I spoke Spanish, and when I said no, he told Officer Stone Bear to arrest me.

Chapter 22

The next morning we were having breakfast with the staff—about an hour before twenty-nine guests were scheduled to arrive from Minneapolis—when the radio phone squawked. Mike took the call in Albert's office, and when he returned, I could tell by the look on his face that whatever he'd heard wasn't good. He stood in the doorway for a moment, looking at Pop and Louie. Then he spoke to all of us.

"That was Dutch's attorney on the phone. He was calling from Illinois to let us know that Dutch died last night about eight o'clock. He was in a coma. He never ... knew anything." Mike started to sit down. Then he changed his mind, picked up his coffee cup and walked out the door.

Pop and Louie looked at each other, but neither spoke. I was surprised, although a little uncertain why. Mike and I had known from the beginning that Dutch didn't have long to live, but we'd always supposed he'd make it through the season somehow. I think only half the people eating breakfast at that moment actually knew Dutch, but no one said a word. As I sat there thinking about what his death meant for Mike and me, the only sound was the soft clink and squeak of silverware.

After a few minutes, Louie caught my eye and motioned toward the door, and Louie, Pop and I left the dining room and headed for our cabin, where we always met when there was a problem. When we got there, Mike was sitting on the steps, staring at the river. I sat down beside him.

"I'm sorry about Dutch," I said. "I just can't believe it."

"Neither can I," he said. "There aren't too many of his kind left—just Morgan, Kassel and Lamb."

"And Hawley," Louie said. "But ol' Dutchie, he was somethin', eh. I'm gonna miss him."

"It's strange," Pop said, "but I had a feeling last November, when Dutch and I shook hands, that I'd never see him again. He was pretty sick even then."

Looking at no one in particular, Mike said, "This is bad—*really* bad."

"You got that right, kid. It's like gettin' kicked in the arse with a frozen boot."

I touched Mike's arm. "What happens to Kettle Falls?"

"I don't know, but whatever it is, I'm pretty sure I won't like it."

Pop had taken off his glasses and was wiping them with his shirttail. "Let's not get ahead of ourselves here. Did Dutch have any living kin?"

Mike shook his head. "All he had was this place."

"What about Katherine?"

"She has no claim on the camp. That was part of the divorce settlement."

Pop inspected his glasses and put them back on. "Then I'd say that makes the Scotia Bank the new owner of Kettle Falls, wouldn't you?"

Mike nodded. "They hold the paper on it."

"Well, Michael, what would you do if you were the bank?"

"I don't know, Pop. Close the camp, I guess. Then sell it."

"And that's exactly what they'll do," Pop said. "But not right now."

I could tell Pop was several moves ahead of us. So could Mike, who stood up and began pacing back and forth at the foot of the stairs, sort of thinking aloud.

"You're right," Mike said. "You're absolutely right. The bank could have repossessed this place any time they wanted, but they didn't. And why not? Because we're booked. The bank wouldn't let that income slip through their fingers whether Dutch was alive or not."

"'Specially with all this hullabaloo about mercury," Louie said. "This camp is worth more to 'em open than closed, eh. They prob'ly couldn't sell it for half of what it's worth. Hell, they prob'ly couldn't sell it at all."

"That's my read," Pop said.

A lot of the tension had disappeared from their faces, but the immediate future still seemed unclear.

"So what do we do now?"

"We don't have to do anything, Allie," Pop said. "It's the bank's move."

"They'll want to meet with us soon," Mike said. "And unless they have a hotshot camp operator in their pocket, they'll probably ask us to run Kettle Falls for the rest of the season. After that, they may try to sell it—but like Louie says, that won't be easy."

Louie pulled a crumpled box of Players from his pocket. "Kid, you're all they got. Nobody but you'd be crazy enough to keep this place open with things the way they are, eh."

"We'll know soon enough," Mike said.

Louie lit a cigarette and looked at Mike. "I feel bad about the funeral. All Dutchie's friends, they're up here, eh."

"This is where he'd want us. We'll send flowers."

We stood there for a few minutes, talking about Dutch and speculating on the future, until we were interrupted by the drone of approaching float planes.

"Minneapolis?" I said.

Mike looked at his watch. "Gopher Plumbing and Heating, right on time."

We all headed down to the docks, and in a few minutes, we were shaking hands with twenty-nine pale, smiling Minnesotans who squinted in the bright sunlight and spoke of Watergate in reassuring Midwestern tones. They were all very excited, and as we showed them to their cabins, they made us promise to have them fed, licensed and on the water in two hours' time.

It was a difficult week for those on the staff who had known Dutch, but the Gophers, as we called them, were never aware of it. Kettle Falls simply did what it did best—provide fishing, food and relaxation for people who were fortunate enough or wealthy enough to stay there.

Four days later, the same morning we packed our guests into two Twin Otters bound for International Falls, we got the call from the Scotia Bank asking if they could fly out and meet with us the following day. We had another group arriving in the morning, so Mike set the meeting for one o'clock, by which time we would have our guests out fishing and the shore crew fed.

Three of them, two men and a woman, arrived in a Piper Cherokee that was so small we literally had to pull the woman, who was handicapped by a tight skirt, from the rear seat. The pilot said, "Yeah, she's not very big, eh, but what a write-off!" The other man laughed knowingly, but the woman scowled as she rearranged her rumpled clothing.

The men introduced themselves as McChesney and Hasbrouck, and the woman as Miss Gilbertson. I'd seen McChesney, the owner of the plane, when I'd been in the bank on routine business, so I knew he was a vice president. But neither Mike nor I had seen the other two before. Miss Gilbertson, it turned out, was a notary public and loan officer, and Hasbrouck was an attorney for the bank. We all shook hands and headed for the lodge, where Albert served us lunch.

Our meeting lasted about two hours, and Hasbrouck did most of the talking. He was like a lot of the salesmen who came to Kettle Falls—the punishing handshake, the practiced habit of beginning every third sentence with your name. The deal he laid out was pre-cooked, of course, and the paperwork was already drawn up. All we had to do was sign on the dotted line.

We'd called it pretty close. Kettle Falls was to be placed in re-ceivership, but we would run it for the rest of the season. After that, McChesney said the bank would probably put the camp on the mar-ket. In the meantime, they would hold the financial reins, and Mike and I would receive a salary. The salary was a third less than we'd been averaging each month in our partnership with Dutch, but we signed the papers anyway. We didn't have much choice. It was my job the bank was taking over, so I was being paid reasonably well to perform only a fraction of my former duties. That took some of the sting out of the terms.

We asked for only one concession—that Louie be allowed to stay in his cabin at Kettle Falls until a new owner took over who could then decide what to do with him. The three of them were happy to oblige us on that point, McChesney even saying it was a good idea to have a resident caretaker over the winter, considering all the sabotage in the district.

By the time Albert served sherbet and coffee, the meeting was over. Not long after that, we walked the three of them down to the dock, where they squeezed themselves into the little plane—Miss Gilbertson in the front seat this time—and took off.

"And that's that," Mike said as the Cherokee banked south.

"We should tell Louie. He's more concerned than he lets on."

We found Louie, along with Pop, sitting at the table in Louie's cabin. They were waiting for us.

"Well?" Louie said. "Let's have it, eh."

"It's about what we expected," Mike said. "We run the place until the end of the season. You get to stay here until the camp sells, and then you can make your own deal with the new owner. Any owner would want somebody living here, so you're okay."

Louie nodded and rubbed his eyes. "That's good news, eh." He got up and went over to the window, where he stood with his back to us.

"They didn't care that you two are Americans, did they?" Pop asked.

"Hell, no," Mike said. "They've known that from the beginning. It's all about the money with them."

"So, other than my job, nothing has really changed, has it?" I said.

Mike frowned. "I wouldn't say that. We took a hefty cut in pay, but there's probably a way around it."

That evening at dinner we told the crew everything we knew about the fate of the camp and assured them that, no matter what might happen down the road, it would be business as usual for the rest of the season. There was some clapping, some thank-yous, and nothing more was said. Other than Louie, no one really cared. For the kids, next year would be part of another lifetime. They were like escapees from a Kerouac novel, and uncertainty was the poetry of their lives. The Indians never talked about next year, either, but not because they found uncertainty liberating. They were just inured to it.

Three or four days after our visit from the bankers, I found Mike sitting in the office with our booking calendar, punching buttons on the adding machine as though he were punishing it for something.

"What are you doing?" I asked.

"Oh, I'm glad you're here. I just figured out how we can get our money back."

171

"What money?"

"The money we're losing since we agreed to fetch and tote for the Scotia Bank. I think I can turn that around."

"How?" I asked, not really caring.

"Our moose hunters. I'd forgotten about them until one called a few minutes ago to make a reservation."

"Whatever you do, the Scotia Bank will find out about it."

Mike tore the tape from the adding machine. "No, they won't. Our moose hunting isn't corporate. It's small groups that have been hunting out of Kettle Falls for years. They don't even stay here. We put them on planes and fly them to our outpost cabins. But here's the best part—it's a cash business. It was Dutch's way of keeping some income off the books."

"So your plan is to pocket the money?"

"Why not? It worked for Dutch, and now that he's gone, it's the easiest way to get our money back."

"But it isn't *our* money."

Mike looked hurt and angry at the same time. "We had a deal with Dutch. We didn't come up here to work for the Scotia Bank."

"Things have changed," I said.

"And I'm going to change them back." Mike looked down at the papers on the desk. His right hand sought the adding machine, then he lost interest and swiveled his chair around. "I should've known what you'd say. We have a right to this money. Have you forgotten everything we did to keep this place open?"

"What a stupid question. I wish I could forget."

Mike started to say something, but I left.

That's how things went with Mike and me. We'd have a few good days, maybe even a good week, and then our relationship would suddenly crumble and whatever ground we might have regained was immediately lost.

It was the same with our sex life. Before Leon Thin Bird, Mike and I could hardly wait for the guests to abandon the lodge every evening and head for their cabins. After I'd closed the store, I would come up to hurry them along, and the moment the last one was out the door, Mike and I would race to our cabin, where we'd make love in the big log bed as though we'd been apart for weeks. Sometimes, we didn't make it to our cabin, and we'd make love right there in the lodge on the bearskin rug—the one that had frightened Molly when Mike showed me around that first day.

Now, our lovemaking was a function of the day we'd had. If it had been a decent day, one unmarred by any unpleasantness between us, we might make love. But there were fewer and fewer days like that.

I missed the way things used to be. I liked who I was then, even though who I was didn't always seem to be me. I think that's what I liked most about it. It was fun to be me and to *not* be me at the same time—like that day at the Laurentian Divide, when another car could have driven in at any moment.

But that was over now. That part of me, like a lot of other parts, was buried somewhere behind the substation.

Chapter 23

Around the middle of August, and much to my surprise, fall arrived. It announced itself with little splashes of crimson on the maple trees and hints of yellow among the birches and aspens. Only the oak trees gave no sign of turning. They clung stubbornly to summer and held their green against the cold nights and shortening days.

The cooler weather brought an end to the mosquitoes and flies, and I came to enjoy taking walks in the afternoons. Sometimes, I'd walk all the way to the main road, and I would always see deer. A couple of times I saw moose, and once, two timber wolves ran into the road, literally skidding to a stop in front of me. They didn't look anything like the pictures I'd seen or the shy, small-boned wolves I remembered from zoos in Chicago. These two were huge—big heads, deep chests, enormous feet—and there was no fear in them. They studied me for a moment, but before I had a chance to be afraid, they melted back into the forest.

The walks helped, but with the bulk of my daily responsibilities now in the hands of the Scotia Bank, I found that, for the first time in my life, I was mentally underemployed, and the last thing I needed was more time to think. My principal role now was that of a courier, and at least twice a week I was in Kenora, turning our bills over to the bank, along with enormous checks from our clients. I also gave them the staff's time cards, and they would look them over and cut the paychecks, which I would bring back to camp and distribute.

One afternoon toward the end of August, I was helping Albert in the kitchen when I heard the crunch of tires on gravel and looked out the window to see Officer Stone Bear pulling up in his truck. I'd been peeling apples, and the paring knife I was holding clattered to the floor.

Albert came right over. "Is anything wrong, Mrs. Bowman?"

"No, no," I said, nodding toward the window. "I just didn't expect to see him again. There's something creepy about that guy."

Mike was down at the store, where he couldn't have seen Stone Bear drive in, so I sent Albert to get him. I was expecting Stone Bear to walk into the staff dining room, but he didn't. He just leaned against his truck, as he'd done before, and waited for someone to come out and see what he wanted. I let him stand there for a minute, composing myself as best I could, then went outside.

"Hello," I said. "I'm surprised to see you."

Stone Bear grunted something but didn't look at me. He was looking at the kitchen door, as though he was expecting someone else to come through it.

"Dutch isn't here," I said.

"No shit, eh—he's dead. Where's your husband?"

I could see Mike coming, not nearly fast enough, and pointed down the hill. "Right there."

When he was still a few paces away, Mike started shaking his head. "What do you want, Stone Bear?"

"Zimmerman's dead, eh. And you're no hired hand. You been runnin' this camp all season."

"That's top-notch detective work," Mike said, "but it doesn't change anything. Have you figured out what happens if you turn us in?"

Stone Bear's little eyes narrowed. "Yeah, this place would close, eh. All the Indians who work here, they'd lose their jobs."

"Every last one."

"You're pretty smart, aren't you, Yank? You had any sabotage since I was here last time?"

"Not since May."

"We've been very lucky," I said. "We keep expecting—"

"Why do you think that is, eh? Every camp that's still open in this district gets hit every couple weeks. Except Kettle Falls."

Mike shrugged. "Like my wife said, we've been lucky."

"You been *real* lucky. It's almost like …" Stone Bear stopped. He smiled and seemed to be staring at something a thousand miles away. "I got a daughter back home in Hollow Water, Yank."

"You're a lucky man, Stone Bear. What are you doing here?"

"She's fourteen and real pretty. You know, them young bucks back home, they've taken notice, eh. They knock on the door and bring my little girl presents, but I run 'em off. I told my wife I was gonna put a stop to all these boys sniffin' around. And my wife, she just laughed, eh. 'How you gonna do that?' she said."

"This is really interesting, but what—"

"And I told my wife I could stop it any time I wanted, eh—it's easy. I told her I'd just shoot one of 'em. Then the others, they'd get the message and stay away."

"That's very creative parenting," Mike said. "Let us know how it works out for you. In the meantime, why don't you tell us what the hell you want?"

"I wanna know why Kettle Falls is the only camp in the district that isn't bein' hit, eh. And I wanna take a look around—if you don't mind."

"I won't even ask if you have a search warrant, because I know you don't. But if you want to look around, be my guest."

Stone Bear pulled a notebook from his pocket and opened it. "You know, I been down at Twin Rivers a few times since I was here before. There's over four hundred people on that reserve, eh, but I finally found two men who said Thin Bird had been there—got their names right here." He held the open notebook out, but Mike refused to take it. "Thin Bird spent the night at their place, eh. That was two days after he was seen in Minaki."

"So what? That doesn't mean he was ever at Kettle Falls."

"That's right, Yank. But it puts a known saboteur only seven miles from this camp—the only one that hasn't been hit since May. I can't figure that out, eh. Thin Bird's Cree—he's got no blood at Twin Rivers. No friends, either. What was he doing in this country?"

"How the hell should I know?" Mike looked at Stone Bear with genuine wonder. "Why the heavy interest in this guy? If Thin Bird killed somebody in Broken Head, he was off the reservation. Why not let the Provincial Police deal with it?"

Stone bear laughed. "Because the Provincials don't give a damn. That store owner, he was an Indian, too, eh."

"I don't know what else to tell you," Mike said. "Thin Bird was never here. He's probably back at God's Lake by now."

Stone Bear had been thumbing through his notebook but looked up suddenly. "I never told you where Thin Bird was from, eh."

"It must've been on that poster."

Stone Bear's mouth tightened into a mean little smile. "There was nothin' on it like that."

"Then it was something Sinclair said."

"I don't think so, Yank. I think you came up with that all on your own, eh. And I think Thin Bird was here—up to no good—and you killed him. Either that or you know who did." Stone Bear's voice became confidential. "Did you throw his body in the river?"

"Give it up, Stone Bear. For the last time, Thin Bird was never here."

"Yank, I don't believe nothin' you say."

"Try to imagine how little I care."

Stone Bear spit on the ground, and both men stood there, glowering at each other.

"Thank you for not reporting us to Immigration," I said. "It's really better for everyone this way."

Stone Bear tried to smile, but it was more of a sneer. "'Specially for me, eh. Like I told you before, I wanna know where you are—now more than ever."

"Take a look around, then beat it," Mike said. "I don't want you here when our guests come in from fishing."

"It won't take me long, eh." Stone Bear turned and walked down the hill toward the marina.

When he was out of earshot, I grabbed Mike's arm. "He knows what happened. He'll never leave us alone now. He's a policeman, and he'll—"

"He's a First Nation cop," Mike said. "He has less clout out here than a crossing guard, and he knows it."

"Do you think he'll go to the substation?"

"He will if he knows how these camps are being sabotaged."

"Do you think he'll find anything? I mean—he won't, will he? He won't find the ..." I couldn't bring myself to say *grave*.

"He could walk right over it and never know it's there," Mike said. "I checked yesterday—there's no trace of it."

"He knows. He knows what we did."

Mike looked at me in disbelief. "Allie, he doesn't know anything, and he never will. Anyway, it isn't about what he knows. It's about what he can prove, which is absolutely nothing."

Despite Mike's assurances, it was unnerving to have Stone Bear wandering around the camp that afternoon. It was silly, but I would have felt better if Stone Bear had been a white man. I worried that, as an Indian, he might possess some strange shamanistic power that would be our undoing. I imagined him communing with the trees, listening to the wind and imploring the spirits to lead him to Thin Bird's grave.

I tried to keep an eye on him that day, but I was in the lodge most of the time, so it was hard. Every now and then, I'd look out a window and see Stone Bear passing by or speaking to someone, but I never knew if he'd been to the substation. Later that afternoon I looked out and his truck was gone. When Mike came into the lodge for dinner that evening, I asked him if Stone Bear had said anything to him before he'd left.

"The only thing he said was that we had a little problem in the attic of the garage. I didn't know what he was talking about, so I climbed up there and looked. Guess what I found?"

"Just tell me."

"Louie's gill net. It's illegal to have an unlicensed net, so I boxed it up and hid it under Louie's cabin. Wait until he—"

"Is there anything he can do about it?"

"Stone Bear? He can't do a damn thing here, except make you nervous, and he's very good at that."

"I can't help it. I don't like having him around."

"I don't either," Mike said, "and if he ever comes back, I'll order him off the property. He's worn out his welcome."

As I had done after Stone Bear's first visit, I worried for several days about what he knew, what he *thought* he knew and what he might have supposed. Then I returned to the old, familiar business of living with myself, which was the same as living with Mike. It wasn't getting any easier.

The last week of August and the first two weeks of September we were booked solid—large groups from St. Louis, Chicago, Topeka and Houston. The fishing, which had slowed down a bit during what I called the seven days of summer, came roaring back in a way that rivaled what it had been in June. The rain held off, and the weather was beautiful.

The blueberries were so thick that in many places the ground was actually blue with them—big, luscious berries the size of a dime. The kitchen crew picked buckets full of them every morning after breakfast, so that Albert could incorporate them in his menus. The guests got into the act, too, and when they came off the water, they would often spend half an hour picking berries, which they would take home along with their fish.

Because a couple of kids on Albert's crew had returned to school for the fall term, he was occasionally short-handed, so Mike and I did our best to help out. One September afternoon we were cleaning up the dining room when Mike picked up a newspaper that one of our guests had left on a table. He was about to throw it away when something caught his eye.

"Do you remember when Nick and Jamie told us that the president of Chile's days were numbered?"

"Yes," I said. "They predicted a coup."

"Well, it happened—he's dead. It says, 'Chilean president Salvador Allende took his own life this morning as government forces led by General Augusto Pinochet stormed La Moneda Presidential Palace in Santiago.' It goes on to say that a lot of his cabinet members and senior military officers were purged—now *there's* a euphemism."

"That ought to make Nixon happy," I said. "But Nick and Jamie liked Allende."

"Yeah, they did. I'm sure if we asked them, they could tell us the next regime that's about to topple."

"Let's not ask. Does the article say anything about the CIA?"

Mike handed me the paper. "I don't know. I didn't read it all."

I sat down to read the story, but there was another piece on the front page that I found myself reading instead. It was about Abbie

Hoffman, the firebrand I'd heard in Chicago during the Democratic National Convention. The article didn't make sense at first, because it was about all the celebrities who had contributed to his bail—Dr. Spock, Jack Nicholson, Paul Newman—and I hadn't known he was in jail. The last paragraph, though, restated the two-week-old facts: Abbie Hoffman had been arrested in New York City for selling cocaine. He'd been caught in a sting and was likely to spend the next twenty years behind bars.

I couldn't imagine what bizarre circumstances had transformed Abbie Hoffman from a political revolutionary into a coke dealer, but there didn't seem to be any doubt about his guilt. The paper said he'd been caught red-handed.

And for some reason it made me sad.

Chapter 24

The next week was cold, and the wind blew hard out of the northwest. Our guests, who had expected typical fall weather, joked that they'd been warmer on ice-fishing trips. At the end of the day, they would arrive at the docks wringing their hands and rubbing their faces, which were nearly frozen from the boat ride back to camp. Heaters ran all day in the cabins, and the fire never went out in the big fireplace in the lodge. Most of the time, Albert had a cauldron of soup or mulled cider simmering over it.

The third Saturday in September we had an empty camp. In fact, we would never be full again. We had some small, hardy groups of fisherman and quite a few moose hunters booked, but the moose hunters would be flown to outpost cabins, along with their guides, and all we had to do was get them there and retrieve them again at the end of their trip.

When Mike and I woke up that Saturday, the first words out of his mouth were "Empty camp today."

"I know," I said. "And it's a good thing. It's been almost a month since we had a break."

"That's why you're going to enjoy my surprise."

"What surprise?"

"Rise and shine. We have to get going."

I pulled the blanket over my head. "If you're about to tell me we're going to Kenora—"

"We're going duck hunting, just the two of us. What do you say?"

"I'd love to, but we don't have licenses."

Mike tugged at the blanket. "Yes, we do. I got licenses for both of us when I was in town last week."

"We don't have shotguns."

"We'll borrow a couple of Dutch's."

"Well, what about decoys? We don't have any."

He laughed. "Wrong again. Remember when I found Louie's gill net in the attic of the garage?"

I pulled the blanket down. "Officer Stone Bear had a role in that, as I recall."

"Yeah, well, when I was up there, I noticed a bunch of duck decoys in the corner—those old fibercast jobs. They've probably been there twenty years, and the mice have chewed the hell out of them, but they're better than nothing. Since that cold snap, there's been a lot of ducks moving around. Have you noticed?"

"Every morning they fly over going *that* direction." I pointed southwest.

"And that's the direction we're headed—if I can get you out of bed."

"I can be ready in half an hour."

"Great! I'm glad you want to go."

"Did you think I wouldn't?"

Mike shrugged. "I really wasn't sure. There are a lot of things that you don't seem to enjoy much anymore."

I sat up and put a pillow in my lap. "Listen, Mike ... I want to go, and I'm glad you thought of it. Can we please leave it at that?"

"Sure."

We showered quickly, hauled our guns, shells and heavy coats down to the marina and put them into a boat—number eleven again—that had two lumpy potato sacks full of decoys in the bow. Then we ate breakfast standing up in the kitchen. Albert handed Mike a picnic basket—the same modified shore lunch box we'd used in May—and we headed out.

It looked like a good day for duck hunting. It was cold, though not nearly as cold as it had been the week before, and the sky was a flat, battleship gray. As we pulled away from the dock, I asked Mike where we were going.

"North Bay," he said. "George had some people in there casting for northerns a few days ago, and he told me there were a lot of ducks up at the west end."

"Do we have to go through those rapids to get there?"

Mike pointed to a flock of ducks overhead. "Yeah, but it won't be bad. They've been drawing the rivers down all summer in case there's a spring flood. There isn't much current in the fall."

And there wasn't. In the places where I remembered current from before, there was only a trace of it now, and there were black marks on the rocks indicating the water was at least two feet lower than it had been in the spring. Even the pinch point at North Boundary Rapids didn't look all that forbidding. The current tossed us around some, and the motor whined and complained as it had in May, but it wasn't bad. After we'd made it through the narrow channel and crossed the turbulent stretch beyond it, we went another half mile before Mike angled the boat off to the right toward what I supposed was North Bay.

It was a big bay, a mile wide at the mouth, and we entered it from the east side, passing through a cluster of small islands that stretched across the entrance. There were a few little islands in the bay, too, and there were lily roots and logs sticking up everywhere.

When I looked over the side of the boat, I could see weeds just below the surface.

"Be careful," I said.

"We're okay. Let's see if we can find those ducks George was talking about."

We headed for the west end, and when we were a couple hundred yards from shore, ducks began to get up from a thin fringe of rice near the water's edge. Mike throttled back and we watched them. There were perhaps three hundred altogether, mostly ring-bills, and they made a big circle and tried to come in again, but they were nervous about the boat.

"There's plenty of ducks," Mike said, "but the prop's already churning mud, and even if we could get to that rice, we couldn't hide the boat in it."

"Could one of us stand on shore?"

Mike shook his head. "It's just muskeg. You'd sink out of sight in thirty seconds. We'll have to hunt from that little island over there." He was looking off to his left at an island about the size of a basketball court. There was quite a bit of rice around it, and it was as close to the action as we could get.

We motored over to it, and it looked good. It was just rock, with a few scraggly trees here and there, but there was a muddy notch on the back side to hide the boat in. Mike put the motor in reverse, and as we skirted the edge of the rice, I set the decoys out in two little clusters where any returning ducks would see them. After I'd set the last decoy in the water, Mike looked them over and laughed.

"Have you ever seen a more pathetic sight in your life?" he said.

The mice had chewed the bills off most of the decoys, and they were full of holes. By the time I'd put the last one out, a couple of the first ones had already sunk, and most of the others were riding suspiciously low in the water or listing badly. There was nothing we could do about it, so we hid the boat on the far side of the island, gathered everything we could carry and walked back across to where the decoys were. By the time we got there, three more had vanished.

"The ducks better come in the next few minutes," Mike said, "or our entire spread will be on the bottom of the bay."

I loaded the guns while Mike threw some driftwood and branches together around a scrub oak that was growing near the water. It was a nice blind—good places to sit—and we hunkered down on each side of the little tree and waited. The ducks we'd put up earlier were still circling the bay, but after we quit moving around, they began landing, four or five at a time, in precisely the place they'd taken off from. They didn't even look at our decoys. After half a dozen little flocks gave us the cold shoulder and glided into the end of the bay, I leaned my shotgun against the tree and sat back.

"They sure like that place," I said.

"They've been there for a few days—that probably has something to do with it." Mike pointed to the spread. "And then there's the issue of our decoys."

"I wonder how much they even matter." I reached behind me and broke off a little branch that was poking me in the back. "Jimmy told me a story one time about how he went hunting and forgot the decoys. But he had a bag of grapefruit someone had given him in the back of his truck, so he threw all the grapefruit in the water and used them for decoys. He said he shot his limit in twenty minutes."

Mike laughed. "That's definitely a Jimmy story. Have you heard anything from him lately?"

"I got a letter just before the cold snap. He never answers my questions, but the letters are interesting. He said he wants to start a wind farm."

"What's that?"

"According to Jimmy, it's a piece of open land that you build a whole bunch of windmills on to generate electricity. Then you sell it to the highest bidder. He says it's the wave of the future, but I imagine it's just the latest in a long line of silly dreams."

"Nothing wrong with dreams."

"You should try some of mine."

There was a beaver swimming around in the decoys. He sensed we were there and was very curious. At one point he swam within fifteen feet of us and stared blindly in our direction with myopic little eyes that looked like onyx. Then he raised his head up out of the water and made odd snuffling noises as he tried to smell us.

"You know what I miss most about Jimmy?" I said. "I miss the way I used to feel about him."

"I know—ever since he lost the point."

I took off my hat and folded the earflaps up. "It started with the smuggling, but you're right—the point is personal, and there are only two ways to look at it. Either Jimmy didn't know what it meant to me—and he should have—or he knew, but he just didn't care."

"Maybe he knew, but he couldn't help it. Why does it matter so much?"

"It's hard to explain. All I know is that I wouldn't be here now if it weren't for the point and those windy mornings I spent there with Hedley. You and I wouldn't be married, either. Actually, we never would've met."

Mike peered at me around the tree.

"It's true," I said. "I followed you out the door at that party because I heard you tell someone you were going hunting. The point is part of that. Without it, you would've been just another guy at a party."

"I'd like to think there's a little more to it than that. *Damn*— we just lost another decoy. Look, I don't really care why we met. I'm just glad we did. There's always something that brings people together."

"Yes, but that 'something' is a big part of who I am." It felt good to be talking but also strange, and it made me nervous. "And it's all connected—the point, me, Cloverdale, the two of us. Even what we're doing now is part of it."

"The point may explain certain choices you made," Mike said, "but once you made them, what difference does it make?"

"You think it should be *was*?"

"I didn't say that."

"It makes a difference," I said slowly, "because even when I was ten, I never imagined a life without both of you in it. I always believed the point would stay in the family, just like I always knew I'd marry you someday—not *you* specifically but you in the abstract. You know what I mean?"

Mike leaned around the tree again. "Of course. It's the same way I feel about you."

"So I always knew we'd love each other—this nameless man and I—and the point would be there, and it would be part of my life—part of *our* life. I used to imagine the two of us very old, walking along that beach after a storm, watching the ducks fly and looking at what had blown ashore in the night. There would be little shells and net floats or maybe a weather balloon from someplace far away or a fisherman's hat with a funny button pinned to it. Or maybe just a big smelly fish. There would always be fish. Whenever there was a storm ..."

And then I was crying. My whole body started to shake, and I couldn't make it stop. I'd been right to be nervous.

"What's wrong?" Mike said. "What is it?"

"I don't have that anymore! I don't have *any* of it! All I've got is Leon Thin Bird. How did that happen? How did it fucking *happen*?"

I was sobbing uncontrollably. I was beyond pain, beyond grief, beyond anything I'd ever known.

Mike scrambled over to me, knocking the blind apart in the process. He tried to put his arms around me, but my forehead was practically between my knees, and I was hunched up in a little ball.

"Allie, for God's sake, what's going on?"

But all I could do was cry. Eventually, Mike got me sitting up straight again, and in a few minutes it was better. He held me for a long time, and I felt the same as I had on that day many years ago, when I left Cape Vincent for Chicago with Tom and my mother. It was as though I could feel the cold car window pressed against my cheek.

When I was finally able to talk again, I said, "That was awful. I don't know why I did that."

"It's okay. I've never seen you like that before, though. You scared me."

"I know. I'm really sorry. I just—"

"Don't worry about it," Mike said. "It doesn't matter."

"Yes, it does."

After a while, we left the blind and sat in the open, where we could watch large flocks of ducks coming into the bay from the north. They would circle the whole bay once or twice, then join the others at the west end. I was tired and limp, but I felt better. I even managed to eat some of the lunch Albert had made for us. When Mike and I had eaten what we could of it, we shared the rest with three pelicans that swam over from a nearby reef, hoping for a handout.

Mike wasn't saying much, but I knew what he wanted to ask. He poured each of us a cup of coffee from the thermos and stretched out on the ground beside me. "What I want to know is whether I'm still that guy—the guy you always thought you'd marry."

"He wasn't real," I said, "so our relationship wasn't very complicated. He was just someone who liked to walk along the beach, hunt ducks, refinish rocking chairs—stuff like that."

"Now I'm *really* worried," Mike said. "I don't even understand the concept of rocking chairs. What's the point of moving if you don't go anywhere?"

I tossed a piece of bread to the nearest pelican. "I could be wrong about the rocking chairs. It was a long time ago, and I never knew him that well. But ... I honestly don't know if you're that guy anymore."

"Because I shot Thin Bird before he could shut the camp down or shoot one of us?"

"It's not that simple. It never has been. I get sick when I think about Thin Bird, but at least I know why. Your lack of reflection ... now that's a little scary."

"It shouldn't be. Reflection is highly overrated. It can't change anything."

"No, but it can help you understand things better. Whenever you don't want to deal with something, you shut it out like it never happened."

Mike threw the dregs of his coffee on the ground. "That isn't true. It's just that there are things you can change and things—"

"If it isn't true, then why do you always say that Vietnam is *was*? You say it as though the past isn't real—like it doesn't matter."

"It doesn't—not in the way you mean."

I shook my head. "The past matters a lot. Who was it that said, 'What's past is prologue'?"

"Shakespeare."

"Well, he was right. The past matters because everything is connected to it. It shapes the present, and it can destroy the future. From what you told me about Vietnam, you should know that."

"I do. And I'll go along with you up to a point. But learning from the past is one thing. Allowing it to hold your life hostage is another. You gotta keep on truckin'."

"No matter what's in the truck?"

Mike raised one eyebrow.

"Some loads are heavier than others," I said.

"Ah ... a metaphor. So whose psychic burdens are we talking about—yours or mine?"

"I don't think there's much we can do about mine. But there are groups of Vietnam veterans who meet and talk. Maybe when we get back in the States, you should—"

Mike was instantly on his feet. "Just what I need—to sit around and listen to a bunch of vets crying in their beer. C'mon, it's time to go."

"Why is it such a bad idea?"

"Because I don't have any problem with who I am, and I can live with what I've done. Hell, a little self-loathing is good for the soul. I repeat—*a little*." Mike looked at me and shook his head. "Maybe *you* should talk to a bunch of Vietnam vets. You're the one who's consumed with guilt and hung up on the past. Let's get outta here."

There was a splash as two mallards landed in the decoys. I don't know where they came from, and neither Mike nor I had seen them until they landed. They sat nervously for a few seconds, looking this way and that among the remaining decoys, then took off, quacking for all they were worth.

A few minutes later, we loaded up the gear, pulled the seven decoys still afloat and headed back to camp. Neither of us said anything, and it was a long boat ride. I kept wishing on the way home that I had a place to go, a life to return to. But it was just a mental exercise. I had no other life. And I still clung to the unfounded hope that things would get better.

Chapter 25

We never went duck hunting again, but when the trees shed their leaves, Mike and I declared a truce and went grouse hunting a few times. After several hard frosts, the grouse had come out of the deep woods to eat berries in the little clearings and clover at the edges of our road, and Mike and I would walk on either side of it, guns at the ready, our fingers on the safeties. Grouse explode from cover at top speed, but Mike soon became an excellent snap shot, and he would get a couple birds every time we went hunting. But I couldn't suppress my instinct to aim, so by the time I pulled the trigger, I was aiming at nothing.

The first week of October, we had to prepare all five of the outpost cabins for our moose hunters, so Mike flew two-man crews into each one to perform routine maintenance, cut firewood and drop off supplies. Because Kettle Falls was empty, Mike asked me if I'd like to go with him to the outpost on Snowshoe Lake. I was surprised he asked, because other than our little grouse hunting outings, he wasn't looking for excuses to be with me, and I didn't blame him. But I thought he probably wanted to talk, so I went along.

We'd been in the air less than twenty minutes when the pilot landed the plane on a swampy little lake and taxied up to a short dock in front of a log cabin. The pilot, whom we'd used a lot over the summer, helped us unload and said, "Pick you up late tomorrow, eh?"

"You got it," Mike said. "Don't forget us, Gus—I know where you live."

Gus laughed, climbed into the plane and started the engine. A few minutes later he was a tiny dot above the trees, heading back to Whiteshell.

We checked out the cabin, and other than a couple rotten boards in the front steps, it looked all right, at least on the outside. It was maybe twenty-four feet square with pieces of plywood bristling with nails over the door and windows.

"Bear scares," Mike said. "And they worked."

After we'd removed them, we began hauling all the supplies from the dock to the cabin, where we piled everything outside the door—food, water, chainsaw, sleeping bags, splitting maul, toolbox, foam mattresses, propane. We moved quickly because it looked like rain, and after we'd rolled the propane tank up the hill, Mike unlocked the door and we stepped inside.

"Oh, my God," I said.

Mike pointed to the roof. "No wonder."

The roof was a patchwork of corrugated metal, and near the peak, one of the sheets had been torn loose, probably by a raccoon, and we could see the sky. Birds and animals of every kind had taken advantage of it, turning the cabin into their personal refuge. The contents of the drawers and cupboards—mostly pots, pans and cooking utensils—were scattered all over the place, and there were feathers everywhere.

"It looks like a chicken coop," I said.

Mike reached down and removed a butcher knife that was stuck, perfectly straight, in the floor. "A chicken coop that was sublet to a poltergeist. At least I know what to fix first. I'd better get up there before it rains."

"Please be careful."

On his way out, Mike opened and closed the cabin door a couple times and scowled at the hinges. "Here's my next job."

The cabin was primitive, but it had the essentials—a table, chairs, bunk beds, a barrel stove for heat and a propane stove for cooking. In addition to a layer of dirt and feathers, there were bird droppings everywhere. I heard Mike on the roof, and shortly after that, I started a fire in the barrel stove.

"Does it draw okay?"

I was startled and looked up to see Mike's face framed by the hole in the roof.

"It seems to," I said.

"Good."

While Mike banged away on the roof, I swept the place out, then hauled water from the lake and washed everything down. By late afternoon, I thought the cabin looked pretty good. I'd removed a dozen mouse nests, several bird nests, one old hornet's nest, and a few other nests I couldn't identify. I'd scrubbed the floor, the propane stove, the counter, the globes on the gas lights—I even washed the windows. After Mike had finished repairing the front steps, he came inside and told me to stop.

"If you get it any cleaner in here," he said, "it'll be bad for business."

I wiped my forehead with my sleeve. "Nonsense. I need another bucket of—"

"No, really." Mike laughed and thumped his chest. "Moose hunter no like frills." He pointed to the propane stove. "A lot of them complained when we put these in the cabins."

"Our fishermen would die in a place like this," I said. "Moose hunters must be a strange breed."

"They are." Mike took the broom from my hands and set it in

the corner. "But we're going to make good money on 'em."

"I don't want to hear about it."

When it started to get dark, Mike hooked up the new propane tank, which gave us lights and a cook stove. It had been a long day, but the rain held off until we were having dinner; then it drummed noisily on the metal roof.

Throughout the meal we talked, and as we did, I realized how much I'd missed conversations over dinner. You can't really talk in a mess hall, not in a meaningful way, and that's where Mike and I had been eating for the last six months. In fact, we'd eaten no more than a dozen meals alone together since we were married, and half of those were on the way to Kettle Falls after our wedding. When we finished eating, Mike got around to asking me what I knew he would.

"How are you doing, Allie?"

"As in how's my head?"

"Yes."

"Today it was good. I was busy all day today, and that makes a big difference. Yesterday was bad. Tomorrow … who knows?"

"Do you think about it all the time?"

"About that night? Not all the time. I spend more time thinking about us, and I spend a lot of time thinking about my thinking. Sometimes, I think about Cape Vincent and the point—that's when I'm tired of thinking about everything else. I know you're worried."

Mike pushed his plate aside. "Of course I'm worried. I didn't really understand the size of the problem until you fell apart in North Bay. Maybe you're having … a *breakdown* or something." He was clearly uncomfortable with the possibility.

"I'm sorry about North Bay … that was bad. But whether or not I'm having a breakdown, I really couldn't say. All I know is that I'm confused and afraid—and I feel like guilt covered with skin."

Mike reached across the table and covered my hand with his. "I wish I could help you. I wish that more than anything. I hate being the cause of this."

"You're not ... not entirely. And I know you want to help. But there are limits to what even you can do."

"I've told you this a hundred times, Allie—what's done is done."

"Yes, and I should move on, forget all about it. I know the drill—I just can't do it. I don't even *want* to do it." Then I said what I'd been thinking for some time. "If we can't fix this, you and I are headed for a very bad place."

Mike nodded. After a moment or two, he stood up and began clearing the table. "Look, I don't know what you're planning to do, but I need you to stick with me until we finish the season. After that, we can talk about what comes next."

"All right," I said, "but you didn't need to say that. I would never leave you in the lurch."

As we lay in bed that night, I could hear wolves howling as I had so many times since that first night in Louie's cabin, and I wondered if Mike was awake and hearing them, too. But it was different this time. They were close and they were moving, slipping through the forest like vapors. As their many voices melded into one, it became an aria of unfathomable loneliness.

Sometime before morning, I knew the rain had turned to sleet because I could hear it sizzling on the roof, and when we got up, there was a quarter inch of ice on everything. The trees were sagging beneath the beautiful weight of it, and it was as if I'd awakened in a wilderness of glass. The little lake was covered with Canada geese that had arrived silently in the night but who were now honking incessantly, filling the morning with goose music. It continued until Mike had to start the chainsaw. After a couple minutes of that, the geese lifted off the water en masse and headed south, no doubt in search of quieter neighbors.

It was another busy day for us, especially for Mike, who spent hours cutting and splitting firewood, which I stacked outside the door—when I wasn't cutting brush, stocking the shelves with canned goods or cleaning up around the cabin, where a year's worth of limbs and branches lay strewn about. At four o'clock that afternoon, Gus finessed his Otter into our little lake again and flew us back to camp.

I never saw much of our moose hunters. They would fly out of Kettle Falls, looking about the same as anyone else, but upon returning a few days later, they looked as though they'd crash-landed in the bush and crawled all the way back. But they seemed better for it, even if they hadn't seen a moose. And Mike was all smiles, so I knew he was making money and evening the score with the Scotia Bank.

We had a few fishermen during the last two weeks of October—two or three cabins' worth—but it was quiet around camp, and Mike and the remaining crew were doing things every day in preparation of closing. I had always thought we'd have a big party at the end of October—an end of the season blow-out—but I soon discovered that camps close with more of a whimper than a bang.

By October 20, we had only a dozen employees left. Some had taken jobs in town. Others had become restless and drifted away as they had arrived, in twos and threes. The only significant difference was in the pairing. Young men who had arrived in camp alone or with other young men now left with girls who had arrived the same way. That seemed like a good thing.

Marcy and Collette, whom I'd met when they were hitchhiking to Nova Scotia, decided to hitchhike to Florida. And my college boys, Duncan and Neil, who'd been their boyfriends for the summer, promised to join them in Fort Lauderdale during spring break. Albert was now working with a crew of three, and although Albert would be one of the last to leave, he had already landed a job as a *saucier* on a cruise ship for the winter.

Pop was still around, winterizing the outboards for what he

assumed would be the last time. But in three weeks he would be back home in Brandon, Manitoba, where he repaired snowmobiles during the off-season.

There simply weren't enough people left to have a party, and in truth there was little to celebrate, other than the fact that Mike and I had run a very complicated business for seven months—a business that might never open again.

Chapter 26

With our time at Kettle Falls coming to an end, Mike and I were very much aware of the enormous decisions we'd soon have to make, but we did our best to avoid talking about them. That was okay for now. There was a lot of work to do. Everything we had done to open Kettle Falls now had to be done in reverse. But very soon, we would have to confront the unknown shape of our future.

One nice thing about October, though, was the fact that we could finally go fishing and spend some time with our friends at Twin Rivers, which we managed to do at least once a week. We had them over for a grouse dinner—the last serious cooking that Albert did that fall—and they had us over for chicken curry, which involved a secret recipe that Nick and Jamie had acquired on their travels and which, according to Mike, might better have remained a secret. With the camp nearly empty, our friends dropped by more often, and we would sit in the bar and talk or shoot pool in the store.

It was Halloween, and we were down at the marina with the

remaining crew, pulling the boats and carting the motors to Pop's shop, when all four of them arrived. I looked up and saw them standing in front of the store, and I could tell by their faces that something was wrong. I got Mike's attention, and together we walked over to say hello.

"Can you take a break for a minute?" Jack asked.

"Sure," Mike said. "Let's have a beer. Are you guys trick-or-treating?"

"In a way," Jack said.

They followed us into the store, and after we'd gotten everyone a beer, the six of us stood rather awkwardly at the counter.

"I can tell you've got something on your minds," Mike said. "What is it?"

"We have to leave," Nick said.

Mike laughed. "You just got here."

"No, I mean *Canada*. We have another assignment."

"We're going to Iran," Jamie said. "We leave in four days."

"Oh, no," I said. "We're going to miss you so much." I gave them each a hug. "Mike and I are leaving in a couple weeks, too."

Jack looked at Suzanne, who gave him a little nod. "Yeah … that's what we want to talk to you about. With Nick and Jamie leaving, I have to hire two more teachers. If you two aren't in a hurry to get home, I was wondering what you'd think about teaching at Twin Rivers. We're in a real—"

"It wouldn't matter that you're Americans," Suzanne said. "Jack could give you work permits. They're the same as temporary visas. Everything would be perfectly legal."

"That's right," Jack said. "It's easy because you wouldn't be displacing Canadian citizens. The paperwork comes with the job."

Mike and I looked at each other. Neither of us knew what to say.

"It's pretty good pay," Nick said, "considering your housing is free. It's fun, too. What do you think?"

Jamie pressed her hands together. "We're just praying you'll say yes. We feel awful leaving like this. Plus, you'd be real assets at Twin Rivers."

"Slow down, everybody," Mike said. "We need some time to talk it over."

"We haven't really discussed life after Kettle Falls," I said. "Could we let you know in a couple days?"

"Sure," Jack said, "as long as the answer is yes."

Mike turned to Nick and Jamie. "Why Iran?"

"Beats me," Nick said. "It was either Iran or Nigeria. As much as we hate to leave, I'm excited about returning to the Mideast—the people, the mild winter, the food. You know, most men have *sexual* fantasies, but mine are about pomegranates, kiwis and casaba melons."

"That may be more sexual than you think," Jamie said. "Tell them about Mary Fast Owl."

Nick smiled. "This is funny and sad at the same time. I was trying to explain to the kids where Jamie and I were going, and I wasn't doing very well. Those children have no concept of Winnipeg, let alone the eastern Mediterranean. But I thought they might be able to grasp the biblical notion of the Levant, so I explained that we were going to a faraway place where an invisible line runs through a land where people once believed the sun rose. All of a sudden Mary Fast Owl, whose English is none too good, burst into tears. I said, 'Mary, what is it?' And she said, 'You go bad place. Lion you cannot see will eat you.'"

We laughed, and I understood why Nick had said it was both funny and sad.

"I'll bet those kids are really going to miss you," I said.

Jamie grabbed my hand. "That's why Nick and I are so anxious for you two to take over."

"Hey," Nick said, "this is probably a stupid question to ask a couple in the throes of atavism, but did you hear what happened

Saturday?"

Mike and I shook our heads.

"No, of course not. Nixon fired Archibald Cox, the special prosecutor—he wouldn't settle for edited tapes."

"Can he just fire him like that?" I asked.

"Probably not," Nick said, "but either way, Nixon's finished."

Jamie held up crossed fingers. "We can only hope. He also fired the attorney general and another guy—somebody big."

"Ruckelshaus," Nick said.

"Yes. Nixon canned him, too. The press is calling it the 'Saturday Night Massacre.'"

"How ... dramatic." I shuddered at the thought of our own Saturday night massacre and looked at Mike, but he wasn't making any personal connections.

"Who's Ruckelshaus?" he said.

The six of us talked about Watergate until Mike and I had to get back to work. And that evening we discussed our future, not because we wanted to, but because with Jack and Suzanne awaiting our decision, there was no more putting it off. We sat on the front steps of the lodge after dinner, as we sometimes did on quiet nights. It was a good place to listen to the river, to the laughter of the loons and the mating calls of moose from the far shore. And although it was too dark to see them, we could always hear large flocks of ducks overhead.

"I guess it's come down to the wire," Mike said. "What happens next?"

"What do you want to happen?"

Mike leaned back on his elbows. "Well, all day I've been thinking about teaching at Twin Rivers, and I think we should do it. I don't have any reason to go back to Chicago."

"Do you remember what you told me when we were driving up here? You said Kettle Falls was the end of the line."

"I was talking about the roads."

"Yes, but it isn't just the roads that end here—it's everything I've ever known, everything I used to believe in. I think it might be best if we didn't see each other for a while after we close the camp."

"I know that's what you think, Allie. I just don't understand it. You're mad at me, so your first impulse is to run away. What kind of solution is that?" Mike nudged me. "I know you still love me."

"Of course I love you," I said. "And I'm not *mad* at you. I just feel like I'm ... drowning."

Mike groaned. "I don't want to talk about Thin Bird, if that's where you're going."

"I know—it's *was*. But you look at what happened—you look at everything—in a way that doesn't allow for alternatives. You're doing it now. That's just who you are, Mike. But it takes up a lot of space sometimes, and it doesn't leave any room for the way *I* see things."

"And how do you see things?"

I hooked two fingers together. "Connected. I see things connected in time and connected to each other. But I also see them connected to something that makes them right or wrong, no matter what. A lot of what I believed in doesn't make sense anymore, but that still does."

"Every situation is different, Allie."

"Yes, but for you every situation means a different set of rules." I half turned so I could face him. "Or as you put it once, you just 'navigate by the stars.' That can't be the answer."

"Are you willing to bet our marriage on it?"

"I already have. That's why I thought it might be better if we were apart for a while. Maybe then I could figure it out."

"I think that's the worst idea you ever had."

Mike said this in a casual, off-hand way, as though he were telling me I'd missed a button, and I could tell from the look on his face that he was already thinking about something else, arranging and rearranging his thoughts, getting all the wrinkles out.

"In spite of everything that's happened," he said, "you like it up here, don't you?"

"Ye-es," I said warily. "Just listen to it. But it's a beautiful place that does ugly things to people. Sometimes, I feel like Mr. Kurtz."

Mike didn't take the bait. "You say you still love me, and I love you way too much to give up without a fight. So what about a compromise?"

"What kind of compromise?"

"Let's go to Twin Rivers and forget about Kettle Falls for a few months. Things will be different there. We can have a real life—a *married* life—and if you still feel the same way in the spring, then we can talk about divorce or whatever it is you want to do."

"I never said anything about divorce."

"I'm just reading between the lines," Mike said. "What about my idea—isn't it worth a try? Our lives will be completely different without this place hanging around our necks twenty-four hours a day. What do you say?"

"What about Stone Bear? When I think about him nosing around here, I'm not sure staying in Canada is such a good idea."

"To hell with Stone Bear. In a month this place will be under four feet of ice and snow, and he won't find it so interesting. How about it?"

I leaned forward and clasped my knees to my chest. "I can't decide if Twin Rivers would be a compromise or an attempt to delay the inevitable."

"Nothing is inevitable."

"I'll probably regret this," I said, "but okay—let's give it a try."

"Great!" Mike said. "That's wonderful! You won't be sorry. I promise."

"You can't promise something like that. How cold does it get up here?"

"I've never wintered over," he said, "but I know forty below isn't unusual."

"Forty below? Can I reconsider?"

"No—a deal's a deal."

"What if I'm a bad teacher?"

Mike put his arm around me. "After what you've done here, teaching will be a walk in the park."

"We'll have to tell Jack and Suzanne in the morning," I said. "What do you suppose is going on in Iran and Nigeria?"

"I haven't the foggiest, but I'll bet our government doesn't like it. I'm sure we'll read about it in the newspaper eventually."

"Is this meeting over?"

"Yes," Mike said, "and I couldn't be happier."

On the way back to the cabin, we held hands, and that night we made love like we actually meant it. And for the first time in several weeks, I didn't dream at all. I hoped that Mike was right about our having a "real" life at Twin Rivers. It would be nice to live like normal people, to eat dinner alone together, to have regular jobs. As Mike had said, it was worth a try. Plus, I had nothing to lose. That was the real reason I'd said yes.

The next day we told Jack and Suzanne, and they were delighted. So was Louie, who looked forward to having us as neighbors over the winter. He asked when we'd be leaving Kettle Falls, and we said in a week or so, whenever we finished buttoning up the camp.

On November second, the last guests left, and after we'd closed the outpost camps, we had our final meeting with McChesney at the Scotia Bank. I was a little apprehensive in light of Mike's creative bookkeeping, but it went fine, and McChesney thanked us repeatedly for seeing the season through. After that we cut the rest of the crew loose, and with only five of us in camp—Mike, Pop, Louie, Albert and me—we ate our meals together in the main dining room with Molly on the floor beside us. It took four long days to tie up all the loose ends, but by evening of the fourth day, the job was done, and the following afternoon, November 7, Pop and Albert left. They had planned to leave on the eighth, but there was a snowstorm headed in our direction, so they thought it best to go before they got caught in it.

Mike and I helped them load their cars, and we said our good-byes up at the gas pump, where Mike insisted they fill their tanks, courtesy of the Scotia Bank. Louie, who said he didn't do good-byes, remained in his cabin, but I'd seen him talking to Albert earlier, and he and Pop had stayed up late the night before, playing cards.

Molly didn't seem to like good-byes either, but she showed up after a few minutes. In the past two weeks Molly had been confused by the camp's dwindling population, and she spent most of her time trying to keep track of the few people who remained, especially me.

The four of us talked for a few minutes at the pump. Then I hugged each of them a long time, starting with Albert. Albert didn't know what to make of that and stood patiently in my embrace, his arms at his sides. Finally, he put one arm around my waist and gave me the tiniest little squeeze.

"It's been a great pleasure, Mrs. Bowman," he said.

"I'm going to miss you so much, Albert—you and your wonderful cooking. Could you please call me Allie just once before you leave?"

Albert's mouth worked nervously. "I'll miss you, too … Allie." Then he shook hands with Pop and Mike, got in his car and drove away.

"He's a good egg," Pop said, chuckling.

"*You're* a good egg." We hugged, and by then I was crying a little.

"Don't cry, Allie," he said. "We'll stay in touch. Remember, I'm the one person on this crew with a real address and telephone number."

"I know, Pop. I know."

"Michael," he said, "I don't think anybody—and that includes the late Mr. Zimmerman—could have run this camp any better than the two of you did. It was a good season."

"Thanks, Pop," Mike said as they shook hands. "I appreciate that."

"Remember to look in on Louie every once in a while."

We promised we would, and just before he got in his car, Pop reached down, gave Molly a pat on the head and said, "I wonder what I've got for a good dog like you." Then he reached in his pocket and pulled out a dog biscuit.

Pop was the kindest person I've ever known.

Chapter 27

t snowed that night, but it was hardly a blizzard. Most of the storm passed to the south of us, and what little snow we got was melting fast by mid-morning. By ten o'clock we'd packed the little squareback to its roof, and we were ready to leave, ready to drive seven miles down a washed-out gravel road to begin a new life or add a coda to the old one. Mike and I said good-bye to Louie—as much as he would permit us—and to Molly, who seemed to sense that something out of the ordinary was happening. It was very hard.

"You two be careful down there," Louie said. "Twin Rivers ain't no church social, eh."

"We'll be careful, Mom," Mike said.

"Don't sass me, Yank. Just watch your step."

"We'll come back to see you every chance we get," I said. "We're only a few minutes away."

"Well, if you're fixin' to come for dinner, you better do it before I'm down to nothin' but moose liver again. Your husband, he's pretty finicky, eh."

"I'm going to miss you, Louie," Mike said.

"Me, too, kid. But I'm gonna miss your wife more, eh. You'd best be goin'."

The two of them shook hands, and I gave Louie a hug. Then we drove away from the place that had been our home and our life for seven unbelievable months.

We were no strangers to Twin Rivers, but as we drove onto the reservation that morning, we were looking at our new home, and it was like seeing the place for the first time. Nick and Jamie had described Twin Rivers as a little piece of the Third World in the middle of Canada. And they were right.

One of the more striking things was the absence of trees. The reservation was about as far off the main road as Kettle Falls, but after the first mile, the landscape—more of a moonscape, really—was nearly devoid of vegetation. It was like entering a surreal version of some cheap Chicago subdivision—the kind where they cut down all the trees and name the streets after them. Except here all the trees had been cut for easy firewood, and there were only three streets—Cedar, Tamarack and Willow. The streets formed a perfect H, the top of which became two boat ramps that plunged into the Winnipeg River. Cedar and Tamarack, the two sides of the H, ran perfectly parallel, with Willow connecting them neatly in the middle. The roads made sense, but the houses were scattered all over the place, wherever the rocks were flat enough to accommodate them.

We didn't see many people, but there were dogs everywhere—dogs, discarded tires and empty oil drums, which rose into tottering mountains of red, yellow and blue. There were few dwellings on the reservation's outskirts, but as we approached the river, the number of houses increased geometrically, as though the water were a living principle that had caused them to cluster there. Almost all of them were blue. They had cheap plastic lap-siding that obviously shattered if it was struck by anything, because most of the houses had jagged, star-shaped holes in them that revealed the black fiberboard underneath. A metal chimney poked through every tar-paper roof, and the windows, mostly broken, were covered over with pieces of plywood.

Strangely, almost every house had fifteen feet of beautiful new sidewalk, but it didn't go anywhere. It ran straight and true from the front doors, then stopped in the middle of nowhere, often in the mud. There may have been front yards at one time, but over the years they had turned into overgrown gardens of junk, where old bedsprings, washing machines and even automobiles grew into rusty rows and hedges.

"I can't believe we're going to live in this shithole," Mike said.

"Well, look on the bright side. This job isn't like Kettle Falls— we can leave whenever we want."

"How about now?"

"Hey, this was your idea," I said. "Besides, it may not be so bad. Nick and Jamie liked it here."

"Nick and Jamie once lived on rice and rat meat for two weeks. They're hardly a fair test."

We parked on the back side of a large building that housed the school and infirmary. There were three little apartments that ran along the back of the building like motel rooms, all of them facing the river, and they were so close to the water there was barely room to park in front of them. We knocked on Jack and Suzanne's door, but no one answered.

"They're working," I said. "Let's go around to the infirmary. That's where Suzanne will be."

We went around the corner to the little infirmary and walked in, and we could hear Suzanne's voice behind a curtain that screened what was obviously the treatment room from our view.

"I don't think you need any stitches, Luther," she said. "But you definitely need a tetanus shot. Once we get your hand bandaged, I'll give you something to put on it, and I need you to apply it three times a day. I want you to come back and see me on Thursday, so we can make sure this wound doesn't infect."

"It hurts like hell, eh."

"I know it does," Suzanne said, her voice soothing and professional. "But you can't expect to run a fishhook through your hand and not have it hurt, can you, Luther?"

"I dunno."

"Yes, you do, and you're going to be just fine. Roll up your sleeve."

A few minutes later, the unfortunate Luther emerged from behind the screen, elevating his bandaged hand. He nodded at us on his way out the door. Then Suzanne came out holding a badly bent treble hook that must have been four inches long.

She saw us and smiled. "I'm so glad you're here. Jack and I will never be able to thank you."

"There's no need to thank us," I said. "We're happy to be here."

Mike was looking at the fishhook. "What was he trying to catch with that? It looks like a grappling hook."

"He said something like *kenojay*," Suzanne said, "but I don't know what it means."

"*Ginoozhe*," Mike said. "It means 'jackfish.' Can I see that?"

Suzanne handed him the fishhook. "Does the *Ginoo* part mean 'Jack'?"

"I don't think it works that way."

"Too bad," she said. "I like the sound of it. We should tell him you're here. Jack has the fourth and fifth graders right now. He'll be very glad to see you."

The school was just down the hall from the infirmary. Basically, it was three classrooms separated by partitioning curtains, one of which had been pushed open. Jack was writing on the chalkboard, his back to us, explaining something to about twenty students who were quietly watching him. We stood just inside the doorway.

"Excuse me, Mr. Kohl," Suzanne said. "Our new teachers are here."

Jack turned around and smiled. "Excellent! Be right with you."

The children stared at Mike and me intently, and Jack handed the chalk to a teenage girl. "Marie, would you please take over?" Then he excused himself and joined us in the hallway, shaking our hands as though he hadn't seen us in years. "Am I ever glad to see you two. I've been running the school in three shifts since Nick and Jamie left. I've even had Suzanne helping out in the afternoons."

"How many kids go to school here?" I asked.

"Oh, about seventy on a regular basis," Jack said. "It makes for three nice classes. Our enrollment will go up when winter comes." He looked at Suzanne. "Anybody in the infirmary?"

"Not right now."

"Good. Let's go back to our place for a few minutes."

On the way to their apartment, Jack suggested—in fact, insisted—that we move into the nurse's apartment, which had been empty all year. It was directly behind the infirmary, and Jack pointed out that because it was on a corner, it had more windows and a much nicer view. He was really selling it. Mike and I said we could just move into Nick and Jamie's old place, but Jack was strangely adamant and finally admitted that it would improve his and Suzanne's sex life considerably to have Nick and Jamie's empty apartment between us as a buffer.

"These interior walls aren't insulated, you know," he said. "It sure as hell didn't matter to Nick and Jamie, but you know how they were about stuff like that."

Mike laughed. "I sure do. We'll stay wherever you want."

"Where do these doors go?" I asked.

Suzanne pointed to the nearest one. "That's the laundry room. The other one is storage. This is the back door to our place right here."

We entered Jack and Suzanne's apartment through the kitchen and sat down at the table. Jack, who hadn't stopped smiling since we got there, got us all a cup of coffee.

"I can't tell you how happy I am to have you on the payroll," he said. "Please tell me you can start tomorrow?"

"Tomorrow's fine," Mike said. "All we have to do is move in, and that won't take an hour."

"Who's teaching what?" I asked.

Jack was primed and ready. "Here's what I was thinking. I've had grades six through eight all year, so I should stick with 'em. Jamie had first and second grade, and since those kids are used to being taught by a woman, I thought that would be a good place for you. Mike can have Nick's kids—the third, fourth and fifth graders. Sound okay?"

"That's fine by me," Mike said.

"Me, too," I said. "Isn't there any school here after eighth grade?"

Jack shook his head. "On most reservations if a student completes eighth grade—and not many do—the parents receive a stipend from the government. There isn't much inducement to send a child to school after that."

"Jack, I'm really nervous about this," I said. "What do I *do*?"

"Well … the first thing you'll do is clean the kids up and give them something to eat every day when they get to school. Then you look them over for cuts and bruises—signs of abuse—which you report to me. As for what you teach, it's the alphabet for the youngest kids, reading with the others. You'll tell stories, sing songs, do a little geography, a little arithmetic—nothing fancy." Jack looked at me and smiled. "Allie, anything you can teach these kids will be something they don't know. You have a background in art, so have them draw a lot. Just do whatever works."

"There's no curriculum?"

"*You're* the curriculum."

Mike, his eyes widening, looked at Jack. "Do we at least have materials to work with?"

"Sure," Jack said, "but it's sort of a hodgepodge. I mean you have books, but probably not enough of any one edition to go around. The government sends us whatever they don't need anymore. That's how it works out here."

My face must have mirrored my fear, because Suzanne said, "Don't worry, Allie. It's not as bad as it sounds. You'll do just fine." It was the same reassuring voice I'd heard coming from behind the curtain in the treatment room.

"I hope so. I'm really scared."

Jack was sort of stroking his chin. "Tell you what I'll do. I'll give you my teaching assistant—the girl you saw helping me in there. Her name is Marie Pale Wolf. At least it was—she changes it every week. She's very bright, and her brother Rennie will be one of your students. With Marie to help you, you won't have any problems."

"Thank you. I accept."

Mike stuck out his lower lip. "Don't I get an assistant?"

"Sorry, buddy," Jack said. "You and I gotta tough it out—assistants are in short supply."

"Oh, I almost forgot." Suzanne got up from the table and returned with a large scroll. "Nick and Jamie wanted you guys to have this."

"What is it?" I asked.

"A poster. They said it was one of their favorites."

The four of us talked until Jack had to get back to his kids, and then Mike and I checked out our apartment. Mike had barely set foot in it when he said, "This place has all the charm of a dentist's office."

"Or an operating room."

He closed his eyes and sniffed. "You're right—it smells sort of like a hospital."

It smelled exactly like a hospital, due to its shared wall with the infirmary—one of those uninsulated walls that Jack had just told us about. It wasn't a bad smell. It was just wrong. It was the lifeless smell of sterility, and it wafted in from the infirmary because it had nowhere else to go.

"I guess we'll get used to it," I said. "I'm more concerned about the lack of color. It's so ... *white* in here."

"White" was an understatement. The apartment was a lustrous, icy alabaster—the walls, ceilings, appliances, counter tops—everything but the carpet. The carpet was blue, but that only made the place seem colder—and whiter.

"When we get a chance, we'll have to paint it," Mike said.

"In the meantime, this might help." I unfurled the poster and held it up. "What do you think?"

Mike did a double take. "Che Guevara? Great! Maybe we can get Ho Chi Minh for the bedroom."

"I like his beret," I said. "And unless you help me put this up, I'm going to get you one just like it. The red will break up the arctic feel of the place."

"Fine," Mike said, "but I'm not as big on Che as the Ralstons are. They probably left him behind rather than explain him to the CIA in Iran."

"Their life is a bundle of contradictions."

"Whose isn't? I'm gonna back the car up to the door so we can unload it."

I would eventually learn that the entire complex in which we were living was modular. It was a "gift" from the Canadian government that had arrived on a caravan of flatbed trucks from Thunder Bay and been bolted together in less than a week. It was a model of architectural functionalism, which went a long way, I thought, toward explaining its sameness, as well as our white apartment. The commissary, the community center and the post office were the same sort of prefab structures, and while all four buildings were perfectly adequate—perhaps even nice—they looked peculiar amid all the blue houses.

When we'd finished moving in, our apartment was nearly as white as before, but it had begun to acquire the feeling of home, if not the smell. We never won that battle. But years later it made me appreciate Marcel Proust in a new way. Proust wrote that smells are like resilient souls that linger in our memory long after everything else is broken and scattered. He's right. Even today, if I'm visiting someone in the hospital, one whiff of the lobby takes me back to Twin Rivers and the white antisepsis of our apartment.

Chapter 28

ater that first afternoon, Jack took us to meet Roy Charging Moon, chief of the Twin Rivers Ojibwe. According to Jack, it was a matter of etiquette that could not be breached, so when the students were dismissed for the day, the three of us walked over to the chief's house. He lived on a little rise near the river, so he had one of the nicer views, but his house was the same as every other on the reservation, except that none of its windows had been broken, which I assumed was owing to his office.

"How should we address him?" I asked. "Do we call him 'Chief' or 'Your Highness' or what?"

"For white people," Jack said, "'sir' or 'Chief,' is best. Charging Moon is a very smart guy. You'll know you're in the presence of a leader."

I found Chief Charging Moon to be pleasant, soft-spoken and very dignified. He was about seventy years old, well over six feet, and he wore his gray hair in a ponytail that reached nearly to his waist. Resting low on his aquiline nose was a pair of half-glasses, and after a few minutes, I noticed one of the lenses was missing.

Jack introduced us, and the three of us sat on the sofa opposite the chief's dilapidated easy chair. There was no other furniture in the living room and only worn linoleum on the floor. Overhead, a single light bulb dangled by its cord from the ceiling.

"*Bowman*," the chief said. "I like your name, eh. It is an Ojibwe name. Did you know that?"

"No, sir," Mike said.

"In our language it is *mitigwaabi inini*—man with a bow. Mr. Kohl tells me that you are Americans. From what American city do you come?"

"From Chicago, sir."

"*Ah*, the Windy City. There are many Indians in Chicago, eh. Mostly Mohawk, I believe. They build your skyscrapers. Have you seen our people up there, scraping the sky?"

"I have, sir," Mike said. "They're called high-steel workers. I understand they have no fear of heights."

"I have heard that, too, Mr. Bowman. The Mohawk, they are a proud people—it is depths, not heights, that frighten them. But how strange and wonderful, eh—to have no fear of that which can destroy you. I myself dislike even standing on a step stool, but then, I am old." Charging Moon touched his fingertips together. "Tell me, Mr. Bowman, what will you teach our children?"

The question came out of nowhere, but Mike seemed ready for it. "I hope I can teach them to think, sir. A student who thinks will never stop learning."

"And you believe in learning?"

"Yes, sir. Very much."

Charging Moon smiled. "Young people always believe in learning. They rush through life so hard, eh—there is so much to learn. It was no different with me. But now that I am old, I think we must *un*learn. Then we must *re*learn. It is like untying and retying a knot, and we must do it many times before we know a thing truly." Charging Moon chuckled and gave a slight wave of his hand. "Pay no attention to me, Mr. Bowman. I would have you believe that old age and wisdom are one, eh. Such is not the case, I assure you."

Most of Chief Charging Moon's questions during the brief interview probed our reasons for having taken the jobs there, which, by his silent nodding, I think we explained satisfactorily. When Charging Moon stood up, indicating that the interview was over, we jumped to our feet.

"In my grandfather's time," he said, "and even in my father's, our education came in dreams, eh. But that is no longer the thing it was, and the dreams, they are different now. I tell Mr. Kohl that education is a path." He was looking at me. "Does that make sense to you?"

"Sir," Jack said, "the Bowman's are highly educated. In fact—"

"I was speaking to Mrs. Bowman. She has said very little, eh— the sign of an excellent teacher. Do you understand what I mean, Mrs. Bowman, about education being a path?"

"I think so, sir. Education is a path that leads … to the future."

Charging Moon helped me with my coat. "Yes, that is true. But like all paths, it leads in two directions, eh. It is good to teach our children about the future but also good to teach them about the past. Remembering is part of learning. Do you not think so, Mrs. Bowman?"

"I do, sir, and we'll do the best job we know how."

"I know you will, and if I can be of service, please come see me again. My power is limited, but it is still power, eh."

As the three of us were walking back to our apartments, Mike said, "You're right about Charging Moon. He's an unusual man."

"He was educated by the Jesuits at Spanish River," Jack said, "and his ancestry goes all the way back to Chief Hole-in-the-Day. If you're Ojibwe, that's a very big deal."

"I liked what he said about education being a path," I said. "A path that leads in two directions."

Jack chuckled. "And Charging Moon has to walk both of them at the same time. Half of this reservation—and the more influential clans—wants to return to the days of the birchbark canoe and the bow and arrow. The other half thinks Charging Moon is right to embrace the future. It's a delicate balancing act."

Mike and I got up very early the next morning for our first day of school and were in our classrooms an hour before the students arrived. I wrote my name on the blackboard, which seemed very safe and professional, and then made sure I had enough milk and soda crackers for my students when they arrived.

"Why crackers?" I had asked, and Jack explained that we had crackers because that's what Diane had sent. She always sent milk, but it might be accompanied by crackers one week, melba toast the next and hotdog buns after that. According to Jack, there was no rhyme or reason to anything Diane did, and he complained about her daily, blaming her for everything that Twin Rivers lacked and for everything she sent us that was of no real use, like twenty thousand tongue depressors or fifty bottles of Dramamine. The mere mention of her name seemed to raise Jack's blood pressure, so I avoided the subject as long as I could. Then, one morning in desperation, I asked him if Diane might be willing to send me a few boxes of crayons.

"You don't have to call her," I said. "I'll do it myself. Just give me her number in Thunder Bay."

Jack had looked very confused, and then he began to laugh. "It isn't *Diane* who sends our supplies. It's D-I-A-N-D, the Department of Indian Affairs and Northern Development."

It was all very funny and reminded me of the time I'd listened to my first hockey game in French.

On that first day, my assistant, the young girl I'd seen helping Jack, arrived a half-hour early. She walked into my classroom, self-assured and pretty, holding the hand of her little brother. She had beautiful long hair, which she parted in the middle, and her face—the high cheekbones, the dark, almond-shaped eyes—reminded me of Gauguin's Tahitian women. Except this girl had clothes on. And makeup.

"Good morning, Mrs. Bowman," she said in perfect, uninflected English. "I'm so happy to meet you. My name is Marie Wolf—well, that's not exactly true. Actually, my name is Marie *Pale* Wolf, but I don't like those adjective-noun reservation names, do you? The Kohls have told me so much about you. I love that you're American, and I was so excited to hear you're a college graduate. This is Rennie, my half-brother. He's an introvert. Is that the right word?"

I'm sure I stood there with my mouth open, overwhelmed by this girl and the machine-gun cadence of her speech. "The right word? Yes, yes."

Marie shook my hand vigorously, but Rennie wanted none of it and retreated behind his sister, studying me with large, curious eyes. He was a cute little boy with a button nose and what my mother used to call a pumpkin-shell haircut.

"Don't you want to shake hands with me, Rennie?" I said.

He squirmed and buried his head in his sister's sleeve.

"Rennie's a little shy and ... *aloof*," Marie said. "But he'll come around once he gets to know you—won't you, Rennie?"

But there was no sign of assent from Rennie, who was pretending, or perhaps wishing, he were invisible.

"Marie, your English is excellent. How old are you? Eighteen?"

"Thank you," she said. "I've worked very hard on my English, and my accent is almost gone. I'm seventeen, but I've always been very precocious. Is that the right word?"

"Yes—and you certainly are."

Marie beamed. "I'm not really from here, Mrs. Bowman. I was

born at Twin Rivers, but my father died of tuberculosis when I was little, and after that my mother and I moved to Kenora—she got a really good job at the hospital. I even went to Beaver Brae High School for two years." The thought of it made her smile.

"That explains some things," I said.

"I hope you don't think I'm bragging, but I had the largest vocabulary of any student in my grade. They gave us a *grueling* test."

"And now you're my student, as well as my assistant. I don't know what I can teach you."

"Everything," Marie said. "And I'm so excited, because all three of my teachers this year are college graduates, and Mr. and Mrs. Ralston were college graduates, too, so that makes six college graduates I've met this year, and we almost never get college graduates at Twin Rivers, especially Americans, because all you have to do to teach here is complete a six-month program." Marie drew a much needed breath. "It's such a sham. Is that the right word?"

"Yes, I suppose it is," I said. "But if you were attending school in Kenora, why did you come back here?"

Marie looked away.

"I'm sorry. I didn't mean to pry."

"No, it's okay. It's not a secret or anything. Before we moved to Kenora, my mother got involved with a man here at Twin Rivers—Thomas Red Feather—and he—"

"*Nimbaabaa,*" Rennie said.

"Yes, Rennie—your father." Marie rolled her eyes. "They had Rennie when I was ten, but my mother finally left him, thank God. That's when we moved into town. It was hard, though, because Thomas wouldn't let Rennie come with us. He didn't want Rennie around white people."

"*Nimbaabaa.*"

"That's right, Rennie." Marie looked at me and whispered, "His *baabaa* is a real asshole." Then she clapped her hand over her mouth. "I'm sorry, Mrs. Bowman."

"No problem," I said, laughing. "That was probably the right word, by the way."

Marie nodded. "Anyway, my mother got laid off at the hospital and went to Winnipeg looking for work. Rennie still lives with his father, and I came back here to live with my grandmother—and to keep an eye on this little troublemaker." She threw one arm around Rennie and held him in a playful headlock. Rennie tried to wriggle away but not very hard.

"Well, I'm grateful that you're going to help me out for a while," I said. "I've never taught school before. I don't know what to do—not even the first thing—and the kids will be here any minute."

"We'll do it together. First, we'll wash their faces and check for lice. Then we'll have milk and whatever. After that we'll sing our song and—"

"Song?" I asked in horror. "I have to *sing*?"

"The children learn a song from a different country every two weeks. This week it's 'The Kookaburra.' After that, you should tell everyone about yourself. They love stories, especially if they can ask questions. Then we should continue with our geography. They must learn the names of our ten provinces and three territories and eventually all the port cities. They're also learning colors, the days of the week, and how to tell time. For the *coup de grace*, we'll read them a story. Is that the right word?"

And that's pretty much what Marie and I did on my first day of school. By three o'clock, when the children were dismissed, I felt as though I'd been pulled through a knothole. But everything had gone well enough, I thought, except for when I'd greeted my class initially.

"*Aanii*, Mrs. Bowman *ndish nikaaz*," I had said, introducing myself. "*Aniish na?* How are you?"

I had worked very hard to learn a few Ojibwe phrases at Kettle Falls, and it seemed like a nice thing to do—to address the children in their native language. But before I'd even finished, Marie was glowering at me from the back of the room. Later that day she explained why.

"It is *imperative* that we speak only English here at school, Mrs. Bowman. Ojibwe will keep the children on this reservation forever."

"Okay, Marie," I said. "Never again, I promise." But when Marie and Rennie were heading out the door to go home that afternoon, I couldn't resist. "Hey, Marie, *gigawabamin nagutch.*"

Marie looked over her shoulder and smiled like an indulgent parent. I expected her to say I was intractable or some such thing, but all she said was, "Yes, until later."

That evening Mike and I compared notes, and both of us agreed that teaching was a good deal harder than we'd expected.

Mike had collapsed on the sofa. "I think the trick is to do something different about every forty-five minutes. That's all the attention span a little kid has."

"Yes, but it takes a lot of planning and organization to do that many different things."

"Especially with so few resources," he said. "My God, I can't feel my feet. I haven't been on concrete for seven months."

We had a phone in the apartment, and that night I called my mother. It was a radio phone, like the one at Kettle Falls, but it was more sophisticated, so we didn't have to say "over" every time we finished a sentence. That made my mother happy. We had written to each other often while Mike and I were at Kettle Falls, but we tried to avoid using the "overphone," as my mother called it.

I told her that Mike and I had arrived at Twin Rivers, and I kept everything so upbeat that, when we ended our conversation, she thought Mike and I were real teachers in a real school. She didn't know anything about Hap and Jimmy, other than what a friend from Chaumont had written in a letter, which was that the two of them spent a lot of time in court suing each other. I suspected some of it had to do with the point, but I didn't allow myself to think about that.

Chapter 29

We'd been at Twin Rivers a little less than a week when I heard a car one evening and looked out to see Louie pulling up in the jeep with Molly in the passenger seat. Molly looked very confused, but Louie just looked cold, even though he was wearing a parka. Mike let them in, and Molly, whimpering with excitement, jumped up and began licking my face.

Louie pushed back his hood. "Smells like a hospital in here, eh."

"Never mind about the smell," Mike said. "It's good to see you. Isn't it kind of cold to be riding around in an open jeep?"

"Damn right it is." Louie blew on his fingers. "But everything else in camp has 'Kettle Falls Lodge' painted on it, eh. I ain't gonna park anything around here with *that* on the side. We lost a truck in here once."

"It's wonderful that you and Molly decided to pay us a visit," I said. "Let me take your coat."

"This ain't exactly a social call, Allie. I came to see if you could keep Molly, eh. All that poor critter does from morning 'til night is run around camp lookin' for you. She doesn't sleep. Hell, she won't even eat. I was hopin' you'd take her—I brought her food, eh."

I knelt down and took Molly's head in my hands. "Oh, Molly, that's so sad. We can have a dog here, can't we, Mike?"

Mike looked at the two of us and laughed. "There's a thousand of them on this reserve already. I can't see where one more would hurt anything."

"Good," Louie said. "Then it's settled, eh. The other reason I'm here is to tell you that Stone Bear paid me a little visit, day before yesterday."

"What did he want?" Mike and I said together.

"I dunno for sure. He asked where you were, and I told him, eh. I wish to hell I hadn't, but I just wasn't thinkin'. He asked if he could take another look around, and I told him to get the hell out."

Mike shrugged. "I don't care if he knows we're here. We aren't breaking any laws. Not anymore."

"I just thought you oughta know, eh. Everything okay here?"

"Yes," I said. "It's strange but nice."

"Hope you're stayin' put after dark, eh."

"We are," Mike said. "We were told not to go out at night without an Indian escort."

Louie gave a little snort. "*Police* escort's more like it. Say, I was kinda hopin' you'd offer me a drink."

"I would," Mike said, "but there's no liquor allowed at Twin Rivers."

Louie laughed. "Maybe so, kid, but I expect you're the only one livin' here that ain't got any."

After only half an hour, Louie said he had to be getting back to camp. Molly investigated every nook and cranny of the apartment and slept happily on the bed that night between Mike and me. At one point, though, she began to twitch and whimper in her sleep, so I reached over and gave her leg a shake. She sighed deeply and never made another sound.

I kept Molly on a leash at first because I was worried about all the other dogs, but after a couple days I realized she'd have to work that out for herself, and I let her loose.

After a while, I found that she was almost always in the company of the same three or four dogs, all of which looked so lean and hungry that we frequently fed them, too. I hadn't been aware of a social order among the reservation dogs before, but now I noticed that most of them traveled in little clutches that were surprisingly stable. They were like people in a city—there were a lot of them, but it was really just a collection of little groups.

Our new life at Twin Rivers was quite an adjustment, and it was two weeks before Mike and I had enough energy at the end of the day to carry on a conversation, let alone to make dinner or do laundry without falling asleep in the process.

In my classroom—after we'd constructed everything imaginable out of tongue depressors—I found myself spending more and more time on reading, which was difficult, because I was forced to use two different books. Half of my class was learning to read with Dick, Jane and Spot, while the other half struggled with British books featuring their opposite numbers, David, Dora and Nip. But my students found it impossible to identify with the neatly dressed, rosy-cheeked children in the books, so I eventually quit using them and tried other strategies. I think I was teaching an alphabet-based version of phonics, but because I didn't really know what phonics was, I was never sure.

From our discussions, it sounded as though Mike was spending a lot of time on math and science, and one evening over dinner he said in frustration, "Can you imagine trying to explain the mechanics of rainfall to a group of children who believe that a turtle and a muskrat teamed up to save mankind from the Great Flood?"

"Does that make any less sense than a story about a man who builds a boat and fills it with pairs of animals?"

"Not a bit. But it's a question of common currency. Life would be a lot easier if we all disbelieved the same story."

I started to laugh. "You'll have to explain that."

Mike laughed, too. "There was a point in there someplace, but ... I forgot what it was."

Most evenings Mike and I would talk about school or goings-on at Twin Rivers, but since we now had a more serviceable telephone, we could also stay in touch with the outside world. All we had to do was use the phone as a radio to reach an operator in Kenora, who would then do something on her end that turned the radio into a conventional phone. And instead of squawking when there was an incoming call, like the phone at Kettle Falls, our new phone had a familiar ring which, when I heard it for the first time, made me realize how much I'd missed that sound.

One evening the phone rang and it was Paula. She had met someone or, as she put it, *met* someone. She was deliriously happy, and whenever Paula was happy or excited, she talked so fast it was hard to understand her. I kept hearing the words "work" and "umbrella," but beyond that I was totally lost.

Finally, I said, "Zee, I'm so happy for you, but please slow down. Does he work at Marshall Field's? Is that where you met him?"

"Yes," she said. "I mean, no. I mean *I* was at work, but he was on his way to work. My God, Allie, he works at First Chicago, and it was raining—coming down in *buckets*—and I was headed to women's sportswear when this soaking-wet guy comes up to me and asks where he might find the umbrellas—jeez, even wet he was cute—and he said all his life he'd sworn he would never be an umbrella person, but this morning had changed his mind, so I asked him what was wrong with umbrella people, because Chicago is full of umbrella people—"

"So was it love at first sight?" By then I was laughing and nearly as excited as Paula.

"It was! It really was. That was two weeks ago, and we've seen each other almost every day since."

"What's his name?"

"Jerry Kaczmarek—he's Polish, just like me. My father's thrilled, naturally."

"Tall, dark and handsome?"

"Of course."

"That's wonderful, Zee."

And it was. When I hung up the phone, I was lonesome for her.

But Marie Pale Wolf—a continual source of amazement— helped take the edge off. After the first week Marie calmed down considerably and realized she could impress me even if she reined in her vocabulary, which she made an honest effort to do. At the end of my second week, her brother Rennie spoke to me for the first time. Marie and I were grading papers, and I'd just asked her what she planned to do with her life. But before she could answer, Rennie, who was playing with some blocks at her feet, said something that sounded like "an ape in Haiti."

"What did you say, Rennie?" I asked. But Rennie wouldn't repeat it.

Marie laughed. "He said 'an airplane lady.' I want to be a stewardess, but Rennie can't say that."

"That's a terrific idea, Marie. Is it something you've always wanted to do?"

"Since I was fourteen—that's when I got to ride in an airplane. It was amazing! Everything looked so different, so beautiful. And the reservation seemed … tiny and unimportant. I wanted to stay up there forever." Marie sighed, and her expression became wistful. "Anyway … that's when I decided to become a stewardess."

"Airplane lady," Rennie said.

"That's right, Rennie." She put her hand on his head. "An airplane lady in a pretty uniform who flies all over the world."

"And what will the name tag say on that pretty uniform?"

Marie drew a line on the paper she was grading, then put her pencil down. "It won't say 'Pale Wolf,' that's for sure. I've pretty much decided on just 'Wolf,' but I was thinking I might put a gratuitous 'e' on the end. Is that the right word?"

"It's a stretch," I said. "You're talking about a silent 'e.' Maybe you could double the o's, like Virginia Woolf."

"Who's she?"

"A writer."

Marie made a face. "I don't think I want to double the o's. Almost every word in Ojibwe has double vowels. It takes four o's just to say hello—*boohzoo*."

"*Boohzoo gegin.*"

"*I'iw ate aapiji*," Marie said. "Very good—but please stop."

Rennie had quit playing with his blocks and was staring up at us. "*Gwa nan da abahmidimon? Anish ougi ojibwemunug?*"

I looked at Marie.

"He asked what we're talking about, and he wonders why we're speaking Ojibwe—and so do I." Marie looked down at him. "It's nothing, Rennie. Never mind."

"Rennie seems comfortable enough speaking in Ojibwe," I said. "I don't think he dislikes speaking as much as he dislikes speaking English."

"Rennie, would you please wait for me in the hall?" Rennie did as he was asked, and when he'd left the room, Marie became very serious. "It doesn't matter whether Rennie likes to speak English or not, Mrs. Bowman. He *has* to speak it. His father, Thomas Red Feather, is the problem, not English. He wants Rennie to be an Indian."

"But Rennie *is* an Indian."

Marie closed her eyes. "You know what I mean. Thomas won't even let him speak English at home."

"And we won't allow him to speak Ojibwe at school," I said. "Poor Rennie—he can't win. He'll forget his own language before he ever learns mine. That isn't fair."

Marie gave me a look, mostly of frustration, then swept her hair over both shoulders with the backs of her hands. "You don't understand, Mrs. Bowman. What isn't fair is what Rennie's life will become if he doesn't learn English. Without it, he'll end up just like his father—stuck on this reservation, spraying hair spray into a paper bag and breathing the fumes because he can't afford whiskey and because he can never leave."

"That isn't fair, either. But if Rennie's father doesn't want him educated, why send him to school? Is it the stipend?"

"Mostly. And to get rid of him during the day."

I looked out the window at the blue houses. "I'm beginning to see why everyone here is so suspicious of us—we're destroying their culture. It's no wonder we can't go out at night."

"That isn't why," Marie said. "It's because a lot of people here are like Thomas—they hate your world because it's better than their world. They're dumb and they're mean and they're bigoted. Is that the right word?"

"I'm not sure," I said. "They aren't bigots just because they resent people who are paid to help them forget they're Indians. They aren't bigots for wanting to be who they really are."

"But don't you see? There's no place left where they can be who they really are—not even this place." Marie was uncomfortable arguing with me. She picked up her pencil and tried to get back to work. "I'm sorry, Mrs. Bowman. It just seems so obvious to me—if who you are isn't working, then you have to become someone else."

"I don't know, Marie. We can choose a lot of things, but not who we are."

She shook her head. "I don't believe that—I can't. We are who we *become*."

When I told Mike at dinner that night about my conversation with Marie—and its paradoxical tensions—he was in Marie's corner, which surprised me.

"Everyone on this reservation should do whatever it takes to get the hell out of here," he said. "As for the cultural paradox, I wouldn't worry about it. This whole place is a paradox."

"In what way?"

Mike was buttering a piece of bread, but he stopped. "Well, if you look out our front window, you see one of the most beautiful rivers in the world, but if you walk out the back door, you enter a wasteland that would rival the slums of Calcutta. That's a paradox. I think you should listen to Marie Wolf or Pale Wolf or whatever her name is. She's the resident expert on Twin Rivers."

"I know," I said. "And she's very smart. I'm just not always sure she's right."

Mike gave me a sly little smile. "Any time you get tired of having an assistant, just tell Miss Gatsby she's welcome in my room."

"Not a chance," I said. "I couldn't do this without her. Besides, I think Marie and I are going to be friends."

Mike was right about Twin Rivers being a wasteland, but even so, it was good for me in certain ways. For one thing, I was generally too busy to think, and I wasn't dreaming as much. I was so tired after a day of teaching that I usually fell asleep the instant my head touched the pillow. The only exception was when I saw Stone Bear's truck one afternoon on my way home from the commissary. When I walked in the door, Mike was standing in front of the open refrigerator, staring at the shelves.

"I thought there was some tomato juice in here," he said.

"You might have to move something."

"Your buddy just left."

"Stone Bear?" I asked.

"No. Suzanne. Why would Stone Bear be here?"

"I just saw his truck."

"Don't worry about it," Mike said. "He's probably still looking for some connection he'll never find between Thin Bird and Kettle

Falls. Do we really need to keep the coffee in here?"

"What did Suzanne want?"

"She knows you're an Abbie Hoffman fan, so she wanted to tell you that a new judge dropped all the charges against him and the Chicago Seven."

"I'm not an Abbie Hoffman fan, but I'm pleased just the same. You're not worried that Stone Bear is here?"

Mike went to one knee. "Not at all. You want a glass of tomato juice? I know we've got some."

But other than my Stone Bear sighting, which cost me a couple nights' sleep, things went well, and I was beginning to think Mike might have been right about the promise of life beyond Kettle Falls. For whatever reason, teaching enabled me to relegate my problems to some nether region of my mind, at least during the week. Weekends were more difficult, but Mike and I always had plenty of school work to keep us busy.

It was almost Christmas before the blizzards came, and when they did, we had one storm after another. By New Year there was over three feet of snow on the flat, and Twin Rivers—along with a good deal of its ugliness and squalor—lay buried beneath it. That was a good thing.

What wasn't a good thing was the fact that I no longer had anywhere to rest my eyes. Everything was white, including, of course, our apartment, and the whiter it became outside, the more I detested it inside. I complained to Mike until he agreed to help me paint the place, but on the weekend we planned to do it, it snowed so much that we couldn't get to Kenora to buy the paint and brushes. The next weekend we had too much schoolwork, and the weekend after that it was something else.

So I found myself walking around our apartment like a penitent, my head bowed, my eyes on the carpet, which provided the only color in my world, other than Che Guevara, who stared imperiously from the living room wall. I think the smell became worse, too, but perhaps I only imagined it. Some days I felt as though I were living in a psychic storm cellar, waiting for the "all clear." Other days I felt like a patient in an asylum or a soul in purgatory, hoping to be cleansed, processed and shipped out.

Jack and Suzanne went to Sudbury for Christmas, so Mike and I spent much of our weeklong Christmas break with Marie, and the more I got to know her, the more I liked her. She was the only secondary student in the history of the school, and if Jack hadn't been a high school instructor in his former life, we wouldn't have known what to do with her. He taught her math and social studies; Mike handled most of the science, and Mike and I together assumed responsibility for her English. Marie had read the usual high school fare—plus everything on the reservation—so we let her read what few books we'd brought with us and those we were able to scrounge in the Kenora Library. She loved everything she read, and we could usually tell by her diction which author she was reading.

After Christmas break, one of the things I did in my classroom was introduce the students to children's stories from all over the world. I had twenty-five tattered copies of an anthology filled with them, but the twenty-five copies weren't the same edition. Both contained the same stories, but the versions of the stories were often different. Most of the time, though, this didn't get in the way.

What I'd do was have the class read a story together, then we'd talk about it. I also included a number of Ojibwe stories in our discussions, so that when we'd finished "Hansel and Gretel," for example, we might talk about "Wenabojo and the Birch Tree" or some other Ojibwe story that I had asked Chief Charging Moon or one of the tribal elders to tell me. Marie wasn't especially pleased with this, but she knew I was excited about it, so she didn't complain.

We did all the other things we were supposed to be doing, too, but I really liked the way these stories were working. Everything was fine until we got to "Jack and the Beanstalk." That's when the two editions—and two radically different versions of the story—became a problem, at least for me.

In both versions, Jack climbed the beanstalk three times and stole the same three things from the giant—a bag of gold coins, a chicken that laid golden eggs and a golden harp. And in both versions, Jack killed the giant, who was pursuing him as he fled down the beanstalk.

But in one edition, the giant had killed Jack's father, the original owner of the three items. In the other, there was no mention of this. So depending on which version my students were reading, Jack was either a legitimate instrument of justice or a thief and a cold-blooded killer. My students realized the accounts differed with respect to these details, but it didn't bother them the way it should have. It was, as they say today, a teachable moment; unfortunately, I couldn't get much traction on it.

"You can't just kill someone because he's a giant," I told them.

"Why not?" one little boy said. "He is like a windigo."

"And what is a windigo?"

"It is a monster made of ice."

"Isn't that quite a bit different?"

"It is the same," he said. "Windigos are giants."

That syllogism, which I was unable to defeat, worked perfectly for my students, who, for reasons of their own, were predisposed against giants. When I told Mike about all the problems I was having with the two versions of "Jack and the Beanstalk," he laughed.

"I don't know what your kids have against giants," he said. "But you're missing the point of the story."

"What do you mean?"

"You're treating it like an Aesop object lesson. 'Jack and the Beanstalk' is an old British allegory about the evolution of the middle class—there are a hundred of them just like it."

"You're making that up."

"No, I'm not. It's about money. Everything Jack steals is made of gold."

"So?"

"So there's an order to the thefts. The first thing a rising middle class seeks is wealth, so Jack steals a bag of gold. But in no time he and his mother are poor again, because what they really need isn't wealth—it's income. That's why Jack steals a chicken that lays an endless supply of golden eggs."

"And the golden harp? I can't wait to hear this one."

Mike thought about it for a moment. "Well ... the harp is the last thing Jack takes, and he wants it only after his material needs have been met. The harp is the possibility of culture and refinement that exists for the middle class once it achieves financial security."

"That's very clever," I said. "But your way of looking at it ignores the facts—the moral implications of what Jack does."

Mike was getting frustrated. "The so-called 'facts' don't matter—they're just a delivery system for the idea. Everything isn't always about morality, Allie. 'Jack and the Beanstalk' is about economics. Look at the big picture once in a while."

"Don't you mean *your* big picture—the one where everyone's allowed to paint outside the lines?"

"No, I mean ..." Mike shook his head. "What the hell did you ask me for?"

Chapter 30

It was so cold toward the end of January that the ground cracked—literally. The temperature fell to 48° below zero several nights, and there was an entire week when it never got above 25° below zero, even during the day. At those temperatures poplar trees explode, and we could hear what sounded like cannon fire on the far side of the river, the only side with trees on it. Twenty-five degrees below zero—fifty-seven degrees of frost—is more than a temperature. It's blunt-force cold that hits you in the solar plexus and doubles you over the moment you step outside. People scuttled from their blue houses to the commissary, then back again, in a defensive half-crouch, their breath hanging in the air like smoke.

We quickly learned that Twin River's prefab buildings weren't designed for temperatures like that. Our complex had electric heat, but we had to set the dials at "10" just to keep our apartment and classrooms above 60°. Yet as cold as it was, we never canceled school.

The first Monday in February, Marie and I were performing our "ablutions," as she called them, which meant we were getting the kids cleaned up before giving them milk and whatever. I was running a Q-tip around in the folds of Rennie's ear—something that never failed to make him giggle—when I felt a large bump on his head.

"Rennie, how did you hurt your head? You've got quite a lump there."

"Faw down," he said.

"He fell off a chair trying to reach something," Marie said.

"Faw down."

I forgot about it until the next week, when Rennie came to school with a black eye and puffy lip. I had Marie watch the class while I took him down the hall to the infirmary, where I caught Suzanne between patients.

"Suzanne, do you have a minute to check Rennie's eye? It looks like someone may have hit him."

"Sure," she said. "Rennie, let's get you up here." She lifted Rennie onto the exam table and had him sit on the edge while she shined a little light in his eye. "The retina is okay … I don't see any blood in there." Then she pulled up his shirt in back and motioned for me to take a look.

Rennie's back was covered with angry welts and bruises, some old, others more recent. I was practically ill.

"Okay, Rennie," Suzanne said. "You go on back to class now. I want to talk to Mrs. Bowman."

Rennie headed for the door, and as soon as he was gone, I said, "This is horrible! What do we do?"

"I'll tell Jack," Suzanne said, "and he'll have a talk with Rennie's father. The first step is to confront the parents."

"What if it doesn't work?"

"Then we'll try something else. There's a protocol for child abuse. I'll let you know what happens."

When I returned to my classroom, Marie seemed very nervous, and the first chance I had, I pulled her aside and told her what I'd just learned. I also asked her about the bump I'd noticed on Rennie's head the week before.

"He didn't fall off a chair, did he?"

Marie had trouble looking at me. "No, Mrs. Bowman, he didn't, and I'm sorry I lied to you. I just didn't want to get you involved. It's not like you can do anything."

"How do you know? Maybe I can. We have to try."

Marie shook her head. "This isn't anything new. It would be best if you stayed out of it." Her eyes were bright with tears, and as she turned and walked away, I had the feeling she was angry with me.

When I told Mike about it, he didn't have much to say. Mike hadn't seen any signs of abuse among his students so far, and he was hopeful it would stay that way for any number of reasons.

"Child abuse is a tricky issue, even in Chicago," he said. "It's probably ten times more complicated on an Indian reservation."

Even though Mike wasn't helpful, I knew Jack would do the right thing, and the next day he knocked on the back door of our apartment to let us know he'd spoken to Thomas Red Feather. I asked him to come in, and the three of us sat down at the kitchen table.

"So what did he say?" I asked. "Did he promise to stop beating Rennie?"

Jack looked down. "Not exactly. It's hard to talk to Red Feather—he doesn't speak English very well. Basically, he told me it was none of my business—none of my *fucking* business, to be precise."

"And what did you say?"

"I said if the abuse didn't stop, I'd contact the tribal police."

"*Biggie?*" I said.

"He's the law. He's actually been pretty effective at this sort of thing."

The police chief at Twin Rivers was a gentle giant named

Big-Too-Much Crow, but everyone called him "Biggie." Because he was a head taller than anyone else on the reservation, Biggie had been made chief of police, but small children followed him around as though he were the village idiot.

"If Biggie is the next step," Mike said, "why don't we go to him now?"

"It's better to give a warning first," Jack said. "I made it very clear to Red Feather that this has to stop. Who knows? Maybe it will."

"I hope so," I said.

The next day when Rennie came to school, both his eyes were black and there was a cut under his right ear.

"Oh, Rennie," I said, hugging him. "We're not going to let this happen to you anymore. I promise."

"Faw down," he said.

"I know, Rennie. I know. Everything will be all right."

But it wasn't. After Biggie had talked to Rennie's father without stopping the beatings, I went to Jack about the possibility of involving DIAND. When Jack wasn't teaching, he was usually in the tiny headmaster's office behind his classroom, and that's where I found him. When I walked in, he looked up and smiled from behind a desk covered with forms and papers.

"Thank you," he said. "Thank you for giving me a break from this tedium. You know, when I took this job, I had no idea there would be so much paperwork. Have a seat."

"Thanks. What are you working on?"

"Enrollment reports. Every week I have to report the number of students we have to DIAND so they can reimburse us. The money we get is based on a head count."

"What's our enrollment been?"

Jack leaned back and rubbed his eyes. "Oh, it's been hovering around eighty this winter. Of course I report it as being between eighty-five and ninety."

"Why would you misrepresent the number of students we have?"

He rubbed his thumb against two fingers. "For money. If I inflate the number of pupil units, we receive more funding for the school. That's how you got colored paper, crayons, finger paint—all those other things you wanted. That's how Mike got his new science books. Pretty soon, we'll have a little library because anything extra goes into a book fund."

"It's a shame we have to falsify reports in order to have a library." I was surprised not only by Jack's revelation but also by his nonchalance.

Jack shrugged. "So what's on your mind?"

"I wanted to ask you if there was anything DIAND could do to stop Red Feather from abusing Rennie. Could we talk to them about it?"

"We could." Jack picked up a paper clip and began straightening it. "But here's the problem. DIAND offers social services to the reservations, but they don't have a legal arm, so anything they proposed to Red Feather would be voluntary on his part. And DIAND would never take a child away from his biological father, if that's what you're thinking."

"Well, who would? What about the law? I mean the *real* law—the Department of Justice, the OPP, the Mounties?"

"Nobody on that list has any authority here," Jack said. "And not even the Department of Justice would be likely to remove a child from his home. The DOJ is very timid about that sort of thing, no matter what kind of home it is."

"And the real police?"

Jack tossed the mangled paper clip into his waste basket. "The OPP wouldn't have jurisdiction unless we were talking about a felony or a crime committed off the reservation. The Mounties couldn't do anything unless a federal crime was committed. The OPP and the Mounties would turn a reservation child abuse case over to DIAND."

"Who isn't empowered to do anything."

"DIAND would contact the tribal police," Jack said. "But ... we've already done that."

I shook my head. "To very little effect. Did you know that after Biggie had that little chat with Red Feather, he refused to give Rennie anything to eat for two days?"

"I had no idea." Jack was as frustrated as I was. He looked down at the clutter on his desk, then at me. "Allie, I wish we could throw Red Feather in jail where he belongs, but it's a vicious, bureaucratic circle. DIAND is relatively new, and where we are right now isn't Ontario or even Canada—it's Ojibwe land."

I didn't know where to turn after that, but the more I tried to stop Rennie's beatings, the more cool and reserved Marie became. I couldn't figure out what I had done to make her act that way, so one day during lunch I asked her.

Marie, expressionless, put her sandwich down and looked at me. "Mrs. Bowman, I don't know what to tell you. I know how much you want to help Rennie, but it's like I said—what's happening isn't anything new. People have tried to help before, but all they did was make it worse."

"What people?"

"The teachers who were here three years ago. I was living in Kenora with my mother, and I don't know exactly what they did, but it's probably the same things you're trying to do—things like going to the tribal police. But it only made Thomas angry—angry and crazier than he already was."

"But, Marie—"

"No, no, let me tell you what happened. Three years ago, my mother and I were delivering groceries to my grandmother, like we did every weekend when we lived in town. Ten minutes after we got here, Rennie walked in the door. He was covered with blood, and there was ..." Marie covered her face with her hands. "There was a bone sticking out of his arm."

I got up and put my arms around her. I could feel her shoulders shaking, and when she uncovered her face, she was crying.

"It was so awful," she said.

"That won't happen again, Marie. I promise."

Marie struggled to catch her breath. "Do you remember when I told you I wanted to be a stewardess?"

"Of course. You were in an airplane. You looked down and—"

"It was the air ambulance that took Rennie to the hospital that day. Rennie was on a stretcher, scared to death, and I was sitting beside him, thinking no matter what, I was going to get as far from this place as I could. I know you want to help, Mrs. Bowman, but just the opposite could happen. It's already happening." Marie started to cry again but not as hard as before. She picked up her napkin and dabbed her eyes. "So much for my mascara."

"Don't get it on your blouse. Here, let me." I took a kleenex from my pocket and wiped away the dark, streaky tears. "How long has Rennie's father been abusing him?"

"Maybe four years, off and on. That's the thing—he doesn't do it all the time. It's something that happens mostly in the winter, when Thomas can't get work or when he's high on something and starts worrying that Rennie is becoming a white boy." Marie tried to smile. "Because of you, Rennie loves school this year, and that's good—unless you're Thomas Red Feather."

I squeezed her hand. "Everything will be all right, Marie. But we can't just cross our fingers and hope the beatings stop. We have to make them stop."

"We might not be able to do that, Mrs. Bowman—that's what I'm trying to tell you. The more we interfere, the worse it could get for Rennie."

"We have to do something," I said. "Doing nothing is never the right thing."

"It is if it stops the beatings. Or keeps them from getting worse."

"But what if we did nothing and Rennie's father hit him one too many times and ... *killed* him? How could we live with ourselves, Marie?"

She nodded in a way that wasn't entirely convincing. "I just hope you know what you're doing."

"I do."

I told Mike about my conversation with Marie and asked him for help, but he didn't react the way I'd expected.

"I don't know, Allie," he kept saying. "I just don't know. It might be better if you stayed out of this one."

"I can't accept that," I said.

It was the next day that I decided to bring the matter to the attention of the tribal elders. I wasn't permitted to attend the monthly council meeting, but I met with several of the elders in their homes and explained the situation to them. Most were suspicious and had no desire to get in the middle of a domestic matter involving a man and his son. But Sam Yellow Hawk, the most receptive of the bunch, promised to speak with Rennie's father, which I thought was a lot better than nothing.

The result was another beating for Rennie.

Marie begged me to drop the matter, but it had gone too far for that. Marie said that whatever Red Feather's initial motives might have been for beating Rennie, he was now doing it to spite me, to show me that he could do whatever he wanted.

But I didn't believe it was that simple, and the idea of ignoring the situation was unthinkable. Rennie had received beatings before I came to Twin Rivers, and he would receive them long after I left— unless I could find a way to stop them.

In the end, I convinced myself that Marie finally agreed with me.

Chapter 31

In the middle of all my efforts to help Rennie, Officer Stone Bear showed up again, which was the last thing I needed. Since Louie had told him where we were, I'd been waiting for him to drop in on us, and in late February he did. Mike and I had just finished dinner when we saw him walk past the window on the way to our front door. Every muscle in my body tensed.

"Just our luck," Mike said. "Chief Bad Penny."

I jumped up from the table. "Every time I see him, I start shaking."

Stone Bear knocked on the door, and Mike let him in. "How's tricks, Stone Bear? Things a little slow over in Hollow Water?"

Stone Bear looked around the apartment, inventorying its contents. "I had business in Kenora, so I decided to come out and say hello, eh."

"Well, we're delighted you stopped by. I'd ask you to sit down, but you won't be staying that long."

"I got a little news for you, Yank. I found a man here at Twin Rivers who says he drove Thin Bird to Kettle Falls last June, eh. He couldn't remember exactly when, but he said there was a big storm that night. Said he waited for him a long time, but Thin Bird, he never came back, eh." Stone Bear stared into Mike's face, looking for something I knew he'd never find there.

"Maybe Thin Bird fell in the river and drowned," Mike said flatly. "Did you ever think of that?"

"Not even once, eh."

"Look, even if this guy at Twin Rivers did what he says he did, it doesn't make a damn bit of difference, and you know it. I've never seen Thin Bird, and you'll never find anyone who says I did."

Stone Bear was looking at the poster of Che Guevara. "You don't never know, eh. Who's that? He looks like an Indian."

"He's from Argentina. You wouldn't know him."

"I'm gettin' closer to you, Yank."

Mike laughed. "You sure are. All you're missing is evidence."

"That's gonna change, eh. Maybe it'll be somebody who saw somethin', or maybe it'll be somebody who gets pissed-up and talks too much. But I'm gonna get a break. I wanted you to know that."

Mike motioned him toward the door. "So long, Stone Bear."

"You shoulda left Canada a long time ago, Yank. I'm goin' back to Kettle Falls in the spring, eh, and I'm gonna find somethin'. I can feel it."

"Feel it all you want—there's nothing to find. None of the crew will ever be back, and we're leaving in the spring." Mike put his hand on the doorknob. "What are you gonna do for fun when we're gone?"

Stone Bear smiled. "It won't be as easy as that, Yank. You gotta cross the border, eh. I'm gonna make sure every port of entry has your plate number. You're a material witness."

"A witness to *what*?"

"How 'bout murder?"

"Take your best shot, Stone Bear," Mike said. "And get the hell out of our apartment."

"Be glad to. This place smells like a hospital, eh."

Stone Bear left, and we watched him through the window as he bent over in front of the squareback and wrote down the license number.

That really spooked me. "What did he mean? Did he just say we can't go back to the States? Can he do that?"

"He's just blowing smoke. He's afraid we'll leave, and he doesn't have anything linking us to Thin Bird. If he did, he would've gone to the Provincials."

I tried hard to believe that, and I might have worried more about Stone Bear if I hadn't been so preoccupied with Rennie.

One night I was tossing and turning in bed, and Mike said, "Which one is it?"

"What?" I mumbled.

"Who's keeping you awake—Thin Bird, Stone Bear or Rennie?"

"All three. Mostly Rennie."

Mike reached over and turned on the light. "I don't like your odds on that one. It might be time to fold the tent."

"I'm not going to stand by and do nothing while that little boy is abused. Remember what happened when *you* did nothing?" I felt instantly awful to have said it. "I'm sorry. I didn't mean that."

Mike, trying hard to keep his cool, propped himself up on one elbow. "Yes, Allie, I remember. But unless you're planning to *shoot* Red Feather, you're comparing apples and oranges. The whole thing with Rennie looks like a lose/lose proposition to me, and you're out of ideas—you said so yourself."

"Please turn off the light."

"Okay, I'm just afraid that—"

"I don't want to talk about it now."

But Mike was right. I'd done everything I could think of and come up empty. Then, in late March, I decided the high court of appeals in the matter might be Chief Charging Moon, so I went to see him one day after school. I didn't ask the tribal elders for permission, as I was supposed to, nor did I tell Mike or Marie where I was going.

"What a pleasure, Mrs. Bowman," Charging Moon said. "Do you come to hear the old stories? It is good to share them with the children, eh. Please sit. We will drink the Postum."

"Thank you, Chief."

We sat as we always did, with me on the sofa and him ensconced in his worn-out easy chair. On each of my visits, Charging Moon, with much fanfare, would make Postum and serve it in his best cups, the two that matched.

"Would you like to hear the story of Manabozho and the buzzard?" he asked. "It is one of my favorites, eh, and children always like it."

"Actually, sir, I've come to ask your help with a problem at school. I don't know where else to turn."

"You are wondering if I can get Thomas Red Feather to stop beating his son."

"Yes, sir, but how did you—"

"I am chief," Charging Moon said. "I hear everything. And the elders, they are like old women, eh. There are no secrets with them. I understand you have been very busy, Mrs. Bowman. You are like a spring bear, eh."

"Is it wrong of me to want Rennie's father to stop beating him?"

Charging Moon shook his head. "Such a thing could never be wrong. But Thomas Red Feather, he is a bad man, eh—a disappointed man. It is difficult to step between a man and his son, even a man like him."

"But, sir, there must be something we can do."

"What you really believe, Mrs. Bowman, is that there must be something *I* can do."

Embarrassed, I stared at the floor. "That's true, sir. I was thinking that because you're the chief, Red Feather would have to listen to you. Could you at least talk to him?"

"I could do as you ask, but it is very bad politics." Charging Moon looked into his cup and frowned. "As I told you when we met, my power, it is limited, eh."

"Yes, sir. I remember. Have you ever been asked to speak with Red Feather before, perhaps by teachers in the past?"

"The other teachers, they never came to me. The elders would not allow it. Yet this time they do. That puzzles me, eh." Charging Moon looked at me as though he were posing a question.

"I didn't ask the elders if I could discuss this with you, sir. I'm sorry."

Charging Moon laughed softly. "They will not be pleased. Then again, they cannot protect me from everything, eh." He pulled his glasses to the end of his nose and looked at me closely. "You must help me to understand something, Mrs. Bowman. With so much injustice here at Twin Rivers, how is it that you seize upon this problem and not another? The people say *boo ni tuun mah noo*— that you are like a dog with a bone, eh."

"I suppose I am, sir. And it's true there are a lot of problems here, but Rennie is one of my students. I feel like I have to do something."

"That much is clear, Mrs. Bowman."

Charging Moon folded his hands in his lap and closed his eyes. Neither of us spoke, and after two or three minutes I was beginning to think he'd fallen asleep. Then he opened his eyes and looked at me. "I will speak with Thomas Red Feather, but I must warn you there are no guarantees, eh. There is a saying among my people, Mrs. Bowman. 'The river is fast, but winter is patient.' Do you understand?"

"No, sir."

"It means the river may freeze, no matter how hard it tries not to."

"I understand that. I really do, sir. Thank you, Chief. I'm so grateful to you for helping."

I was zipping up my coat and must have looked puzzled, because Charging Moon said, "There is more you wish to say?"

"Oh, no, sir. Not really. I was … just wondering if I'm the fast river or the patient winter."

"That is up to you, Mrs. Bowman."

I was so excited when I left Chief Charging Moon's house that I could scarcely feel my feet on the path as I raced home to tell Mike. No one had ever asked for Charging Moon's help before, and I was sure Red Feather would listen to the chief. When I burst through the door, Mike was on the sofa, reading the *Miner*.

"Where did you go after school?" he said. "I lost track of you."

"I went to see Chief Charging Moon, and he agreed to speak with Rennie's father."

Before I'd even removed my coat, I told Mike the whole story. But by the time I'd finished, I knew something was wrong.

"I wish you hadn't done that," he said.

"But the chief could be the answer to everything."

Mike set the newspaper aside. "Or he could fail. You don't realize it, but you just backed Charging Moon and Red Feather into a corner—the *same* corner."

"That isn't true. I didn't force anyone to do anything."

"Sure you did. You put Charging Moon in a position where he has to act, and when he does, Red Feather will have to prove that nobody, not even the chief, can push him around. That's the kind of asshole he is." Mike's expression was commingled sadness and dismay. "Haven't you figured that out yet?"

I hung my coat in the closet and turned around slowly. "I was thinking that doing anything is better than doing nothing, which seems to be your solution."

"Allie, there *is* no solution. That's what I'm trying to tell you, but you're so hell-bent on saving the day that you can't see it. This has become an obsession with you."

"Why is it an obsession if I try to make a little boy's father stop beating him?"

Mike threw up his hands. "I don't know—you tell me. It's all you care about. You don't even eat any more. And now you've put Charging Moon's credibility on the line."

"Instead of criticizing everything I do, you should be helping me. Don't you care about what's happening to Rennie?"

"Of course I care." Mike got off the sofa and came over to me. "But I care more about what's happening to you. Plus, I don't know how to help Rennie. Nobody does." He tried to put his arms around me.

"I guess you don't know how to help me, either," I said, turning away.

I was so angry I didn't eat dinner that night, and I don't think I ever really slept. Trying to protect Rennie was the only right thing I'd done in months. What was wrong was the fact that Rennie was being beaten for liking school, for speaking English, for learning a few things about the world beyond Twin Rivers. Marie was scared because of what had happened before. I understood that. But I wasn't here then, and those who were had failed to enlist the help of Chief Charging Moon. He would be the difference this time.

Chapter 32

The next morning before school I told Marie that the chief had agreed to speak to Rennie's father, and she informed me he already had.

"How do you know that?" I asked, and she said at Twin Rivers everyone knew everything as soon as it happened, sometimes before. But Marie didn't share my confidence in the chief's ability to stop the beatings. When I tried to talk to her, she grabbed a box of colored pencils and walked over to the pencil sharpener.

"It's going to be all right, Marie. Red Feather will listen to the chief."

Marie spun around and the pencils flew out of the box like arrows and rattled across the floor. "How do you know? There are tribal politics involved, Mrs. Bowman. Clan politics, too. Do you know the first thing about clan politics here at Twin Rivers?" She knelt down and began picking up the pencils.

"A couple went under the bookcase," I said. "I'll get them. No, I don't know anything about clan politics."

"I didn't think so. There are seven different clans here, and some don't like taking orders from others—even when a chief is involved." She put the last pencil in the box and counted them. "Charging Moon isn't a king, you know. He's just a chief, and he isn't all that popular, especially with Red Feather's clan. There are reasons why Chief Charging Moon has stayed out of this in the past."

"I believe you, Marie," I said. "And you're right—I had no idea of the politics involved. But the chief wouldn't have agreed to speak with Red Feather if he didn't think it would help."

"I don't know how you can be so sure."

But I *was* sure, and when the beatings stopped, I was also convinced I'd been right, although I'd been pretty much convinced of that from the beginning. On the basis of what I could see, and according to what Rennie told Marie, Red Feather didn't lay a hand on him for almost two weeks. I was jubilant, vindicated, nearly giddy with relief.

Then Red Feather beat Rennie so severely that he was rushed to the Kenora hospital in a coma.

Marie's grandmother told me that Marie had stopped at Rennie's house to walk him to school, as she did every weekday morning, and found him dizzy and vomiting. She tried to get him to the infirmary, but Rennie had collapsed at the end of his father's fifteen feet of sidewalk. He was seizuring, so Marie put him in a neighbor's truck and drove him to the hospital.

I called the nurses' station and tried to speak with Marie, but I was told she wouldn't talk to me. Somehow, I made it through lunch, but at one o'clock I told Mike I wasn't feeling well and dismissed my students for the day. Back at the apartment, sick with worry and guilt, I cried and looked out the window at the frozen river.

By two-thirty, my worry and guilt had been displaced by rage, and Thomas Red Feather was its focal point. When I could stand it no longer, I went to Red Feather's house and stormed up the steps with no idea of what I'd say when I confronted him. I could see him through the window, sitting at the kitchen table, peeling the foil off a TV dinner. It was like something snapped inside me, and I barged in without even knocking. The look on Red Feather's face was one of complete astonishment.

"You're a disgusting, despicable piece of human trash!" I screamed. "You're a monster, and anyone like you who abuses a child doesn't deserve to live. If I were a man, I'd beat you senseless, the way you did to Rennie."

Red Feather was too surprised to say anything at first. Then, in a heavy Ojibwe accent, he said, "Get out, bitch, or I beat you like dog."

"You'd love that, wouldn't you, you bastard. I'll bet you like to beat up women almost as much as you like beating up children."

Red Feather started to get out of his chair, but I left, and he made no attempt to follow.

When Mike walked into the apartment after school, he was very worried about me and asked at least half a dozen times how I was feeling. I should have told him I'd gone to Red Feather's house that afternoon, but I didn't. He would have been furious, and we were so busy trying to get information about Rennie that I never mentioned it. Because we weren't family members, the hospital wouldn't tell us anything, and Marie still refused to come to the phone.

Mike finally said, "Let's try guile," and he called the nurses' station, identifying himself as Rennie's uncle. That was good enough for the duty nurse, who told him that Rennie had been taken into surgery, and it would be several hours, perhaps even days, before they knew anything.

Jack and Suzanne had come over, and I was making a pot of coffee when there was a loud knock at the door. Mike answered it, and when he did, Red Feather and a man I'd never seen before burst into the apartment. Red Feather had a lever-action rifle, which he pointed at Mike's chest. The other man held a knife. Their eyes were nothing but pupils.

"*No move!*" Red Feather said. "I knock, eh—not like woman."

Mike had no idea what the men were doing there, but unlike the Kohls and me, he didn't seem frightened—just confused.

"*Whoa,*" he said. "Put the rifle down. What's this all about?"

"Woman know," Red Feather said.

"What woman? What are you talking about?"

Red Feather didn't answer. He was staring at me with crazy, hate-filled eyes.

"Goddammit," Mike said. "Are you gonna tell me what you're doing here?"

The man with the knife looked at Red Feather. "His woman, eh?"

Red Feather nodded.

"Your woman, she broke into Thomas's house—bitched him out at his own table. When we're done with her—"

"Who the hell are you?"

"Frankie Five Bears. You're gonna remember that name, *zhaagnaash.*" He made a slicing motion with the knife. "I'm gonna carve it into your face, eh."

Mike never looked at Five Bears, not even when he spoke to him. He never looked at anything but Red Feather and the rifle.

"Listen, Thomas," Mike said. "I don't know anything about this. Lower the gun and we'll talk."

Red Feather stepped toward Mike and jabbed the barrel into his chest, pushing him backward. "No talk, *waabooz.* Woman come."

Five Bears looked at Suzanne, then at me. "Which one is she?"

"Yellow hair," Red Feather said. "You come now, *gishkishe.*"

Like Suzanne and I, Jack hadn't said a word. I was standing with my back to the sink, the coffee pot still in my hand, and Jack and Suzanne were seated at the table, too afraid to move. But Jack must have felt the need to assert himself in some way.

"Make no mistake, Thomas," he said. "If you two don't leave right now, you'll both go to jail for a long time."

Red Feather sneered and turned his head to say something.

Mike grabbed the rifle by the front stock and snapped the barrel up into Red Feather's forehead. In the same motion, he got his other hand on the gun somewhere behind the trigger and brought the butt up under Red Feather's chin with enough force that he was knocked backward several feet, landing on our coffee table, which exploded beneath him.

The man with the knife lunged at Mike, but before he could close the distance, Mike swung the rifle with both hands and struck him across the side of his face with the barrel, knocking him to the floor.

Mike put the rifle to the man's head, and I thought he was going to pull the trigger.

"Mike, no!"

He looked at me, and I saw the life come back into his eyes, like a well refilling with water. He kicked the knife away from Five Bears' outstretched arm and lowered the rifle.

"Stupid bastards," he muttered.

Jack leaped up from the table. "Fuck *me*! That was beautiful!"

"You ... you could have been killed." Suzanne said.

Mike, his composure returning, tried to laugh. "Not much chance of that. These two are so high I'm surprised they found the apartment. And this one," he nudged Red Feather with his foot, "forgot to pull the hammer back. Hell, I doubt this thing's even loaded."

He threw the lever experimentally, and a live round landed on the carpet.

"So much for that theory," Jack said. "Hey, he's coming to."

Red Feather was moaning and trying to get up on his hands and knees. Mike put one foot in the middle of his back and pushed him down hard.

"Somebody get Biggie," Mike said. "And let's find something to tie these geniuses up with."

"I have tape in the infirmary," Suzanne said. "I'll be right back. My word, you two sure know how to entertain!"

Jack followed her to the front door. "I'll get Biggie—but this is one for the OPP." He was in the open doorway when he stopped and turned around. "You know, for a second there, I thought you were gonna waste old Five Bears."

Mike shook his head slowly. "No."

Jack left and I threw my arms around Mike. "Are you all right? I was so—"

"I'm fine." He unclasped my hands from his neck and held me at arm's length. "What the hell were they talking about? Did you go to Red Feather's house?"

"I did. And I'm sorry." I couldn't look him in the eye. "I knew you'd be angry, so I didn't tell you."

"Angry? You could've been killed."

"I don't know why I did it. I honestly don't. I thought about Rennie all afternoon, and then I just … went over there. I should've told you."

"You should've stayed out of it."

"I couldn't help it. I'm sorry it turned out this way."

But sorry wasn't even close. What I felt was irreducible, bottom-of-the-ocean sorrow—squared. Not only had I failed to protect Rennie, I'd let Marie down and endangered the lives of everyone around me, including Mike. That hurt the most. I never imagined that my efforts to help Rennie would leave Mike looking down the barrel of Red Feather's rifle. But I should have. And yet it didn't matter anymore, because nothing mattered—rewards and punishments were randomly distributed. If you killed someone and disposed of the body, there were no consequences. If you tried to help a child, it turned out badly.

Suzanne returned with a roll of bandaging tape, and we bound the hands of the two men, who were semi-conscious by that time, and put them on the sofa. Red Feather was mumbling incoherently, and there was thick, ropey saliva running down his bloody chin. Five Bears was smiling, looking around as if he'd just awakened and didn't know where he was.

When Biggie got there, he decided to put both men in detox rooms at the community center. Twin Rivers didn't have a jail, but the detox rooms had doors that locked and no windows. We all agreed that would do for the time being.

I finished making the pot of coffee I'd begun an hour before, and the four of us stayed up very late, talking about Rennie and what had just happened.

"The irony of it all," Jack said, "is that Mike may have saved our lives tonight, and I'll probably have to fire him for it."

"Why?" I said. "All he did was stop those men from harming us—from harming *me*."

"I know," Jack said. "But a white teacher just beat the hell out of two First Nation residents. That won't play well with the general public. I feel terrible about this, but I know what's going to happen."

Mike had been very quiet. "You're right. Allie and I should go. Don't worry about it, Jack."

"It isn't fair," Suzanne said. "You had a right to protect yourself—that's all you were doing."

"There's another component to the problem," Mike said.

I raised my hand. "He means me. I was stirring the pot by trying so hard to protect Rennie. That's what started it all. Rennie is in the hospital because of what I did."

After Jack and Suzanne left, I called the Kenora hospital once more to see if Marie would speak to me, but she wouldn't. The nurse said Marie was with Rennie in intensive care, and she'd made it clear that she would take no calls from Allison Bowman.

Before we went to bed, I asked Mike how close he'd come to

shooting Five Bears.

Mike shrugged. "That sonofabitch tried to kill me."

"I know you get angry when I say this, but … maybe you should talk to somebody when we get home. It might—"

"Jesus Christ, Allie! If anybody's screwed up around here, it's *you*. If you'd backed off when everybody told you to, none of this would've happened. Don't you realize that?"

I didn't answer. I wasn't sure *what* I realized. Backing off would have been the smart thing to do, but I couldn't have done it. And it wasn't because Rennie needed me. It was because I needed him— him, his abusive father, his awful beatings, the whole wretched business. I couldn't have let go of that for anything, but I wasn't sure why. It reminded me of a story my mother once read to me about a monkey who got trapped when he reached into a jar to grab a plum. The monkey's hand was small enough to fit through the neck of the jar, which was tethered to a tree, but once he'd grabbed the plum, he couldn't pull his fist back through the hole. To escape, all the monkey had to do was let go of the plum and withdraw his hand, but he wouldn't do it—he was trapped by his own compulsion. I don't remember the moral of the story, something about self-destructive behavior, no doubt. But it ended badly for the monkey.

That night had been terrifying, but once I stopped shaking, I was struck by the irony of it all—the way those qualities in Mike that chilled me to the bone were the same ones that had just saved my life, maybe all our lives. I could appreciate that there was a duality in violence. It was like fire—it could cook your dinner or burn your house down. But as true as that may have been, I couldn't help thinking it might be best if people like Mike were kept in little boxes, the kind with glass fronts that you break in an emergency.

Chapter 33

Red Feather and Five Bears had burst into our apartment on a Friday night. Within twenty-four hours, a dozen different versions of what had happened were circulating all over the reservation, and according to Jack, none of them favored Mike and me. On Sunday, after a few fruitless calls to the hospital, I gave up and went to my classroom to do some work. When I came back to the apartment that afternoon, Mike was in the kitchen, where he had dishes, pans and cooking utensils all over the counter.

"What are you doing?" I asked, horrified.

"Making lasagna. I wanted to have something special for dinner tonight—something you might actually eat. It's our anniversary."

"Oh, Mike, I forgot. I never—"

"I know. You've been a little preoccupied."

I covered my face. "I'm sorry. I can't believe I forgot."

"It's okay. I would've forgotten, too, if Hannah Speaks Twice hadn't brought your present over a couple hours ago. I asked her to make something for you last month, but then I forgot all about it until she showed up at the door. Be right back." Mike disappeared into the bedroom and returned with a package wrapped in newspaper. "Sorry—we don't have any wrapping paper."

I was speechless with shame. I unwrapped the package and inside was a pair of beautiful hand-made moccasins with elaborate beadwork on the vamps.

"They're … lovely," I said. "I don't have anything for you. I'm so sorry." And then I started to cry.

"It's no big deal, Allie. Don't worry about it."

But of course I did.

We taught the following Monday, but very few children showed up for school. Their parents kept them home as a gesture of their displeasure with Mike and me, and at the end of the day, Jack told us the elders had indeed convinced the tribal council that we should be dismissed immediately.

I didn't care. I was much more concerned about Rennie and frustrated by my inability to find out how he was doing. Mike tried to pass himself off as Rennie's uncle again, but by then the hospital had a list of people with whom they were permitted to share information, and there was no uncle on it. What little we knew came from Marie's grandmother, who told us Rennie had come through the surgery but had not regained consciousness. Marie was sleeping in a chair by his bedside.

We left Twin Rivers the next day, March 26. The previous two weeks had been unseasonably warm, and a lot of the snow had melted. There would be more snow to come, of course, and more cold weather, but now there were puddles everywhere, and the air was spring-like and balmy.

We got up early but took our time leaving, mostly because we had no reason not to. We should have hurried or pretended we had a schedule to keep, but we had no idea that morning where we'd be by late afternoon. So we worked in fits and starts, making a couple trips to the car, then taking a break.

I didn't want to leave without speaking to Chief Charging Moon, but it took me quite a while to work up the nerve. I asked Mike if he wanted to come with me, but he didn't, so I went to Charging Moon's house by myself and knocked on the door.

"It is good that you have come to say good-bye," Charging Moon said. "Please, come inside. We will drink the Postum."

I shook my head. "No thank you, sir. I just came to apologize for everything. I'm sorry about ... all of it."

"There is no need to apologize, Mrs. Bowman. But there is something you hide, eh—something *here*." He touched his chest. "And this thing, it compels you. Now, it has hurt you deeply, and I fear you may choose the wrong wolf."

"I'm sorry, sir. I don't understand."

"You will, Mrs. Bowman. The Ojibwe say that in each of us live two wolves. One is filled with anger and sorrow, the other with hope and kindness. And the wolves, they fight to the death, eh."

"So ... which one wins?"

Charging Moon touched his chest again. "The one you feed, Mrs. Bowman."

When I got back to the apartment, Mike and I continued to pack at the same unhurried pace. Jack and Suzanne managed to sneak away from work for a while, so we had a cup of coffee with them, and then Molly disappeared as we were about to leave, no doubt wanting to bid farewell to her skinny friends. It was twenty minutes before she returned and climbed into the nest we'd made for her in the back of the squareback. After we said good-bye to Jack and Suzanne, we stopped at the post office for our mail, and there was a letter from Paula that I stuck in my purse to read later. From Twin Rivers we drove to Kettle Falls to say good-bye to Louie, who was surprised by our sudden decision to return to the States.

"So this is it, eh?"

"This is it," Mike said.

"What the hell happened, kid? I thought you was stayin' at Twin Rivers 'til spring, eh?"

"We had a little trouble."

Louie's face lit up. "What kind of trouble?"

So we told him the whole story, and he enjoyed it immensely, especially the part about Mike subduing our would-be assailants, which he made us repeat several times.

"Goddamn!" he said. "I wish I coulda seen that, eh."

"And our problems aren't over," I said. "There's a chance that Stone Bear flagged our license plate, so we may not be allowed to re-enter the States."

Louie rubbed his stubbled chin. "Why don't you take the winter road, eh?"

"What's the winter road?" I said.

"It's the ice road that runs down the big lake to the States. It starts in Kenora and goes all the way to Warroad and Baudette on the American side. Ain't no customs out there, eh."

Mike had never heard of the winter road. "You're telling us you can get from Kenora to Minnesota by driving the length of Lake of the Woods?"

"That's what I'm sayin', kid. I ain't been on it for years, eh, but the road, she's always there in the winter. Pretty soon it won't be safe to drive, but it oughta be good for a while yet."

"We'll have to give that some thought," Mike said.

I grabbed his sleeve. "I think we should do it."

Then we said good-bye, but it was much harder this time. As I waved to Louie from the car, I thought how much the scene resembled the one from nearly a year ago, when Mike and I had first arrived at Kettle Falls. The first thing I'd seen was Louie's weather-beaten cabin, which was only a little grayer now than it had been last April. And there were the remains of his woodpile, with his ax stuck in the same tree stump, and what might have been the same smoke was coming from the chimney. And then, like now, there had been mud and the same intimations of spring. It had all been magical then. Now, it was hauntingly familiar and would soon become a memory, like everything at Kettle Falls.

As we pulled onto the main road, Mike said, "We did pretty well, financially speaking."

"How much do we have?"

"A little over sixteen thousand dollars cash, but half of it's Canadian. We need to exchange it in Kenora before we leave. Not at the Scotia Bank, of course."

"Definitely not," I said. "I guess we're rich."

Mike laughed. "I wouldn't go that far, but we won't have to worry about money for a while."

"What else do we have to do in Kenora?"

"Just gas up the car. Do you really want to take the winter road?"

"Yes, don't you?"

"I haven't decided," Mike said. "I don't think Stone Bear notified the ports of entry. It isn't his style. I'm more—"

"But he *could* have."

"Yes, it's possible. But I'm more concerned about all the cash we have. If we get caught with that much money, we'll be in trouble."

"Then isn't it better to be safe than sorry? If we don't have to go through customs, why run the risk?"

Mike made a little noise of uncertainty. "First, we need to know if this car can handle the winter road. Then we have to find out how to get on it. Let's get those two questions answered."

When you come into Kenora from the north, one of the first things you see is the hospital, and as we drove by, I looked at the wall of windows and wondered which one was Rennie's room. Somewhere behind that glass was a bed with a little boy in it, beaten and unconscious, and next to the bed was a teenage girl, wondering if he'd ever wake up. I started to cry.

Mike looked at me, then at the hospital. "We can stop if you want."

"Marie doesn't want me there. Let's just … keep going."

So we did. We exchanged our currency at the Bank of Canada and stopped at Pond's Bait to buy a lake map, but the woman behind the counter wasn't able to tell us much about the winter road.

"All I know," she said, "is that it used to start right here at the wharf, eh. But then the warm weather and current, they opened up Devil's Gap, and you can't get through there no more." She also said there were probably accesses to the winter road south of town, but she couldn't say where. "It changes every day, eh."

We drove out of Kenora and stopped at the Husky station, where we filled the car and bought some food for the trip. Mike asked the owner where we might get on the winter road.

"Two days ago, you coulda got on right here, eh," he said. "But then I let some loggers use my access, and them yahoos tore it up with their trucks and skidders. The lake, she's got three feet of ice on it yet, but along the shore she's pretty rotten."

"Got any suggestions?" Mike asked.

He pointed down the highway. "Try Thomson's Motel. It's only a couple minutes from here. They might still have a road, eh. They cater to ice fisherman."

Thomson's Motel not only had a road but also a sign out by the highway advertising it. We pulled in and parked in front of a sawhorse that had been placed between the muddy tire ruts that ran down the hill to the lake. The sign said we were supposed to pay our three-dollar access fee in the motel office, so we went inside, where Mr. Thomson took our money. Then he walked out with us and removed the sawhorse. He didn't even wear a coat.

"Land of Lincoln," he said, reading our license plate. "Don't see many Americans this time of year, eh."

"Are we going to have any trouble out there?" Mike asked.

Mr. Thomson looked at the squareback. "You got plenty of weight in the back. You should be okay. Ain't much snow on the ice now, eh."

"I meant trouble with the border patrol or immigration."

Mr. Thomson put his hands in his pockets and didn't say anything.

"There's an emergency back home," Mike said. "I need to get there fast, and I'm looking for a shortcut. That's all."

"Well, they don't patrol the lake regular, but they're out there, eh—your people and ours. So you're goin' all the way to Minnesota?"

"Yes, to Warroad or Baudette," Mike said. "We haven't decided which."

"Either way there's a whole lot of nothin' between here and the States, eh. And it's mighty big water down there. It's none of my business, but if I was you, I'd steer clear of Baudette, eh. Warroad's a better bet, 'specially if you don't know the lake."

"All right," Mike said. "Warroad it is. How far is it?"

"It's a ways, eh. 'Bout a hundred and twenty kilometers as the crow flies, but on the winter road it's probably closer to a hundred and fifty, maybe more."

"What's that in miles?" I asked.

"'Bout ninety-five." Mr. Thomson pointed to the lake. "Just drive out past my fish houses and you'll hit the road, eh. All you have to do is follow it and pay attention to the ice. There'll be some heaves and pressure ridges out there, but there's always a way around 'em."

We thanked him, got into the car and headed out onto the lake. It was soupy at the edge, and Mr. Thomson had made a bridge from the shore to the ice with some huge planks that flopped noisily as we drove over them.

We made our way to the fish houses, which looked like a little shanty town on ice, and kept going as he'd instructed. Off in the distance we could see a truck heading north, moving perpendicular to us, and we assumed it was on the winter road. There wasn't much snow on the lake, mostly slush and water, but there were steep berms on both sides of the road, where the snowplows had thrown a winter's worth of snow that was still frozen solid. We finally found a place where we could drive across, and when we came down the opposite side, we were on a ribbon of ice at least fifty feet wide that stretched before us like a turnpike.

Mike started to laugh. "Can you believe this? This is *way* better than I expected."

"I know. Me, too."

"We'll be in Warroad in no time."

Chapter 34

Our optimism was short-lived. Ten miles south of Kenora the road narrowed considerably and forked every mile or so, forcing us to make unnerving, almost arbitrary decisions. Twice we followed roads for over half an hour before realizing they led to other accesses or closed resorts. When that happened, there was nothing to do but turn around, retrace our steps and get back on what we hoped was the main road again.

The winter road wasn't on the map, so we tried to get our bearings from the islands. That was difficult, though, because there were so many of them we couldn't tell which one we were looking at—or from what angle. After a while we almost convinced ourselves that it didn't matter where we were, as long as we stayed on the main road. But being lost goes against the grain of human nature, and the first time we stopped to let Molly out of the car, Mike dug around in the back for his binoculars.

"Maybe if I can see these islands better, I can find one on the map," he said. "Right now I can't tell if I'm looking at one big island or a bunch of little ones."

"I have Hedley's compass in my bag. Would that help?"

"It won't work in the car, but it's a good thing to have. I didn't know you brought it up here."

"I've never used it," I said. "I just brought it with me for luck."

"We're gonna need some."

I went through my little duffle bag, found the compass and gave it to Mike.

Fifteen miles south of Kenora, there were no other cars, no cabins, no one to ask for directions. Mr. Thomson was right—there was a "whole lot of nothin'" out there. But even worse, there was more than one winter road. In the preceding months, the road had been rerouted whenever pressure ridges or the gnawing current had made it necessary, and it was hard to tell which roads were old and which one was currently in use.

Because we wanted to go south, we followed one of the old roads for a long time in a brainless way that was rooted in our misplaced faith in the compass, which somehow convinced us that south was all we needed to know. We became suspicious as the road grew progressively worse, but we stuck with it until it stopped in front of the five-foot ice heave that had been its undoing. Another time we followed what turned out to be one of the older roads until it vanished in an acre of open water. That frightened us, and we didn't use the compass when we chose roads after that.

Both of the times we'd followed dead-end roads, we managed to find our way back to the main road, but we were zigzagging down the lake, and we knew it would take hours to reach Warroad that way. It was already three o'clock, and our late start was beginning to catch up with us.

Once, the road went directly across a long, narrow island, and it felt good to be on solid ground, if only for a few minutes. We let Molly out, and she ran around happily, did her business, then ran around some more. It was a nice break for all of us, but when we tried to leave the island, we found open water all along its southern shore, and we couldn't get back on the lake. Finally, we left the island the way we'd come, then drove all the way around it, hoping to pick up the winter road again on the far side. That cost us half an hour, and even when we got back on the road, we weren't sure it was the right one.

"The main road should be farther down the shore than this," Mike said.

I looked back at the island. "I don't know where we were for sure. We should've hung something in a tree where the road came across. Can we get closer to the island and take a better look?"

"We're about as close as I care to get. Let's stick with this road a while and see where it goes."

But a few minutes later the road angled off suspiciously to the east.

"Do you think we're still on the winter road?" I said. "We're wandering around all over the place."

"We're on a road—that's all I know. It'll be dark in an hour or so, and when that happens, things are gonna get—hey, look! Another car."

Off in the distance I could see a dark blob on the ice. It was definitely a car or truck, and it seemed to be heading in our direction.

"I hope he isn't lost," I said.

"I hope he's on the same road we are. Otherwise, I'll have to chase him down to ask directions."

But we didn't have to chase him down. When he was a hundred yards away, he turned his lights on and off several times, signaling us to stop.

"Maybe it's an immigration officer," I said.

"Not in an old truck like that. Grab the map."

We stopped the car, got out, and the truck pulled over across from us. The driver was busy in the cab for a moment, then he climbed out holding a beer in each hand and another pressed between his chest and forearm. He was about forty, and he smiled as though we were just the people he was hoping to see. Painted on the side of his truck were a muskie and the words "Ghost Bay Resort."

"From the land of sky-blue waters," he said, handing Mike and me a beer. "I had to go all the way to Oak Island to get it."

We thanked him and Mike said, "It's a good thing you came along when you did."

The man laughed. "Woman told me that once—got me in a mess of trouble. 'Course, I didn't know she was a deputy sheriff's wife … what's the problem?"

"I don't know where I'm going," Mike said.

"Then one direction's as good as another."

"I mean," Mike said, "that I don't know where I *am*."

"Ain't that a bugger? Happens to me all the time. Woke up in my brother-in-law's garage Sunday morning, and damned if I could figure out where I was. Him and me stopped at the legion for a bump and a snort, and the next thing I remember is waking up on a cement floor. *Uff-da*—thought I was in jail."

"So where are we?" Mike asked.

"You mean right now?"

Mike gave me a little sideways glance, and I could tell he was becoming frustrated.

"Yes. Right now."

"Well … let's see." The man looked around. "We're six miles north of the Northwest Angle, sorta between the Bukete Indian Reserve and the Windigo Reserve. My name's Sven Tollefson, by the way." He pointed to the side of his truck. "Me and the old lady own Ghost Bay Resort. Where are you going?"

"Warroad."

"Goin' the distance—good for you. You're headed right, but you got another problem—that's why I zigged my lights. They got a checkpoint set up at Flag Island. It's not far from here, and this road goes right to it. Them bastards do it every couple weeks—

immigration and the game wardens—and they're *sneaky*, doncha know. They do it just before dark when they can catch ice fishermen coming back across the border into the Angle. Fine the hell out of 'em."

"What's 'the Angle?'" Mike asked.

"You must be a long way from home, pilgrim. The Northwest Angle is a little chunk of Minnesota that has no border with the U.S. of A.—no *land* border, that is. It's got Manitoba on one side and Ontario on the other, so no matter how you slice it, you gotta go through Canada to get in or out—unless you're in a boat or on the ice."

"I can't believe there's a piece of Minnesota up here," Mike said.

"Hell, most Minnesotans don't even know it." Mr. Tollefson looked at me. "Is that a map you're holdin'?"

I gave him the map, which he spread across the hood of his truck. From what I could tell by looking over Mike's shoulder and listening to Mr. Tollefson, we could avoid the checkpoint by going west, sneaking around the end of Flag Island and returning to the main road a few miles south of there at a place called Sugar Point. Our accidental friend said it would be easier for us to drive ashore in the Northwest Angle, then pass through customs at the Manitoba border in Sprague. Mike and I didn't bother explaining why that wasn't an option.

"Did you have any trouble at the checkpoint?" I'd noticed the Minnesota plates on his truck.

"No," he said, "but they all know me, and besides, I'm a landed immigrant. Say, why don't you spend the night with us? It'll be dark in twenty minutes, and our place is only seven miles north of here. It ain't fancy, but we'd be happy to throw another cup of water in the soup."

"Thanks," Mike said, "but we want to get off the lake."

I glowered at Mike. Mr. Tollefson looked disappointed.

He drained his beer and tossed the can in the back of his truck. "Yeah, I can't really blame you for that. Once you get past Driftwood Point, you'll see the glow from Warroad. Just follow it on in. But for chrissake don't veer off toward Baudette. That road's a real bugger."

Before we went our separate ways, Mr. Tollefson got a pencil from above the visor of his truck and drew the route we were supposed to follow on our map. We were a long way from Warroad, but the line on the map was tremendously reassuring. We thanked him and got back in the car.

"It's a lot colder than when we left Kenora," Mike said as he started the engine. "I damn near froze out there talking to Tollefson. Why did you stare daggers at me when I told him we wanted to get off the lake?"

"Because it's a long way to Warroad, and now we have to leave the winter road to make a detour. We get lost in broad daylight, and now you want to drive around in the dark. It would've been safer to stay with him and his wife."

"That's a lot of negative vibes, Moriarty, but it's still more than you've said to me all day."

"I have a lot on my mind."

"Yeah."

We left the winter road and followed the line on the map for seven or eight miles, staying well away from Flag Island and the checkpoint. By the time we reached what we thought was Sugar Point, it was dark, and when the air temperature became colder than the slush and water on the ice, we had fog. It was thick and sudden, as though someone had thrown a switch.

Mike tried the brights, then the dims, then the brights again. "This is like driving around inside a light bulb."

"What are we going to do?"

"The same thing we've been doing, only slower."

Once we had passed Sugar Point—or what we thought was

Sugar Point—we were supposed to turn east in order to pick up the winter road again south of Oak Island, which Mr. Tollefson had circled on the map. It might have been a workable plan two hours earlier, but it fell apart quickly in the darkness and the fog. We turned east at what may have been Sugar Point or what may have been an island. There was no way of knowing. Mike started using the compass again, and we drove east a long time without coming to the winter road, without coming to anything.

"We've been going fifteen miles an hour for over half an hour," I said. "That's seven or eight miles—twice what Tollefson drew on the map."

"I know. I can't figure it out."

"Could we have driven across the road without knowing it? Maybe we didn't see it."

"It's got snowplow ridges on both sides," Mike said. "Sometimes they aren't very high, but we would have felt something. Let's give it another ten minutes."

"Then what?"

"Hell, I don't know. Then we'll try something else."

But we didn't make it ten minutes. We'd driven less than a mile when Mike slammed on the breaks without warning, causing the little squareback to slide sideways until the tires on my side struck something, and we came to a sudden stop. Molly gave a little yelp of surprise.

"Are you okay?" Mike asked.

"Yes," I said, a little shaken. My head had hit the window on my side. "What did we run into?"

"I'm hoping it's the edge of the winter road," Mike said. "I'm sorry. I didn't see it in time."

We found the flashlight, and Mike moved the car so I could open the door to get out. It wasn't the winter road that had stopped us. What we'd hit was a pressure ridge that probably ran for miles north and south, and any idea we had about traveling farther east ended right there. With the flashlight we could see several feet of black, open water in the yawning crack beyond the heave. Mike started to say something, but he was interrupted by a deep booming sound that began very close to us, then rumbled off in opposite directions. We felt the ice shudder.

"Let's get outta here," Mike said.

We jumped into the car and drove as fast as we could in the direction we'd come from. When we were a quarter mile from the pressure ridge, Mike stopped.

"That was close," he said, reaching for the map. "We could've been in serious trouble."

"We *are* in serious trouble."

Mike studied the map under the flashlight. "Let's go west until we hit this shoreline—see it running down the left edge of the map?"

"How will that help us?"

"It's mainland. If we keep it in sight on our right side, I don't see how we can get into too much trouble out here. We'll just follow it south down to Driftwood Point. Maybe we'll find a branch of the winter road down there."

So we crept west through the fog, looking for the shore, but as the temperature dropped, the fog thickened until our visibility was nearly zero. And to make matters worse, it got very cold in the car. I don't know what kind of heater the squareback had, but it was the kind that didn't put out any heat unless the car was going at least forty miles an hour, and most of the time we were doing about ten.

Forty-five minutes after we'd decided to find the mainland, I saw something out my window, but I couldn't tell what it was. I made Mike stop the car, and when we walked back to check, we found a large tree limb sticking out of the ice.

"We're close," Mike said.

To avoid getting too near shore, where the ice might be unsafe, we went more slowly after that, but even so, we couldn't see anything ahead of us but an opaque whiteness in the headlights. We almost hit the rocks on shore before we saw land, which seemed to rise out of the fog like Brigadoon.

Mike threw the car into reverse, floored it, and when we'd retreated a hundred yards, he said, "This should work. We'll stay close enough to the shoreline to follow it and far enough away to be safe."

I looked at the map. "If we're going to follow the shoreline down to Driftwood Point, we have a couple problems. First, we probably won't know when we get there, and second, we'll never see the lights of Warroad in this fog."

"Jesus, could you just let me enjoy the moment? This is one of the few times today that I've actually known where we are."

I didn't say anything more for an hour.

We stuck to the shoreline like glue, moving in close enough to see it every few minutes, then veering away quickly, so that we didn't hit a rock or a log or break through the ice. We had the same blind faith in the mainland that we'd previously placed in the compass, and after a couple hours it, too, had become an addiction. We were supposed to travel from Driftwood Point south to Warroad, thirty-five miles away. But even though we knew that leg of the journey was impossible in the fog, we kept going, partly because we had a rough idea of where we were but mostly because there was no place to stop, even if we'd wanted to.

Eventually, the compass indicated that the shoreline was leading us southwest, and when Mike checked half an hour later, it said we were heading *due* west. At that point, we could no longer kid ourselves about Driftwood Point—it was somewhere behind us in the fog, probably a long way. Mike stopped and looked at the map again.

"The bright side," he said, "is that I still know where we are. We're coming into Big Traverse Bay."

"Let me see."

I leaned over to look at Mike's finger on the map and saw that Big Traverse Bay was a monster. Its mouth was a dozen miles wide, and the bay itself ran north and south for almost thirty miles. Warroad lay at its southern end, but in the fog thirty miles was the same as a thousand.

"We can't take off across this Bay," I said. "Please tell me you aren't considering that."

"I'm not. We'd wander around out there until we fell through the ice. I'm going to stick with the shoreline. If we have to, we can go ashore and make a fire."

It was a half-hour later that we felt the car go over something. There was a slight jolt, nothing more, but it was enough for us to get out and investigate. We hoped it was the edge of a road, but even if it was, we knew it wouldn't be the road we needed. But it wasn't a road at all. It was an old snowmobile trail, sort of etched into the ice.

Mike dug at the trail with his foot. "It looks like it goes to shore. Why would it do that?"

"Maybe there's something on shore near here."

He shined the flashlight into the darkness. "I can't imagine what. We're in the middle of nowhere—that's the only thing I'm sure of."

"We'd better follow it in," I said. "Besides, it's time to make sure we still know where the shoreline is. We haven't checked in a while."

In the fog it would have been easy to lose sight of the trail, so Mike straddled it with the car, and we followed it easily, feeling the turns in the soles of our feet. But when we didn't reach the shore after several minutes, we knew something was wrong.

"We couldn't be this far from the mainland," Mike said. "I need to find out what's going on."

He stopped, and I held the flashlight while he looked at the map again.

"I think I know what happened," he said. "When we crossed that snowmobile trail, I thought we were a long way from this bay—Sand Point Bay." He jabbed at the map with his finger. "But we must have been right in front of it, and then when we turned, we turned *into* it. That's why we lost the shoreline."

"Should we stick with the trail?"

"We can give it a few more minutes," Mike said. "But I'm not keen on driving into a bay—I don't trust the ice, and we weigh a lot more than a snowmobile."

But in less than fifty yards, the trail turned sharply to the right and headed for the eastern edge of the bay. We followed it, and as I stared into the fog, looking for things we might run into, I saw something on the ice ahead of us.

"Slow down," I said. "There's something up there. I don't see it anymore, but it was—"

"I see it. It looks like a dock. This is as far as we go."

Mike angled the car toward the dock, and when he did, we could see our headlights reflecting in the windows of a little cabin.

"I think we just got lucky," he said. "It's probably a trapper's cabin."

We got out of the car and approached the dock cautiously, and when we were close enough, Mike shined the flashlight on the shoreline. There was several feet of open water between the ice and the muddy beach, so we stepped onto the dock and walked its creaky length to shore.

The building wasn't a cabin. It was an odd little structure made of cinder block that looked as if it had been there a hundred years. To us, though, it was as good as a Hilton. As we walked up to it, Mike shined the flashlight on a rusty metal sign next to the front door—*Government Cold Weather Testing Facility*.

"Hardly my idea of a 'facility.'" I knocked on the door and Mike started laughing.

"There's no one here, Allie." He shined the flashlight on the door jamb. The cabin was padlocked from the outside.

"Maybe they hid a key someplace."

We looked everywhere we could think of—behind, under and over things—but there was no key to be found.

"Let's try the windows," Mike said.

So we walked around the cabin, checking each one, but they'd all been nailed shut from the inside. Behind the cabin we noticed an overgrown road—a continuation of the snowmobile trail we'd followed ashore—but judging from the size of the saplings that had grown up in it, it hadn't seen a car or truck in years. Stymied by the windows, we soon found ourselves standing in front of the door again, staring at it.

"What are we going to do?" I said. "It's too cold to—"

Mike took a half-step back and kicked the door in. There was an explosive sound of rending wood, and our door problems were over.

"I think we just passed the first test at this facility," he said.

I followed him inside, and it was like walking into a big icebox—or a tomb. There were several kerosene lanterns hanging from the rafters, so I held the flashlight while Mike got one lighted. It wasn't much of a place, but it had a stove, four walls and a roof.

"You stay here," Mike said. "I'll get Molly and make a couple trips to the car. Maybe you can get a fire going. It's colder in here than it is outside."

I lit the rest of the lanterns, and soon Molly, happy to be anywhere but in the squareback, was cavorting around like a puppy. Next to the stove was a box filled with old newspapers and kindling, and as I crumpled up pieces of newspaper and tossed them into the stove, I began glancing at some of the articles. Then I began reading them.

In a couple minutes Mike came through the door with a sleeping bag under each arm. "What's the problem? We'll freeze to death before you get a fire going."

"I don't think anyone's been here for a long time." I held up a front page with the headline U.S. BLOCKADES CUBA. "Here's one about the overthrow of the Diem regime."

"Do you think you could put them in the stove and start a fire?"

That question, I thought, captured the very essence of Mike's nature.

I finally got the fire going while he made more trips to the car. Then I looked on the shelves and in the cupboard to see if there was anything to eat, but all I found were three cans of beans and a can of Franco-American spaghetti. The cans were frozen, their tops ominously domed. When Mike returned the next time, I asked him if he'd brought in whatever food we had in the car.

"Yes," he said. "And unless you found something to eat in here, we have half a bag of Fritos, a cinnamon roll and a Cadbury bar."

"I'm not hungry. Eat whatever you want."

"It's hard to imagine three things that go together so poorly," he said. "I don't know whether to eat the Fritos before or after the cinnamon roll. How can you not be hungry?"

"I don't know. I'm just not. The only one who'll get a decent meal tonight is Molly. Did you bring her food in?"

"It's on the table."

"What do you think they tested here?"

Mike pointed to a garbage can full of beer cans and whiskey bottles. "Their livers."

"Seriously."

He shrugged. "It could be anything—car batteries, wheel-bearing grease, antifreeze. We built a lot of places like this after the war. I suppose Canada did, too."

"I wonder where that road out back goes."

"Hard to say. It doesn't really matter, though, because we're still in Canada. We'd still have to go through customs someplace."

I fed Molly while Mike put some big chunks of wood in the

stove, and it was nice once the place warmed up, a lot nicer than spending the night in the car or huddled beside a fire on shore. I sat at the table while Mike wired the front door closed, and when he was finished, he unrolled our sleeping bags on two of the folding cots that served as the beds.

"I don't know when I've seen you so quiet," he said.

I nodded.

"I said I don't know when I've seen you so—"

"I heard you," I said. "Look, I'm worried sick about Rennie. And I'm upset that Marie won't talk to me. As soon as we get to a phone, I'm going to call the hospital again. I can't stand not knowing anything. Until we got lost in the fog, that's all I could think about."

"Did you ever read that letter from Paula?"

"No, I forgot all about it." I reached for my purse. "I can't believe I did that."

"We've been a little busy since we picked up the mail."

I opened the letter and began to read. Like all of Paula's letters, it sounded as if she were there in the room with me, so much so that I could hear the words in her own irrepressible voice. When I'd finished reading, I put the letter down on the table and looked over at Mike.

"Paula's getting married."

"That's great. When?"

"December."

"Good for her. You don't seem very excited."

"I am. I'm happy for her. It just seems so … ironic."

"What's ironic about it?" Mike said, yawning. "I wonder if it'll be a Polish wedding. I've never been to one."

"I'm sure it will."

I didn't bother explaining my irony remark to Mike, who had begun blowing out the lanterns. I heard him zip himself into his sleeping bag, and I could tell by his breathing that he'd fallen asleep almost immediately. But I didn't sleep much that night. I lay there thinking about tomorrow, and each time I closed my eyes, I would see the fog and dark shapes in the fog that frightened me.

Chapter 35

The next morning when I woke up, I could hear fire crackling in the stove, so I knew Mike was already tending to things. But neither Mike nor Molly was in the cabin. The fog had lifted, and when I looked out the window, I could see them on the ice next to the car, where Mike was looking at something through the binoculars. He would stare across the huge expanse of ice, check the compass, look at the map, then repeat the process. He was preparing to do battle with the lake again, and it looked as though he was enjoying himself. There had been a couple times in the fog when I also got the impression that he found our predicament a good deal more exciting than I did. A few minutes later, he and Molly came through the door.

"It got cold last night." He went to the stove and held his hands over it. "There's ice all the way to the shore this morning. I wouldn't want to walk on it, though."

"Do you know where we are?"

"I knew that last night. I just didn't know where anything else was. We're in Sand Point Bay—I could see the opposite shore."

"Could you see Warroad?"

"Warroad is still a long way from here," he said. "According to the map, everything to the west of us is called Buffalo Bay. It's in Manitoba. If we drive across the bay to Buffalo Point, we might be able to see Warroad from there, but I wouldn't bet on it."

"We'd better get going."

Mike put both hands on his stomach. "Last night I dreamed about food—ham, eggs and hash browns. I haven't had a food dream since Vietnam. Aren't you hungry?"

"Not really. What are we going to do about the broken door?"

"When we go, I'll wire it shut—that's all I can do. We should probably leave the Canadian government ten bucks so they can fix it."

"Make it twenty."

Mike laughed. "All right, but for twenty dollars they could rebuild the place."

A half-hour later we were in the car again, heading south toward Buffalo Point. We could see the shoreline on the other side of the bay, but just barely. It appeared as a thin, wispy band of gray that struggled to separate the lake from the sky, both of which were about the same color. After a few minutes, we could see it much better.

"It's like a different lake down here," I said. "No islands."

"And no shoreline to the east. It might as well be the Atlantic Ocean out there."

"Is that a flag?"

Mike handed me the binoculars, and although it was difficult with the car bouncing around, I focused them on the far shore.

"There's some kind of building with a Canadian flag flying from it," I said.

"Maybe it's a restaurant."

"Whatever it is, I hope it's on Buffalo Point. I don't want to be lost anymore."

As we got closer, we could see an occasional car drive onto the lake from somewhere near the building, and when we were about a mile from shore, Mike stopped the car and stepped outside to get a compass reading. Then he took the binoculars and glassed the whole point.

"It looks like ... a bait shop with a landing to the lake. There's a big sign on the roof ... Buffalo Point Marina. You gotta love that."

"I do. What am I seeing to the right, way over there?"

"It's ... cars and fish houses. The last two cars that drove onto the lake both headed that direction."

"Do you want to stop and get something to eat?"

Mike lowered the binoculars. "As much as I'd like to, it's probably a bad idea. With our luck there'd be a CO or a border patrol officer there checking fishermen."

"I agree. We've come too far to get careless now."

Buffalo Point proved to be more of a peninsula than a point. It took quite a while to drive around it, and even when we had, we couldn't see Warroad. That was a little unsettling, but we'd found the winter road again, and we knew the United States lay at the end of it.

On a good day you can see ten miles across open water, but on the ice you're lucky if you can see half that far. So even when we could see the lake's southern shoreline, we couldn't see Warroad or anything that looked like a town. It wasn't until we could make out a water tower rising above the trees that we knew where Warroad was. Soon after that we saw a slender communications tower of some kind, and we began to relax.

"Are we in the States yet?" I asked.

"I think so. On the map it looks like we were in the States as soon as we came around Buffalo Point—but you have to be completely past it."

"Then we've made it."

"In a way," Mike said. "But I won't feel safe until this car is on dry land a hundred yards from the lake. Once it is, we're just two Americans in Warroad."

"I hope there isn't a checkpoint where we come off."

"If there is, we'll have to find someplace to sneak ashore."

As we approached Warroad, we could see a few fishermen standing on the ice and seven or eight snowmobiles crossing the bay in a little convoy. We even passed another car heading north—something that hadn't happened since our chance encounter with Sven Tollefson. When we were a half mile from shore, we saw a car drive off the lake, and from that we could tell where the access was.

Mike watched the car through the binoculars. "He never stopped and nobody checked him. Let's do it."

As we drew closer, we could see that the access was in a little park protected by a riprap jetty that ran into the lake on the big-water side of the landing. Even from where we were, we could see American and Canadian flags on many of the buildings, and in that way Warroad reminded me of Cape Vincent or any little frontier town on international water.

Someone, probably the DNR, had placed a rather elaborate aluminum bridge between the ice and the shore, and we drove across it, right up a concrete boat ramp, and we were home. We drove through the park quickly, turning onto a street that followed the lake in a sweeping curve, and when we came to the Warroad Motel and Restaurant, we stopped. It was ten forty-five.

"I'm going to let Molly out," I said. "Go ahead. I'll join you in a minute."

"I'll be the man eating three breakfasts."

I put Molly on a leash and took her back across the street to the park, where I walked her around for a while in the areas where there wasn't any snow. I felt nauseous. I wanted to enjoy being back in the United States, but that morning it was impossible to feel good about anything.

I sat on a bench for a minute or two, thinking about what I would say. I didn't understand what had happened to me, but I knew that Thin Bird and Rennie were halves of something. That made me uneasy, because I wasn't sure I liked what they added up to. I also knew I'd been on borrowed time since the substation. But until Rennie ended up in the hospital, I'd been like a cartoon character who runs off a cliff but doesn't fall. He just keeps running until he looks down. Then gravity takes over.

I walked across the street, put Molly back in the car and went into the restaurant, where I saw Mike waving to me from a booth by the window. He had a cup of coffee in front of him.

"What took you so long? Did Molly run off?"

"No, nothing like that. Did you order?"

"I was waiting for you."

"You should have ordered. I'm not really hungry."

We had a nice view of the lake that was vastly improved by the fact that we weren't on it. The waitress brought me a cup of coffee and handed us menus.

"I saw you come off a few minutes ago," she said. "You should be goin' out right now, not comin' off ... but I guess you two aren't fishermen."

She was waiting for a reply of some sort, so Mike said, "We just came down from up north." As vague as his explanation was, it seemed to satisfy her, and she smiled, saying that she'd be back in a minute to take our orders.

"Allie, this is your kind of place—fish on the wall and ketchup on the table."

"And a stuffed bear wearing an apron over in the corner."

Mike craned his neck around. "Oh yeah. I missed that. I can't believe you aren't hungry. We haven't eaten since the day before yesterday."

The waitress returned and Mike ordered an enormous breakfast, but all I wanted was some toast. Mike shook his head in disbelief.

"I'm going to find a phone and call the hospital," I said.

"Tell them you're with DIAND—a case worker or something."

"All right."

I found a phone in the hallway that joined the motel to the restaurant and made the call from there, playing the DIAND card, as Mike had suggested. I don't think the nurse knew what DIAND was, but she told me Rennie was still unconscious and that his condition had been downgraded from critical to serious. It was very encouraging news, she said. I knew Marie was almost certainly nearby, and I considered having the nurse put her on the phone but decided it was a bad idea to trick Marie into talking to me.

When I went back to the restaurant, Mike had bought a newspaper, which he was reading while he waited for me and his food. When he saw me, he put it down.

"I can tell by your face it's good news," he said. "The DIAND ruse must have worked."

"It did. And it's wonderful news. Rennie is still unconscious, but the nurse said his vitals are good. There's no way of knowing how long it'll be before he wakes up, but she said the doctors are optimistic. I'm so relieved. I can't tell you how—"

"That's great, Allie. I know how worried you've been. Maybe now you can—"

"Yes, maybe. Anything of interest in the paper?"

Mike picked it up again. "This is the *Grand Forks Herald*—I don't even know where that is. Let's see … here's a front-page story about a peat fire that burned underground all winter. Right underneath that is an article about the SLA wanting Patty Hearst's father to feed the unwashed masses." He opened the paper and folded it in half. "This is interesting—there have been several sightings of a white moose near a town called Greenbush … *What the hell?* Abbie Hoffman jumped bail yesterday. I didn't know he'd been arrested."

"He got caught selling cocaine. It was some kind of sting."

"Well, he's too famous to get very far."

"Abbie Hoffman? I wouldn't bet on it."

Our food came and Mike ate like a man who'd been thinking about breakfast a long time. I let him finish. Then, with my voice shaking, I said, "I have something to say that's going to be very hard for me. I know it won't come out the way I want, but please don't say anything until I've finished."

Mike put his forearms on the table and looked at me. "I know what you're going to say. I thought you were going to tell me last night—the irony comment."

"I couldn't last night. It's hard enough now."

"Let's have it."

I spoke very slowly, concentrating on each word. "I think we need to be apart for a while. We had a deal. You asked me to give Twin Rivers a try, and I did. But it didn't work. It was all I could do before to live with what *you* did, but now I have to live with what *I* did. I can't be with you and do that. I'm sure of it."

"Can I talk now?"

"No, please, not yet. Three months after we were married, I watched you kill a man without giving it a thought. And I sort of held my breath, waiting for something to happen."

"Like what?"

"I wasn't sure. But I knew you couldn't kill someone for free."

"So you were expecting divine retribution?"

"No, not at all. It's more like physics—some kind of equal and opposite reaction. I kept waiting for the other shoe to drop."

Mike shook his head. "There is no other shoe. When are you going to realize that?"

"You're wrong," I said, edging closer to tears. "*I'm* the other shoe. How many times did I tell you how guilty I felt about Thin Bird—how I wished I could press a button and make things right?"

"A thousand. But I don't see—"

"*Rennie was that button.* And I kept pressing it until it blew up in my face. Mike, this isn't about you anymore. It's about me—about *us*—and I've ruined everything. Rennie's in the hospital, Marie won't speak to me, and you … I almost got you killed. My God, I hate myself." I wasn't crying, but I was close.

The waitress came and cleared our table without a word. She knew something was going on and wanted no part of it.

When she was gone, Mike said, "So a divorce will solve all your problems?"

"You're the one who keeps bringing up divorce. But you don't realize that if I stayed with you now, we'd be looking at a divorce in a few months anyway—and you'd be the one asking for it."

"I don't quit that easy," Mike said. "Look, you might hate yourself, but I still love you, and I know we can work this out."

"But it isn't a *we* thing. I have to do this myself. I'm just asking for a little time. I don't think that's—"

"Why is it always about what *you* think? You wanna know what *I* think?" Mike looked at me as though I'd stolen something from him. "I think you're out of your fucking mind."

I reached out to touch his hand, but he pulled it away.

"Please don't make me cry," I said. "Not here. I need you to understand."

"Forget it," he said, still glowering. "I'll never understand, not any of it. You've said what you wanted to say, and so have I. Do whatever the hell you want."

We didn't talk any more after that. We looked out the window at the lake, and I'm sure we both wondered what would happen next. When we paid for our meal, Mike bought two area newspapers and picked up some brochures that were in a wire rack by the cashier's station. We were both tired, so we decided to get a room at the motel and sleep for a few hours.

I had the rudiments of a plan. I would ask my mother and Tom if I could stay with them for a while, and I knew they'd say yes. But I couldn't imagine what Mike would do. He didn't have anyone who would smile understandingly and take him in no matter what. All he had was me.

We took showers and slept for three hours with Molly on the bed between us. When we woke up, we watched TV until late afternoon. It had been a year since we'd watched television, and even though the motel got only one channel, we couldn't get enough of it.

Finally, when it was getting dark, Mike said, "I know you're probably not hungry, but I am, and according to the paper, Warroad has two pizza parlors. Should we get a pizza and a six-pack and watch TV?"

"All right," I said, "but let's walk. And let's take Molly."

So we put on our coats, and the three of us walked up Warroad's Main Street, which led directly away from the lake. It was cool, and there was no smell of earth or flowers or grass yet, but even so, it felt like spring. We passed a grocery store, a couple bars and a sport shop before coming to the Bossa Nova Pizzeria.

Mike looked in the window. "Works for me. I'm too hungry to check out the competition."

I tied Molly by her leash to a bicycle rack, and we went inside, where we were immediately greeted by the aroma of American pizza. The place was empty, except for some high school kids, talking and laughing at a table in the corner. We ordered a large pizza and would have eaten it there, but Molly looked so forlorn sitting out front that we stuck to the plan and took the pizza back to the motel, stopping on the way for a six-pack.

Dinner was awkwardly circumspect.

"Good pizza," Mike said. "I didn't realize how tired I was of Canadian pizza until now. I think it's the feta cheese."

"I know what you mean. It's nice to see the toppings again, too—Canadians hide everything."

"I guess a country that eats poutine and puts vinegar on its French fries is bound to have a different concept of pizza."

We watched TV until late. I finally went to bed, leaving Mike to pore over the brochures and newspapers he'd bought that morning. There was something strangely purposeful about his reading, and his face bore the same expression I'd seen so often when he was working on his thesis.

The next morning, after I'd taken Molly for a walk, I called the Kenora hospital again, but there was no change in Rennie's condition. I told the nurse I was with DIAND, as I'd done before, and she promised to call me if Rennie regained consciousness. But when I was unable to provide her with a phone number, she became suspicious and I hung up, knowing that the DIAND masquerade was over.

We had breakfast at the motel restaurant again. In fact, we sat at the same booth and had the same waitress, who looked us over closely to see if things had improved in the last twenty-four hours. When she decided they hadn't, she became nervous, and although she was polite, she spoke as little as possible. After we ordered, Mike laid out his plan, and the moment he did, it became clear to me why he'd looked as though he were studying the night before.

"Here's what we do," he said. "You need a car, so we're going to buy you one this morning."

"That's crazy! Why do we need two cars?"

"Because we sold your car before we came up here, and this is as far as I go. I'm not going back to Chicago."

If I'd been standing, that revelation would've put me on the ground. "You can't stay *here*. What are you going to do? I was thinking we'd both be in Chicago."

Mike broke the paper band around his napkin and silverware and placed the napkin in his lap. "I know the feeling. The day before yesterday, I was thinking we'd always be together. Now the only thing I'm sure of is that there's nothing for me back home."

"But you can't just—"

"There are some huge resorts in Baudette—that's thirty-eight miles from here. With my experience, I'm sure I can get a decent job at one of them. They're probably hiring right now." Mike looked out at the lake, and when he spoke again, the edge was gone from his voice. "I don't expect you to understand this, but when we were out there in the dark, lost in the fog, it was the first time in months that I actually felt … *alive*. I don't want to leave this lake."

I almost smiled. "I understand that. I do. But how will we stay in touch?"

"Is that important?" he said, the edge back.

"Don't be ridiculous. I need to know where you are. It's not like I'm—"

"Leaving me? That's exactly what you're doing. But if you want, I'll let you know where I end up."

"Won't you call to see if I got home safely?"

He shrugged. "I will if you want me to. Look, I don't know the rules here. This is your show."

"All right," I said. "If you want to be cruel, go ahead. If you want to stay up here, then stay. But don't disappear. This is too important."

"You need to remember who wants to do the disappearing."

I nodded and lowered my head. "I know you're angry. But when I leave, try to remember how much I love you. It's just that … everything is different now. *I'm* different, and I can't stand it."

Mike started to say something, then changed his mind and signaled our waitress for more coffee. I looked at the lake, where the sun on the ice made it shimmer like a parking lot. The few cars that ventured out on it looked wavy and distorted after they got a hundred yards from shore.

I hadn't eaten much of my breakfast that morning, either, and when the waitress came to take our plates, she asked me if there was anything wrong with my food, which was funny in a way, because it was just toast. I told her it was fine, that I wasn't really hungry. I'm sure she was hoping we'd either leave town or sit at someone else's station if we showed up again.

On the way to the car, Mike said, "Look, if you want to stay in touch, that's fine. I don't hold out much hope that things will ever work out, but ..."

"Then please call me tomorrow night."

We went directly from the restaurant to Warroad's only car dealership. I wasn't surprised that Mike knew where it was, and I assumed this was one of the things he'd gleaned from last night's reading. We had hardly stepped from the car when a salesman came out to greet us. He was putting on his jacket as he passed through the door, and although he was just a kid, he was eager to please and listened carefully as Mike explained what we were looking for—or rather, what Mike was looking for.

It was cold and blustery in the lot, and as we walked between the rows of used cars, I wasn't paying much attention to Mike or the salesman. Instead, I found myself listening to the big American flag that flew above the showroom. It snapped loudly in the wind, and there was something mesmerizing in the sprung rhythm of its halyard clanging against the pole.

The salesman showed Mike three cars, all of which appeared to be in good condition despite being several years old. There was a Camaro, which didn't have enough trunk space to be practical, a Pontiac Tempest with a Jesus fish and ninety thousand miles on it and a yellow Chevelle wagon with a slightly crumpled front fender, which Mike knelt down to examine.

"Moose hit," the salesman said.

"What?"

"*Moose* hit. That's my Uncle Howard's car. He hit a moose on the way back from Roseau last month—grazed it was all. I can make you a really good deal on that one."

Mike turned to me.

"This is stupid."

But it didn't matter what I thought, and negotiations were soon underway. The salesman ran back and forth to his boss a few times with Mike's offers, and after he'd agreed to put new tires on it, we bought Uncle Howard's car. As Mike counted out the money in hundred-dollar bills, the salesman gaped as though we were Bonnie and Clyde.

I don't know why, but I wanted us to be together until Chicago—I never imagined we'd split up in Warroad—but things were falling apart so fast there was no way to stop it or even slow it down. I drove the Chevelle back to the motel, and on the way, we pulled into a gas station. Mike got out of his car, said he'd just be a minute, and returned with road maps of Minnesota and Wisconsin, which he handed to me through the window.

"You might need these."

Back at the motel, neither of us spoke much. I took Molly for a walk, gathered up my things and wondered what Mike and I would say to each other when I left. Mike gave me almost all the money we'd made, and when I protested, he said, "Take it. You earned it."

Our good-byes didn't amount to much. When Molly and everything I owned was in the Chevelle, Mike and I embraced for a moment, and I said, "I love you, and I hope you get a job at one of those big resorts. Please remember to call me."

"You're trembling," he said.

"I'm scared."

"Then don't go."

"I have to."

"Take Highway 11 through Baudette to International Falls."

And then I left.

Chapter 36

I don't remember anything about the drive from Warroad to Baudette except the eagles. The road followed the railroad tracks closely, and bald eagles were sitting all along the embankment and even on the rails. They were migrating north again, just as they'd done a year ago when Mike and I had arrived in Kenora. I couldn't figure out what attracted them to the railroad tracks until I realized they were feeding on the carcasses of deer and moose that had been hit by trains. In a few places I could see the carnage—a leg here, a hindquarter there—and I didn't look at the eagles after that.

Coming into Baudette, I saw the signs for all the resorts Mike had talked about but nothing of the resorts themselves. Most of them were at the mouth of the Rainy River or on the points that stretched into Lake of the Woods from its southern shore, which was a few miles north of where I was.

When I reached International Falls an hour and a half later, it was time to call my mother—something I'd been dreading. I knew she and Tom would welcome me with open arms, but I wished I could've given them more than twenty-four hours notice that they were about to have a semi-permanent house guest. The worst part would be explaining why I was alone. My mother had no idea that was coming. But until the fog, I hadn't known it myself.

When I called her and delivered what were, by then, carefully rehearsed lines, my mother was shocked, and there were some long pauses as she considered my sketchy, unsatisfying explanations. But she asked no questions. She said "I see," when she clearly didn't, and "I'm sure everything will be fine," when neither of us had any reason to think so.

Heading south from International Falls was hard because I was on the same road that Mike and I had taken a year ago when we'd been so happy. I tried not to think about that, but then I'd pass a restaurant where we'd eaten or a gas station where we'd stopped, and it all came rushing back. After a while, I started thinking about the people I'd met in the last year—people like Pop and Louie, who had so much sadness in their pasts. Men like Kenny Morgan, who threw people out of airplanes. And Marie, whom I had failed in every way imaginable.

I didn't see the wayside rest at the Laurentian Divide, where Mike and I had made love, but I knew I'd passed it when I saw a sign that said Duluth was only forty-nine miles away. It was all downhill from there, all the way to the Gulf of Mexico. When I thought about how Mike had pulled me across that line a year ago and kissed me, I felt dry and empty.

I crossed the St. Louis River in Duluth, and Molly and I spent the night in a motel on the other side of the bridge in Superior, Wisconsin. As soon as I checked in, I called the Kenora hospital again, only this time I didn't pretend to be anyone else. When I got the head nurse on Rennie's floor, I gave her my name and insisted that she put Marie on the phone. And she did.

It wasn't a pleasant call. Marie was distant, but she said Rennie was awake, and the doctors had told her he could expect a full recovery. He'd awakened very hungry, she said, and had already eaten some pudding and a bowl of cereal. I started to cry, and I think Marie was crying, too, but it was hard to tell, because a lot of the time she wasn't saying anything. I told her how sorry I was, and she told me I was like certain characters in the books we'd read together.

"Which characters?" I said.

"The ones with such good reasons for all the trouble they cause." Then she said, "I'm sorry, Allie. I didn't mean it like that."

It was the first time she'd ever called me by my first name.

I spent the next day driving the length of Wisconsin. Size seemed to matter in Wisconsin—every few miles I would encounter some colossus by the side of the road, an enormous likeness of something placed there by the chamber of commerce or by some business hoping to attract attention, if not customers. There were big fish, big geese, big deer, big wedges of cheese and things that didn't make sense at first, like a big mouse—two big mice, actually—just outside of Mauston. That afternoon I had a bowl of soup in a restaurant with a big steer on its roof. I hadn't noticed all that hyperbole a year ago.

Several hours later, I pulled into my mother and Tom's driveway. They had been watching for me and ran out of the house before I could open the car door. My mother hugged me a long time, and Tom hugged me self-consciously, the way he always did. There were very few questions initially, except about Molly, who was running happily around the front yard, having sensed somehow that we'd reached our destination. We went inside and talked until dark. Tom disappeared after a couple hours and returned with two big bags of Chinese food, which we ate with chopsticks in the living room.

"Allie, eat some more," my mother said. "You're skinny as a rail."

"Maybe later," I said. "Is it really okay about Molly? She could probably stay with Paula if it's a problem."

Molly came over to me at the mention of her name and put her head in my lap.

"We're happy to have you both," Tom said. "What kind of dog is she?"

"You're a mutt, aren't you, Molly?" I said, scratching her behind her ears. "A beautiful, beautiful mutt."

"Well, you and your beautiful mutt can stay in your old bedroom," my mother said. "It's all ready for you."

"Thank you. I'm sorry to impose on you like this. As soon as—"

"You could never impose on us," Tom said. "We're your parents, and this is your home for as long as you want." Then he looked embarrassed. "I'm going to get your stuff out of the car, Allie."

When he was gone, my mother said, "He's right, you know—*as long as you want.*"

Before I went to bed that night, Mike called, and I told him about Rennie, and he was very relieved, though probably more for my sake than Rennie's. In the day and a half since we'd parted, he'd gotten a job at a big resort in Baudette called Bittner's. That's where he was calling from.

"What will you be doing?" I asked.

"All I know right now is that I'm in charge of the guides, the boats and the marina. It pays good, and they've given me an apartment right here in the main lodge. I've got a kitchen, a telephone, a TV. The interview lasted all of five minutes."

"They're lucky to have you. Is it a nice camp?"

"Bittner's is no camp," he said. "It's a corporation. They put a hundred guests a day on the water in thirty-foot Sportcrafts. They've got everything—golf course, tennis courts, an indoor pool. They say the fishing is pretty good. In the spring—"

"I miss you," I said.

"In the spring they catch their fish right on the sand in six feet of water, just like at Kettle Falls."

"I said I miss you."

"I heard you."

The next day I slept until one o'clock in the afternoon, and the day after that until eleven. But by the end of the week, I was getting up with my mother in time to see Tom off to work, and at least physically, I was beginning to feel better. Naturally, Tom and my mother were worried about me, but Tom lacked the ability to conceal it, which made things awkward for both of us. Sometimes at breakfast, I would catch him peeping over the top of his newspaper, checking to see if I was okay.

A couple days after I got home, Paula came to the house, and we spent the evening together. It was wonderful to see her again, and no doubt for my benefit, Paula did her best to suppress her own excitement over her forthcoming wedding.

"You've gotta meet Jerry," she said. "I mean, when you feel up to it. I've told him so much about you."

"I'm anxious to meet him, Zee. I just need a few days to get my feet on the ground. Then we can have dinner or something."

Like my mother and Tom, Paula asked few questions about Mike or my marriage, which must have been really hard for her. I knew they'd all get around to asking eventually, but I appreciated their holding off awhile, if only because I didn't know what to tell them.

Mike, who had been understandably guarded the first time we talked on the phone, took to calling once a week, and I was grateful. I looked forward to his calls, even though our conversations were often filled with awkward silences. Mike, like nature, abhorred a void and did his best to fill these lulls with stories of big fish, big storms and even bigger opportunities that awaited him on Lake of the Woods. He was doing well at Bittner's, and his responsibilities, as well as his paycheck, were increasing rapidly.

"In a couple of years," he said, "I could be running this operation. Would you like to come up and see it?"

And that's when I tried to explain how pointless it was for us to pick up where we'd left off and ignore the reasons we were speaking on the telephone instead of face-to-face. Invariably, these phone calls would end with the same series of questions, to which I would give the same evasive answers.

"Do you want a divorce?" Mike would ask.

"No, do you?"

"No. Are we ever going to get back together?"

"I hope so."

"What does *that* mean?"

"I'm not sure."

And soon after that, we'd hang up. I didn't know where things were headed for Mike and me, but I remembered why I'd left him, and I knew if I went back, it would be forever. It would have to be. And I would need to know that what happened to me before would never happen again. But how could I be sure? The fact that there were things about Mike that frightened me—and things about myself that I deplored—didn't mean those things would change just because I wanted them to.

I had read somewhere—in Mike's science book at Twin Rivers, I think—that all the cells in the human body are replaced every seven years, which meant at the end of that time, we were different people. I liked the concept, especially the part about becoming someone new. But seven years was a long time to wait.

Still, it would be wonderful to be reborn. Perhaps in seven years, I could come up with something more practical than my mother's ideas about the inherent rightness and wrongness of what we do and the karmic consequences that supposedly follow from it. And perhaps in another seven, I'd understand what Hedley meant when he said that people always had a choice, even when it didn't seem that way. If it wasn't my fate to be reborn, then, at the very least, I hoped for a sign. But since none was forthcoming, I braced myself against the pain and waited. And all the while, I had increasing doubts about my marriage, my future and myself.

Oddly enough, the beneficiary of all this introspection was Jimmy. I was clearly no better than he was, and I now felt ashamed to have judged him as I did. We had both smashed up people and relationships, but I'd been forewarned of the risks. And although both of us had intruded into situations where we didn't belong, Jimmy had only wanted to put some money in my father's pocket. I wasn't sure what my motives had been with Rennie, but the whole thing smacked of atonement, arithmetic and bookkeeping. There were gooey streaks of self-righteousness in it, too, and this bothered me the most. On balance, Jimmy looked pretty good compared to me. Yes, he broke laws, but I broke *everything*. I was like Mr. Magoo walking through a construction site. And I was miserable.

Jimmy, for all his shortcomings, was delighted with his life, and it fit him like one of his bespoke suits. That made me wonder about the things we believe in—those things that make us who we are. I believed in many things, but few of them had made me happy in the way that Jimmy was happy. Or even in the way that Mike was happy. It's not that the things we believe in should necessarily fill our hearts with joy, but they ought to make our lives better. And if not better, certainly not worse.

I tried to put all this in a letter to Jimmy, but I tore it up when I imagined him reading it.

Perhaps in seven more years, it would all make sense.

Chapter 37

One morning my mother and I were tidying up the kitchen after breakfast when she announced that we were going to Geneva for the day. "You always liked Geneva," she said.

That was true. Geneva was a pretty little town an hour and a half west of the city on the Fox River. It was full of little gift shops and boutiques, and against all odds, Geneva had somehow escaped the sprawl of Chicago, retaining much of its bucolic charm.

"What do you need there?" I asked.

My mother was loading the dishwasher. "I don't need anything. You do. You don't have any clothes—at least none that fit—and I made an appointment for you to have your hair and nails done. There's a cute little restaurant there, too, down by the river. They say Al Capone used it as a hideout. I thought we'd have lunch there."

I got up and brought her Tom's plate. "This is your way of saying I look awful, isn't it?"

"Allie, you have to *rinse* things first. Let's just say you look like Twiggy—with bad hair. Are you done with your ..."

I handed her my coffee cup and sat back down. "I saw how shocked you were when you first saw me. And I see the way you look at me when you don't think I know. Zee did the same thing the other night."

"We're worried about you. Paula called here, you know, the morning after she came by. You were still asleep. She asked me if you were all right."

"What did you say?"

"I said I didn't think so." My mother closed the dishwasher and turned it on. "What happened in Canada, anyway?"

"I'd rather not talk about it. And I don't need new clothes."

"This isn't a discussion," she said. "I want you to feed your beautiful mutt, get in the shower and try to do something with that ... *hair*. Good heavens, you're not living in the tules anymore."

"Mom, you've used that expression all my life, and I've always meant to ask—where *are* the tules?"

"Don't change the subject, Allison. Get a move on."

So I got a move on, and despite my initial objections, we had a good time. My mother insisted on driving, and I had some of the same feelings I used to get when Mike and I would leave the city for a day of hunting. As we neared the Fox River, the suburbs melted away. There were hills and wooded ravines, and although there were few leaves on the trees, many of them were budding.

"It's pretty out here," I said. "Have you ever thought maybe you and Tom should buy something out this way when he retires, maybe something on the river?"

My mother laughed. "He'll never retire. And I've had enough of living in the country for one lifetime. I've had enough of rivers, too."

"Have you heard anything from Jimmy? The last letter I got from him was two months ago."

"I don't really hear from Jimmy," she said. "I just hear *about* him once in a while from my Cape Vincent friends."

"I was just wondering if you knew what's going on with the point, that's all."

"Allie, forget about the point. You've got enough to worry about."

"I can't help it. I love that place."

My mother sighed. "Always the river rat. You know, from the time you were six, you'd come home after school, get your fishing pole and walk down to the lighthouse or the docks to fish—you and all the old men. What was it you used to catch?"

"Sunnies, mostly. Once I caught—"

"And then when you were older, the highlight of your week was when Hedley or Jimmy would take you fishing in a boat or duck hunting, which you loved more than anything. I used to think you'd lose that, living in Chicago, but you never did. You're smart and sophisticated, and you talk city. But sometimes, when I look in your eyes, I can see the river."

"I'm glad. I like that."

My mother gave me her God-help-you look. "Like it all you want, Allie, but forgive me if I don't share your enthusiasm. I never cared for any of it. I don't have good memories of the Cape like you do."

"I was a little girl."

"And I lost a husband there. I'm glad you have good memories, but I've never missed anything about that miserable, hardscrabble country."

"For me it's kind of … an anchor."

"That's lovely, dear. Just don't tie it around your neck."

When we arrived in Geneva, my mother parked the car and led me directly to a beauty parlor, where she disclosed that I had an appointment in five minutes.

"We should probably have them write up an estimate first," she said as we hurried along.

"You're very funny, Mom. I don't look *that* bad."

"Allie, you look like a soup sandwich, but we're going to take care of it. Have you even had a haircut in the last year?"

"As a matter of fact, yes," I said. "I had Mike cut my hair about a month after we got to Kettle Falls. I had to. There were literally clouds of black flies."

"How awful."

"They weren't around long."

"I didn't mean that. I meant the idea of a man with a pair of scissors."

At the beauty parlor my mother introduced me to a girl named Leanne, whom she seemed to know. Leanne led me to her chair and asked how I wanted my hair cut, but I couldn't think of anything to say.

"I don't really care," I said, finally. "Whatever you think."

She gave me a strange look and didn't ask many questions after that—until she was shampooing my hair and discovered the scar above my ear.

"*Ouch*," she said. "How'd you get that?"

"I fell and hit my head. It was a year ago."

"It's healed, but it's still red. Does it hurt?"

"Only when I think about it."

After that I had trouble staying awake. It was very warm in the shop and warm under the dryer, and everything smelled of lemons, strawberries and flowers. Somewhere in the process, another girl came and did my nails, and then I was done.

Leanne held a mirror behind my head. "What do you think? I think it's really cute."

"It's fine," I said. "It looks great."

And it must have, considering my mother's reaction when I stepped into the waiting room. Either that, or I'd looked so bad before that she would have regarded anything as an improvement.

She turned me around by the elbow. "It's *perfect*. A bit of a shag—not too long, not too short. Now that you're beautiful again, let's go shopping."

Before we'd even stopped for lunch, my mother had bought me more clothes than I ever remembered having at one time. I'd lost a lot of weight, and most of the things I tried on seemed to hang on me, but my mother bought them anyway.

"They're your size," she said. "You're a ten. You'll grow into them—you know, once you start eating again."

"I can pay for this stuff myself," I said at the first store, when my mother had thrust her credit card across the counter. "I actually have a lot of money."

"Good. You can buy lunch. The clothes are my treat, and we haven't scratched the surface yet."

We had lunch in a dark little restaurant festooned with Capone memorabilia that included a grainy photograph of the man himself, standing in what may have been the restaurant's kitchen with a big spoon in his hand. The menus looked like wanted posters, and on the back was a story about how Capone had used the restaurant as a place to hide from rivals like Bugs Moran and "G-men" like Eliot Ness.

"The food's good here," my mother said. "I don't know why they have to play up the Capone angle so much. I mean, let's face it, the man was a gangster."

"But a huge celebrity."

My mother closed her menu. "I suppose so. But people shouldn't get the two confused. A couple days ago, Patty Hearst robbed a bank, and it took up the whole front page. And yesterday that young man ... what's his name? The one who always wears the flag?"

"Abbie Hoffman."

"Yes. Yesterday, he didn't show up for his hearing, and it's all they want to talk about. You'd think he was a movie star. Are you ready to order?"

"No one expected him to show up—it was just a formality. He's on the run."

My mother looked around for our waitress. "Exactly my point—he's a fugitive. But for two weeks it's been Abbie Hoffman *this* and Abbie Hoffman *that*. It'll be the same thing now with Patty Hearst. Honestly, I don't know what all the fuss is about. They may be famous, but they're both criminals. What goes around comes around."

A thousand bedtime stories roared in my ears, and suddenly I was back in Cape Vincent, where no sin went unpunished and everyone got what he deserved.

I put my menu down. "I don't know what that means anymore. Patty Hearst was kidnapped—who knows what she's been through. And the police have been trying to put Abbie Hoffman in jail since I was in high school. Maybe he was set up. How do we know they're even guilty?"

My mother raised her eyebrows. "Because the police are after them. What are you having?"

I let it go. I wasn't looking for a prickly conversation with my mother, but I was surprised by my feelings, which were new and unfamiliar. After lunch we continued to shop until I refused to enter another store.

"We're done," I said. "I love all the things you've bought me, but it's time to go home. It's late."

My mother glanced down the darkening street. "Just one more stop. It's right around the corner. They have the cutest—"

"We're going home now," I said. "Thank you for all the clothes."

"Well, all right," she said. "*Be* a party pooper. I haven't had this much fun in a long time."

"Tom will have to open another store to pay for all this."

"Actually, today was his idea."

"You mean he thinks I look awful, too?"

My mother linked arms with me as we walked. "Of course not. He just thought it might cheer you up to have some new things.

Tom's like most men. He thinks a good shopping spree will solve every woman's problems."

"Well, it was very nice of him."

When we'd put the last of my new clothes in the car, I offered to drive home.

"Thank you," my mother said. "I don't see as well at night as I used to. I think I'm getting old."

"You'll never get old."

"That's what I thought when I was your age," she said.

I found my way out of town, and in a few minutes we were back on the narrow two-lane highway that led to the interstate. It was dark by then, and I had the lights on. The last thing I expected to see was a deer, but right after we crossed the river, one stepped from the edge of the road directly into my lane. I wasn't going very fast and had plenty of time to slow down.

But when the deer crossed into the oncoming lane, it was struck by a car heading in the opposite direction.

The car must have hit the deer in the head and neck, because I saw its left headlight disappear for an instant; then the deer spun 180 degrees in the air and landed in front of us as the other car passed by. Its hind legs were kicking, but I knew it was dead.

I pulled onto the shoulder and turned on the warning flasher.

"How sad," my mother said as we got out of the car. "There's getting to be so many of them. I almost hit one last year."

"Do we have a flashlight?"

"In the glove compartment. I'll get it."

The other car had pulled over soon after it passed us, and I could see a woman, silhouetted by her tail lights, walking toward us. She was saying something, but I couldn't hear what it was. Two cars whizzed past before she reached us, one from each direction, and the second car didn't slow down enough. When its driver finally saw the deer in front of him, he hit the brakes hard, and his car fishtailed, nearly sideswiping ours.

A few seconds later the woman joined my mother and me. She was crying.

"I never even saw it." She was smartly dressed—raincoat, heels, white scarf. "It just ... *appeared.* I feel terrible."

"We have to get that deer off the highway," I said. "And we have to hurry. If we leave it there, it'll cause an accident."

We walked to the front of the car and looked at the dead deer in the pulsing light of the flashers. It was a doe. Its neck was broken, and it was very big in the belly from the fawn it was carrying.

"Oh, my God. *Look!*"

The woman pointed to the doe's abdomen, where the unborn fawn was waging a desperate battle for its life. It was moving and kicking violently inside its dead mother, which now seemed alive with the struggle.

"What are we going to do?" the woman said.

"We have to drag it off the highway—*right now.*"

"We should call a vet. Maybe we could—"

"There's no time," I said. "Grab a leg. Let's get this over with."

"I can't touch it. *Oh, God, it just keeps moving!*"

"I can help, Allie," my mother said.

"No," I said. "I need you to signal the cars behind us with the flashlight. If they don't slow down ..." I looked at the woman. "C'mon! Grab hold."

"I'm sorry," she said. "I can't. I just *can't.*"

I let go of the doe's leg and stood up. My mother was walking down the shoulder on our side, waving the flashlight, and I could see the headlights of oncoming cars. Without thinking about it, I grabbed the lapels of the woman's raincoat and shook her very hard.

"You're going to stop crying and help me," I said. "And you're going to do it *now.* People could get killed out here, maybe even us. Do you understand that?"

I let go of her raincoat, and she looked at me with huge, frightened eyes and nodded.

"Good. Now grab the other leg."

Together we dragged the deer to the shoulder and rolled it into the ditch. There were cars going past, but not as fast as before, and I knew my mother had succeeded in getting their attention.

When it was over, the woman wouldn't look at me. She had stopped crying, but there was blood on her hands, which she held in front of her like a surgeon who'd just finished scrubbing. She stood in front of my mother's car and stared at the blood in a bewildered way, looking at her palms, then the backs of her hands, turning them over in the headlights. Then, without a word, she took off her scarf and wiped her hands on it several times before walking back down the shoulder in the direction of her car. After she left, one driver stopped to ask if there was anything he could do, but there wasn't. And there never had been.

"Are you okay?" my mother asked.

"Yes," I said. "You?"

"I guess so."

"You're shining that in my face."

She lowered the flashlight. "I'm sorry. How did you get that woman to help you?"

"I threatened her."

"With what?"

"With ... violence. I led her to believe I would harm her in some way if she didn't help me. It was very liberating. Effective, too."

"My God."

I opened the passenger door for her. "Let's get out of here."

We drove a long time in silence. Then, when we were halfway home, my mother said, "It was a shame about the fawn, but I guess we did the right thing."

I went off like a firecracker. "The right thing? The right thing would've been to deliver the fawn by C-section with a Swiss Army knife or maybe a broken bottle. Then we could've turned it over to a petting zoo, where it could live happily ever after. *Reader's Digest* would kill for a story like that. Next month we could read about how compassionate and resourceful we were—and what a miracle it was!" I was practically shouting. I took a breath and fought for my composure. "But things just … didn't work out that way."

My mother stared at me. "Are you sure you're okay?"

"I'm fine. I'm just—"

"What in God's name happened to you up there?"

But I didn't tell her. I never told her much of anything about Canada, except that I didn't want to talk about it. I didn't even want to think about it.

I thought a lot about the fawn, though, and the raincoat lady, and I wondered what Hedley would've said about the whole thing. Maybe I'd made one of his ever-present choices that night. If so, it hadn't felt like it. There had only been that one horrible thing to do—no options, no prerogatives.

Eventually, I began to think maybe that's the way it worked. Maybe having a choice didn't mean having the luxury of choosing one potential solution over another. Maybe it meant doing the only thing you could do—a choiceless choice but still an alternative of sorts.

Chapter 38

When I came downstairs the morning after the deer episode, Tom and my mother were sitting at the kitchen table, doing what they'd probably done every morning since I got there—wondering how the mad woman living upstairs was feeling today. I began banging around in one of the cupboards, and when my mother asked me what I was doing, my answer surprised even me.

"I'm hungry," I said. "I'm looking for the waffle iron."

When Tom heard that, he jumped up from the table, reminding me that waffles were his specialty. He made me sit down and in no time had prepared an enormous breakfast that he set before me on two plates. Then he and my mother watched me eat as though they were watching the final seconds of a Super Bowl that could go either way.

When I was finished, my mother said, "Allie, that was breathtaking—inspiring, actually. Tomorrow we'll concentrate on chewing our food before we swallow it."

"I'm sorry. I was hungry."

"I'm delighted," she said. "If you keep it up, your new clothes may even fit someday." Then she announced she had errands to run, and I started working on the dishes while Tom had another cup of coffee.

"I'll make you the same breakfast tomorrow," he said. "I don't get to do that very often."

"Thanks, but I probably won't be able to eat for a week."

While I was rinsing the dishes, Tom asked me if I'd be interested in working at one of his stores. I sensed he'd been thinking about this for a while, waiting for the right moment to bring it up.

"You'd be good at it," he said, "and I thought it might … you know, help to keep your mind off things."

"It's nice of you to ask, but I don't know the first thing about furniture."

Tom laughed. "Most of the people who work for me don't, either. All you have to do is convince people there are colors other than persimmon and chairs other than Barcaloungers. Nothing to it."

"I don't know, Tom. Things are kind of crazy right now."

"I understand," he said. "And if you had to quit suddenly, it wouldn't be a problem. Just think about it."

Tom got up from the table and headed into the living room.

"Hey," I said. "Thanks for the shopping spree yesterday. And thanks for making my breakfast."

He turned around in the doorway and smiled. "Let's do it again tomorrow."

I took the job Tom offered—mostly because he'd been so kind to offer it—and read everything about furnishing and interior design I could lay my hands on. I studied furniture until I could draw eleven different chair styles from memory, including the feet, and distinguish Hepplewhite from Chippendale at twenty paces. In time, I even developed a salesman's patter, as well as their soft powers of persuasion. "Yes, these earth tones are lovely, but don't you find it amazing how pastels never seem to go out of style?" If my inner life hadn't been ripped from its moorings, my new job would have been fun.

But I was adrift, rudderless, and the growing emptiness I felt being away from Mike made it even worse. Whenever he would call, my mother would always ask me how he was doing, but she kept all questions about our marriage to a judicious minimum. Still, I sensed that she was growing impatient with me, and one afternoon she said as much.

"Maybe you should fly up to Baudette for the weekend. You know, just to see how he's doing."

"There's no airport anywhere near there."

"Then drive up. You can take my car."

"I have a car."

"Then *use* it. I'm sure Mike would love to see you."

"I don't think that's a good idea."

"Why not?"

"Because I'm afraid I might stay there, and that would be a mistake."

"And there's nothing you hate more than making a mistake, is there?"

"What's that supposed to mean?"

"Nothing," my mother said. "Just don't be stupid. And don't get it in your head that he'll wait around for you forever, because he won't."

If Paula had feelings like my mother's, she kept them to herself. And she never asked anything specific about what had happened in Canada. Paula knew where the boundaries were, but she also knew she had a best friend's right to ask questions within those boundaries, and she exercised that right freely. A lot of our conversations were like the one we had in the car after looking at wedding dresses.

"I don't understand," she said. "Is it a trial separation?"

"I don't know what it is, Zee. I just can't be with anybody right now. I'm an emotional basket case, and Mike and I are very different."

"As in … irreconcilably different?"

"As in fundamentally different."

"But you still love him, and you say he loves you."

"That's true," I said. "But John Lennon is wrong—love isn't all you need."

"But you don't have to agree on everything. If you love each other, you have to work out the problems."

"I need to work out my own problems first." The traffic was bad, and it reminded me of something. "Do you remember what you told me a couple weeks ago—that you hate yourself every time you take the Dan Ryan Expressway?"

Paula shook her head. "That isn't what I said. I said I hate myself when I'm on the Dan Ryan at rush hour. There's a big difference."

"Yes, but you said you cut people off, honk the horn constantly and swear at everybody."

"Yeah, I do. I scare myself. What's that got to do with anything?"

"Well, that's how I feel. But it's like I'm on the Dan Ryan all day long. I want to take an exit, but I can't."

Paula smothered a laugh. "You could get off at West 47th and take it over to Halsted, but I wouldn't recommend it late in the day."

"You're a big help."

"I'm sorry, Allie. I just want you to be happy. I want you to have what Jerry and I have."

But that was the problem. I'd already had all that and lost it.

Right after the House Judiciary Committee recommended Nixon's impeachment—and five months before she and Jerry were to be married—Paula almost lost it, too. I hadn't heard from her for a few days when she called one evening, very upset.

"You busy?" she asked.

"Not really. I was just sketching some ideas for a customer. What's wrong?"

"Everything. I can't talk about this on the phone. Could we please meet somewhere?"

"Sure. Are you at your apartment?"

"Yes, but don't come over here. Jerry thinks I'm sick, and he might drop by. I told him not to but ..."

"What's the name of that little place where we used to meet on Lake Street? It's about halfway."

"Donovan's?"

"Right. I'll meet you there in half an hour."

It was July, and even though it was early evening, the rush of heat when I stepped outside nearly took my breath away. The Chevelle didn't have air conditioning, so I drove very fast with all the windows down, and Chicago smelled the way it always does after it's baked all day under the summer sun—melting tar, overheated automobiles and Lake Michigan, hot and funky. It's something you don't often notice until nightfall; then it washes over you with the onshore breeze.

As I steered the Chevelle through traffic, I supposed Paula would tell me that she and Jerry had just had a huge fight—something to do with the wedding—and now she never wanted to see him again for the rest of her life, that it was a terrible mistake to have believed she could ever be happy with him. If that's what it was, I knew I could bring her around in an hour or so.

But when I saw her sitting at a table in a dark corner of the bar, I wasn't so sure. She didn't seem angry. She seemed ... broken. There was a red tealight candle on the table, and the light it cast on her face made her look grotesquely sorrowful.

I leaned down and hugged her. "What happened?"

"I don't even know how to tell you. I've been crying for two days."

"Afraid Nixon will beat the rap?"

Paula tried to smile. "None of that matters anymore."

We each ordered a glass of iced tea, and when the waitress left, I said, "I've never seen you so upset. What's wrong?"

Paula's mouth began to work, but at first no words came out. Then, very quietly, she said, "I slept with someone," and she started to cry.

Through her tears, Paula explained that the evening had begun with a little cake and ice cream party after work for a co-worker who'd received a long-awaited promotion. After a couple hours, the party migrated to Rush Street, where a good deal of bar-hopping had gone on, and Paula, who'd had several Wallbangers too many, wound up in the apartment of a handsome young law clerk.

"What was I *thinking*?" she said. "I'm in love with a wonderful guy—the guy I want to marry—and I sleep with some stranger I met at the Scotch Mist. God, I'm such a tramp."

I'd been sitting across the table but moved to the chair beside her. "You're not a tramp. You were drunk and you did a stupid thing. It happens."

"Did you hear what I said? I screwed some guy I didn't even know." She put her head in her hands. "What am I going to tell Jerry?"

"Nothing." The word came out so easily it surprised me.

It surprised Paula, too. She looked at me in astonishment.

"What good would it do?" I said.

"I have to tell him. I can't just go on as if nothing happened."

I could hear the substation humming in my ears. "Believe me, you won't. But this doesn't have to ruin your life. Or Jerry's."

"What about little things like honesty? It's wrong not to tell him."

"It's wrong either way, Zee. Look, if telling the truth is more important to you than Jerry's feelings and your life together, then you should do it. But sometimes truth is the easy way out."

Paula shook her head. "I can't believe you're saying this. Jeez, you're the girl who found a ten-dollar bill in the locker room and turned it in to lost-and-found. And now you're—Hayes, are you even *listening* to me?"

"Of course I am—I'd still turn the money in. I was just ... thinking about something."

"What?"

"Wolves."

"Hayes, don't do this to me."

"No, no, listen. I learned something about pain in Canada—never feed it. If you do, it just gets bigger. What if because you're in pain, you inflict it on Jerry? Then it's twice the size. And what if because he's in pain, he does something foolish, like break off the engagement and never see you again? The pain just keeps growing. Is that what you want?"

"That's what I deserve."

Under any other circumstances, I might have laughed. "Zee, this isn't about deserving. It's about living. Besides, you already got what you deserve—look at yourself. The question is how much company you need in order to live with it."

Paula looked confused, but she wasn't crying anymore. "I don't know what to do. I thought you were gonna tell me to do the right thing."

"I'm pretty sure I just did."

"But I want to be forgiven. Haven't you ever felt that way?"

"Yes. But I gave into it, and ... things didn't turn out well."

When Paula and I left Donovan's that night, she hadn't decided whether or not to tell Jerry. But when I saw them together three days later, it was clear—at least for the time being—that she'd chosen the right wolf.

Chapter 39

By the end of July, I had a fairly comfortable routine and was even thinking about finding an apartment, an idea that didn't sit well with my mother. Mike continued to call, though not as often, so I took to calling him. I could usually reach him in the evening, except on Sundays, which puzzled me. I couldn't help remembering what my mother had said—*he won't wait around for you forever*—and at first I thought maybe Mike had a girlfriend. But it was hard to imagine a romance that confined itself to a single night per week, especially the same one. Even so, when I asked Mike about his Sunday nights, he became sullen and changed the subject. I didn't ask again.

Neither of us had any idea what lay ahead, but I think we both clung to the hope that things might eventually work out. Mike was waiting for me to say something, but I was just waiting. Perhaps I was still waiting for a sign, like the prophetic flock of blackbirds Mike and I had seen that time at Cloverdale. Or perhaps I was waiting because I didn't know what else to do.

Not long after Zee had told me about her night on Rush Street, my mother heard that the Bayside Pub had burned to the ground under somewhat suspicious circumstances.

"I hope Jimmy didn't have anything to do with it," she said. "He owned that place with Hap, you know."

I would have forgotten all about the pub, but the day before Nixon announced his resignation, Gabby called. She was actually calling my mother to find out where Mike and I were living, and she was surprised when I answered the phone. Her French-Canadian accent confused me, and at first I thought the call had something to do with Kettle Falls. But once we got past that, Gabby explained she was trying to get ahold of me because Jimmy was in "a little trouble."

"What kind of trouble? Is he okay?"

"He's fine ... I just don't know how long he can stay that way."

"Does it have anything to do with the pub?"

"*Oui et non*. It's really complicated, Allie, and Jimmy doesn't know I've called you—he wouldn't want that. It's just that he always says you're the only family he really has, so I—"

"But he's okay?"

"Yes, he wouldn't go to *hôpital*, but he's—"

"The *hospital*? What happened?"

"Somebody hit him on the head here at Sable, and Stokes found him. I was out of town."

"Who's Stokes?"

"He works for Jimmy—he's been here forever. Jimmy will be angry that I called you."

"Then tell him I called you. Do you mind if I come out there in a couple days?"

"*C'est splendide!* We'd love to have you. I travel a lot, but Jimmy's always here."

For several minutes, I tried to wring more details from Gabby about what had happened, but she was reluctant to say much. Jimmy had been knocked unconscious and robbed. That, and the fact that the break-in had taken place two weeks ago, was all I could get out of her.

After I got off the phone, I felt bad about inviting myself to Sable Island, yet I also had the feeling that may have been what Gabby wanted. I had nothing to offer Jimmy—I knew that. It was just time to go home. Gabby's phone call might not have been the sign I was looking for, but it was the perfect excuse to head east, to return to the fountainhead, the scene of the crime—whatever it was I'd abandoned.

I'd wanted to leave by noon the next day, but of course I didn't. There were some things I had to tell Tom about—things from work—and then there was the inevitable confrontation with my mother, who made it very clear that she didn't want me within a hundred miles of Jimmy.

She was standing in the doorway of my bedroom, watching me throw my clothes into two suitcases.

"What's going on out there that you have to leave all of a sudden? Why can't you go in a week or so?"

"I have to go now."

"He's in trouble, isn't he?"

I was struggling to close the first suitcase. "I'm not sure. I got a call from Gabby, and I didn't like the sound of it. I don't really know the whole story."

"I don't like the sound of it, either," she said, "and I don't know *any* of the story. Try folding things before you put them in there."

When I turned around, my mother was gone. I knew she was angry, but I thought that was the end of it. I should've known she was just marshaling her resources. Moments later, she burst back into the room.

"You're making a big mistake, Allison. Jimmy destroys people."

"You can say what you mean. I know what happened to my

father."

My mother glared. "Then you know enough to stay away from your uncle."

"You don't need to worry about me."

"That's what your father said."

I tried to embrace her. "Everything will be fine."

My mother backed away. "Don't you dare give me a hug while you pack a bag to run off and save Jimmy from whatever mess he's in. Just stay out of it."

"I can't."

"You'll wish you had." Then she left again, only this time she didn't come back.

It was almost two o'clock by the time I was ready to leave. Tom urged me to wait until the following morning, and I probably would have, if my mother had reacted differently. But it was tense in the house, so I decided that as long as I was going, I might as well leave right away. Besides, it was a two-day trip no matter when I left. I asked Tom if he'd mind taking care of Molly while I was gone, and of course he didn't. He even offered me his car for the trip, but by then the Chevelle and I had a certain history, so I threw my suitcases in the back and left just ahead of a storm.

By the time I reached Gary, Indiana, it was pouring, and, according to the radio, several tornados had touched down in the state. East of Gary, some of the underpasses were beginning to flood, and there was an abandoned vehicle in the deepest one. I drove through it very slowly, so as not to swamp the Chevelle's engine, and as I passed the stalled car, I noticed there were two rats perched on its vinyl roof. They stared at me with little red eyes, and I laughed out loud at the indignant looks on their faces. It was the same look you get from hitchhikers that you drive past in bad weather.

I made it through all the underpasses without incident, but the rain came down so hard I could barely see the road, and a lot of the cars had pulled off on the shoulder. Somewhere between South

Bend and Elkhart, my windshield wipers wore out—or whatever wipers do when they start smearing water all over the place. So I pulled into a gas station, bought new ones from an attendant who was nice enough to put them on and drove from there to a motel, where I sat in my room and watched the rain.

The next morning I remembered to set my watch ahead an hour before starting out. That seemed like a strange thing to do—to propel myself into the future in order to reclaim my past. Time zones may mend the little rents and tears that our travels leave in the fabric of the universe, but there's a troublesome trade-off—they turn every day into two days. If I traveled far enough, it wouldn't be today anymore. It would be tomorrow. Somewhere, it already was.

Time zones were like the angle of declination and the two norths—crude and compensatory, like a matchbook under the short leg of a wobbly table. Yet it was these same clunky concepts that enabled us to live in the world, to find our way, to arrive at our destination in sync with the solar system. Our relationship to the universe shouldn't require constant tweaking, but it does. I thought about that a lot as I drove east toward tomorrow—and yesterday.

I made it the rest of the way to New York that day, but it was brutal, since I'd put so little of the trip behind me the first day. The highlight of day two was the swearing-in of Gerald Ford, and I must have heard him announce the end of our "long national nightmare" at least fifty times on the radio. I was happy about Nixon's resignation, but everyone had seen it coming.

Just south of Henderson Harbor I crossed Sandy Creek, the ancient southern boundary of my childhood and gateway to my little corner of the world, an insular province of wind, water and forgotten wars. It was good to be back, and I headed directly to Sackets Harbor, the nearest town to Sable Island, where I hoped someone from the club could pick me up at Jimmy's landing. I'd never driven across the ford myself, and I had no intention of attempting it in the Chevelle.

At Sackets I saw a pay phone in front of a bait shop and stopped to make my call. The instant I opened the car door, I could smell the lake, and when the wind hit me, it brought with it my childhood.

Gabby answered on the first ring. She was excited that I'd arrived, though she was starting to worry a little, and I explained how yesterday's storms had slowed me down. She said Jimmy had been angry that she'd called me, accusing her of making everything sound worse than it actually was. But he'd come around quickly, she said, and was really looking forward to seeing me.

"Do you know how to get to the landing from where you are?" she asked.

"I think so."

"Good. I'm going to have Stokes pick you up. Jimmy wanted to do it, but he just walked in covered with grease—*il est immonde!* He's been working on the boat."

"That's fine," I said. "I'll see you soon."

Two wrong turns later, I was standing on the dock, looking across the narrows at Sable Island, thinking about the time Jimmy had driven me out there when I was eleven. The sun was on the trees, and both the lake and the sky were turning pink in anticipation of the sunset. Above the ford, terns were hunting minnows in the shallows, flapping their wings in a frantic attempt to hover before plopping headfirst into the water.

It was cool for August, especially near the lake, so when I returned to the car, I put on my jacket before lugging my suitcases out on the dock. By then I could see a small skiff motoring toward me from the island, and I knew it was my ride. As it swung into the dock, I grabbed the gunnel, and a bald, smiling man in his sixties stepped out.

"I'm Stokes," he said, offering me his hand. "And I'm bettin' you're Allie."

"I am. I'm happy to meet you, Mr. Stokes."

He laughed. "Just plain 'Stokes' will do. I sure ain't no

mister."

"Then Stokes it is," I said. "I think we actually met a long time ago when I was a little girl."

"You don't say. Well, I don't recall, but that's kinda how it goes." Stokes looked down at his feet. "I got CRS, Allie. There ain't a damn thing I can do about it."

I could tell I was supposed to ask. "What's CRS?"

"Can't remember shit." Stokes' face broke into a broad smile. "Hell, I couldn't tell you what I had for breakfast." He eyed my suitcases. "Is that everything?"

"Yep."

"Well, Allie, let's get crackin'."

We put the bags in the boat and pushed away from the dock.

"I thought maybe you'd come over in a truck," I said, "but I'm glad you didn't."

Stokes pulled the starter rope. "You know, I was gonna, but then Jimmy told me about the time he drove you out here when you was little." He started to laugh. "He said you was scared to death."

"It's true. I was."

And as we left the landing, I realized I'd never known real fear until I was eleven. Now, I was afraid all the time.

Chapter 40

When we got to Sable Island, Jimmy and Gabby were standing on the dock. They had to look directly into the setting sun to see us, and each of them held one hand in front of their eyes and waved with the other. I jumped out of the boat before Stokes had even killed the engine and hugged Jimmy a long time, then Gabby.

"I can't believe you're really here," Jimmy said. "You look terrific."

"So do you," I said. "Both of you."

And they did. Jimmy had acquired a few more gray hairs, but he never seemed to age. And Gabby—she was even more beautiful than I remembered. She looked as though she should be sashaying down the runway at a fashion show instead of standing on the dock at a hunt club.

She grabbed one of my suitcases. "Here, let me take this. Thank you, Stokes."

"Yes, thanks," I said. "I enjoyed the ride."

"My pleasure, ladies," he said.

Jimmy took the larger of my bags, and the three of us walked up the hill to the house—to the *mansion*. The last rays of the sun were striking the tall windows in a way that made it look as though every light was on. We entered the rear of the house through a columned portico and a massive door with an elaborate fanlight. Inside, the house was gorgeous—classical and carefully balanced but very homey. Gabby and I sat down in front of the fireplace in the great room while Jimmy carried my bags upstairs.

"I'm putting you in the executive suite," he hollered.

"Thank you," I said, "but anyplace will do."

"Nonsense, *mon amie*," Gabby whispered. "He wants to impress you because he knows how fancy that place was in Ontario." She pointed to the huge fireplace. "He even laid a fire, and it's August. Let me make you something to eat. What would you like?"

"Just a sandwich. Whatever you have."

When Jimmy came downstairs, he went behind the bar. "Name your poison."

"A beer would be good," I said.

Jimmy pulled three bottles from the big glass cooler, and when he handed me one, I started to laugh.

"*It's UC for me*," I said, reciting the old jingle. "I haven't seen a bottle of Utica Club since I was a little girl."

"They're still making it. So how have you been?"

"Oh, God, Jimmy, I don't know. How have *you* been?"

"Good, I've been good. What do you think of the place?"

"It's magnificent! Sable Island must be the fanciest club on the Seaway."

He smiled. "We're getting there. Tomorrow I'll show you around—you gotta see the new trap and skeet range." He nodded toward the fireplace. "You want a fire?"

"Sure, that would be great. I forgot how it cools off here at night."

Jimmy jumped up to light the fire, and a few minutes after that,

Gabby brought me a ham sandwich, the crusts neatly trimmed.

"*Madame, le dîner est servi.*"

"Thank you. It looks good."

Gabby glanced at the fire and gave me a little smile. "America certainly made history today. Did you ever think you'd see a *président* resign?"

"Not until a couple weeks ago," I said. "He didn't have much choice."

Jimmy leaned back in his chair. "Yeah, you gotta know when to fold 'em. He damn near wrecked the country before he figured that out."

"So how's Mike?" Gabby asked. "How come he made you come out here by yourself?"

Gabby's question blindsided me—I'd told her nothing about Mike and me on the phone. Stammering with embarrassment, I gave them the bottom line—that we'd been apart since the end of March.

Jimmy shook his head. "Jesus, Allie. I'm really sorry. I hope everything works out."

"Me, too," I said.

"I never saw two people more in love than you and Mike," Gabby said. "You were … *un couple parfait*. Are you in touch?"

"Yes," I said. "It isn't that we don't love each other. It's just that we … I don't know—it's hard to explain."

"Well, you don't have to explain a thing to us," Gabby said. "We're just happy you're here."

It was almost an hour before the conversation turned, as it had to, toward the robbery. Jimmy brought it up.

"So how much did Gabby tell you about what's going on out here? She must have made it sound pretty bad for you to jump in your car and drive all this way."

"*Je suis innocente,*" Gabby said. "I told her I was worried, that's all."

"Who broke in here?" I asked. "Did you see the guy?"

Jimmy looked at Gabby, who shook her head emphatically. "I never said a word."

Jimmy bit his lower lip. "The guy didn't have to break in, Allie. It was Hap. My business partner hit me over the head with a bottle of whiskey and emptied my safe. Then he split."

"*Why?*"

"The usual reasons. He was broke. And he was in trouble." Jimmy got up and jabbed at the fire with the poker. "Hap was in over his head—*way* over. He ran up a bunch of gambling debts and couldn't pay his bookies. He was betting on football, horses and—"

"Tell her about the Bayside Pub," Gabby said.

"I'm getting to that." Jimmy returned the poker to its rack and sat back down. "Hap torched the Bayside for the insurance, but the company wouldn't pay—they claimed an accelerant had been used. I'm half-owner of the place, so now everybody, including the police, thinks I had something to do with it."

"But we weren't even in town," Gabby said.

Jimmy tried to laugh. "After the Bayside didn't pay off, Hap really got desperate. He borrowed money from a loan shark in Jersey, but of course he couldn't pay the juice, so they put the screws to him."

"And he wanted Jimmy to bail him out," Gabby said.

"But I couldn't do it. Hell, I'm mortgaged to the roof of my mouth, and he needed fifty thousand dollars. When he realized I didn't have it, he started in on me about the point for the hundredth time. He promised to—"

"Please tell me Hap didn't sell it," I said.

"He didn't. The point's in joint tenancy—that's one of a dozen things we went to court over. He also tried to force me to buy him out of the club. You should see my legal bills."

"And when everything else failed, he came out here and robbed you?"

Jimmy nodded. "That's how it turned out, but I don't think he planned it that way. Hap showed up that night with a bottle of rye that he was drinking like water. He told me there were some very nasty people looking all over Jefferson County for him, and they were either gonna break his legs or kill him, so he needed money to get out of town. His plan was to head for the Maritimes, and from there he said he was going to get on a plane and disappear for a while. Anybody want another beer?"

"I'm fine."

"So am I," Gabby said.

"I'm sure as hell not." Jimmy got up and headed for the bar.

Gabby mouthed the words "There's more," and when Jimmy returned with his beer, I asked him to finish the part about when Hap came out to Sable Island.

Jimmy settled back in his chair. "Well ... like I said, Hap was drunk as a lord, but I finally agreed to lend him three thousand—that's all I could spare—so I opened up the safe in my office, and that's when he let me have it with the Overholt. I had almost twenty grand in there, and he took it all."

"What's an Overholt?"

He and Gabby laughed.

"Welcome to northern New York," Jimmy said. "Old Overholt is rye whiskey. I've still got a lump where—"

"The gun," Gabby said. "He took a gun, *n'est-ce pas?*"

"Yeah, but not just any gun. He stole a Parker shotgun that Gable gave me when—"

"*Clark* Gable?" I said. "You knew *Clark Gable?*"

"Everybody knew him. He used to come up here in the old days. I guided him on Wolfe Island when I was a kid. One day we were on Brewster's Marsh, and he told me it was the best duck hunting he'd ever had. He said he'd never forget it, and he gave me his Parker so *I'd* never forget. His name was engraved on the receiver. I never shot it, I just—"

"Why would Hap steal his shotgun?"

Jimmy frowned. "It was *my* shotgun, and Hap can get five or six grand for it easy."

"And afterward Stokes found you on the floor?"

"Right in there." He pointed to his office. "Stokes was in town having dinner with his sister, like he does sometimes, and when he got back, he found me on the floor and the safe open."

"And naturally," Gabby said, "neither of them thought to call the police."

"Stokes wanted to," Jimmy said. "I had to threaten to fire him before he shut up about it. I didn't want the cops around here ... but of course the bastards showed up anyway."

I looked at him, confused.

"Didn't Gabby tell you about that either?"

"I most certainly did not," Gabby said. "I left all the best parts for you."

Jimmy folded his hands behind his head. "When Hap went missing, somebody filed a missing person's report—probably the guys he owed the money to—and the cops came out here to ask me some questions. 'Did Mr. Strattner tell you where he was going?' 'Do you know when Mr. Strattner might be coming back?' Stuff like that. They didn't really ask me much the first time."

"The *first* time?" I said.

"Yeah, the second time was last week. They had me come to the police station, and from the things they asked, I sort of got the feeling they thought I might have ... *killed* him."

"That's crazy," I said. "He isn't dead. All they have to do is get ahold of him, and he can clear the whole thing up. Don't you have any idea where he is?"

"Not really," Jimmy said, a trace of frustration in his voice. "Hap's plan was to go someplace where no one could find him— that was the whole idea."

"Okay, but he'll show up eventually, and when he does, that will be the end of it."

"We know that, but the cops don't. Jesus, I wish they'd get off my back."

I thought of Stone Bear—the eyes, the riveting stare. "They might if ... they believed you."

"Well," Jimmy said, "I told 'em the truth. I said Hap was into a loan shark for some serious money and that he was on the run, headed up to Halifax. I said I didn't know what his plan was after that, and I don't."

Gabby turned to me. "But the police don't know anything about Hap coming out here that night."

"Why the hell should they?" Jimmy said. "It wouldn't have looked too good if Hap went missing right after he'd robbed me."

"What about the people Hap borrowed the money from? Aren't the police interested in them?"

"I don't think the police believe they exist," Jimmy said. "Even if they did, they'd never find those guys. I don't know who they were, and there's no way of finding out now."

"I still don't understand why *you're* a suspect."

"I don't know that I am. They've never used that word. But it's no secret that Hap and I have been at each other's throats—we spent the last year suing each other. And then there was that tiff at the Chicken Shack last—"

"What tiff?"

Jimmy groaned. "The day before he showed up out here, Hap and I got into a fight at the Chicken Shack—it's a little dive out on Route 3. He called me to meet him there for dinner, and he was already drunk when I walked in. He kept asking me for money, and I kept telling him I didn't have any. Then he started yelling and took a swing at me when I tried to leave. It wasn't a fight, really. I just clipped him on the chin and he fell over the table."

"But everybody saw it," Gabby said.

"The owner must have called the cops after I left, because they asked me about it. It was no big deal." Jimmy picked at the label on his beer bottle. "I screwed up when I talked to the insurance investigator, though. The cops asked me about that, too."

"*Quoi*? You never told me about that."

"No, I ... forgot. The investigator who told me the Bayside fire was arson asked if I had any idea who might have done it. I said it was probably Hap."

"And that's how you screwed up?" I said.

Jimmy squirmed in his chair. "I was mad, you know? I told him when I caught up with Hap, I was gonna kill him."

"*Ah, mon Dieu!*" Gabby said.

"Yeah, well, like I said—I was mad. I didn't mean I was actually going to *kill* him. The police don't have anything on me, and they know it."

"Even if they did," I said, "they'd have a hard time proving you killed someone who isn't dead."

"But how can we be sure?" Gabby said. "What if these New Jersey *truands* who were looking for Hap caught up with him? If his body turns up in a dumpster, it will be *très mauvais* for Jimmy."

"I think you need a lawyer," I said.

Gabby looked triumphant. "See? That's what I told you."

"I've got a lawyer."

"You need a *criminal* lawyer," she said.

Jimmy put his hands in the air. "What the hell do I need *any* lawyer for? Hap isn't dead, and I haven't done anything. Hap's smart, and thanks to me he has enough money to hide for a long time. He's probably in Rio by now or on some little island drinking rum out of a coconut."

"I still think you need a lawyer," I said.

"Look, if it makes you two feel any better, I'm meeting a guy tomorrow who knows all about that stuff. I'll ask him for a couple of names. I promise."

We sat there and didn't say anything for a while. Jimmy let the fire die down, and we all had another beer and talked about the fishing, which had been good, and about the upcoming duck season, which Jimmy said looked very promising in terms of his bookings. The wind picked up, as it so often did on the lake at night, and it wasn't long before we could hear it howling in the chimney and buffeting the windows.

"I think I'm going to bed," Gabby said. "You two stay up as long as you like. I'll see you in the morning. Allie, I'm so glad you're here. *Bonne nuit.*"

"Me, too," I said. "Good night."

"We'll be along soon," Jimmy said. "I'd better go down and check the *Merganser*. I didn't put it in the boathouse. Care to join me?"

"Sure. Is the *Merganser* the big Chris-Craft that was at the dock when I got here?"

"The very same." Jimmy finished his beer in one swallow and stood up. "I left it out because I was thinking you might get here early enough to run over to Henderson Harbor for dinner."

"Can I have a rain check?"

"You bet."

Jimmy and I walked down to the dock under a full moon, and the boat was fine, snug in its moorings, which creaked softly as the boat rose and fell with the swells.

"Offshore wind," Jimmy said. "We're okay."

"I've missed that sound. The wind here is different than anywhere else."

"That's because there's so much of it." He knelt down and checked the bow line. "I'm really sorry about you and Mike. What happened?"

"I jumped."

Jimmy cocked his head. "I don't follow."

"Do you remember telling me how you kept yelling at my father to jump just before the barge exploded, but he wouldn't do it? Well … I jumped. I don't know how else to put it."

"I hope you can swim better than he could."

"I'm sort of treading water at the moment."

Jimmy stepped into the boat and offered me his hand, which I took and hopped in beside him. We sat down in the big captain's chairs and swiveled them around to face the open water.

"This is a big boat," I said. "Much bigger than I'm used to."

"Twenty-eight feet and tight as a drum." Jimmy looked at me closely. "You seem different, Allie. You even look different."

"In what way?"

"I'm not sure. Your eyes, maybe. They remind me of your father."

"I've been thinking about him a lot lately," I said. "It's a new thing. Do you ever think about Hedley?"

Jimmy laughed. "I was thinking about him as we walked down here—when I saw the full moon. I was thinking how he used to call it a barley moon."

"Why barley?"

"I haven't a clue. That's just what they call the full moon in August. They have names for all of them. The full moon in October is a hunter's moon."

"I know about the hunter's moon," I said. "I wish I had memories like that. I wish my father had told me the name of the moon or a constellation or something. I'd be happy if he'd told me the name of a single star. That way it would be mine. I'd have that forever."

"If it wasn't for me, he might have."

"I didn't mean it like that. Besides, I have you to tell me about the barley moon. I didn't know there was such a thing."

"Well, you're looking at it."

By any name it was a beautiful moon, and in its tranquility, it seemed out of place amidst the wind and tumult. Later that night, as I lay in bed, the moon made its way to my window and woke me up.

I watched it through the swaying trees, thinking that to paint it, you would first have to paint the wind and then the sound of the wind. Only then could you paint the moon.

But there are other things that you cannot capture with pigment or even with words. I fell back to sleep looking at the barley moon, thinking about those things.

Chapter 41

The wind blew itself out during the night, and when I looked out the window the next morning, the trees weren't moving at all, and there was a low-hanging blanket of fog on the lake that was burning off as I watched. It was early, but I got up anyway, took a long shower and went down to the kitchen, where Stokes was having a cup of coffee.

"What strikes your fancy this morning, Allie?" he said. "We got some good back bacon. Or I could whip you up an omelet."

"Thanks, Stokes, but I think I'll just have a cup of coffee. I can get it."

"Sit yourself down," he said. "Have your coffee while I scramble you some eggs. I can't let you sit here and not eat somethin'."

"All right. Thank you."

Stokes brought me coffee in a big mug, got some eggs out of the refrigerator and cracked them into a bowl.

"What else do you do at Sable Island besides the cooking?"

"Oh, we got a real cook for hunting season. I just fill in a little. Mostly, I do whatever needs doin'." Stokes hesitated for a moment.

"Did Jimmy give you the skinny on what happened out here?"

"Yes," I said, "if you're talking about Hap Strattner."

He looked relieved. "Good. I didn't know if I was supposed to talk about it or not. You know, I told Jimmy we should report it to the police, but he wouldn't hear of it." He poured the eggs into a frying pan and started to laugh. "Jimmy says to me, 'Goddammit, Stokes, I'd pay twice what Hap stole from me just to keep the cops *off* this island.'"

"Jimmy and the authorities go way back."

"Yeah, but he's too smart for 'em. Hell, he's the best in the business."

"The business?" I said without thinking.

"Smuggling. He's the best."

"Oh, smuggling. Sure. Absolutely the best."

Stokes brought me my eggs, and we sat by ourselves and talked until Gabby and Jimmy joined us. They were both wearing camouflage bathrobes with "Sable Island Hunt Club" printed on them in little red letters. Stokes got each of them a cup of coffee, then set about the business of making their breakfast.

"She blew pretty hard last night," Jimmy said. "I thought maybe we'd get rain today, but it doesn't look like it."

"How did you sleep?" Gabby asked me. "Did the wind keep you up?"

"No, but the moon was awfully bright."

"*Désolée.* Those west windows—I should have pulled the shades in your room."

"No, I enjoyed it. I haven't seen a moon like that for a long time."

"What's on your list today, Stokes?" Jimmy said. "You need anything from town?"

Stokes set a plate down in front of Gabby. "I don't think so. I'm gonna do some mowin', and after that I should probably work in the carriage house. Everything was just kinda throwed in there at the end of the season."

"If you need anything, let me know. I'm headed to Watertown after we show Allie around."

"Okay, boss," Stokes said. "But I think I'm set."

"What's in Watertown?" Gabby asked.

"I want to pick up some props that I had rebuilt, and I'm meeting somebody for lunch."

"Barry?"

"How'd you know?"

Gabby laughed. "You told us last night you were meeting someone today who could recommend a lawyer. Who else could it be?"

Stokes looked up from the stove. "A lawyer? Now we're screwed."

"I just need a little advice," Jimmy said. "Don't get excited."

"Whatever you say, boss."

The three of them finished breakfast, and while Gabby and Jimmy went upstairs to get dressed, I went into the bar to call Mike, who had no idea I was in New York, and my mother, who'd be relieved to hear I'd arrived safely.

My mother seemed to be over the fit of choler, or whatever it was, that she'd had the day I left. I didn't tell her very much on the phone but promised to call again soon. Mike didn't answer, so I assumed he was at breakfast or already working. I decided to try him again that night, when there was a better chance of his being there.

The phone calls made, I sat down in one of the big leather chairs by the window and watched the lake—and Stokes, who would silently appear, then disappear every few minutes on a riding lawnmower. Hundreds of dragonflies were darting and crisscrossing very low over where he'd mowed, looking for mosquitoes. They were careful to stay in the warm sunlight, but they probed the edges of every morning shadow.

In a few minutes Jimmy and Gabby found me and provided a tour of the house, which, like many of the big places in that country, consisted of an original limestone structure that had become a hyphen connecting huge postbellum additions.

"The lighthouse and the keeper's home were both built in 1823," Jimmy said as we entered through a low doorway.

The hand-hewn timbers and uncut stone gave the rooms a feeling of incredible mass and antiquity. As I looked around, a century and a half seemed to melt away.

"It's hard to believe," I said. "When this place was built, America stopped at the Mississippi, and Thomas Jefferson was alive. Thomas Cole was still painting portraits."

"This is one of the oldest buildings in the county," Jimmy said with pride. "It's listed in the National Registry."

"It's good that you restored it. History is … everything."

Jimmy laughed. "The state of New York felt the same way. They gave me a lot of money to fix it up."

"I wish they'd give us some money to heat it," Gabby said.

Jimmy led the way from the keeper's home into the older of the two additions, and in every room the furnishings were perfect, a mélange of antiques that came together beautifully.

I pointed to a chair. "Is that a real Phyfe?"

"Yes, you know furniture?"

"I've been working for Tom."

"That's great—we've got a couple Eastlake tables around here someplace. I'll bet you've never seen one. Of course, I'm partial to Stickley myself." Jimmy motioned us forward. "Keep moving, folks. Stay together. There's much more to see."

The last time I was there, the club had seemed grand, but I was only eleven and must have failed to see the decrepitude that Jimmy, by his account, had struggled to eliminate over the years. Now, there wasn't so much as a blister in its glistening paint or a crack in its leaded windows. All the woodwork, including the doors and floors, had been refurbished, and everything was as close to original as Jimmy could get it.

When we were done inside, we walked the grounds, grasshoppers clattering at our feet. The late summer perennials were a riot of color—purple asters, black-eyed Susans and hollyhocks of every hue.

Jimmy pointed to a bed of mums. "All this is Gabby's doing. I've got as much into the landscaping as I do in the house."

Gabby took his hand. "You said money was no object, *mon amour*."

"I know, but *Jesus* ..."

"It's beautiful," I said. "I hope you charge your duck hunters top dollar."

"I do. I just wish I'd had all this back in the glory days. Too many hunters today are willing to stay in a motel."

After they'd shown me the new trap and skeet range, Jimmy asked Gabby if she wanted to run into Watertown with us.

"You two go," Gabby said. "I was thinking I'd work on my tan before I go back to Toronto."

"You're leaving?" I said.

"Yes, the day after tomorrow. I wish we could have overlapped longer, but I'll only be gone a couple days." She put her arm around Jimmy. "*J'ai un vrai boulot*."

"You travel too much," Jimmy said. "And I have a 'real job,' by the way."

"Of course you do, *mon cher*."

Within an hour, Jimmy and I were leaving for Watertown, and because he didn't have a vehicle at the landing, we had to take the truck, which also meant we had to cross on the ford. I didn't like that part, but it wasn't as bad as I'd expected. It was bumpy, and the water came in under the doors, but this time it was more strange than scary. When we drove past the dock and up onto the landing, the only car there was mine, and I took the opportunity to retrieve my sunglasses from above the visor, where I'd forgotten them the day before.

"I know it's out of the way," I said, "but would you mind driving through the Cape?"

"I was planning to," Jimmy said. "Anything special you want to see?"

"Yes."

"Your house and Hedley's house?"

"Yes."

As we reached the outskirts of the Cape, what struck me immediately was the number of mobile homes, which were unheard of when my mother and I lived there. It made sense, though. Once affluent and fashionable, Cape Vincent had been succumbing to a generic American poverty for a long time now. The hunt clubs had slowed the process down, but they couldn't stop it, and the only jobs left—most of them hourly or part-time—were in Watertown. The mobile homes were simply the latest symptom of the old disease, which now manifested itself as a tug-of-war between a romantic past and a minimum-wage future. As Jimmy drove through town, it was easy to see which one was winning.

"There's your old house."

"It looks about the same," I said, "only it's smaller than I remember. And there used to be a big tree outside my bedroom window."

"We had a bad ice storm here about five years ago. Lost a lot of trees. You know, I could count on my fingers the number of times I was in that house after ... you were born."

"You were going to say after my father died."

"Yeah."

When we got to Hedley's house, it didn't look the same at all. It had been added on to, and it was beige now with brown trim. There were two children splashing around in a little inflatable pool in the front yard and a big Chesapeake lying nearby in the shade of a lilac bush. I wondered if perhaps the dog was a distant relative of Ace and decided it probably was. The last thing we did in the Cape was drive down to the docks, and I was glad we did, because heading downriver was the biggest laker I'd ever seen.

"Do you know that ship?" I asked.

"Everybody knows that ship. She's the *Stewart Cort*, the first thousand-footer on the Seaway."

I took off my sunglasses and tried to take it in. "It's almost … overwhelming. I've never seen so much burnt sienna in one place before."

"She's even bigger than the *Edmund Fitzgerald*."

We walked down to the harbor, and it was like running into an old friend.

"See that pier next to the breakwater?" I said. "That was my favorite place to fish when I was little. I did very well there."

"You and all the old-timers. You were quite the tomboy."

"River rat," I said. "I still am."

"Anything else you want to see in the Cape, river rat?"

"No, but thank you for bringing me here. I'm ready for Watertown."

Jimmy drove east, back toward Sackets, and just before we crossed the Black River, he picked up his props at a little shop with a sign out front that said WELDING ALL KINDS. Then we went on to Watertown, which didn't appear to have changed very much, although the same economic tension I'd seen in the Cape was also present in Watertown's business district. Where I remembered booteries and little markets, there were now karate studios and head shops, which were sadly incongruous with the nineteenth-century buildings that housed them.

"Where are we going?"

"The Crystal," Jimmy said. "That's where we're meeting Barry."

"Great! I love that place. Barry is the person you're going to talk to about an attorney, right?"

"Yeah, yeah."

The Crystal looked exactly the same as when Hedley used to

take my mother and me there for special occasions, like my birthdays, which he felt were too big to be absorbed locally. Jimmy and I walked past the bar at the front of the restaurant and sat down at a table covered with red formica that wasn't really red anymore. Many years and many cleanings—along with several million plates and elbows—had worn most of the color away, leaving only splotchy traces of the original finish. Jimmy's friend wasn't there yet.

"Do you think he forgot?" I asked.

"No, he'll be along. We're a little early."

A waitress brought us menus, and we explained that there would be three of us. Half a minute later, Jimmy waved to someone behind me.

I turned to see a man with a closely cropped beard making his way past the bar. He was about forty, wearing blue jeans and a faded work shirt, and when he saw Jimmy, he smiled. Jimmy and the man greeted each other familiarly, without shaking hands, as though they saw each other often or knew each other well.

"Allie," Jimmy said, "this is my friend Barry Freed."

"It's nice to meet you," I said.

"The pleasure's mine, Allie. Jimmy told me you were coming." He put his hand on Jimmy's shoulder. "Did you really drive all the way from Illinois just to see this guy?"

"I did—all the way from Chicago. Do you live here in Watertown?"

Barry pulled up a chair. "In my dreams. I've actually been living in Mexico, but my girlfriend's grandmother has a home on Wellesley Island. We're visiting."

"Barry's checking out the area," Jimmy said. "He wants to move here."

"I do," Barry said. "The St. Lawrence is the most beautiful thing I've ever seen. I can't imagine anything better than waking up and seeing it from my bedroom window."

I looked at his eyes, which were sad and kind. "I hope that happens for you."

There was something strangely familiar about Barry, and all through lunch I tried to put my finger on it. He had a Jewish, New York accent, and except for his deep tan, he looked like a college professor—like *most* college professors. Finally, I decided that was why he seemed familiar.

During lunch we talked mostly about Watergate, Nixon and what Ford would do. Barry knew more about politics and American history than anyone I'd ever met. At one point I asked him if he was a teacher, and he looked at Jimmy, then at me and said he'd tried teaching but found it impossible to educate people with closed minds.

Eventually, as he was supposed to do, Jimmy asked Barry about attorneys, and Barry asked him what kind of attorney he needed.

"Criminal."

Barry raised his eyebrows but didn't say anything. He wrote several names on a napkin and slid it across the table. When we'd finished lunch, Barry said he had to meet Johanna, his girlfriend, so they could catch the ferry back to Wellesley Island.

He shook my hand again. "I enjoyed meeting you, Allie. I hope to see you again sometime."

"Thank you," I said. "I hope you wake up soon with the river outside your window."

He smiled. "So do I. I'll be in touch, Jimmy."

Later, as Jimmy and I were walking to the truck, I said, "Barry seems like a nice person. How do you know him?"

"We've done a little business," Jimmy said.

"What business is he in?"

Jimmy started to laugh. "You don't have any idea who that was, do you?"

"Should I?"

"That was Abbie Hoffman, Allie."

I stopped dead in my tracks. "*What*? That *couldn't* be Abbie

Hoffman. Abbie Hoffman jumped bail. He's ..."

"That's right—on the run, using 'Barry Freed' as an alias. Your mouth's open."

I put both hands to my head. "I just met *Abbie Hoffman*? I can't believe it! I heard him speak once in Chicago. He was amazing and terrible at the same time."

"And now he's Barry Freed. You know, when he told me who he was, I had to go to the library and look him up. Barry Freed doesn't have much in common with the guy I read about."

"He's changed," I said. "A lot."

"Can people really do that?" Jimmy looked at me as though I knew the answer. "I mean, how can you change who you are?"

"I don't know," I said, "but I met an amazing girl in Canada who told me if who you are isn't working, then you'd be a fool not to become somebody else. And she was an expert."

When we got to the truck, Jimmy unlocked the driver's door, got in and reached over to unlock mine. As I climbed in, he started laughing again.

"I knew you'd get a kick out of that," he said. "You know, one time I asked Barry if he ever missed being Abbie Hoffman, and he said, 'Sure, I miss a lot of things about my old life, but it was too damn hard being me.'"

"I'll bet it was," I said.

On the way back to Sable Island, I asked Jimmy what kind of "business" he'd done with Barry. Jimmy was vague, but he said Barry had needed to get back and forth from Canada a couple times, so Jimmy had taken him. Jimmy never used the word *smuggle*. He made it sound as though he'd given a friend a ride to work, as opposed to spiriting a fugitive in and out of another country.

"It's not like he can just go through customs and cross at the border," Jimmy said.

"No, I understand. I hope one of the lawyers he wrote down can help you with the Hap Strattner mess. He probably recommended

William Kunstler."

"It isn't *that* big of a mess."

"It will be if Hap turns up dead."

"He won't."

"How do you know?"

"I just do," he said. "Hap always lands on his feet."

"Tell me something … since Hap is gone and may never come back, does that mean you can dissolve the partnership?"

Jimmy looked over and smiled. "And claim all of Hap's assets, including his half of the point?"

"I was just wondering."

"I could go to court and try, but there are a couple reasons why I won't. For one thing, Hap will be back some day. For another, if I made a move like that, the police would climb all over me. Hell, they'd have more motive than they knew what to do with."

"Hey, look. There's the place you were talking about last night— the Chicken Shack. I must have missed it on the way in."

On my side of the highway, tucked back in the trees, was a ramshackle, low-roofed structure with neon beer signs all over the front. It was covered with the kind of tar paper that's supposed to look like bricks but never does.

"You didn't miss it," Jimmy said. "We didn't come this way. The Shack has damn good chicken if you go there on a Friday, when they change the grease. By about Wednesday things start to taste funny."

"*Yuck.*"

A few minutes later we were driving down the little road that led to the landing, and when Jimmy pulled into the clearing, he stopped in front of the ramp and turned off the engine. He put both hands on the wheel and stared across the water at Sable Island.

"I'm in kind of a jam right now, Allie, but I don't want you to worry about anything."

I did my best to smile. "That's a tall order. You know, if Hedley were here, he'd say you're in a pickle."

"Or he'd say that I chose to be in this situation when I got involved with Hap. Maybe I did, but it doesn't matter anymore … right or wrong, that's just the way it is."

"Right or wrong," I said. "Or both. Or neither. I used to spend a lot of time thinking about things like that."

"So what made you quit?"

"I don't know that I have. I wish I could, though. It's too damn hard being me."

Jimmy laughed and turned the key in the ignition. "Lift up your feet, river rat. Let's go back to the club. The three of us should do something fun this afternoon. What would you say to a couple rounds of skeet?"

"Trap," I said, "but only if you spot me four birds."

"You're on."

And with that he put the truck in gear, and we drove down the ramp into the lake.

Chapter 42

We had fun shooting trap that afternoon. Both Jimmy's trap and skeet ranges were so new they hadn't been painted yet, but they were regulation, fully automated and state of the art. Gabby joined us and shot well for someone who'd never fired a gun before she met Jimmy. I shot okay, but even with a four-bird handicap, Jimmy won easily with two perfect rounds of twenty-five. Gabby even made him hold his shotgun at his waist until each bird was thrown, but it didn't make any difference. Jimmy's shooting was fast and effortless, and his gun seemed to fire the instant the stock touched his shoulder.

"You hustled me," I said. "Do you *ever* miss?"

"Once in a while on the skeet range."

Gabby rubbed her shoulder. "I've never seen him miss. Every time I do this, my shoulder turns black and blue."

"Mine hurts, too," I said. "Jimmy, your guests are going to love this—their own shooting range."

"Yeah, now all I have to do is pay for it. That's a little tricky since Hap ran off with my operating capital."

"Can you borrow more? Maybe get a note?"

Jimmy zipped his shotgun into its case. "It's just a cash-flow problem. I'll raise the money somehow."

"*Somehow?*" Gabby said. "Tell the truth, *amoureux.*"

He looked at her but didn't say anything.

"Hey, I already know the truth," I said. "I thought maybe he'd given it up."

"I'm standing right here," Jimmy said.

"It used to bother me, too, Allie," Gabby said. "But he'll never change—*qui a bu boira.*"

Jimmy looked puzzled. "Who drank will drink? If that's supposed to be French-Canadian wisdom, it doesn't make a lick of sense."

Gabby laughed. "Yes, it does—it's like leopards and their spots."

"If you say so," Jimmy said, "but I like my spots the way they are."

After we'd picked up our casings, Gabby said she had to make some phone calls, so Jimmy decided the two of us should walk down to the boathouse.

"You haven't seen it yet," he said, "and I want to show you something—something I don't show to just anybody."

"Ooh, mysterious."

The boathouse was a newer building, not far from the dock, that sat at the end of a dredged, L-shaped channel leading to the lake. I'd seen it from a distance, but it wasn't part of my earlier tour. The boathouse had a walkway on one side, where the service door was, and an open stairway that led up to its flat roof, which was actually a sundeck with a white balustraded railing.

Jimmy unlocked the door. "This wasn't here when I bought the place."

We stepped inside, and when he turned on the lights, half a dozen startled swallows swooped down and flew under the big double doors, which closed to within a foot of the water. The boathouse had a full floor with a workbench at one end and two boat slips, only one of which had a boat in it. In the empty slip the water was jet black and filled with little gasoline rainbows that seemed to swirl and change colors under the lights.

Jimmy gestured toward the boat. "What do you think?"

I was looking at a nondescript fiberglass runabout—maybe twenty-two feet long—that was painted flat gray right down to the deck cleats. I couldn't tell if it was a new boat or an old one. There was nothing on it that indicated the make or model. There wasn't even a name on the stern.

"It's ... nice," I said. "Another Chris-Craft?"

"No, it's basically a Thompson—with a few modifications."

"You're rebuilding it?"

"Already did. Hang on a minute." Jimmy got inside the boat and lifted the engine cover. The engine was bright orange and so clean it actually gleamed. "*Now* what do you think?"

I had no idea what to say. "Jimmy, I'm really sorry. I don't know anything about engines. It's very clean. I've never seen such a—"

"It's a Chevy big-block," he said. "A four-fifty-four. I put it in last year."

"So it's fast?"

"Fast?" Jimmy looked at the engine the way some men look at women. "It's got 500 horsepower at the crankshaft, and it pushes this boat seventy miles an hour. The hull can take every bit of it, too—I reinforced it with aluminum."

"I'm sure it's very useful, but maybe you should paint it. It looks kind of ... plain."

Jimmy laughed. "I just did. I change the color a couple times a year, but I want it to look like every other rig on the river."

"Oh, I get it—you want to blend in."

"I want to be invisible, but blending in is usually enough."

"You should have a name on it, at least."

Jimmy lowered the engine cover and sat down on it. "Allie, I can get in this boat any night of the week and make a thousand dollars out there on the river—sometimes a lot more."

I didn't say anything.

"Look, I don't want this to be a problem, especially now, when I have to go back to work. With that twenty grand gone—"

"Work?" I couldn't help laughing. "Is that what you call it?"

Jimmy shook his fist. "*Straight to the moon, Alice.* You're as bad as Gabby."

"Sorry," I said, trying not to smile. "I interrupted you … you were saying?"

"I was saying I have to do a lot of *smuggling* between now and freeze-up to cover my losses. I've got big payments to make, Allie, and I don't want to sneak around behind your back."

"Don't worry about it, Jimmy. I've known for years you were a smuggler."

"And you don't mind?"

"Of course I mind. But it's on the list of a hundred-and-one things I can't change. I probably wouldn't anyway. Smuggling is … *you*."

"You sure?"

"Positive. Besides, I've got a new rule about minding my own business."

Jimmy climbed out of the boat. "Hedley had a real thing about smuggling. He used to say, 'James, honest men work days; smugglers and whores work between them.'"

"Hedley said a lot of things, Jimmy. Most of them were probably true, at least for him. But he told me once that Elvis Presley was a flash in the pan, and he made Kool-Aid without adding sugar. Who would do a thing like that?"

"The same guy who used to tell me the best way to double your money was to fold it in half and put it in your pocket." Jimmy shook his head. "But smuggling for me isn't really about the money—not that I don't need some right now."

"Then what's it about?"

"The excitement, maybe? The risk, the thrill of it. It makes me feel alive. Hell, I'm almost glad I need the money."

"I'm sure my husband would understand that perfectly, but I don't. Not that it matters."

"Let's go up on the deck," Jimmy said. "It's nice up there this time of day."

He turned off the lights, locked the door, and I followed him up the stairs. It was pleasantly cool on the deck, and there were round cedar tables with umbrellas, along with an assortment of chairs and chaise lounges. There was a breeze coming off the lake, and the sun was so low it was beginning to flatten into the water somewhere west of Charity Shoal. Jimmy leaned against the railing while I sat at a table and looked out at the golden water.

I leaned forward, my chin in my hands. "Tell me a smuggling story—one I won't believe."

Jimmy pinched his lower lip and became thoughtful—or pretended to. "Hmm ... a smuggling story. I wish Gib Leroux was here. He could tell you a corker."

"Who's Gib Leroux?"

"Just a guy I know. He's retired now—did it on one big job. Gib was a lucky man ... a *very* lucky man."

Jimmy paused, and I knew what was coming because he told stories the same way Hedley did. And sure enough, when he spoke again, the timbre of his voice had changed—just like Hedley's used to—and all of his words had reorganized themselves at a different pitch.

"It was in 1963," he said, "and Gib took a job late in the year—a big-ticket run just before ice-up. He was the only one of us who hadn't pulled his boat that fall, so we figured he had something in the works, but he wasn't talking and we didn't ask. It was the end of January when I ran into him at Roxy's Bar in the Cape." Jimmy stopped and smiled to himself, musing on whatever had happened at Roxy's.

"And?"

"And I bluffed—I asked Gib straight out how the big job went, like I knew all about it. He said, 'Good, Jimmy. It went real good—big payoff.' So we had a couple beers—he was already lit up—and after a while, he leans across the table and says to me, 'I smuggled two men out, Jimmy—very bad men. I took 'em up the Cataraqui to the bridge.' Gib told me that from the time he picked them up until they got off his boat on the other side, they never spoke a word to him. But he said they were whispering to each other in French the whole time, like they didn't think he'd understand."

"But with a name like Leroux, he did, didn't he?"

"Sure," Jimmy said. "Most river rats speak a little French—it comes in handy now and then. But Gib's a *French* river rat, and these guys hadn't counted on that. Well, Gib overheard just enough to scare the hell out of him." He paused again.

I pointed my finger at him and pretended to shoot. "Ka-pow! What did he hear?"

Jimmy sat down beside me and lowered his voice for effect. "I had to buy Gib three more beers to find that out, but he finally came clean. He said he was pretty sure the men he smuggled across that night were the ones who shot Kennedy. They were Corsican, and they'd spent a month holed-up in Texas. Gib said somebody met them at the bridge and handed him a bag full of hundred-dollar bills." Jimmy chuckled softly. "I'll bet if old Gib had said so much as *au revoir*, he would've been found floating in the Cataraqui."

"Wow! Great story. I take it you're not a big fan of the Warren Commission."

Jimmy scrunched up his face. "If Oswald shot Kennedy, then I'm Deep Throat. There's no way you believe that cock-and-bull nonsense."

"I used to but not anymore. That doesn't mean I believe the whole French Connection thing, though."

"Either way, the moral of the story is when you're smuggling, you never know what you're getting into."

"That isn't exactly a moral."

"Of course it is," he said.

"No, no, a moral would be something like 'Never smuggle Corsicans' or 'Don't speak French in front of a stranger.' Those would be morals."

Jimmy gazed out at the lake. "Maybe you're right. I guess there shouldn't be a moral to a smuggling story anyway."

"Maybe there shouldn't be a moral to *any* story. I've become very suspicious of morals. I mean, why should we expect something from a story that we can't find in life?"

"I couldn't tell you," Jimmy said. "Morals are definitely not my area—ask anybody."

"I meant the other kind," I said, laughing. "What about life?"

"I don't know much about that, either—except that we all have the same goal."

"And that would be ..."

Jimmy looked surprised. "To find happiness, Allie. Everything else is just strategy."

"You're a wise man, Master Po."

Jimmy rolled his eyes. "You can find more wisdom in a fortune cookie. What do you want to do tomorrow?"

"River rat stuff."

"Well ... with the duck season almost two months away, that means you want to fish, shoot, play cards and generally goof-off. That sounds good to me—maybe I can forget about the police for a while."

So for the next three days, goof-off is what we did. Smallmouth bass were biting well on the shoals, and in the *Merganser* there was no place we couldn't go, even in the wind. We ran the river all the way to Ogdensburg one day, just for fun, and the next day Gabby was back, so the three of us went out on the big lake to Prince Edward Point, where we drifted with the wind, got sunburned and caught fish so fast we couldn't keep our lines in the water. After dinner, we'd walk up to the trap range and shoot a round of trap or skeet, and no matter what handicap we imposed on him, Jimmy always won.

When I left Chicago, I had no idea how long I'd be staying in New York, but very quickly one week became two, and then Gabby, who would come and go, was due back for a long weekend, so I'd stay a little longer. It felt right to be there, and I think Jimmy was grateful to have someone to talk to when Gabby was on the road. At the very least, I probably helped him keep his mind off his troubles. I'm sure Jimmy never forgot about Hap and the police—I know Gabby and I didn't—but none of us mentioned it.

Jimmy's legal problems may have weighed on his mind but not heavily enough to keep him from returning to "work." One afternoon, not long after our conversation in the boathouse, he announced that he was going to "take a little nap," which, as Stokes explained, meant Jimmy would be on the river that night. I heard Jimmy downstairs around one in the morning, and a short time later, I heard what I assumed was the Thompson take off across the lake and head west toward the mouth of the river. I don't know what time he got back, but he was exceptionally chipper at breakfast that morning.

"How'd it go?" I asked.

"Great! Couldn't have been better." Then he began singing Pink Floyd's "Money," hammering the bass line into the table top.

"I get it," I said. "Eat your breakfast." But it was too late, and that riff was stuck in my head for the rest of the day.

After a while, I noticed there was no discernible rhythm to Jimmy's late-night escapades. He'd be out on the river two or three nights in a row, then skip a couple, and I supposed it was because he didn't want to become predictable. I don't know if it was the smuggling and excitement that agreed with Jimmy or all the money he was making. But whatever it was, his spirits improved dramatically.

One morning at breakfast I explained to him that it was time for me to think about going home, but he was ready for me.

"Home?" he said. "This is your home. You belong out here."

"But I work. I have to get—"

"Another job. I understand. I'll pay you twice what Tom's paying you to sell furniture. You start tomorrow."

"Jimmy, my marriage is—"

"Exactly! You should get back together with Mike, and the two of you should move out here. How can you not know that?" He set his coffee cup down hard.

I didn't talk about going home anymore after that. I didn't want to go anyway.

In the two or three phone conversations I'd had with Mike since arriving at Sable Island, I hadn't told him anything about my reasons for being there—only that I was visiting Jimmy and Gabby. The phone calls were unremarkable until Mike told me one night that Bittner's did a huge ice-fishing business, and the owners had asked him to stay on and run it while they went south for the winter—something Mike said they'd long dreamed of doing.

"What should I tell them?" he asked.

"I wish I knew, Mike. I really do."

"That doesn't help me," he said. "I need something solid from you one way or the other."

"You have a master's degree from a very prestigious university. Do you really want to run camps forever?"

"Oh, pardon *me*. I didn't know you were teaching art out there in New York. Look, I need to know what I should do, and that depends on what you tell me."

"I understand, but … I'm happy here."

Mike hung up with a sharp click.

So I had two sets of problems, and when I wasn't struggling with decisions about my marriage, I was worrying about Jimmy's predicament. Jimmy had hired a lawyer from Albany named Martin Ingram—one of the attorneys Barry Freed had recommended—and Ingram told us the district attorney might be willing to take the case to the grand jury without a body, but only if the police had identified a crime scene or if it could be proven that Hap Strattner was actually dead. And so far, neither had happened. The police weren't idle, though. They were asking a lot of questions around town, and they'd searched Hap's house in Alexandria Bay a couple times. Ingram said if they'd found Hap's wallet or car keys or something that made his disappearance look coerced, then there might be grounds to launch a murder investigation. But evidently the police didn't find anything like that.

We wondered if they would search Sable Island, but Ingram said it was nearly impossible to obtain a search warrant in a missing-person case. Of course, if the police had known that Hap was at Sable shortly before he disappeared, it would've been a different story. But they didn't, and we weren't about to tell them. So the police investigation was a stand-off.

By mid-August, Jimmy's initial fears had turned to annoyance. It cramped his style to have the police looking over his shoulder all the time, and he damned Hap regularly for that, vowing to get even, no matter how long it took. But Gabby and I weren't convinced Hap was alive, so instead of waiting for him to return or send a postcard from South America, we just hoped whoever had disposed of his body had done a good job of it.

As the end of August approached, we were no longer able to spend all our time playing—only about a third of it. Jimmy, Stokes and I worked hard, if a bit sporadically, getting the club ready for the mid-October opening of duck season. We'd work a couple days sealing floors or repairing duck blinds; then we'd loaf, which is the way Jimmy wanted it. He said he never got too carried away with the work until the middle of September.

I couldn't get over how much different Sable Island was from Kettle Falls Lodge. Both places were posh and expensive, but because Sable Island was a club, many of the guests had memberships, often for a lifetime, which meant they were comparatively low maintenance. At full capacity, Jimmy needed only a dozen staff, including guides and a cook, and a lot of them stayed on the mainland, so that, too, made life simpler. "Sable Island practically runs itself," Jimmy said, and to hear him describe it, the club might have been his alter ego. Kettle Falls was frenetic and hyperactive. The Sable Island Hunt Club was mellow and serene.

The Tuesday after Labor Day, the police wanted to talk to Jimmy again, so he went to Watertown, but this time Mr. Ingram went with him. When he got home, Jimmy found Stokes and me replacing decoy lines in the carriage house.

"So what did they want?" I asked.

Jimmy sighed. "It was the same old thing. But they were a lot nicer about it with Ingram in the room. Last time, I was 'buddy' and 'fella.' Today, I was 'sir' and 'Mr. Addison.'"

"Well, that's an improvement. Do you think that's the end of it?"

"Not a chance."

Stokes tossed another decoy on the ready-to-go pile. "Why the hell not?"

"Because Ingram asked them if anyone else was under investigation, and basically they said no. They said my past makes me a 'person of interest.'" Jimmy managed a little smile. "Ingram went through the roof when he heard that."

"Good," I said. "Did he use the word *harassment*?"

"No, but he chewed on 'em pretty good for not doing their jobs.

It won't change anything, though. As far as they're concerned, I'm the only game in town." Jimmy sat down on an overturned floater and shook his head. "This is never going to end."

"Them sonso'bitches," Stokes said. "All you ever done was smuggle."

Chapter 43

One morning after breakfast, for no particular reason, I took a cup of coffee and climbed the spiral staircase to the top of the lighthouse, where I sat quietly within its hexagon of glass. It was a beautiful morning, perfectly calm, and the lake reflected the sky so faithfully that it was impossible to tell where one ended or the other began. Both held the same clouds, the same hazy sun, and the seagulls that flew over the lake were also flying deep within it.

I could see everything, but I was seeing it twice. Along the shore, the huge overhanging willows, newly minted in the water, grew in and out of themselves, touching at the fingertips. To my right, down on the dock, I could see Jimmy on his hands and knees, swinging a hammer, but he wasn't alone. His left-handed doppelganger was kneeling upside-down on a different dock just beneath the water, driving nails upward into its undisturbed surface. Everything was itself and yet more than itself—*the same but different*. From where I sat, there were twice as many possibilities in the world as usual.

I probably stayed there for twenty minutes, enjoying my double vision, and I would have stayed longer, but I came to feel there was something subtly wrong with the moment or perhaps with me. After a while I realized the only Zen in a lighthouse—or anywhere, for that matter—is the Zen you bring there, and I had come empty-handed. I knew I could do better but not just then. So I left, somewhat reluctantly, and joined Jimmy on the dock.

"Were you up in the lighthouse a few minutes ago?" he asked.

"Yes. I was meditating. What would you like me to do?"

"Are you and Stokes finished at the range?"

"We put two coats on everything, even the trap house. It looks great."

"Thanks," Jimmy said. "I don't know when I would've gotten to it. You want to come with me on an errand?"

"Sure. Where?"

"I have to run into Fletcher's and pick up a new bilge pump for the Thompson. Nobody in Sackets has the right one."

"You working tonight?"

"That's the plan. My truck in ten minutes?"

"Okay," I said. "I'll see if Stokes needs anything."

I finally found him in the garage, putting a new tire on one of the trucks.

"That ford sure beats the hell outta things," he said, pumping the jack handle. "Tires don't last more than a few months, and the alignment's catawampus after one trip over." He wiped his hands on his coveralls and chuckled. "At least you can tell when it's a Sable Island truck comin'—the damn things go down the road sideways."

"Do you need anything from the Cape? Jimmy and I have to pick something up at Fletcher's."

"Naw, I'm good, Allie." Stokes started to laugh. "Jimmy must be hard up."

"It's nothing like that. He just needs a bilge pump. I'll see you later."

Stokes had laughed when I mentioned Fletcher's because Jimmy avoided Fletcher's as much as possible. Fletcher's Marina functioned like a smuggler's clearing house, and everybody knew it. There were a lot of places like that on the Seaway—bait shops, bars, even certain stores in town—but Fletcher's was one of the best known, and they operated practically in the open. Jimmy said they posted smuggling jobs on their bulletin board, but I think that was an exaggeration.

There was a hierarchy among St. Lawrence smugglers, and Jimmy, who occupied the topmost tier, never used any local business as a contact. He joked about having an agent, but I think it was actually true. Jimmy would get phone calls that he always returned from pay phones in town, and I supposed whoever was on the other end of the line got a piece of the action. But I never asked about things like that.

Forty-five minutes from the time I'd left Stokes—and after a bone-jarring trip across the ford—Jimmy and I walked into Fletcher's Marina, where a small drama was unfolding. A red-faced man behind the parts counter was arguing with a young woman holding a baby. He wanted her off the premises, but she wouldn't go.

"Please, Mr. Fletcher," the woman said. "You don't understand. He has to get back into the country."

The man pointed to the door. "Lady, I'm asking you for the last time to leave. Do I have to call the cops?"

The woman stood there for a moment, shifted the baby to her other arm, then turned and walked past Jimmy and me on her way out the door. She didn't look at us, but I could tell she was crying. There was a bench outside the front door, and through the window I watched her lay the baby on it very carefully, then sit down and put her hands over her face.

Jimmy walked over to the counter. "Call the cops? I'd buy a ticket to see that, Fletch."

The man half smiled. "How you been, Jimmy? That broad walks in here outta the blue and says she needs somebody to smuggle her husband over from Canada. It's like she was asking me for a goddamn spark plug. Hell, she could be anybody."

"Why would she set that up over here?"

"That's what I asked her. I told her to find somebody on the Canadian side. I got that pump you called about—I just gotta find it. Gimme a minute."

While Jimmy waited at the parts counter, I went outside. The woman hadn't moved. I walked over to the bench, said hello, and when she uncovered her face, it was the perfect image of despair.

"This is a first," she said. "I've never been kicked out of a marina before." She was sniffling but tried to smile. "Did you see?"

"Yes, I came in right at the end." I sat down next to her. "How old is your baby?"

"Five months, eleven days," she said, with a new mother's precision. "I'm glad she won't remember any of this. Boy, I really caused a scene in there."

"You call *that* a scene? You should see some of mine. I'm Allie Bowman."

"I'm Janice Spencer … and I'm not having a good day." She was younger than she'd seemed inside—mid-twenties, more cute than pretty, with blue eyes and blonde hair that she kept in place with a headband. "Everybody told me if I asked at this marina, they could help me, but that man wouldn't even talk to me."

"It's because he doesn't know you. He said you're trying to get your husband into the States. Is that true?"

Janice nodded. "Yes, but I'm making a perfect mess of it." She looked at me closely, deciding how much to say. "My husband and I have been living in Canada for the past three years. We're draft dodgers—I mean *Warren* is. But now his father has cancer, and Warren wants to go back to Glens Falls and see him before he dies. He has to sneak in somehow."

"But if he gets caught, he'll go to jail."

"Worse—federal prison. One of our friends went back for his brother's wedding, and now he's doing three years in Fort Dix." She shook her head as though she couldn't believe it herself.

Jimmy walked out the door and held up a small box. "We're in business."

"Jimmy, would you mind waiting for me in the truck?"

"Sure thing."

"Your husband?" Janice asked.

"My uncle. So what are you going to do?"

"I have to find a smuggler, even though part of me doesn't want to. Warren and I have a new life now, a *good* life and ... a little girl." Janice's eyes welled up.

I looked down at the baby and imagined Janice bringing her to the prison on visiting days, holding her up to the glass so she could see her father. "Maybe you should tell him you couldn't find anyone."

"I would ... but I know what this means to him."

I didn't know what to say. High above us, a flock of pelicans made a slow, fixed-wing spiral in the quiet sky. I watched them for a moment, then turned to Janice. "You're between the devil and the deep blue sea—that's what my grandfather used to say."

Janice forced a smile. "Hey, it comes with the territory. I mean, you don't love people because they're perfect or sensible or because they always do things you agree with." She pointed to my wedding ring. "But you're married—you already know that."

On some level I might have, but Janice was giving me way more credit than I deserved. "Are you sure you want to do this?"

"I have to."

"Then please don't leave. I know someone who might be able to help. I'll be right back."

I went across the parking lot and approached the driver's side of Jimmy's truck. He took one look at me and said, "Not a chance in hell."

"You don't even know what I'm going to ask."

"Yes, I do—*no!*"

"Just talk to her. Her name is Janice and she needs your help. This is a chance to be a smuggler and do something nice at the same time."

"I don't want to do anything nice."

"I don't believe you."

Jimmy tried to roll the window up, but I put my hand on top of it.

"Didn't you tell me you don't approve of smuggling?" he said. "I seem to remember that. C'mon, get in."

"It isn't that simple. There's smuggling and there's ... *smuggling*." I started to laugh. So did Jimmy.

"Thanks for clearing that up. Let's go."

"Five minutes—just talk to her."

It took a while, but he finally gave in, and I led him over to the bench where Janice was rocking her baby on her lap, talking to it and making little cooing sounds. I introduced them.

Janice stared up at Jimmy, wide-eyed. "Are you a smuggler?"

Jimmy turned to me and smiled. "Your friend has a nice touch. Very subtle."

"I'm sorry," Janice said. "It's just that Allie said you might be able to help me, and no one but a smuggler can do that."

Jimmy nodded at the baby. "Cute little guy. What's his name?"

"Laura."

"Oh ... then he's not ..." Jimmy, distracted, was looking around, watching the cars go by. "Listen, whatever conversation we're about to have, I'd rather not have it in front of Fletcher's. Let's go down by the water."

"Good idea," Janice said. "I've had enough of this place."

"I'll carry Laura," I said. "That is, if it's okay."

"Oh, thank you! She gets heavy after a while."

367

I took Laura and we went down to the docks and walked along the quay, eventually making our way to the breakwater, where we sat on the rocks and talked. There weren't many people around, other than a few tourists who were casting for something with very heavy tackle and a few disgruntled sailboat owners who were scowling at the glassy water.

Janice told Jimmy her story, and he had only one question.

"I'm wondering the same thing Fletch was," he said. "Why aren't you setting this up on the other side of the border? They specialize in this sort of thing at Akwesasne."

"If you're talking about that reservation on St. Regis Island," Janice said, "Warren and I were there yesterday. We drove around for an hour, trying to figure out what to do. Finally, a policeman pulled us over, but we chickened out—we told him we were lost."

Jimmy laughed. "He's the guy you should've asked. The Mohawk do a land-office business up there."

"It's better this way," Janice said. "In a few months, Warren and I will be landed immigrants, but if we break the law in Canada, it could ruin everything. That's why I came over this morning. If there's going to be a problem, I want it to be on this side of the border."

I was still holding the baby, and it had been going fine, but for some reason she started to fuss.

"You have to move," Janice said.

"Move?"

"Your body—it's not moving. You have to rock her or bounce her up and down a little. Here, take these."

She handed me her car keys, but I didn't understand.

"Just dangle them in front of her," she said. "Let her grab them. She'll settle right down."

"Oh, okay," I said, dangling.

Jimmy cleared his throat. "Can we, uh, get back to business? Where's your husband now? Can you get in touch with him?"

"Yes, he's at the Anchor Inn in Kingston."

"Good, that helps. I want you to go to the Seaway Motel in Three Mile Bay—it's not far from here. After you check in, call your husband and give him your room number. Tell him to be on the main dock of the Basin Yacht Club at two o'clock in the morning— that's really important. Can you remember that?"

Janice jumped to her feet. "Does that mean you'll do it?"

"Yeah. If I don't, Allie will never—"

"Oh, *thank* you." She threw her arms around him. "Thank you so much."

Jimmy gently disentangled himself and put a hand on her shoulder. "The Basin Yacht Club at two o'clock."

"I won't forget. Why a yacht club? Is it a secret place?"

A look of amusement spread over Jimmy's face. "The yacht club is across the street from your husband's motel—he can just walk over there."

"Oh, oh, I see," she said. "I'll never be able to thank you." Then she thought of something. "I never asked about your rates."

"My rates?"

"Yes, do you charge by the person?"

Jimmy struggled to keep a straight face. "Usually. Sometimes I charge by the pound—luggage is extra, naturally. How many bags will your husband have?"

"Just one."

"Then how does a hundred bucks sound?"

"Seriously? That sounds like a really good deal."

"It is," Jimmy said. "It's our summer's-end package, plus your friend-of-a-friend discount. And since there's no 'secret place' surcharge, you get another 10 percent off."

Janice looked at me. "He's teasing me, isn't he?"

"Yes," I said. "And he's really enjoying himself."

"Just make sure your husband is on that dock at two o'clock," Jimmy said. "We'll deliver him right to your door."

369

"You make it sound easy." She reached for her purse. "Should I give you the money now?"

"*Jesus*," Jimmy said, looking around. "Please don't."

Janice took the baby and thanked us repeatedly as we walked back to the parking lot. We helped her get Laura squared away in the car and watched as she pulled onto the highway and turned right toward Three Mile Bay.

On the way back to Sable, I thanked Jimmy for helping her.

"Don't mention it," he said. "It's nothing."

"Maybe to you, but it's very important to Janice and her husband."

"And to you, too, for some reason."

When we got to the landing, I asked him to stop for a minute. "I just want to warn you that when we get back to the club, we need to talk."

Jimmy looked at me suspiciously. "If we need to talk, let's do it here."

"We can't. I'll need a couple hours."

"Two hours? I've never talked about *anything* for two hours."

"Well, I'm guessing this will take some time. I have to talk you into letting me come along tonight."

Jimmy slammed the truck into park. "Oh, no you don't—no way!"

"Will it be dangerous?"

"That's not the point. Tonight's a milk run, but I have another load. It's a lot of running around, and you're not going."

"If it isn't dangerous, what's the problem?" Then I understood. I let Jimmy calm down for a few moments. "My father doesn't have anything to do with this."

"Maybe not for you, but what about me? Hedley would rise from the grave if I pulled a stunt like that. And your mother ... I don't even want to *think* about what she'd do."

"Let's not argue about this now. We'll have plenty of time when we get back."

"No, we won't. I have a million things—*two hours*?"

I nodded. "At least two. I'm beginning to think three."

Jimmy sighed and sort of slumped over the wheel. "Okay. If it means that much to you—okay."

"Thank you. I knew you'd understand."

"I don't understand."

"You're a wonderful uncle."

"I'm an idiot."

When we got back, I helped Jimmy install the bilge pump, which meant that I held the flashlight and handed him tools. I've never liked holding flashlights for people, especially men, and that afternoon it seemed the beam was never directed exactly where Jimmy wanted it. Finally, he started laughing.

"What's so funny?" I said, moving the flashlight. "There, is that better?"

"You're not even close," he said. "I was just thinking about the time I helped Hedley put new points in his truck. I was holding the light—just like you are—and he was getting angrier by the minute. Finally, in this really sweet voice, he said, 'James, are you able to see what I'm doing with that flashlight?' And I said, 'No, Pop, not really,' and he said, 'Then how the hell do you expect *me* to see it, ya knucklehead?'"

We laughed, and I told Jimmy that if I'd been holding the flashlight, Hedley would have told me what a good job I was doing and then bought me an ice cream cone.

"Ain't *that* the truth," Jimmy said. "There were two Hedleys— the one you knew and the one I knew. For what it's worth, I think you got the better deal. Now please hold the flashlight so we can *both* see what I'm doing."

"Will you buy me an ice cream cone if I do?"

"No, but I'll leave you standing on the dock tonight if you don't."

At dinner I told Stokes all about Janice Spencer and how I'd be making the run with Jimmy that night. Stokes couldn't stop laughing and asked Jimmy if he could even remember the last time he'd made a hundred-dollar run. Jimmy wasn't sure, but he said he was probably still in high school. About halfway through the meal, Stokes, as he always did, went over to the stove. "Anybody want anything?"

Jimmy raised his coffee cup. "As long as you're up, I'll take another shot."

"Sure, boss. I think it's great you're takin' Allie."

"Oh yeah? What's so great about it?"

"It's just a good thing." He turned to me. "It'll be fun, Allie."

"You think so?"

"Oh, sure. There's nothin' like smugglin'. I used to do a lot of it. One time Jimmy and me—"

"Before your CRS kicked in, I could've sworn you were gonna get me another cup of coffee."

Stokes reached for the pot. "Here you go, boss. Anyway, I'm glad you're takin' Allie. I remember one spring when my sister's boy was maybe fourteen, and I realized—all of a sudden-like—that we'd never really done anything illegal together. So you know what I did? I took him that very day to French Creek, and him and me speared a mess of pickerel."

Jimmy and I laughed, but Stokes was serious. "You can wait too long, you know."

"From what I hear of your nephew," Jimmy said, "I'd say you got there in time." He pushed his chair back from the table. "I need you at the old CCC camp on Mink Point at three o'clock."

"You got it, boss."

"And keep your headlights off." Jimmy turned to me. "Around midnight we'll head out. I have to make a pick-up here and a delivery in Canada. After that we can run ... what's his name?"

"Warren."

"After that we can run Warren across."

"Is that who I'm picking up at Mink Point?" Stokes asked.

"Yes," Jimmy said. "You'll take him to the Seaway Motel. He'll know the room number. Any questions?"

Stokes and I shook our heads.

"Good. Let's hit the sack."

Chapter 44

As I lay awake in bed, I thought about what a strange day it had been. The strangeness had begun that morning in the lighthouse, when I'd seen everything twice, including Jimmy, who had told me there were two Hedleys. I wondered if maybe there were two of everything, in the way that each day was actually two days. There were certainly two Abbie Hoffmans. And two norths.

My heart was pounding. I put my hand on my chest, and I could feel the two wolves in there, circling, sizing each other up.

There was no chance of sleeping. That night was like those nights before duck hunting, when I would lay awake listening for Hedley's truck, listening to the wind working under the eaves and the oak tree groaning outside my window. But tonight there was no wind. The calm that had begun that morning had continued all day, and I hoped it was better for smuggling than it was for duck hunting. Shortly before midnight I heard Jimmy downstairs, so I put on my robe and joined him. He was in the kitchen, eating a bowl of cereal. When I walked in, he held up the box.

"Breakfast of champions," he said. "Someday you'll see my picture right here."

"America's best smuggler?"

"Why not? Get any sleep?"

"Not a wink."

"You want something to eat?"

"I couldn't eat right now."

"Then it's game time." Jimmy finished his cereal and put the bowl in the sink. "You'd better suit up. And dress warm—it's cold on the water at night."

"I'll be there in five minutes. Don't you dare leave without me."

I went upstairs, got dressed and ran all the way to boathouse, where the Thompson was warming up, idling with a deep, loping sound that I could feel in the pit of my stomach. Jimmy was standing beside it, his hands in his coat pockets.

"Are we ready to go?" I said.

"As soon as you get the stern line."

We cast off and Jimmy backed the Thompson out of the boathouse, then swung it around and headed down the channel into the lake, slowly increasing the speed. Late that afternoon, low clouds had rolled in from the east, and the overcast, along with the absence of a moon, made for a dark night on the lake. There were no shapes, no lights, nothing but an inky blackness that seemed almost liquid, as though the air itself had turned black and was staining our lungs as we breathed it.

The darkness didn't bother Jimmy. Like most men, he drove his boat standing up in order to see better, but tonight there was nothing to look at, and the only light came from the glowing instruments— the dials, gauges and compass—that shined softly on his face. I stood beside him and stared at the windshield, which looked like a piece of slate.

"No running lights?"

"Too risky," he said.

"It's so dark out here. How do you know where you're going?"

"The compass and a lot of dead reckoning. In about thirty seconds, you'll see a flashing light off the starboard side. It'll be the blinker south of Point Peninsula."

"Starboard's the right side, isn't it?"

"Yes, river rat. Until you turn around."

About half a minute later, right on cue, I saw the beacon winking faintly in the distance. Jimmy throttled back, slipped the boat into neutral, then turned off the ignition.

"What are you doing?"

"Listening," he said. "I want to make sure we weren't followed from Sable."

"Does that happen often?"

"Almost never. But I have to assume the cops are watching me these days."

We listened, but there was no sound at all and nothing to see in any direction except mute, implacable blackness. Jimmy started the engine and headed north.

"Beautiful night for a boat ride," he said. "It's almost never this calm." Jimmy pushed the throttle forward slightly, and the boat leaped across the water. "I have a pick-up on Point Peninsula. The landing's a couple miles from here."

A few minutes later, he slowed down and turned the running lights on, just for a moment, then off again. Someone on shore signaled with a flashlight, and when we reached the dock at the landing, there was a suitcase on the end of it. Jimmy eased up to the dock in reverse, grabbed the suitcase and handed it to me.

"Put this somewhere out of the way."

"What's in it?"

"It's better you don't know." He pulled away from the dock and headed for the dark safety of the big water.

The suitcase looked harmless enough. It was aluminum and had about the same heft as the smaller bag I'd brought with me from Chicago. Whatever else it may have held—drugs, money, something more sinister—it also contained the accumulated poor decisions and lapses of judgment of everyone associated with it. I hoped whoever packed it had left room in there for mine.

I set the bag at my feet. "Where are we taking it?"

"Just past Marysville—a place called Ferguson Point."

"Is it far?"

"About thirty-five miles. It's across the river from Kingston on Wolfe Island. In a few minutes, you'll see the light at Charity Shoal—that's eight miles from here. You'll see the beacon way up ahead of us on the port side. After that, we're in Canada."

"If you went up past the Cape, there are places where the river is less than a mile across. Wouldn't that be easier?"

"Easier for the police," Jimmy said. "Or for someone trying to rip me off. Bottlenecks are bad—no elbow room."

We rumbled on through the darkness toward Charity Shoal, and it reminded me of last spring, when Mike and I had driven down Lake of the Woods on the ice, looking for Warroad. But tonight I wasn't lost, and Stokes was right—it was fun, at least so far. It would've been fun even in daylight, but the night made it better.

Jimmy was taking his time, traveling at just under thirty miles an hour, but there was no sense of movement because there was nothing to gauge it by, other than the sound of rushing water beneath the hull. Had it been daytime, I would have seen Lake Ontario on my left and dozens of islands on my right, clustered at the mouth of the St. Lawrence. But as it was, all I could see was a tiny pinhole of light up ahead in the darkness.

"Charity Shoal?"

"Yes," Jimmy said. "Do you see the other one? It's on my side at two o'clock."

"No."

"Wait for it—it's a blinker. *There.*"

"I saw it. What's it marking?"

"Otty Shoal. We're going right between them."

But before we did, Jimmy shut down again and we listened.

"I think I hear a boat," I said. "Or maybe it's a plane." But the pitch wasn't right for either one, and the engine had an odd nickels-and-dimes sound to it, like a handful of change rattling around in a can.

"It's a laker," Jimmy said. "It's probably ten miles away. When there's no wind like this, you can hear every boat on the water. The downside is they can hear us, too."

Jimmy started the engine, and when he spoke again, it was to tell me we'd crossed the border. A short time later he reached up and turned a knob on a little box mounted on the dash. It had a circular face, almost like a clock, and the instant he turned it on, a jittery orange light appeared on the circumference of the dial.

"Depth finder?" I'd read about them but had never seen one.

"Yeah. It's shallow around Simcoe Island. In a few minutes this thing will be more help than the compass."

I'd been watching the glow from Kingston for some time, but now the sky to the west was brilliant, as though the entire city were on fire. We entered a long, narrow channel between Simcoe and Wolfe Island, and when we came out the other end, we were on the St. Lawrence River. Kingston was on our left, dazzling but silent, and on the opposite shore we could see the lights from Marysville.

"Where's Ferguson Point?"

"Straight ahead," Jimmy said. "There's an old sawmill there. That's where we drop the case."

The drop-off was different from the pick-up. Jimmy killed the engine a hundred yards offshore, and we drifted in the current until he was sure it was safe. Then he turned the running lights on and off, and someone signaled from shore but with automobile head-lights this time.

As we got closer, I could see a man standing on the end of the dock. Jimmy brought the boat alongside the dock, again in reverse, and swung the suitcase up onto it.

The man picked it up and pointed at me. "Who the hell's she?"

"Don't worry about it," Jimmy said. "C'mon, don't make me sit here."

The man handed Jimmy a bulky envelope, which he put in his jacket pocket, and that was it. We pulled quickly away from the dock and headed across the river to Kingston for the second pick-up, the one I was there for.

"One down, one to go," Jimmy said. "I hope your passenger shows up."

"He will."

Ten minutes later we were moving along Kingston's brightly lighted waterfront, past huge piers and breakwaters, on our way to the Basin Yacht Club which, from a distance, looked like a forest of sailboat masts. The only activity in the marina was at the far end, where a party was still underway on an enormous yacht, and even with our engine running, I could hear "Jumpin' Jack Flash" thumping across the water. Jimmy angled toward the main dock, where we could see someone standing beside a small duffle.

"That must be him," I said.

I waved and the man waved back.

Jimmy brought us in close, then swung the boat around, keeping the prow pointed toward open water.

The man on the dock approached cautiously.

"Are you Warren?" I said, and when I did, I could see the relief on his face.

"You must be Allie. Thanks for doing this. I'm so glad Janice found—"

"Get in," Jimmy said. "Let's get going."

With our passenger aboard, Jimmy returned us quickly to the offshore darkness of the channel, where he killed the engine and listened for boats again. We introduced ourselves, and Warren was a pleasant surprise. Because he was a draft dodger, I was expecting long hair, beads and a beard. But he wasn't like that at all. He was clean-shaven, very polite and looked like someone who'd been president of his high school science club. Jimmy told Warren to take the seat behind him, then eased the boat to half-throttle and headed upriver, back toward Simcoe Island and the lake.

I couldn't see Warren very well, but I turned toward him. "Janice told me about your father. I'm really sorry. I hope you get to see him."

"Thanks," Warren said. "I want my dad to see his grandchild before he dies. And I want to thank him—I'd be in jail if it weren't for him."

"You may end up there anyway, if you aren't careful."

"Maybe," Warren said, "but I meant before. I almost came back two years ago when my mother died."

"Your father talked you out of it?"

Warren laughed. "He was pretty persuasive. He said if I came home, he'd disown me and burn my baseball cards. The thing is, Janice and I weren't doing well in Canada—no friends, no money—and when my mother died, it kind of pushed me over the edge. I was ready to come back and go to jail, but my dad ... he wouldn't even discuss it with me."

"Good for him," I said. "It sounds like things worked out for you."

"They did, but only because he started sending us money after that—a lot of it. He told us he got a big raise, but what he'd done was take out a second mortgage on his house." Warren paused for a moment. "He was going to retire. Now, he has cancer and more debt than he could pay off in two lifetimes."

"But he has a son who didn't get killed in Vietnam or end up in a federal penitentiary—and he has a granddaughter."

I couldn't really see Warren's face, but I saw him take a swipe at his eyes.

"Fathers sure do some crazy shit, don't they?" he said.

By then we were back on the big water, bound for Charity Shoal and the border. There was still very little wind. We were going faster than we had on the trip over, but Jimmy wasn't pushing it. It wasn't long before I could see the light on Charity Shoal, and when we were half a mile from it, Jimmy shut down again.

Warren looked around nervously. "What's wrong?"

"Nothing," Jimmy said. "We're about to cross the border. I want to make sure we don't have company."

"I don't hear anything," I said.

"Neither do I. Let's go home."

We were barely across the border when, fifty yards to our left, a boat turned on its running lights and put a spotlight on us. There was a squeal, then a crackling voice on a bullhorn. "*Gray runabout, heave to. This is the police.*"

There was more, but I couldn't hear it because Jimmy shoved the throttle all the way forward, and the Thompson exploded across the water. I heard Warren say, "*Holy shit,*" but after that, all I could hear was the engine, which roared like a jumbo jet on take-off. In five seconds we were going so fast I thought the speed would suck me right out of my seat, and I clung to it with both hands. Warren wasn't so lucky. He ended up on the floor and slid all the way to the stern, where I could see him wedged between the engine compartment and the side of the boat. Jimmy was now sitting down. He took off his hat and sat on it, then looked over and said something I couldn't hear. He was smiling, though, which made no sense to me.

After two or three minutes of terrifying speed, Jimmy slowed down, and when I looked back, I could see the police boat, now a mile behind us, lit up like a Christmas tree. I was scared, and I knew that Warren, who by then had climbed back into his seat, was terrified. Jimmy, however, seemed unconcerned. We were cruising at

perhaps three-quarter throttle, and he would look back at our pursu-
ers, nudge the lever one way or the other, then look back again.

Warren leaned over Jimmy's shoulder. "Why have we slowed
down? Let's go. You can outrun them."

"I will. I just need to—"

"You turned on the running lights," I said. "They can *see* us."

"Calm down," Jimmy said. "Both of you. I want them to see us.
Sure, we can outrun them—and we will—but not until I lure them
away from the Cape Vincent Channel. That's where we're meeting
Stokes, and I don't want any cops within ten miles of it." Jimmy
looked back and laughed. "Those boys sure took the bait. Look at
'em."

"Where are we going?" I said. "It felt like you turned back
there."

"I did. We're heading out into the lake. See that light dead
ahead? That's the buoy on Galloo Shoal."

Warren leaned forward again. "What's the plan? Whatever you
do is fine with me, just so I don't—"

"The plan is to swing by that beacon, kill the lights and disappear behind Galloo Island. Once we get behind it, they won't be able
to hear us. They'll never know we doubled back to the channel."

The police were very determined and, from Jimmy's perspective,
very cooperative. He stayed a mile or so ahead of them, occasionally allowing them to draw closer to keep their interest piqued.

"They probably think we live on Galloo," he said, looking over
his shoulder. "They think they're gonna arrest us on our dock."

We were in front of the Galloo beacon, just about to make our
turn, when we lost power suddenly. Warren tumbled off his seat—
forward this time—and I nearly went over the windshield. It was as
if a gigantic hand had reached up from the lake bottom and grabbed
us.

The boat was shuddering so badly I thought it would break into
pieces. Jimmy throttled back until it stopped.

"What happened?" I said.

"I don't know." He switched off the running lights and looked at the gauges. "It's not the engine." Then he turned the wheel both directions. "I must have hit a net. I've got steering, but there's something wrapped around the shaft."

We all looked back at the police boat. It was closing fast and in two or three minutes would be alongside. All I could think of was Warren behind bars, and it was all my fault.

Warren was frantic. "We have to *do* something."

Jimmy pointed to the beacon. "We have to get over there. *Now.*"

He put the boat in gear and coaxed as much speed from it as he could, but everything began to shake and vibrate again.

"Too much cavitation," he said, easing back on the throttle. "We're gonna break the shaft. What are our friends doing?"

Warren had never taken his eyes off the other boat. "I think they're slowing down. Why would they—"

"They can't see us anymore—no running lights." Jimmy pulled a slicker out of the compartment at his knees and handed it to Warren. "I'm going to pull up to that marker buoy, and when I do, I want you to put this over the light on top of it. Can you do that?"

"Yes," Warren said.

But when we came alongside the buoy, Warren couldn't reach the top of it, even by standing on the gunnel. I grabbed the boat hook, and together we draped the slicker over the light.

"So far, so good," Jimmy said. "Now we need a little luck."

He pushed the throttle forward as far as he dared and began circling around the shoal to the far side, putting it—and the now invisible beacon—between us and the police. They were quartering, looking around with the spotlight less than three hundred yards away. But they'd changed course slightly and were now headed more toward Galloo Island than the shoal.

"It's now or never," Jimmy said. "Keep your fingers crossed."

He turned on the running lights.

The police swung around and came straight for us, wide open. We were still moving away from the shoal, but they closed on us like we were dead in the water. Within seconds, they passed the place where we thought the beacon was, and for a terrifying moment, I thought they'd missed the reef.

Then we heard the impact. The first sound was metallic. The ones that followed were hollow and resonant, like a truck backing over a bass fiddle. Then it was quiet, except for Jimmy's laughter.

"I think they've actually run aground." He jumped up on the engine compartment to see better. "They *have*. Those boys just fell for the oldest trick in the book."

Warren had collapsed into his seat. "I didn't know what you were doing until five seconds ago. That was ... *amazing*. I just can't ..." He looked at me. "Janice won't believe it." Deep oceans of relief filled his voice.

"I can't believe it myself." I was shaking from the adrenaline. "Jimmy, a Wheaties box isn't good enough for you. I hope those guys are okay."

From what we could tell, the police boat had remained upright. There was a lot of commotion onboard—a lot of flashlights and hollering—but they weren't going anywhere. One of the men shining a light in our direction was standing on the reef several feet from their boat.

"Time to blow this pop stand," Jimmy said.

We limped along until we'd put a quarter mile between us and them. Then Jimmy turned off the engine.

"The cops have radioed for help by now, so we have to get that net, or whatever it is, off the shaft." He turned to Warren. "Can you swim?"

"Sure. What do you want me to do?"

"We have to get wet." Jimmy raised his seat, dug around underneath it for a moment and came up with a knife and a flashlight.

"Allie, there's a bunch of flares in a green metal box in the cuddy. Would you go up there and get me one?" He gave me the flashlight. "You'll need this."

I crawled under the front deck, found the green box and removed a flare—or what I assumed was a flare. It was a tube—aluminum, I think—with a cap on one end. By the time I'd crawled out again, both men had stripped down to their underwear.

I stood up, pretending to stagger, and put a hand to my chest. "Be still, my heart!"

Warren gave me a sheepish grin. "I used to have an underwear dream like this in junior high, but I was always on an escalator."

"Going up or going down?"

"Up, I think. I don't really—"

"Did you find a flare?" Jimmy said.

"Yes." I gave it to him.

"Thanks." Jimmy showed the flare to Warren. "I'll need both hands down there, so your job is to hold this thing so I can see what I'm doing. They burn hot, so keep it out in front of you—away from the hull and away from me. It'll last about three minutes—that should be plenty." Jimmy gave him the flare.

"How do I light it?"

"Twist the cap off and bang it on the end of the flare—kind of scrape it at the same time. Go ahead."

Warren's first attempt was unsuccessful, but the second time he struck the flare, it ignited with a sharp crack that quickly softened to a hiss. There was light everywhere—a white, blinding brightness. The men jumped into the water—Jimmy with a knife, Warren with the flare—and I could see the light moving underwater toward the stern. For a full minute the boat was surrounded by a glimmering nimbus that radiated thirty feet in every direction. Then the light began to move again, and both men popped to the surface.

"Almost done," Jimmy said.

They gulped some air and submerged again, and the next time

they came up, they climbed in the stern. Warren let go of the flare, and I watched the light become smaller and smaller as it sank out of sight.

"I was right." Jimmy said. "It was a net. If it had fouled the rudder, we'd be in handcuffs right now. You did a good job, Warren."

Warren was shivering. "Thanks. I'm glad I could help. Can we go now?"

Jimmy laughed and threw him a towel. "You mean you aren't having fun?"

"I've been too busy being terrified. Hey, I just thought of something." He grabbed his duffle bag and began going through it. "I've got extra underwear in here. You want some?"

"Sure," Jimmy said. "That'd be great."

They both looked at me.

"Not to worry," I said, turning around. "I won't peek—word of honor."

The men pulled on their clothes, and twenty minutes later we were in the Cape Vincent Channel, heading toward the CCC camp. When we got there, Stokes was waiting for us.

"I was startin' to worry, boss. What took you so long?"

Jimmy tossed him the bow line. "We got tangled up in a white-fish net. Stokes, this is Warren. His wife's waiting for him at the Seaway Motel."

"I'll have you there in fifteen minutes, young fella. Lemme give you a hand."

Warren tried to pay, but Jimmy wouldn't take his money. "I never charge a customer who ends up in the water. Besides, you're like family—I'm wearing your underwear."

Stokes shook his head. "I ain't even gonna ask."

We said good-bye to Warren, shook hands and stood on the dock as he drove off with Stokes.

"He's a nice kid," Jimmy said. "I hope he makes it."

"Me, too." But I wasn't worried about Warren anymore. He was doing what he had to. Or what he wanted to. I was thinking about something else. "How far from here did my father die?"

Jimmy took off his cap and ran his hand through his hair. "A couple miles. Why?"

"At Featherbed Shoal?"

"That's right."

"Could we go there?"

"Now?"

"Yes."

"If we went tomorrow, you could see better. Haven't you ever been there?"

"I never wanted to go before. Would you please take me?"

Jimmy didn't answer right away. Then he put his arm around my shoulders. "Of course I will."

It was still pitch black as we headed downriver, but it was beginning to smell like morning. In the last hour the wind had come up a little, and there was a light chop on the water. We were a long way from the shipping lanes, and when Jimmy turned the depth-finder on, the little orange light told us we were shallow. Less than a minute later, Jimmy throttled down to a troll and began to circle, looking for something.

"The reef we hit is right around here someplace," he said. "It's as big as a house, but they don't mark shoals this far from the channel."

"Please don't hit it again."

"The water's deeper now. I couldn't hit it if I—*there it is*." He pointed to the depth-finder. Its orange light had jumped from fourteen feet to less than five. "It was right about here, Allie. This is where the shit hit the fan twenty-two years ago."

"Where's Carleton Island? Isn't that where you swam to?"

Jimmy peered into the dark and pointed. "It's about a hundred yards off the bow. You can just make out the tree line against the sky."

"I see it. Please hold the boat here."

I went into the cuddy and emerged with the box of flares. Jimmy watched in silent fascination as I lit one and tossed it over the side. The aura of light spread across the shallow water as though it were a living thing.

Jimmy turned off the engine. "Do it again."

And I did, throwing the second flare as far as I could. "You do one."

Jimmy lit a flare and lobbed it behind the boat, where it created another glorious island of light.

"Hell," he said. "Let's do 'em all."

We lit the remaining flares as fast as we could and hurled them onto the shoal. I don't know how many there were, maybe a dozen, but we threw the last one into the water before the first one had gone out. It was beautiful. The water over the entire shoal pulsed and quivered with light that pushed back hard against the darkness and broke through the surface, where it shimmered on the waves. It was green and gold and magnificent—as though the bottom of the lake had burst into sudden tongues of flame.

Neither of us said a word. Then, one by one, the flares went out, the light paled, and too soon the night—and the cold, blind river—were whole again.

Jimmy looked over at me. "Are you crying?"

"They never found his body."

"No."

"But they buried something. What did they bury?"

It took him a long time to answer. "It was a little casket full of personal effects—the suit he was married in, a baseball he caught at a Yankee's game. Stuff like that. There was a picture of you in there." He stared at the invisible shoal. "I never should have brought him along."

"My mother and I are the reason he was here that night, not you." I drew a ragged breath. "Fathers sure do some crazy shit, don't they?"

I couldn't see Jimmy's face, but I heard him laugh. "So do daughters. But you know—crazy or not—that was the prettiest three minutes I can remember. I wish your mother could've seen it."

"Me, too. Thanks for bringing me here."

By the time we got back on the big lake, it was light in the east, and as we came around Grenadier Island, Jimmy pointed toward shore.

"There's a sight Hedley would've enjoyed."

Over on Addison Point, I could see a large flock of ducks, low on the water, passing in front of the old blind. From where we were, they looked like a swarm of bees. They circled twice and landed.

"What kind are they?"

"Broadbills," Jimmy said. "They're already moving onto the big water. Winter's coming early this year."

Chapter 45

When we got back to Sable, the sun was coming up. We put the boat in the boathouse, and with the last of our strength, dragged ourselves up the hill. Jimmy went straight to bed, but I went into the kitchen and watched the clock on the wall for half an hour. At exactly six o'clock I called Mike, hoping to catch him before he left his apartment. When he answered, I knew I'd awakened him.

"Is this *you*?" he said hoarsely. "What time is it?"

"I'm sorry to wake you, but it's Sunday. I can't reach you during the day, and you're never there on Sunday night."

Mike didn't answer, and I thought we'd been cut off.

"Are you there?"

"Yeah, I'm here," he said.

"Where do you go? If it's a girl, just tell me. I know I haven't been—"

"I go to meetings."

"Meetings?" I wound the telephone cord around my finger. "What kind of meetings?"

"A bunch of us Vietnam vets get together on Sunday nights and just … talk. We meet in Warroad or Roseau. Once in a while in Baudette."

I almost asked if the meetings helped, then thought better of it. "That's … great. That's really great."

"It's asinine. You don't understand, Allie—these guys are really screwed up. I don't have anything in common with them. They can't hold jobs, they drink too much, all of them …"

"All of them what?"

He made a noise, a little cough. "All of them are divorced. Anyway, it's nothing but touchy-feely bullshit, and I'm tired of feeling guilty for not having nightmares, flashbacks and all the rest of it. I can't figure out what I'm doing there."

"Then I'm glad you—"

"I only did it because you wanted me to, but if you don't like who I am, there isn't a damn thing I can do about it." Mike lowered his voice. "One thing's for sure—this *I'm OK—You're OK* crap isn't the answer."

"You're right. It isn't. But maybe it's true—maybe we *are* okay, even if we're both casualties. What matters is that we have each other, and we love each other … don't we? Please say we do. I was wrong to—"

"What's going on, Allie?"

I slowly unwound the telephone cord from my finger. "I was wondering if you'd like to come to New York. I need to see you. Actually, I just need you. The duck season opens soon. I was hoping you'd come out here."

Mike exhaled loudly. "I can't do that—this isn't a job I can just leave. I already told the owners I'd stay through the winter. Look, I tried to talk to you about it, but you never gave me much feedback."

"I don't think you understand what I'm saying. Let me—"

"What's to understand? You haven't said a meaningful thing

to me for five months. Now I'm supposed to drop everything so we can discuss our future? It's five o'clock in the morning here. Couldn't you—"

"I'm sorry," I said. "I shouldn't have called." I hung up the phone. I could hear Mike saying something, but I hung up anyway.

I went upstairs and slept until noon, and when I came downstairs, I found Jimmy doing an inventory in the bar, where duck hunters would soon be standing shoulder to shoulder. The radio was on, but when he saw me, he turned it off.

"I'm surprised you're up," he said. "I thought you might sleep for a hundred years—you know, like the princess in the story."

"I have … a hundred years and then some."

Jimmy pointed to the rows of bottles. "There isn't anything in this bar that I don't need at least two cases of. I'll have to make a couple runs just to stock it. Sit down. I'll make you a bloody Mary."

"No thanks. I'm not even awake yet." I slid onto a stool. "Was there anything on the radio about last night?"

"A little bit. One of the cops has a broken arm, and we destroyed a very expensive boat. The police think we're Canadians—I love that." Jimmy's smile faded away. "I'll have to paint the Thompson again, though. They got a pretty good look at it."

"*Gray runabout, heave to,*" I said.

"Yeah, don't remind me. Hey, guess what else I heard?"

"The Yankees won the World Series?"

Jimmy laughed. "The Yankees will be lucky to win the division. Ford pardoned Nixon. Can you believe it? I wonder what the hell he was thinking."

"He was thinking enough is enough."

"Maybe so. We can hear all about it on the news tonight."

"I won't be here tonight. I have to leave."

Jimmy's head snapped around. "You can't just *leave*. I was hoping you'd stick around and help me run this place. And what about

Gabby? She'll be home in a couple days."

"You'll have to say good-bye for me. Tell her ... I'm sorry."

"Don't you want to see what happens with the police investigation?"

"Of course. But until Hap turns up, nothing's likely to change. Anyway, I'll be in touch. Where's Stokes?"

Jimmy jerked his thumb in the direction of Sackets. "After he made me tell him about last night a dozen times, I sent him to town on errands. He said he can't wait to hear the story from you, so be prepared." Jimmy came out from behind the bar and sat down on the stool beside me. "What's so important in Chicago that it can't wait until after duck season?"

"I'm not going to Chicago. I'm going to Minnesota. I talked to Mike this morning, and it didn't go very well."

"Oh," Jimmy said. "That's different. That's a *lot* different. Why don't you rest up and leave tomorrow?"

"I need to get there."

"I don't know what to say, Allie."

"Just tell me that you'll miss me."

"I *will* miss you, but you'll be back."

"How can you be sure?"

Jimmy smiled. "Some things you just know."

"How do I get to Minnesota from here?"

"Minnesota? You, uh, cross the bridge, take a left, drive for twenty-four hours, then take another left."

I shook my head. "I can't go through Canada, Jimmy. Someday I'll tell you why."

I could tell he really wanted to know about Canada, but he didn't press me. "Then go through Michigan—drive across the UP."

"We did a nice thing last night, helping Warren and Janice. Thank you for doing that. And thanks for taking me. I'll never forget it."

"No regrets?"

"Of course not. It was all good—*better* than good."

Jimmy gave me a funny look. "Aren't you forgetting something?"

"Like what? I wish that guy on the boat hadn't broken his arm, but—"

"We made two runs last night. Remember the suitcase? You don't even know what was in it."

"It doesn't matter. Like you said, we made two runs."

Jimmy thought about it, took a handful of peanuts from a little dish on the bar and popped them into his mouth. "So they cancel each other out?"

"Not really. I think you have to add them together."

"What do they add up to?"

"I'm not sure ... the truth, maybe?"

But I knew it wasn't that simple. The suitcase and what we'd done for Warren and Janice didn't really add up to anything because they weren't values that could be combined. They were just two fragments of one night, two aspects of a single thing, separate yet entirely reliant on one another—the same but different.

"*There* you are!" Stokes came through the door, a big smile on his face, and sat down beside me. "I been lookin' all over for you. Tell me the whole story, Allie, right from the start. Don't leave nothin' out."

But I hardly knew where to begin. Or where it would end.

Chapter 46

I n the summer of 1978, a photographer named Leonard Walsh
arrived in Sackets Harbor to complete a photo essay he was
doing on lighthouses of the Great Lakes. He had intended to
photograph the lighthouse at Sable Island, among others in the area,
but quickly discovered that it can't be seen from anywhere on the
mainland. Not knowing what else to do, Walsh tried to rent a boat,
but there was none to be had, and finally, someone who should have
known better told him he could "just drive out there," which is what
he did. Or rather, what he tried to do. Mr. Walsh made it about a
third of the way to Sable before slipping off the edge of the ford. He
was fortunate enough to get the car door open and escape, but his
Oldsmobile Cutlass sank like ... well, like an Oldsmobile Cutlass.

Jimmy, Stokes and I watched the salvage operation from lawn
chairs on the beach at Sable Island. Salvage operations are a spectator
sport along the Seaway, and from where we sat, it looked as though
half the population of Sackets was over on Jimmy's landing. After
the Coast Guard failed to snag Walsh's car with grappling hooks,
they brought in a big crane on pontoons, which they anchored on

the ford. Then they sent divers down to attach a cable to the car. Eventually, we heard faint applause, and shortly after that, we could hear the big crane rev its engine and begin to labor under the load it was lifting from the lake bottom. It didn't take long. In a few minutes we could see the hood of a vehicle emerging slowly from the water.

It wasn't an Oldsmobile.

"Oooh, *shit*," Jimmy said. "I think that's Hap's truck."

It was Hap's truck, all right, complete with Hap's body.

That certainly woke the police up, and they wasted no time in questioning Jimmy again. But in addition to Hap's body, there was also twenty thousand dollars in the truck, along with a shotgun that had once belonged to Clark Gable. These things proved very helpful to Jimmy's case, and after he told the police the whole story—and after Stokes backed it up—the district attorney must have known he was fighting an uphill battle. When Jimmy's lawyer said Jimmy was willing to take a polygraph test, that was the end of it. Hap's death was ruled an accidental drowning.

With Hap officially dead, Jimmy had no need to dissolve Seaway, Ltd. The partnership came to a legal conclusion all on its own, and when it did, the entire point was once again in Jimmy's hands. But not for long, because he gave it to me. Actually, he sold it to me for one dollar, which he thumbtacked to the wall at Sable Island—the one covered with photographs of famous people.

Hap's death resolved a lot of issues, but it raised some questions, too, especially when it came to certain details in the police report. For instance, Hap's headlights weren't on at the time of the accident, and his truck was in reverse. The headlights didn't make sense because we knew Hap had driven off the ford well after dark on the night he disappeared. And why reverse?

The answer came to me one morning when I found myself toe-to-toe with a road grader on the narrow, unpaved driveway of a friend. In order for the grader and me to get around each other, I had to back up all the way to my friend's house.

I called Jimmy right away. "I know what happened that night."

"You mean to Hap?"

"Yes. You said Stokes found you on the floor that night after Hap hit you with the bottle, right?"

"Yeah, he'd been in town—"

"But you don't know how long you'd been unconscious."

"I don't think I was ever really out. If I was, it wasn't very long."

"Probably less than five minutes," I said.

"How do you know that?"

"Because when Hap was on the ford heading back to the mainland with your money, I think he saw Stokes' headlights coming toward him from the landing."

"Maybe," Jimmy said. "But there's enough room on the ford that Hap could have squeezed by Stokes, waved and kept right on going. Our people pass each other all the time out there, even at night."

"Yes, but Hap didn't *know* it was Stokes. He probably thought it was the people he owed money to—the ones who were looking for him. That's why he turned his headlights off."

"And then he put the car in reverse to back up, but he was drunk and—"

"And he drove off the ford. Stokes never saw him. A few minutes later, Stokes walked into the club and found you on the floor."

"That's pretty good, Allie. It's probably as close as we'll ever get to the truth."

Chapter 47

Alot of years have passed since all this happened. And the characters, almost all of whom were real people, are mostly gone now. If this were a movie, the screen would fade to black and you might see a few white sentences, little postscripts, explaining what happened to them in later life. I want to do something like that. I owe it to them.

Paula Zarobsky Kaczmarek died of ovarian cancer on February 6, 1994. She was forty-four years old. Her parents, Jerry and their two beautiful teenage sons were in the room with her when she died, and a few minutes before that, I'd been there, too. Paula was unconscious, but as I sat by her bedside and held her hand, I half expected her to open her eyes and say, "Jeez, Hayes, it's about time you got here." But she didn't.

Paula had the best marriage of anyone I've ever known. She never told Jerry about what happened that night after work. I would've known if she had.

Louie Labonté remained at Kettle Falls through two more changes of ownership, but when he was eventually told his services would no longer be required, he disappeared that winter and was found the following spring in a little clearing not far from his cabin.

According to Pop, Louie had walked into the woods, lain belly-down on his rifle, and fired a bullet upward beneath his chin. Neither Pop nor I thought Louie had chosen to die in that clearing by chance. It was a pretty spot—I'd often picked blueberries there—and we believed Louie ended his life in the same place he'd buried Angelique many years before.

Edward "Pop" Smith died in a nursing home in Brandon, Manitoba. I saw him shortly before he passed away, and he told me he had reconciled with his son, who—because of Pop's alcoholic past—had been forced to grow up without him. Pop said his son's forgiveness had made the last few years of his life the happiest he could remember. A couple hundred pages ago, I said something about Pop being the kindest person I had ever known. It's true. He was.

Marie Pale Wolf and I corresponded off and on for a few years, and then I lost track of her. But I know she became the "airplane lady" she'd long wanted to be. She was a flight attendant for Ozark Airlines until they went out of business, and after that she worked for Northwest. In the last letter I received from her, she said she'd finally changed her name. Marie Pale Wolf had become Marie Swenson, and she did it the easy way, by getting married. Marie wrote that her husband was a pilot, "a blond Adonis," as she put it, whom she'd met at the Grand Forks Air Force Base in Minnesota.

I know very little about Rennie, other than the fact that he made a full recovery. The last thing Marie told me about him was that he was working on a First Nation construction crew in Winnipeg.

Nick and Jamie Ralston's wanderlust left no room for permanent attachments, and I knew on the day they left Twin Rivers for Iran that I would never see them again. But I stay in touch with Jack and Suzanne Kohl, the onetime headmaster and nurse at Twin

Rivers. They eventually moved to North Bay, Ontario, where they continued their careers for many years. On the refrigerator I have a picture of them standing at the wheel of their sailboat, *Second Wind*. They look very happy.

Barry Freed, a.k.a. Abbie Hoffman, did indeed have the opportunity to wake up with the river outside his window. He and Johanna Lawrenson moved to the tiny town of Fineview on Wellesley Island in 1978, and though still a fugitive, Barry conceived and organized the Save the River campaign that ultimately prevented the Army Corps of Engineers from turning the St. Lawrence into a barge canal. In 1980, after the success of Save the River—and after winning the praise of Governor Carey and Senator Moynihan—Barry Freed turned himself in. But not before setting the stage in an interview with Barbara Walters that aired September 4 on *20/20*.

Jimmy insisted I watch *20/20* that night, because he appeared in a portion of it. Actually, his hand and forearm appeared, but that was enough for Jimmy, who had driven one of the two boats that took Walters and her production crew out to Wellesley Island for the interview—after first running them all over the river in case they were being followed. There was a short scene before the interview began in which Walters met Barry, to her genuine surprise, out on the river. Barry was in his own boat, which he brought alongside Walters and the *Merganser* to make sure there were no police aboard. After both boats had cut their engines and drifted within a couple feet of each other, Jimmy reached out and grabbed the side rail of Barry's boat to draw it closer. The camera was rolling, and it was this small gesture on Jimmy's part that caused his hand and forearm to be immortalized.

In time, Barry and Johanna would leave the river, and of course Barry became Abbie Hoffman again, but he was unable to reprise his role as Angry Young Man of the Sixties. Perhaps he no longer cared. In the spring of 1989, Abbie emptied a hundred and fifty Phenobarbital capsules into a glass of Glenlivet and drank it down, demonstrating once and for all that it was just too damn hard being Abbie Hoffman.

Jimmy received a Christmas card, addressed to both of us, from Warren and Janice Spencer the year Warren returned to the States to see his father. There was a nice note with the card that said they'd done what they set out to do and then slipped back safely into Canada. That one Christmas card is all I've ever heard from Warren and Janice. Perhaps they will read this book and drop me a line. I hope so. I've changed their names, but they won't have any trouble recognizing themselves.

Jimmy married Gabby in 1975, and they lived on Sable Island until he was killed in an automobile accident on Route 81, just north of the Lake Oneida bridge. It nearly broke my heart. Gabby eventually sold the Sable Island Hunt Club to a consortium of its wealthiest members, but after two seasons, they found themselves unable to run the place, their best intentions notwithstanding. The property was parceled into lots and sold, and the mansion itself had a succession of owners, all of whom were seduced by its beauty and nearly pauperized by its upkeep. I believe it's on the market again right now.

I did my best to bring about some kind of reconciliation between my mother and Jimmy, but I succeeded only to the extent that Jimmy and Gabby were included in two rather awkward Thanksgivings in Chicago. After that, I didn't try anymore. My mother was incapable of forgiving Jimmy for his role in my father's death, and that would never change. I still think about the stories she read to me when I was little, those stories about right and wrong, with their elegant moral simplicity. They were true, in their narrow way, but real truths are often double truths, like the two norths. And unless you know the angle of declination, it's easy to lose your bearings.

As for Mike Bowman, my husband of over thirty years, he came in from splitting wood only moments ago. We have a little hydraulic wood splitter, but Mike rarely uses it, even though splitting wood by hand sometimes makes his back sore. We have a perfectly good gas furnace, too, but he doesn't use that much, either. He enjoys the feel of a maul in his hands, just as he enjoys the smell of wood smoke, which I agree is very pleasant.

Mike has been working outside a lot this week because the second half of duck season opens tomorrow, and he wants to give it his undivided attention. We have a split season where we live—duck hunting begins in October, closes for the first three weeks of November and then resumes just before Thanksgiving. That's one of the reasons Mike has been trying to get everything done—raking, wood-splitting, winterizing.

The other reason is that Dale Olsen, Mike's friend from Vietnam, and his wife Annie will be here visiting for a few days. We see them a couple times a year, and the men enjoy hunting and fishing together. I don't remember when Dale quit being *was*, but it was a long time ago. Mike got his number from information one evening and called him. I've never asked what prompted him to do it, but I'm glad he did.

I can hear Mike in the mudroom, shedding his coat and boots, and very soon he will begin looking for me, as he always does after coming in from outside. He'll look in the kitchen, the living room, possibly the laundry room, before finding me upstairs in the spare bedroom, which we turned into a little office after our daughter Lindsey was married.

I can now say, without reservation, that it was worth everything we went through in our first year together—a year in which so many things happened to us that our marriage couldn't contain them all. The only real fight we had after that was three years later, when a friend of Mike's from UC—a friend who happened to be the English Department Chairman at the University of Alaska in Anchorage—called to offer Mike a professorship there. Mike had been very interested. The pay was almost twice what he was making at the college where he still teaches, and he told me if we went to

Alaska, he could get his pilot's license, buy a float plane and maybe someday open a fly-in fishing and hunting lodge out in the bush. I'm not ashamed to say I was a poor audience for this idea, but when we look back on it, Mike says he's glad I talked him out of it, and I believe him. The life we chose is a good one.

It didn't take Mike long to find me in the spare bedroom. I heard him on the stairs, and then he was at my side.

"It's cold out there," he said, rubbing his hands together. "How's the book coming?"

"I don't know ... it's hard. Everything happened such a long time ago. Do you realize when we met, America had just put a man on the moon with a slide rule? Now we have a president with a BlackBerry."

"None of that should matter, Allie. Just remember what Faulkner said about the eternal verities of the human heart."

"Do I have to?" I said, laughing. "This is hard enough as it is."

"Maybe you need a break. Let's walk down to the point. You won't believe the ducks. The entire time I was outside there were ducks overhead—thousands of them. Dale's timing couldn't be better."

"A big cold front makes all the difference."

"Yes, yes, it does ... all the difference."

But Mike wasn't paying attention anymore. All the time we'd been talking, he was edging closer to the computer screen, and now he was close enough to read what was on it.

"You're doing it again," I said. "*Shoo.* Go away."

"You spelled 'hydraulic' wrong."

"It's a typo. Go away."

Mike was still reading. "Come with me to the point, or I'll be forced to tell you some things about the past perfect tense that you obviously don't know."

"That does it," I said, activating the screen saver.

"Come with me."

"Oh, all right. Maybe a break will do me good. Just give me fifteen minutes—there's something I want to get down before I forget."

"I hope you're going to address my concern—what we talked about a couple days ago."

"I'm still thinking about that," I said. "I'll meet you outside."

Mike headed for the door. "Fifteen minutes."

Mike's "concern" has to do with my handling of Thin Bird's death at the substation, which he believes is too close to the way it actually happened. I've changed a few of the details, but Mike thinks that scene has the potential to get us in trouble. I reminded him that a novel is a work of fiction, which makes it a perfect hedge against self-incrimination. But he wasn't convinced.

"Your so-called novel is more fact than fiction," he said, "and I'd feel a lot better if you increased the aesthetic distance in that episode."

That's why I asked Mike for fifteen minutes. I've been thinking about what he said since yesterday afternoon, when something happened that I can't get out of my head. I was baby-sitting for our four-year-old granddaughter. Her name is Jennifer, and from where I was sitting at the computer, I could see her on the floor with a coloring book open in front of her. But after a while, I noticed that she wasn't paying any attention to it. She was holding a crayon at arm's length, sort of waving it around in front of her.

At first I couldn't figure out what she was doing. Then I understood. She was writing her name in the air. As I watched her, I could see the smooth *J* flowing into the loop of the *e*, which led to the hill country of a compound *n*, and I thought how beautiful it was to have witnessed that early attempt at self-definition. It also occurred to me that what Jennifer was doing is very much like what I'm doing now.

I suppose everyone hopes to leave a tiny scratch on the surface of anonymity, but when your efforts end up in print, there can be risks. I'd like to believe that Leon Thin Bird has no further power over Mike and me, but now that I've gone out of my way to resurrect him, who knows? Mike could be right—Thin Bird might be like an ancient land mine, buried in haste and long forgotten, still waiting to be stepped on.

That's the problem with writing your name in the air. You can never be sure what you've done.

Fifteen minutes later, Mike and I were walking across the yard toward the lake, which I heard the moment I stepped outside. The wind was blowing hard, and I could see breakers exploding on the rocks, but the noise they made bore no resemblance to the rhythmic sound of waves. It was more like the roar at a football game after a game-winning field goal. When we reached the water's edge, we walked up the shoreline toward the point, which was gauzy and gray a quarter-mile away.

"Every time I walk this beach," Mike said, "I can't believe Jimmy just gave all this to you—to *us*."

"It was part of his plan to get me back here." I pointed to a duck decoy marooned on the rocks in front of us. "Look what washed ashore."

Mike picked it up, turning it over in his hands. "It's wood. It must be an old one. It has G-I-H-C carved into the bottom of it."

"Galloo Island Hunt Club. How many does that make this year?"

"Seven or eight. I don't know where they all come from, but I haven't bought a decoy since we built the house."

"The bounty of the beach," I said. "All right, I found the decoy. Now you have to find something."

"I found two Rapalas and a teak belaying pin yesterday. I suppose they don't count."

I took his arm. "Of course not. You know the rules."

We were almost to the point when Mike walked suddenly toward the water, then retreated in the face of a wave.

"What is it?"

"I'm not sure," he said, backing up again. "I saw something out there between the waves. *Look*, there it is again. It's green." He took off his boots and socks and rolled up his pant legs. "Ripeness is all."

"But timing is everything. Don't get wet."

Mike waited until a receding wave gave him the opportunity he needed. Then he ran out, grabbed something and scurried back with the next wave right behind him.

"I got it!" he said.

"What is it?"

Mike dropped to one knee, very theatrically. "Milady, I know not. Yet humbly I beseech thee to accept this modest token." He nodded toward the lake. "I risked life and limb to get it."

"Such daring," I said. "Let's see."

Mike handed me a piece of green glass that had once been a bottle but was now something else entirely. It must have lain on the bottom for many years, because time and sand had worn away its top half, turning it into a beautifully smooth artifact that resembled a glass serving spoon. It was an amazing transformation.

Mike stuffed his socks into his pocket and sat down on a rock to put his boots on. "Well, does it count?"

"Yes, I love it. Thank you."

When we got to the blind, we entered its magic circle of stone and looked out at the lake.

Mike pointed to a large flock of broadbills that flew by well within range. "See what I mean about tomorrow?"

"Yes," I said. "You did a nice job on the blind this year."

"It took me two days. The ice really did a number on it. Every winter the lake knocks it down, and every summer I rebuild it again."

"It's a cycle," I said, "like everything else. Hedley did it, too. In fact, I'll bet some of these stones are the same ones he used."

Mike nodded. "I'm sure they are. They're probably the same

stones somebody used three hundred years ago—some colonist with a blunderbuss and a three-cornered hat, who walked down here like we just did, saw all the ducks and decided to make a blind."

I closed my eyes halfway and squinted at the lake. "The sheep are grazing. I wonder if the man in the three-cornered hat ever saw them."

"We'll never know."

But as I looked at the lake, I realized he would have seen them. He would have learned a lot by then about how to look at things, just as he would have known that seeing things perfectly is not the same as understanding them. Sometimes, it's good to have your eyes wide open. Other times, it helps to close them a little. That was the secret, and he would have known it, the man in the three-cornered hat. You learn that quickly in the New World.